Collective Identity

Book IV of the Commitment Series

BADGER BLISS BOOKS

DEDICATION

Here is the recipe for a family:

Infinite humor
A ton of tolerance
Unlimited patience
Unconditional love
Boundless determination
Unwavering commitment
The ability to forgive
The ability to accept
A little sugar
A little spice

Mix well and simmer for 6 or 7 decades. Serve warm. Enjoy.

~~~~~~~~~

We all have families we are born into, but for whatever reason, we sometimes become separated from them and form families of our own, unrelated by blood, but families nonetheless. Family is all about belonging to someone. Sometimes we are born into families, and sometimes our families come to us through other means. Shared DNA is not a requirement for a strong and loving family. All you need is a commitment and the willingness to enrich the life of someone you love. All families are important. All families are valid. All families are good.

This book is dedicated to all the families in the world, regardless of tradition, color, creed, ability, orientation, or how you came to be.

In the words of The Captain and Tennille (and Neil Sedaka)……
"Love will keep us together."
~~~~~~~~~

ALSO WRITTEN BY KAREN D. BADGER AND AVAILABLE FROM BADGER BLISS BOOKS:

ON A WING AND A PRAYER
YESTERDAY ONCE MORE
THE BLUE FEATHER
ALL MY TOMORROWS
1140 RUE ROYALE

The Billie/Cat Commitment Series:

IN A FAMILY WAY
UNCHAINED MEMORIES
HAPPY CAMPERS
COLLECTIVE IDENTITY
SWEET ANGEL
RELATIVE-LY SPEAKING

www. badgerblissbooks.com

Collective Identity

Book IV of the Commitment Series

A BADGER BLISS BOOK

By

Karen D. Badger

COLLECTIVE IDENTITY - Book Four of the Commitment Series
by: Karen D. Badger
www.karendbadger.com

Cover design by Karen D. Badger

A Badger Bliss Book
Published by Badger Bliss Books
Georgia, VT 05468

www.badgerblissbooks.com

ISBN 13: 978-1-945761-08-9
ISBN 10: 1-945761-08-3

1st edition published by Badger Bliss Books in January, 2015
2nd edition published by Badger Bliss Books in August, 2016

Printed in the United States of America and in the United Kingdom.

ACKNOWLEDGMENTS

As usual, my beta readers provide an invaluable service. They find my mistakes, express their opinions about my characters and plot, and help me to improve my skills as a writer. I'd like to express my extreme gratitude to my wife, Bliss, my mom, Ellie Atherton and my very good friends, Donna Brown and Carol Poynor, for your hard work and for being forthright and honest in your opinions and feedback. You guys rock!

Many thanks to my editor Nat Burns for helping me to make this book as good as it can be. Thank you for being there for me and for doing such a marvelous job with the edits, my friend.

Finally, many thanks to my family and friends for their unwavering support. You give me the confidence to move forward with my stories… not to mention providing me with lots of fodder for new plot lines! This particular series is about family… about how families come in many varieties… and about how family is not limited by blood relations. Thank you all for being a part of mine.

SPECIAL NOTE: I'd like to thank Iliana Martin, dear friend and author of the beautiful poem, *Come, Take My Hand*. Iliana, you are truly a talented writer. Please continue to share your talent with us, my friend. Love you muchly! SA :-)

Prologue

American Embassy
Saigon
1960

"I'm telling you, General, with a little luck, I can break this code."

Josephine Wycliffe paced back and forth in front of her commanding officer, her worn fedora shoved down low over her brow.

General Stanza crossed his arms in front of his chest. "And just how to do you propose to do that, Miss Wycliffe?" he asked.

"You leave that up to me. All I need is someone proficient in the Vietnamese language and I guarantee I can do it."

* * *

Jo leaned her backside against the table at the far end of the room, her arms crossed, as she waited for the General to arrive with her linguist in tow. Her worn beaver-pelt fedora sat squarely on her head, the brim tilted slightly forward. A lit stogie hung from the corner of her mouth. Her legs were crossed at the ankles.

When the door opened, she stood up, legs splayed apart and hands on her hips, holding the edges of her leather bomber jacket open. She intended to let this new person know who was in charge right from the start as she clamped down on the stogie and narrowed her eyes. All was for naught as her jaw went slack and the stogie fell to the floor.

Josephine Wycliffe was totally unprepared for the arrival of Alexandra Spirakis.

Miss Spirakis was head and shoulders above her in height. Her slim frame sported a smart business suit with a calf-length, form-hugging skirt and short jacket, highlighted with white piping and a rounded Peter Pan collar which was buttoned clear to the top and decorated with a cameo brooch. The small hat adorning her head, and white kid-gloved hands clutching a small purse, reminded Josephine of church-lady attire. She wore moderate heels, which accentuated her already lofty frame, and enhanced the obvious height difference between the two women.

Despite the fact that Spirakis' demeanor screamed prim and proper Southern Belle, Jo was captivated.

Holy Shit! Does this woman know how beautiful she is? Josephine thought to herself. *Damn! I'm going to cream myself just looking into those eyes! Wycliffe, you dog... that's one mountain I'm looking forward to climbing!*

Lecherous thoughts aside, Jo was totally taken with the crystal blue eyes hiding behind cat-eye glasses, and her creamy complexion accented by ruby-red lipstick. And then there was the jet black hair pulled back into a neat bun at the nape of her neck. As unprepared as she was for Miss Spirakis' appearance, she was caught totally off guard when she heard her speak.

"Ah, Miss Wycliffe, I do believe you dropped your cigar on the floor."

Jo's eyes opened wide as a heavily accented Southern voice floated melodiously from the linguist's lips to her ears. She especially liked the way she said 'cee-gar.' All Jo could do was stare.

"Miss Wycliffe, are ya all right?"

Jo suddenly came back to her senses and frowned. She pushed her hat further onto her head. She crushed the cigar under her worn leather boot and extended her hand to Alex without looking directly at her. "Josephine Wycliffe. Nice to make your acquaintance. You can call me Jo."

Miss Spirakis took her hand and tilted her head forward in an attempt to meet Jo's eyes. "Well the feeling is mutual, Miss Wycliffe, but I think I will call you Josie. Jo just sounds to… well, too mannish. It just doesn't feel proper-like to call you Jo. I'm Alexandra Spirakis. Alex is fine."

Jo released her hand and cleared her throat. "Call me what you'd like. What's important here is the job at hand. I trust you are qualified?" she asked gruffly.

Alex raised her eyebrows. "I do declare, you do speak your mind, Miss Wycliffe."

"Jo," Josephine interrupted.

"Yes. I assure you, Josie, I am more than qualified. Now if you'll direct me to the powder room, I'll take care of business, then we can get to work."

The General, who had been watching the exchange, interjected. "Go back out the door… down the hall to the right."

Alex excused herself and left the room.

"What the hell were you thinking?" Jo resounded. "How am I supposed to get any work done with her around?"

General Stanza chuckled. "Don't under estimate her, Wycliffe. She comes highly recommended. If I'm right, she'll give you a run for your money… in more ways than one."

* * *

"Oh, my!" Alex said out loud as she leaned against the bathroom wall. Her heart was beating a mile a minute after her first encounter with Josephine Wycliffe.

She pressed one hand against her heart, feeling it thump through her clothing.

Land sakes, what is wrong with me? she thought. *I've only just met the woman. It's like I was struck by lightning or something. I don't know if I can do this.*

Alex composed herself and checked her reflection the mirror to see if every hair was in place. She flushed the toilet to feign her reason for escaping to the powder room then smoothed the front of her jacket before opening the door.

Jo was alone in the room. Anxiety gripped Alex's stomach as she steeled herself before joining her.

Jo removed a new stogie from between her teeth and spit a small amount of tobacco onto the floor. "Everything come out okay?" she chuckled.

Alex paused, not really knowing how to deal with this brazen woman. "My word, are you always like this?" she asked.

"Like what?"

"So bold and brash."

Jo clamped the cigar between her teeth once more and approached Alex with her hands on her hips. "Get used to it sweetheart. I am who I am," she said.

"And must you smoke that thing? It's quite offensive."

Jo narrowed her eyes into slits. "Don't be telling me what I can and can't do, Miss Spirakis. I'm not pretty when I'm angry."

"Alexandra. My name is Alexandra, and if we are to work together, I think a little respect is warranted."

"You get what you give, Al. Now we've got a job to do. I suggest we get started."

* * *

Two weeks later...

"Damn! We're never going to break this code," Josephine complained as she stomped back and forth across the room. "I thought you were good at this stuff, Al."

Alex stood bent over the table, studying an array of papers spread out before her. On them, was a series of dots, similar to Morse's code, but without the dashes. "There's something not quite right about this," Alex said. "I just can't put my finger on it."

"Every day we fail to break this thing, our forces are dying in ambushes. I need a drink," Jo said.

She poured herself a shot of whiskey from the bar in the corner of the room and downed it in one gulp. "Do you want anything?" she said over her shoulder to Alex.

"A glass of wine would be nice."

Jo poured the wine for Alex and another shot for herself and carried both drinks to the table. She handed the wine to Alex.

"Thank you, Josie." Alex held the glass of wine in one hand, the other hand perched on her hip. "I'm missing something here. Could you play the recording back one more time?"

"For Christ's sake, Al, what good is that going to do? You've reviewed that damned tape a thousand times already. I, for one, am getting sick of listening to it."

"Josephine Wycliffe, I was hired to do a job and I'll not quit until that job is done. Now if you don't want to listen to it again, I suggest you turn in for the night so I can get back to work."

Jo grabbed her bomber jacket then tossed down her shot of whiskey, slamming the shot glass on the table. "Suit yourself. I'll see you in the morning."

* * *

Alex watched Joe as she slammed the door on the way out. She took a deep breath and struggled to retain her composure.

Josephine Wycliffe, if I weren't such a lady, I'd show you just what I think about your Yankee, know-it-all attitude.

Jo had been alternating between trying to intimidate Alex and trying to seduce her since the day she walked in. Alex decided she wouldn't succeed with either attempt if she kept behaving the way she was. A lady has standards, after all.

Alex wiped the tear of frustration from the corner of her eye and rewound the cassette tape one more time. She pressed the 'play' button and picked up her pen and notepad, then sat down to listen. A series of taps and pauses echoed at sporadic intervals from the recording. She strained to listen but still struggled to make sense of the seemingly unrelated series of taps. Finally, she put the pen and paper on the table and closed her eyes, shutting out all visual sensory input so she could focus only on the sounds coming from the recording.

Five minutes later, her eyes flew open. "Oh, my goodness!" Alex exclaimed. "It's not Vietnamese at all! It's English!"

* * *

"You woke me out of a sound sleep, Al. This had better be good," Jo complained when she charged into the briefing room.

Alex sat hunched over a series of sketches spread out before her on the table. She had removed her jacket, revealing a long-sleeved white button-up blouse, tailored to fit her slim waist, only one shirt-tail was hanging out, the collar was open, revealing generous cleavage, and the sleeves were rolled up to her elbows. Tendrils of long dark had hung at the sides of her face, having escaped the elastic holding the bun together at the nape of her neck.

Jo stopped dead in the doorway and took in her disheveled attire. "Holy shit! What did you do with Al?" she asked while trying to repress the stirrings in her abdomen.

Damn! She's even more beautiful all mussed up like that.

Alex looked up and furrowed her brow behind the cat-eye glasses. "I beg ya pardon?"

"Ah… nothing. So what's got your panties in a wad?"

Alex pressed her palms into the tabletop. "Must you always talk that way, Josie? My panties happen to be just fine, thank you very much."

Jo looked at the mess of papers on the table. "So what's this all about?"

"I think I'm onto something here, Josie. We have been working so hard to come up with Vietnamese translations for these series of dashes, when all along, it's not even Vietnamese."

"Then what the hell is it?"

"It's English, American English… at least I think it's a variation on American."

"What the hell are you talking about, woman?" Jo ranted as she paced back and forth. "Jesus-H-Christ. I knew the minute I laid eyes on you that you were all looks and no brains."

Alex stood tall and tilted her head back slightly while cocking an eyebrow at Jo. She placed her hands on her hips for emphasis.

"For your information, Miss Wycliffe, I am fluent in several languages, while you just barely get by on rudimentary English. I resent the implication that I don't know what I'm talkin' about. I'm telling you, this code is American."

Jo walked around the table and pushed Alex back into her chair. She leaned in so her face was close to Alex's. "Are you trying to tell me there's an American traitor working with the Viet Cong?"

Alex sat back. "Heavens, no. That's not what I'm sayin' at all."

Jo took off her fedora and slammed it on the table. "Then damn it, Alex, what *are* you trying to tell me?"

"If you'd lose that chip on your goddamned shoulder long enough to listen, I'd be happy to tell you!" Alex exclaimed. "Now see what you made me do? I cussed. I never cuss!"

Jo held her hands up in front of Alex. "Okay. I'm sorry. I'm ready to listen."

She leaned her backside against the table and crossed her arms.

"The series of taps on the recording appears to be random at first, but if you listen to it carefully, you'll notice a pattern… two series of taps, followed by a pause, then two more series of taps, another pause, and so on."

"And your point is?" Jo said impatiently.

"I believe this series of taps is based on a concept called Polybius Square, which originated in Ancient Greece."

"So what's that got to do with the code being American?" Jo asked.

"I called a friend of mine at the State Department last night and learned that prisoners of war who managed to escape the Viet Cong prison camps reported using a system of taps to communicate with other prisoners in the same compound. It apparently took on a life of its own and was used for virtually all communication between the prisoners. I can only surmise the Viet Cong eventually caught on to it."

"One thing doesn't make sense to me, Al," Jo challenged. "If this is a system of communication used by American POW's… a system the State Department is aware of by the way, why hasn't someone broken it before now?"

"Because if I'm right, the Viet Cong did something very sneaky… they changed the order of the code."

"Changed the order?"

"Yes. You see, the Polybius Square is a five-by-five grid of letters laid out with the characters of the Latin alphabet, except for the letter K. The letter C was used in its place. Without K, there are 25 letters in the alphabet, five letters per row, five rows."

Alex picked up a piece of paper from the table with a grid of numbers and letters on it. "Here is what a normal Polybius Square looks like."

"So, how does this translate into code?"

"Well, let's say you want to tap out the word WATER. The W is right here, in the fifth row, second column, so you would tap five times, followed by two times, then a slight pause. The letter A is in the first row, first column, so you would then tap once, followed by one more tap, then again, a slight pause before moving on to the letter T with four taps, followed by four more taps."

"Seems complicated."

"It is on the surface, but once you memorize the row and column location for each letter, it's really pretty simple. The problem is, when I tried to apply the normal Polybius Square to the taps on the recording, all I got was a bunch of gibberish."

Jo began pacing again. "So where do we go from here?

If you got gibberish, then you are most likely wrong in your assumptions. It looks like we're back to square one."

"I don't think so… at least I *hope* not. Like I said, I think the Viet Cong took this code and changed it so it *would* look like gibberish to anyone trying to decode it. There are countless combinations for the placement of the twenty-five letters in this grid."

Jo stopped in mid-pace and stared at Alex. "Are you telling me this is impossible?"

"No. I'm telling you it will be time-consuming. That's why I called you in. I can't do this on my own. I need your help… and if we get lucky, the Viet Cong will have followed a pattern. We'll look at the most obvious ones first and compare it to the series of taps on the recording."

"I need a drink," Jo said.

"I don't think so. You'll need a clear head for this. Why don't you start putting the series of taps from the recording on paper while I set up the coffee pot, then I'll begin mapping out some of the more obvious modifications of the Polybius Square. Once we have the recording on paper, we'll compare it to the different modifications I come up with, and maybe… just maybe, we'll hit pay dirt before we're old and gray."

"Old and gray, huh? Do you think you can live with me for that long?" Jo asked.

"Heaven forbid!" Alex exclaimed as she went to prepare the coffee.

* * *

Ten hours later….

"I give up. Never in my life did I think I'd admit defeat, but damn it, I quit. We've tried how many combinations now… fifty… a hundred? And still no success?" Jo ranted. "I need a drink… and I need it now!"

Alex lowered her forehead to rest on her arms crossed on the table in front of her. Her hair was a mess, her clothes smelled like perspiration, she was hungry and tired, and she desperately needed a bath so she was in no mood to deal with

Josephine Wycliffe. She sighed deeply as she listened to Josephine rant for the umpteenth time since they began the decoding process.

She lifted her head when Jo paused for a breath. "You want a drink, Josie? Then have one. I'm tired of listening to you complain. I'll have the next combination ready in a few minutes."

Jo sat back in her chair. "I'm sorry for complaining, Al, but it feels like we're hitting our heads against the wall here. The only thing we have for our efforts is one big headache."

"Well, I'm not ready to give in. Here's the next combination," Alex said as she handed the paper to Jo.

"How is this one configured?"

"I basically filled in A through Z, except for K, of course, in a spiral from the upper left corner around to the right until Z finally lands in the center."

Normal Polybius Square

	1	2	3	4	5
1	A	B	C	D	E
2	F	G	H	I	J
3	L	M	N	O	P
4	Q	R	S	T	U
5	V	W	X	Y	Z

Modified Polybius Square

	1	2	3	4	5
1	A	F	O	G	B
2	E	S	X	T	H
3	N	W	Z	Y	P
4	M	R	V	U	I
5	D	L	Q	J	C

Jo took the paper and began applying the recorded tap sequences to the new layout.

"I thought you were getting yourself a drink," Alex said.

"Grrrr…" Jo grumbled as she continued to transfer the recorded tap code to the modified square.

Alex reached for a new piece of paper and began mapping out yet another possible modification, only to be interrupted once more by Jo.

"Holy shit! Holy shit, Al! Holy shit!"

"What is it, Josie?"

"You are not going to believe this. Come here."

Alex jumped to her feet and ran around the table to look over Jo's shoulder. "Oh, my!" she exclaimed.

There on the paper were the words, 'US forces'.

"Give me a hand with this, Al," Jo said, pushing the modified Polybius Square toward her as she translated the recorded tap sequences.

Over the next few minutes a message appeared.

'US forces approaching Ho Chi Minh Trail. Estimated arrival, four-thirty pm. Ambush.'

Josephine jumped to her feet and grabbed Alex, hugging her hard. "We did it! We did it, Al!"

"That we did," Alex replied as she struggled to breath.

Jo held Alex at arm's length and looked into her eyes. Before either of them knew what was happening, their lips met for a kiss that would rock both of them to the depths of their souls.

A few days later, Alex returned to the States and it would be a full five years before they would see each other again.

Part I

At Loose Ends

Chapter 1

2014

Cat rolled onto her back and brushed her sweat-soaked bangs from her forehead. "Damn, that was good!"

"Thank you, my love." Billie kissed Cat lightly on the nose. "I aim to please."

"Where did you learn to do that?"

"I have many skills!" Billie grinned.

"You're pretty proud of yourself, aren't you?" Cat laid on her stomach and propped herself up on her elbows while bending her legs at the knees.

Billie cupped Cat's face. "Yes, I am." She placed several butterfly kisses across Cat's lips.

"You, my love, have more stamina than I know how to deal with. You totally wear me out."

"Just making up for lost time, my love."

"It feels good to make love to you again, Billie. I really missed that. I really missed *you,*" Cat said softly. "I was so worried you would never remember. I couldn't imagine how we were going to move forward with our lives when all of our past had been erased from your memory. It broke my heart to think you might never remember the day we met, or Skylar's birth, or the first night in our new home. So much of who we are is wrapped up in the five years of history we have together. I don't know how I would have coped if your memory hadn't returned."

Billie frowned. "I knew I loved you, Cat. I just didn't remember who you were. I mean, I fell in love with you all over again before my memory returned, and when it did come back, my remembered love for you came flooding in on top of my newly discovered love for you. It was amazingly sweet and intense. In a way, losing my memory was a blessing as it made me really appreciate what we have together."

Cat yawned loudly.

"C'mere, you," Billie said as she invited Cat into her arms. She kissed Cat on the forehead after she snuggled into Billie's shoulder. "Comfy?"

"Yes."

Billie stared at the ceiling as Cat lay in her arms.

Would you really have walked away from me if my memory hadn't returned, Cat? I would have lost my reason to live if you had.

Billie thought about how things had changed since Cat came into her life. They met five years ago, at a time when her life was in turmoil. Her son, Seth was six years old at the time and in a persistent coma from a head injury after being hit by a drunk driver.

Billie met Cat while teaching her aerobics class. Cat was the most uncoordinated student she had ever seen and each morning for the next several weeks, Cat and Billie met at the gym for private lessons and before long, they fell in love. Little did they know, they both harbored secrets that had the potential of changing their lives forever. Unbeknownst to Cat, Billie spent each evening visiting her son in the hospital. Cat, on the other hand, hid the fact that she had a daughter, four year old, Tara.

Several weeks later Cat failed to show up for one of their morning aerobics lessons and when Billie went to Cat's apartment to check on her, she was met at the door by the little girl. Cat was suffering with appendicitis and refused to go to the hospital because she had no one to care for Tara. Needless to say, Billie stepped in and over the next couple of weeks, their secrets were revealed.

Cat's father was a neurosurgeon and he was able to reverse Seth's coma, allowing him to go home with both Billie and Cat who had decided to blend their families. Soon after they moved in together, their worlds were turned upside down when Billie's ex-husband Brian, broke into the house while Billie was at work and raped Cat. Eight months later, Skylar, their beautiful baby girl, entered their lives.

Billie looked at Cat as she slept on her shoulder.

Cat, you have endured so much heartache that you would not have suffered if you had never met me. Yet you continue to devote your life to me. I have never been more in love with anyone than I am with you, she thought.

Soon after Skylar was born, they bought a house in a quiet neighborhood on the outskirts of Albany, New York. They did not anticipate the animosity from neighbors who were unhappy with such an unconventional family living in their midst. It wasn't until Billie rescued some of her neighbors from their burning house that the community began to accept them. Then Billie's ex-husband once again entered their lives and took Cat and the children hostage in exchange for ransom. Billie made an attempt to rescue them, but in the process, Brian shot her in the head, the bullet lodging itself in the frontal lobe. If not for Cat's medical training, she would have died.

Two years later, Billie began to experience crippling headaches and uncharacteristic mood swings, and even went so far as to threaten Cat with physical abuse. It was as if she was a totally different person.

In the midst of the chaos, a series of photographs arrived in the mail depicting her and an unknown female in extremely compromising and pornographic poses. In a fit of blind rage, Cat threw Billie out.

Billie forced Cat to see her side of the story. In truth, the pictures revealed the horrific life that she had lived while still married to Brian… that of a battered wife, forced to endure the humiliation of sex with the female prostitute while her husband photographed them.

Putting the incident behind them was painful, but the healing was quick as their love blossomed anew. After the healing began, the only thing that marred their life together was the constant recurrence of headaches, which often sent Billie to bed.

Then one morning, Cat was unable to wake Billie. Cat

made the heart-wrenching decision for Billie to undergo brain surgery to repair the damage the gunshot wound to the head had incurred two years earlier. Cat's decision saved Billie's life, but could have potentially turned her into and invalid. As it turned out, Billie awoke from a post-surgery coma with promise of a full recovery, but with no memories of her life with Cat nor their daughters.

The journey back was long and arduous. Billie fought to regain her mobility and sense of self, while she watched Cat anguish over the possibility of losing her soul mate forever.

Little by little, the memories returned. When the final barrier fell, the two came together in a tide of passion so strong their lovemaking left them both feeling exhausted and exhilarated at the same time.

Pretty much the way I feel right now, Billie thought. She kissed Cat on the head, causing her to stir from sleep.

"I'm sorry, love. I didn't mean to wake you," Billie said.

Cat smiled. "That's okay. You have a far-away look in your eyes. Do you want to share?"

"I was just thinking about everything that's happened to us since we met. You know Cat, it took losing myself for me to truly appreciate what I have, and who I am," Billie said.

"Who are you, Billie? I mean, really–who *are* you?" Cat asked.

Billie tucked a stray lock of hair behind Cat's ear. "What do you mean?"

"Well, I have a large family, several sisters, parents who are well established in the community, two wonderful grandparents in South Carolina. I know my roots," she explained.

Billie frowned. "I'm sure there's a point in there somewhere."

"Billie, what I'm trying to get at is this: I know where I come from, but you never talk about yourself or your family or where you come from? Do you have any aunts or uncles? Grandparents?" Cat asked.

"My parents never talked about their families," Billie

said. “I never thought much about it until now, but they were pretty evasive about them, in fact.”

"Well, maybe we should look into this further," Cat said. "Maybe we should have a family tree done. You know, trace our genealogies. If we really feel we were destined to be together, maybe the same is true for our ancestors."

Billie closed her eyes and pressed her head into the pillow. "Hmmmm," she murmured, "I'll think about it, but right now we should really get some sleep. We both have to work in the morning."

Cat grinned. "I guess you're right. We both know how hard you are to get up in the morning."

Billie raised her eyebrows. "Me? *I'm* hard to get up? Hell, it takes three men and a boy to get *you* out of bed in the morning, my dear!"

"Three men and a boy, huh? Does that mean you're willing to share me?" Cat asked.

Billie rolled to her side and loomed over Cat. "I will never share you with anyone, sweet thing. Is that clear?"

Cat smiled and placed a quick peck on Billie's lips. "Clear as a bell, love. Clear as a bell," she replied.

Billie gathered Cat into her arms once more and pulled the blanket up around them both. "Sleep well, my love," she said as she closed her own eyes.

Cat rested her head on Billie's shoulder and threw her arm around her waist. "You too," she said before drifting off to sleep.

* * *

"Good Morning, Art," Billie said as she passed her boss's office on her way to her own. She threw her briefcase on her desk and went directly to her coffee maker. After setting up the pot to brew, she turned on her computer and logged on to the Internet. She grabbed the mouse and directed the cursor to her bookmarks and double clicked on a search engine.

"Let's see now," she said to herself. "Search keywords-genealogy, family tree."

After pressing the enter button, poured herself a cup of

coffee as the computer to display the requested items. Within moments, several web sites on the topic of genealogy appeared. She bookmarked the more interesting sites, intending to return to it later in the day during breaks and lunch.

Just before lunch, her boss, and good friend Art, poked his head into Billie office. "Pastrami on rye, or ham and cheese?" he asked.

Billie looked up from her computer. "Huh?"

"We're taking orders for lunch. Pastrami on rye, or ham and cheese?" he asked again.

"Ham and cheese, thanks." Billie turned her eyes back to the screen.

Art looked at his friend and drew his brow together. "You okay, Billie?"

Billie looked up distractedly. "Yeah, I'm fine."

"Hold on, I'll be right back, gotta give Jack our sandwich orders."

Art returned to Billie's office a few moments later and closed the door. He sat in her visitor's chair facing her desk and cleared his voice to get her attention.

Billie looked up. "Is there something I can help you with, Art?"

"Yes. You can tell me what's up with you. Is everything all right? Is Cat all right? The kids?" he questioned.

Billie reached across the desk and covered Art's hand with her own. "I'm fine. Cat's fine. The kids are fine. I've just been busy. Between the case files I'm working on and the research I am doing for Cat, I barely have time for a bathroom break," she explained.

"Research? What kind? Maybe I can help," he volunteered.

Billie looked at Art a little uneasily. "You're going to think I'm crazy, but losing my memory made me question just who I am. I mean, who would I be today if my memory hadn't returned? I have no idea where my family comes from. My parents didn't, or better yet, wouldn't talk about any extended family I may or may not have, so I aim to find out for myself. I am researching how to do a family tree. I want to learn how to trace Cat's and my genealogies into the distant past."

"How distant?" Art asked.

"I don't know, as far back as we can, I guess. Cat has it in her head that our lives have been connected in some way across the generations, so the goal is to keep going back until we find where our ancestors crossed paths."

Art's eyes grew wide. "Now what makes Cat think your ancestors were together?"

Billie looked away nervously, chewing on her bottom lip.

"Come on, Billie, you know I don't play the waiting game well. Spill it," Art demanded.

"Art, do you believe in psychic connections?" Billie asked.

"Psychic connections. You mean, like mind reading?"

"Sort of," Billie said. "I'm talking more along the lines of cross-dimensional communications."

"Charland, what did you put in your coffee this morning?"

"I'm sorry Art. You probably think I'm out of my mind. Let's just drop it, okay?" she said.

"No, I don't think so, Billie. You have definitely piqued my interest," Art replied. "So, what exactly is cross-dimensional communication?"

"It's kind of hard to explain. Cat and I have always had this telepathy thing going on, kind of like a sixth sense. Not long after we met, she fell ill with appendicitis, and I instinctively knew there was something wrong with her. Then there was the day Brian broke into the condo and raped her. I swear I sat here at this desk and a heat wave of fear overcame me when it happened. We've had the same exact dreams, even before we met. It's kind of freaky, but it's like our souls have known one another forever."

"So, you're telling me that you and Cat have a connection of sorts, kind of like the way some twins are connected," he concluded.

"Yes, exactly," Billie said. "Cat and I have believed for a

long time that we have always been destined to be together, and she thinks our ability to know when the other is in danger is so strong that our ancestors might have experienced it as well."

Art looked at his friend with wide eyes. "Well, if I've learned anything over the past several years, it's that a lot of strange things are possible where you and Cat are concerned. If you tell me you are experiencing cross-dimensional communication, then I guess I have to believe you," Art said. "So, how can I help?"

"Are you sure you want to do this, Art? So far what I've found on line is pretty dry reading, and there are thousands of web sites. Who knows how many we'll have to go through before we find anything useful," Billie warned.

"Well, with two of us looking, it's bound to go faster, don't you think?" Art replied.

"You might be right, especially since I'm trying to tie our bloodlines back several generations," she said.

"You do realize you have one hell of a task ahead of you, don't you?" he pointed out. "Heck, I don't think records even exist beyond the eighteen hundreds."

"I know, but the bond is so strong, Art. I have to try. I promised Cat I would."

Art perched on the edge of Billie's desk and crossed his arms. He took a deep breath. "Well, call me crazy, but count me in. I'll do what I can to help."

Billie smiled. "Thanks Art, I know I can always count on you," she said.

Chapter 2

Cat and Jen relaxed on the back porch, enjoying tall glasses of iced tea when Billie pulled her car into the driveway. Seth and Stevie paused from playing basketball, and stepped aside to allow her room to drive the car into the garage.

Billie grabbed her briefcase and pressed the automatic garage door closer on the way out. She put her briefcase down against the closed door. "How about I kick your butts in a game of hoops elimination?" she challenged the two boys.

"You're on, Mom!" Seth replied. He winked at Stevie. "Easy, peasy," he said.

For the next hour, Cat and Jen watched as they passed the ball between them, shooting hoops until finally, it was just Seth and Billie remaining in a one-on-one situation.

"Look at her," Cat exclaimed. "She's out there in a skirt and heels, playing basketball! Sometimes I wonder who the biggest kid *is* in this family," Cat finished, secretly proud of her wife.

"I think it's kind of cute," Jen said. "I mean, if there's one thing you can say about Billie, it's that she's fun. She's not afraid to get right into it with the kids… even my kids! Stevie and Karissa aren't one bit intimidated by the big lug. Parents in general don't do enough of that these days," she observed.

"Yeah, I guess you're right. I should be grateful that she's such a hands-on parent," Cat answered. "Oh, oh, it's come down to the wire. Billie and Seth, one-on-one," Cat pointed out. Their attention was drawn back to the competition in the driveway.

Seth and Stevie stood off to the side while Billie stood at

the free-throw line, bouncing the ball repeatedly on the ground in front of her.

"Okay, Mom. If you make this shot, you win. Miss it, and you bow down to the king, AKA, me!" Seth bragged, trying to intimidate his mother into missing the shot.

Billie looked at Seth out of the corner of her eye and grinned. She bounced the ball a few more times, set herself and tossed the ball up towards the hoop. The ball hit the backboard, almost dead center and came down on the edge of the ring. It bounced back and forth, and swirled around, until it finally fell over the *outside* edge of the ring and onto the blacktop below.

"Aarrgghh!" Billie exclaimed as she watched Seth strut around.

"I'm the man! I'm the man!" Seth high-fived Stevie and retrieved the ball. "Like I said – easy, peasy!" he said as he walked circles around Billie while continuing to bounce the ball.

Billie stood there, arms crossed, tapping one toe, a look of frustration on her face. Finally, giving up the poor loser facade, she grabbed him while he strutted by like a bantam rooster, and planted a big wet kiss on his cheek.

"Aw, Mom!" he complained, wiping his cheek off as she released him.

Stevie stood by the sidelines and laughed at his friend's embarrassment. "Better you than me!" he teased.

"What?" Billie exclaimed. "Can't a Mom be proud of her baby boy?"

Seth turned five shades of red. "Mom, do you *have* to call me that? Geesh! I'm almost twelve, you know!"

"I know how old you are, scamp!" she replied. "But you'll *always* be my baby, like it or not," she teased as she walked away. "Good game, by the way. I really am proud of you, kiddo."

Seth resigned himself to the praise. "Thanks, Mom," he said as he and Stevie returned to their game.

Billie retrieved her briefcase and headed for the house.

She pushed the screen door open and stepped onto the porch, only to be met by Cat. Billie set her briefcase down and took Cat into her arms. "Hey love," she said.

"Hey, yourself," Cat said. "How was your day?"

"Better now that I'm home," Billie replied. Billie took Cat's hand and walked her to the empty chair next to Jen. She sat down and pulled Cat onto her lap where they exchanged several kisses.

"Ahem," Jen said from just a few feet away. "You two *really* need to get a room!"

Billie and Cat turned their faces toward the sound, their cheeks touching side by side. They shot identical looks of innocence at Jen.

Jen raised her eyebrows at the two women. "Oh, come on now. You can just wipe those innocent looks off your faces. Don't forget, I was there when the two of you were screaming like banshees in the campground showers not too long ago, remember?"

Billie looked toward the floor and grinned as her face turned a lovely shade of pink.

"Busted!" Cat said.

"Busted is right!" Jen said. "Well, I guess I need to collect my brats and head home. Fred should have the grill going by now." She rose from her chair and walked just inside the kitchen. "Karissa, honey. Time to go home before Daddy grills the burgers to a crisp!" she called to her daughter.

"Okay, Mom. I'll be right there," Karissa answered.

Jen turned back toward the porch, only to see her two friends in another lip lock. She shook her head side to side. "Don't you two ever get enough?" she asked.

Cat smiled at their friend as she climbed off Billie's lap. "The day we get enough, Jen, is the day you can write our obituaries," Cat chuckled. She looked at Billie. "Iced tea or beer?" she asked.

"Beer. Help me up and I'll get it myself," she said, extending her hand to Cat.

Cat pulled Billie to her feet then headed inside, only to have Billie follow close behind, pinching her backside along the way.

"Stop that!" Cat complained as she half-heartedly avoided Billie's reach.

"Stop what?" Billie teased, chasing her into the kitchen and pinning her against the cupboard for a kiss.

"I am so jealous!" Jen said. "Do me a favor and have a heart to heart with Fred, will you? If he was half as passionate as either of you, I'd never get out of bed!"

Billie chuckled at Jen's exclamation.

Jen took exception at being laughed at, and grabbed the dishtowel from the counter top. She quickly rolled it up and snapped Billie on the behind as Cat cringed.

"Yeow! What the hell!" Billie exclaimed. She turned around sharply to look at Jen.

Jen had an evil look in her eyes as she rolled up the towel once more, ready for round two.

"You are a dead woman, Swenson!" Billie exclaimed as her eyes darted around, looking for a weapon to use against her.

Cat stepped between them. "Come on now, girls," she said, trying to diffuse the situation.

"If I were you, I'd get out of the line of fire, Cat," Jen said as she grinned and swirled the towel even tighter.

"She's right, Cat. You don't want to get Jen's blood on that nice blouse you're wearing," Billie agreed as her eyes settled on the perfect weapon.

"Okay! Okay! Have at it. Kill each other!" Cat exclaimed as she stepped back to watch.

Billie and Jen never took their eyes off one another as they circled, sizing each other up and maneuvering for an advantage. Finally, Jen made a slight movement forward.

That move was Billie cue to act. She shifted her weight quickly to the right, turned on the cold water and grabbed the sprayer on the sink, directing it full throttle into Jen's face.

Jen shrieked as the cold water soaked her face, hair and clothing. Cat held one hand over her mouth, the other one holding her stomach as hysterical laughter nearly overtook her. Billie stood, sprayer in hand, a wicked look on her face, ready to douse the flames once more should Jen decide to re-ignite.

Jen started rolling up the now-soaked towel once more, the look on her face even more determined than ever. A malicious grin spread across Billie's face. Just as Jen raised the towel, and Billie raised the sprayer, Karissa, Tara and Skylar entered the kitchen from the living room.

"Okay, Mom. I'm ready to go home," Karissa said, drawing Jen's attention away from the impending battle. She looked at her mother in open-mouthed surprise. "Mom, you're wet," she said unnecessarily.

Jen looked from her daughter, back to her friend. She placed the towel on the counter and leaned in to whisper into Billie's ear, "You haven't heard the last from me yet, oh Tall One. Watch your back. Paybacks are a bitch!"

She planted a kiss on Billie's cheek and then repeated the gesture on Cat.

"Come on, honey," she said to Karissa. "Time to rescue our dinner from Dad. I'll see you all later!" She looked meaningfully at Billie. "I'll see *you* later."

Cat opened her arms to Billie once more as they watched their friend leave. Her hands cupped the sides of Billie's face. "Billie, you are so bad. I think you've really done it this time. I could see the wheels turning in that wicked little mind of Jen's. You'd better be careful around her."

Billie just chuckled. "Have faith, woman. I can handle Blondie."

"Well, one of these days Blondie is going to give Dagwood a run for her money," Cat replied.

Billie turned to Tara and Skylar who were rummaging through the refrigerator for a snack. "What am I, chopped liver? Don't I get a hug?" she asked.

Both girls quickly hugged Billie then immediately turned their attention back to the refrigerator.

Billie raised her eyebrows at her daughters' quick dismissal. "I guess I know how I rate," she said.

"Nothing comes before food," Cat chuckled. "Why don't you go change into something more comfortable while I clean up the mess you and Jen made."

"Something more comfortable?" Billie stepped in close to Cat so the girls couldn't hear. "Are you trying to seduce me, Mrs. Charland?" Billie whispered.

"Busted again!" Cat exclaimed as she claimed Billie's lips once more. "Now go change your clothes," she ordered.

"Yes, Boss," Billie replied after placing a quick kiss on Cat's mouth.

* * *

After dinner, Cat and Billie relaxed on the front porch swing with a couple of iced teas as the children played croquet in the front yard. Billie pushed the swing back and forth with her toes while Cat sat sideways on the bench, her back resting against Billie's shoulder and her knees bent. A sense of peace and serenity pervaded the air around them.

"Cat?" Billie said.

Cat tilted her head back to look up at her wife. "Yeah?"

"Were you serious about researching our genealogies?"

Cat sat up and swung her legs over the seat of the swing. She looked at Billie. "Yes, that is, if you want to. It might be fun. Why do you ask?"

"I spent time doing some research on the subject today. There is a ton of information on the Internet, almost too much. I found a lot of useful material, some guidelines, some worksheets, you know, general information on how to get started. There are even software packages available to subscribe to that will help you build family trees. Art even gave me a hand," Billie replied.

"Art? What does he think of all this?"

"I had to tell him about the connection between us. You know how persistent he is. He wouldn't leave me alone until I told him why we were tracing our bloodlines."

"He must think we're nuts!" Cat remarked.

"At first, I think he did, but after I explained everything, he was ready to offer his full support. In any case, I think we have the essentials to get started, so if you're serious, then let's do it. Maybe we can get started this weekend?" Billie offered.

"This weekend? Why wait 'til then?"

"Because according to the literature, the first step is to research our immediate families. Considering I don't have any immediately family, we'll start with yours. The research suggested we start with something as simple as old family records. So, we'll invite ourselves to Doc and Mom's for a cookout on Saturday, and then dump the kids on them while we comb through the attic looking for old family records. What do you think?" Billie explained.

"Sound like you've got it all planned out, but what *I* think is that you have an ulterior motive behind getting me alone in the attic, Ms. Tall, Dark and Dangerous," Cat teased.

"Am I that transparent?" Billie asked.

"As clear as glass, my love. You should know better than to try to hide a libido as big as yours," Cat exclaimed.

"Nothing is as big as mine," Billie smiled. "You know, we *could* find out that I come from a long line of sexy, lecherous, characters that spend their lives seducing beautiful, young women," Billie wiggled her eyes brows up and down.

Cat laughed out loud. "One can only hope, Don Juanita. One can only hope!"

Chapter 3

Two days later, Billie and Cat sat at Ida and Doc's kitchen table drinking coffee and planning an approach to their ancestral search.

"So tell me again dear, why are you researching our family tree?" Ida asked as she poured coffee for the ladies.

"Thanks, Mom," Cat sipped her coffee. "Oh, this is good!" she exclaimed. "We're researching our family tree to see if there is some connection between us in the past."

"A connection? What makes you think there is a connection in the past?" Ida asked.

"Mom, have you ever met someone that you instantly click with?" Cat asked.

"Or the feeling of knowing someone for a life time even though you've just met?" added Billie.

Ida returned the coffeepot to the warming pad before carrying her own cup to the table. She sat and contemplated the questions for a moment before answering. "Yes, I guess I have had those feelings about people before," she said.

Cat placed a hand on her mother's arm. "Well, the feeling between Billie and me when we first met was so strong it was scary. After our first date, we both felt like we had known one another for a million lifetimes," Cat explained.

"I know this is going to sound odd, but it was almost as though our souls had met long before our bodies did," Billie said.

"So do you think that feeling of familiarity comes from your ancestors knowing one another?" Ida asked.

"Yes, we do," Cat replied. "I mean, what other explanation could there be? Unless, of course, you believe in reincarnation or something like that."

"Well, I guess you have nothing to lose by trying. Is there anything I can help with?" Ida offered.

"The first thing we need to do is to sketch out a family tree, as far back as we can without searching records. Mom, we'll need your help with that part of it," Billie replied.

Ida patted Billie's hand. "Sure, Honey. I'll give you all the help I can."

"Okay. The guidelines Billie found on line suggest that we start with our immediate families then go backward," Cat explained. "We can use this worksheet to keep track of the genealogy," she added, reaching into the folder on the table for the family tree worksheet Billie printed out.

Cat picked up a pencil and started writing in names as she talked. "Let's see; there's Billie and me, and our kids," Cat said.

Suddenly, Cat looked up at the other two women and grinned.

"Boy, the historians would have a field day with this one, years down the line. Two women in the same family tree are parents to three children. Who do you want to be Billie, the mom or the dad?" she asked, tongue in cheek.

"Well, let's see. I've got the androgynous name, I'm bigger, and I *did* cut the cord when Sky was born, so I guess I'll be the dad. Works for me," Billie mused.

"Okay," Cat said. "Dad: Billie Jean Charland. Mom: Caitlain Maureen O'Grady Charland. Children: Seth Michael, Tara Marie and Skylar Jean Charland. Maternal parents…"

"Should we include the other parentages of the kids, Cat?" Billie interrupted.

"If you'd like." Cat went back and wrote Brian Charland next to Seth and Skylar's names and Frozen Pop next to Tara's.

"There," she said. "Now where was I? Oh yeah, maternal parents: Michael O'Grady and Ida Wycliffe O'Grady. Maternal grandparents, father's side: Joseph O'Grady and Martha Anderson O'Grady. Maternal grandparents, mother's side: Josephine Wycliffe and Alexandra Spirakis. Matern..."

"It tickles me that your maternal grandparents are two women!" Billie interrupted.

Cat grinned. "Yep. It seems that I am their living legacy," she replied.

"I can understand why your parents were so accepting of our relationship," Billie replied.

"Now we couldn't very well have objected when I, too, am a product of such a union, could we?" Ida interjected, taking a sip of her coffee.

"I guess not," Billie said. "I hope you don't mind me asking, Mom, but do you know who your real father is?"

"I'm afraid not. It was never very important to me, so I never asked. As far as I was concerned, I have two very loving parents. It didn't matter to me that they were both women. Josephine is my birth mother, but Alexandra is the more maternal one. I guess if either of them played the 'daddy' role, it was Josephine," Ida explained. "I called Josephine, Mom, and Alexandra, Nona. I would sit for hours just to listen to Nona talk. She used to read bedtime stories to me in that South Carolina accent of hers. I loved her voice," Ida reminisced.

"She sounds like a wonderful person. Do you see much of them?" Billie asked.

Ida shook her head. "Not as much as I'd like to. They travel so much, it's tough to nail them down long enough for a decent visit," Ida explained. "They were in Greece when you and Caitlain were married, so they couldn't make the wedding."

"Yes, I remember. They're in their seventies, right? I'm surprised they're still traveling so much," Billie commented.

"They continue to travel the world history lecture circuit. Mom is a professor of history at The Citadel in South Carolina, and she is often invited to deliver keynote addresses and lectures around the world. Even at her advanced age, she just won't give up and retire... and Nona won't stay home without her, or at least that's what Mom says, although I secretly think she uses that as an excuse to have Nona with her. They go everywhere together," Ida explained.

"Sounds like they're very much in love," Billie observed.

"They are true soul mates, Billie. I never thought I would see that again until my Caitlain met you," Ida said.

Cat, who had been sitting there quietly, watching the interaction between the two women she loved, smiled and reached her hand across the table to Billie, who took it in her own and squeezed it lightly.

Ida looked back and forth between her daughter and daughter-in-law. "You know, Billie, you look exactly the way Nona did in her younger years. You could be twins, in fact."

"Cat has mentioned that before. Do I really look that much like her?" Billie asked.

Cat nodded vigorously. "Billie, maybe that's why you felt so familiar to me when we first met. You *do* look a lot like Grams. No wonder I fell in love with you the moment I laid eyes on you. I love my Grams very much."

"Maybe," Billie replied.

"Mom, are you sure you don't mind watching the kids for a few hours while Billie and I go through the old documents in the attic?" Cat asked.

"Caitlain, I've already said I don't mind. Now, you and Billie take your coffee cups with you and head upstairs. I'm sure you'll find a lot of interesting information in the old trunks up there. Don't worry about the kids, your father and I have plans to take them to the movies in a little while. Knowing your father, a stop at the miniature golf course afterwards is also a strong possibility. We'll be gone for several hours, so enjoy your time alone, okay?" Ida said with a sparkle in her eyes.

Cat picked up her Mother's hidden meaning and blushed to the roots of her hair. Billie just smiled and sat contemplating her coffee cup.

"Thanks, Mom," Cat kissed her mother on the cheek then turned to Billie. "Ready?" she asked.

Billie picked up her cup. "Lead the way."

Cat led Billie to the second story hallway and pointed at the ceiling. "We need to pull the steps down," she said.

Billie contemplated the recessed panel in the ceiling.

"Do you have a hook of some type?" she asked.

"Duh! That would be helpful, wouldn't it?" Cat said, gently chastising herself. She opened the closet door just a few feet away and retrieved the hook that hung on the inside wall. She handed it to Billie. "You'll have to do this. I'm afraid I'm a little too vertically challenged for the job."

Billie took the bar from Cat and worked the hooked end into the ring on the panel above them. She pulled down steadily until the folding stairs were low enough to complete the job by hand.

"After you," she said to Cat as she stepped aside.

Cat and Billie stepped into a very dusty, but intriguing attic. Countless boxes and trunks lined nearly every inch of wall space, in addition to old furniture, toys and clothing. The bright sunlight shone at both ends of the attic through windows covered by a thin layer of dust. Particles of dust danced along the sunbeams.

Billie was in awe of her surroundings. "Wow, this is really cool!" she exclaimed as she lazily walked around touching box after box and picking up a stray toy to examine.

Cat watched Billie investigate, sensing her child-like vibes of excitement.

"We used to play up here on rainy days," Cat said. "In fact, if you take a more global look at that end of the attic, you'll see how Daddy painted and decorated the walls to make it look like a fun-house. My sisters and I spent countless hours up here playing house or pretending to be famous movie stars. We would even give occasional performances for our parents," Cat said wistfully as she recalled some of her fondest childhood memories.

Billie felt the pangs of envy fill her heart as she silently mourned her more stoic childhood.

"Did you have a special place like this, Billie?" Cat asked.

Billie shook her head no. "Unfortunately, Cat, we moved around a lot when I was really young. I was a military brat. We never stayed in one place long enough to create these kinds of memories. Anyhow, with no brothers or sisters to share it with, what fun would it have been?" she reasoned.

"Didn't you have a best friend you were close to?" Cat inquired.

"I had friends at school, but no one I would call a best friend. My parents pretty much frowned on kids hanging out at the house," Billie explained.

"No sleep-overs or anything like that?" Cat asked.

"Nope. They didn't believe in that. They pretty much kept to themselves, and as a result, I was kind of a loner," Billie replied sadly.

Cat touched the side of Billie's face. "It must have been a lonely childhood, my love. I'm sorry," she whispered.

Billie smiled to relieve the dismal mood the discussion had put them in. "It had its moments, Cat. I was an only child, so I had my parents' full attention. I certainly didn't lack for love and comfort. It could have been worse."

"I guess," Cat replied skeptically before changing the subject. "We'd better get to work before we lose our light."

Moments later, Billie and Cat sat cross-legged on the floor, surrounded by several dusty boxes, whose contents had been half emptied around them.

Somewhere during the search, the quest to reconstruct Cat's family tree was lost amid the mounds of pictures of Cat as a baby… Cat as a toddler… Cat in grade school. Ida was a fanatic about taking and keeping photographs of her children. Dozens of photo albums and loose pictures were jammed into boxes all over the room.

"Awwww, look at this," Billie said, handing a picture to Cat. "You were so cute! You looked just like Tara does today."

The picture was of Cat at nine years old, dressed in a pinafore dress with a large bow in her hair and a flower basket hooked over her left arm. Three other children dressed as a lion, a scarecrow, and a tin man surrounded her.

"Oh, god! I was in the fourth grade. We were doing a class production of the Wizard of Oz," she explained, blushing.

Billie took Cat's chin in her hand. "You made a cute

Dorothy, my love."

"I love you, Billie," Cat said.

"Wait a minute!" Billie reached beyond Cat and grabbed a yellowed copy of a very old newspaper article. She pulled herself into a sitting position and held the paper in front of her.

"Billie, what is it?" Cat asked.

"Cat, look!" Billie exclaimed as she held the newspaper for Cat to see.

There, across the headlines, in bold Gothic print, were the words *Local Hero Breaks Secret Viet Cong Code.* Under the headline, was a large, fuzzy black and white photograph of a light-haired woman dressed in dark trousers and a leather bomber jacket. Her hair in disarray under a tattered hat and a there was a cigar clamped between her teeth. Standing beside her was a slim, dark haired woman clothed in a matronly dress which was graced by a string of pearls. The dress had a lapel collar and was belted at the waist. She was wearing high-heeled shoes and her hair was tied neatly into a bun at the nape of her long, slender neck. A caption ran under the photo.

"Local resident, Josephine Wycliffe (right) and Greek liaison, Alexandra Spirakis are awarded the Distinguished Civilian Service Award after successfully assisting the U.S. Navy in breaking a Vietnamese communication code. This code has resulted in the deaths of many US forces over the past several months."

The article was dated May thirtieth, nineteen sixty.

Cat took the paper from Billie and read it out loud.

"Local historian and professor of History at The Citadel, Josephine Wycliffe, and Greek liaison and resident of Charleston, South Carolina, Alexandra Spirakis, accomplished what scores of intelligence officers failed to do. They broke the secret military code used to communicate instructions to the Vietnamese fighters as to the location of SEATO (South East Asia Treaty Organization) forces in the field.

"Wycliffe, a renowned historian, worked with Spirakis, an interpreter fluent in five languages, to decipher the previously unbreakable code. When asked how she did it, Wycliffe simply said, "The power of history was behind us. Al [Miss Spirakis] simply researched the history of a similar ancient Greek communication system that was developed hundreds of years ago. From there it was easy. It ain't brain surgery!"

Cat smiled at Josephine's bold speech. "Grandma Jo is quite a character," she said. "Sometimes I wonder why Grams has been with her for so many years."

Billie's interest was piqued. "What do you mean?" she asked.

"Well, they're like night and day. Grams towers over Grandma Jo by about eight inches, and though she's relatively small in comparison, Grandma Jo is a ball of fire that just *cannot* be extinguished. I swear that woman will never grow up. The highlight of every family get together is a lively football game with Grandma Jo as quarterback. She's quite butch, preferring to dress in trousers and button-down shirts, and *always* sports that old worn fedora of hers. She swears like a sailor and until recently, her bad habits included smoking old stogie cigars that Grams absolutely detests."

"And Alexandra? What is she like?" Billie asked, fascinated with the idea that Cat's grandparents were elderly lesbians.

Cat smiled broadly. "Grams is absolutely beautiful. Tall and regal, but at the same time a perfectly dainty southern belle. She is quite a contrast to Grandma Jo. I don't believe I have ever seen her in anything less than properly starched dresses, with neatly coifed hair, and the faint smell of jasmine and lavender. And her voice... her voice is melodious and very heavily laden with Southern twang. When I was little, I used to sit cuddled up against her for hours just enjoying the smell and sound of her."

Billie watched Cat closely, a sense of homesickness for her own absent family settling in the pit of her stomach. She found herself absorbed in the stories Cat was weaving and yearned to know more about the elderly ladies who obviously loved each other very much.

"So is Jo from the South too?" Billie asked.

Cat threw her head back and laughed. "Heavens no!" she exclaimed. "Grandma Jo is definitely a Yankee and makes no secret of the fact that she thinks her Northern roots are far superior to anyone in the South!"

"That must have gone over big with Alex!" Billie exclaimed.

"Nowadays Grams lets it run right off her back. In her younger years, she allowed Grandma Jo to get to her, but now she just calls her an old poop, or something equally as funny, then dismisses what she obviously considers to be Yankee rambling," Cat described through chuckles. "They certainly are a pair!"

"How did they meet?" Billie asked.

Cat picked up the article Billie discarded and looked at the picture once more. "This is how they met," Cat said.

"Really?" Billie asked. "They met during the war?"

"Yes. As the article says, Grandma Jo is an historian, and a very vocal one at that. At the onset of the war, she pestered the Department of Defense on a regular basis, insisting she could help win the war. More than fifty years ago, she was a very vibrant, outspoken, young professor with a very large chip on her shoulder…not that the chip isn't still there today, mind you," Cat joked before continuing. "On top of her colossal ego, and being a woman, she felt she had something to prove, so she pestered the Department of Defense, and they, of course, wrote her off as some kind of whacko. It wasn't until she became an instructor at the Citadel that they actually took notice of her and listened."

"How did she do that?" Billie said incredulously.

"Well, actually," Cat replied, "she used her connections at the Citadel to get access to a general officer at the Pentagon. She pestered that poor man mercilessly until he finally gave her a chance to state her case."

"And her case was…?" Billie asked.

"She felt that given the opportunity, and the assistance of a linguist, she could break the secret code the Viet Cong were using to communicate tactical locations of SEATO forces to ground troops who were waiting in ambush. Being a professor of history, she claimed she had the knowledge and the know-how to break the code," Cat explained.

"Let me guess," Billie interrupted. "The linguist was Alex."

"Yes," confirmed Cat. "As I said, Grams is fluent in five languages, Vietnamese being one of them. Since Alex already had top secret clearance in her role as the Greek liaison, the military brass was able to bypass all the bureaucracy, and simply assigned her to work with Jo on the code."

"So, Jo and Alex met and it was love at first sight," Billie guessed.

"Not exactly," Cat replied. "They were like oil and water at first. Jo had little use for helpless women, which she mistakenly thought Alex was at first. That is, until one evening while eating dinner at a local restaurant, Jo had a little too much to drink and Alex quite easily threw her over her shoulder and carried her home. She had a new respect for the southern belle from that point on. Pretty soon, one thing led to another and before they knew what hit them, they realized they were in love. They've been together ever since," Cat finished.

"Jo *does* sound like a character. I'll bet life with her was quite interesting," Billie commented.

"Interesting is an understatement, my love. The stories I have heard about their exploits! Remind me to tell you a few of them someday."

"They sound wonderful. I'd like to meet them one day," Billie replied. "Someday soon, because I don't think we're getting very far in this attic."

"Let's not give up so fast. I know there's more information here. We just need to look." Cat looked around once more at the array of boxes stacked neatly around the attic. "Why don't you start over there, while I look over here," Cat suggested, indicating the boxes located at the far end of the room.

Several hours later, they had collected a sizeable stack of papers and photographs, all containing information to help fill in the lower branches of Cat's family tree.

Billie looked at the stack of information and sighed. "We've just started on the tip of the iceberg, and I'll bet the portion still under the water is huge! I'd like to talk to your grandmothers at some point. Maybe they can fill in the blanks for us."

Cat nodded in agreement then picked up the discarded article they read earlier. She carefully scanned the picture then looked at Billie and smiled. "You *do* look like her, you know."

Billie looked at the faded photograph one more time. "You think so?" she asked.

"Yes, I do."

Billie chuckled. "Well then love, we have a problem."

"Huh?" Cat said, confused.

"Yeah, you're in love with, and routinely make love to, someone who reminds you of your grandmother. You, my darling, need serious counseling!" she said, grinning from ear to ear.

Billie suddenly found herself buried under a mound of old and dusty photographs as Cat made a hasty exit before Billie could catch her.

Chapter 4

Later that evening, after the children were fast asleep, Billie once more teased Cat about having a thing for her grandmother. Once again, Cat stomped off, leaving Billie alone, chuckling, in the family room. After she waited what she considered an appropriate amount of time for Cat to cool down, Billie extinguished the flames in the fireplace, checked and secured the house, then went upstairs to their bedroom. She stopped in front of the bedroom door, inhaled deeply and mentally steeled herself for dealing with Cat, should she still be upset about the teasing earlier in the evening. She reached for the handle and found it to be locked.

"Sweetheart, may I come in?"

Silence ...

"Please?"

Silence ...

"Cat, honey, please. I'm sorry. I was only teasing."

Silence ...

"Cat?"

Silence ...

Billie sighed and resigned herself to spend the night in the guest room downstairs. She turned around and took one step down the hall toward the stairs when suddenly, the door behind her opened and she felt herself pulled into the bedroom by her collar. The door shut and she found her face pressed against it.

"Hands on the door, grandma. Feet apart," said a sultry voice.

Slim hands found their way around Billie's waist then came to rest on her abdomen. The firm body behind her pressed her harder into the cold wood as the hands continued to roam. Billie's eyes closed as a desire ignited deep within her core and spread through her entire being, following the path that the hands were trailing up and down her body. Her knees weakened under the onslaught as the hands found their way up to cup full breasts.

"My, what firm breasts you have, grandma," a raspy voice said in her ear.

"All the more to please you with," Billie said.

The hands were on the move once more, trailing a path of fire from breasts to hips. Billie felt nimble fingers snake around to the front to release the catch at her waist and lower her zipper. All Billie could do was moan in a deep throaty voice into the wood panel her face was pressed against.

Suddenly, the hands were at her waistband, sliding down inside the edge of her jeans. They found their way around the back to cup firm cheeks, sliding the denim and silk off as they massaged the succulent flesh.

"My, what firm cheeks you have, grandma," said the voice.

Again, Billie answered. "All the more to please you with, wolf."

The reference to wolf drew a deep chuckle from the disembodied voice behind her.

Moments later, the jeans and panties lay in a heap around Billie's ankles.

"Kick them off," the voice whispered into her ear, sending shivers of desire coursing through her.

The jeans were soon in a pile against the wall.

Next, the hands moved under the front of Billie's T-shirt and massaged her breasts before moving around to the back, kneading the firm muscles across her shoulders. Billie soon found her shirt being pulled upward over her head, only to join the pile of denim against the wall. The unseen force grabbed Billie's wrists and pressed Billie's hands against the door once more, then trailed a path of desire up and down her biceps.

"My, what strong arms you have, Grandma," the sultry voice said again from over her shoulder.

Billie's eyes were squeezed shut. She took a deep breath and said shakily, "All the more to pl—Oh God!" she cried as she felt teeth sink into the taut muscle stretched across her shoulder blade. "God!" she said again as her knees buckled.

Suddenly, in one movement, she felt the clasp of her bra release as her breasts were freed from their lace prison. The hands grabbed her shoulders and spun her around, forcing her back into the door. Billie opened her eyes and looked into the passion filled depths of Cat's smoldering green eyes, realizing for the first time that Cat was totally naked. Neither could look away.

Cat's chest rose up and down rapidly. "Could I do this to my grandmother, Billie?" She took Billie's breast into her mouth and clamped down on the nipple until Billie cried out in ecstasy.

Billie was helpless, paralyzed by desire where she stood.

Cat let her hands freely roam around Billie's body, pushing her closer and closer to the edge of oblivion. Cat suddenly dropped to her knees and invaded the very depths of her core with such abandon, that Billie literally sank to the floor in a boneless puddle of flesh, her body wracked with spasms. Cat lay with her and held her close while whispering words of endearment until Billie slowly returned to herself. Several moments passed before Cat could convince Billie to rise from the floor and move to the bed. As they lay entwined, she pulled Cat close and held her tight.

"Cat, I have never felt so complete and fulfilled in my life. Just when I think I know you inside and out, you do this to me. I love you with everything I am, even if I do remind you of your grandmother," Billie said, chuckling at the personal joke. "Let me love you, Cat. I want to make you feel as good as I do right now. Please," she added.

Cat raised herself onto her knees and leaned over Billie. She placed kisses along her breastbone to Billie's neck, working her way up her throat to her left ear. "I love you," she whispered before clamping down on Billie's earlobe with her teeth.

"Oh, god!" Billie exclaimed. Her chest thrust upward as bolts of desire invaded the depths of her core once more. She tightened her hold on Cat. "Cat, do you know what you're doing to me?" she asked. "I'm supposed to be making love to you!"

"I can't get enough of you, Billie," Cat said. She lay there, breast to breast, resting her elbows on either side of Billie's head. She placed several kisses on her mouth, gently exploring Billie's lips and finally demanding entrance into the moist depth.

Billie's hands roamed up and down Cat's naked back as their tongues danced in exploration, entwining, probing, thrusting, tasting and evoking a raging tide of emotions within both women.

Soon, the battle escalated from passionate kissing to vigorous caresses. Hands roamed freely and aggressively over bare skin. Cat's nails raked in a crisscrossing pattern over Billie's back, leaving raised welts in their wake. Bolts of desire followed in the wake of Cat's nails, settling in her groin and driving her mad with need. Locking their legs together, Billie flipped them over until she was lying on top of Cat.

"My turn," Billie said before diving into Cat's mouth, shoving her tongue deep into Cat's throat, while Cat squirmed with desire beneath her.

"Billie. Billie, please. I need you," Cat pleaded between kisses. Cat wove her fingers into Billie's long black hair, and held her head close.

Billie moved her caresses to Cat's neck, nipping and biting a trail down her neck and across her collar bone. With each bite, Cat moaned loudly, praising any god that would listen, for bringing this remarkable woman into her life.

Billie began a very slow descent down the length of Cat's body. She stopped to savor Cat's breasts, teasing and nipping, until the nipples were standing at attention. Cat squealed with desire as Billie pinched and suckled each one between her teeth, pulling at them until the pain exceeded the point of comfortable tolerance. Cat cried out as the pain became too intense to bear, providing Billie with the signal she needed to back off.

Releasing the swollen nub suddenly, Billie watched as the now red nipple throbbed and pulsed in time with Cat's ragged breathing.

By the time she repeated the process on the other breast, Cat was beside herself with need and longing. Her own seduction of Billie, combined with the assault she was presently undergoing, pushed her to the limits of endurance. She was about to go over the edge, with or without Billie's help. She placed her hands on Billie's shoulders and pushed her down toward her throbbing center.

"Oh god, Billie, please take me. I can't wait any longer!"

Billie looked into Cat's face and smiled.

"Patience, my love. I will make you mine... soon," she teased before continuing to place a trail of kisses down Cat's abdomen.

Cat thrust her hips upward toward Billie, begging for fulfillment. Cat's head was thrown back into the pillows. Her hands clutched the bed sheets on both sides of her hips as her chest arched upward… eyes closed, lips moist and parted as her brow creased with the effort to contain the desire that threatened to overcome her.

Billie was awestruck at the sight before her eyes. The pure seductive nature of Cat's appearance nearly pushed Billie over the edge. Unable to control herself any longer, Billie dove into Cat, tasting, biting, caressing, and feasting on the uniqueness that could only be described as Cat.

Cat screamed Billie's name over and over as desire surged in her loins, growing with intensity and spreading throughout her entire being until it overwhelmed her senses. Finally, when Billie sensed that Cat could not withstand any more, she filled her core with an intensity that surprised them both.

The sudden, unexpected invasion pushed Cat completely to climax. The frenzy that had started in her loins suddenly exploded into a multimedia light show inside Cat's brain. Billie continued her ministrations as spasms uncontrollably wracked Cat's body, sending her into sensory overload, and causing her to momentarily lose consciousness. Retracting her fingers, Billie gathered Cat in her arms and held her tenderly as Cat came back to earth and slowly returned to herself.

As Billie held Cat close, she could feel wetness on her shoulder where Cat rested her head. She arched her head back and tilted Cat's chin upward. She was immediately alarmed by the tears flowing from Cat's eyes.

"Cat, what is it? Did I hurt you?"

Cat shuddered slightly in Billie's arms.

"No, love. You could never hurt me. I am just so overwhelmed by what I feel right now, that I can't contain it. Billie, I love you like I have never loved another soul. Promise me that we will always be together. I love you with everything I am."

Billie lowered her head and placed gentle kisses across Cat's lips.

"Cat, never in my life could I possibly express my love for you in such an eloquent way. You have spoken my own heart with your words. I love you too, little one, and I promise I will never leave you. I don't exist without you, Cat."

Billie gathered Cat in her arms.

"Sleep, my love," Billie said as she pulled the sheet up around them both.

"Are you convinced now that I don't think of my grandmother when I make love to you?" Cat asked.

"Grandmother? What grandmother?" Billie answered with a slight chuckle in her voice before drifting off to sleep.

Chapter 5

"More coffee?" Billie asked as she carried the coffee carafe to the table.

"Please." Cat pushed her cup toward Billie without looking up from the papers strewn on the table before her.

Billie smiled as she watched Cat pour over the notes they had taken from information found in Doc and Ida's attic the previous day. After refilling her own cup, she returned the pot to the warmer and rejoined Cat at the table.

"Okay, Billie," Cat said. She looked at the crude sketch on the table in front of her. "We have re-constructed my genealogy at least a generation beyond Grandmas Jo and Alex, except for my maternal grandfather. It's a dead end after that. Mom didn't have any records beyond the great-grandparents, so we'll have to start researching other things like census records, church and military records as well as birth, death and marriage certificates, immigration records and social security records." Cat looked up at Billie with a hint of disappointment on her face.

Billie traced her index finger down the side of Cat's face. "Hey, don't give up, love. We've just started and we have tons of avenues left to explore."

Cat closed her eyes and savored the feel of Billie's touch. "Hmmm, that feels good."

"So, why the disappointed look on your face?" Billie asked.

"We haven't even scratched the surface yet. It seems like such a huge undertaking. After all that time going through box after box in Mom's attic, we've only managed to go back three generations, and we haven't even started to research *your* family yet," Cat replied.

"We'll get to that later," Billie said. "We've actually

made more progress than you think. In fact, we've got a pretty good start on your genealogy. Sure, we've hit a dead end, but I think in addition to pouring over official records, we really should speak with your grandmothers. They might be able to fill in the gaps. At least some of them," Billie suggested.

"Yeah, I guess you're right. We'll have to find out when they'll be home next. It seems like they're on the road more than ever lately. I swear they think they're still kids. Mom keeps track of them by phone every week. I'll give her a call later to see if she knows where they are right now," Cat said.

Billie smiled. "All right. In the meantime, why don't we go to the hall of records at the library and see what we can dig up about your great-great-grandparents. Maybe we can start the search on my family at the same time," Billie suggested.

"I'll gather up the kids. Let's hit the children's section first to get them something to read while we're poring through the dull stuff," Cat suggested.

* * *

As it turned out, the library was hosting a children's read-a-thon that morning, which the three Charland siblings eagerly joined while their mothers went in search of historical records on their families.

"Wycliffe, Jonathan P, born January, eighteen ninety-seven, Norfolk, Virginia. Died, May nineteen fifty-eight in a cave-in in Brazil while researching ancient cave drawings. Occupation: Professor of History, New York University."

Cat paused. "Wow, Billie. I didn't realize Grandma Jo followed in her father's footsteps."

She continued to read. "Married to Helen Folstoy, September fourth, nineteen thirty-two. One child, Josephine, born February fifteenth, nineteen thirty-five. Parents, unknown. No military records. Great! This is just great!" Cat exclaimed after reading Jonathan's statistics out loud to Billie.

"What?" Billie asked.

"Parents, unknown," Cat said. "Without Grandma Jo's help, I don't think we'll find anything more on my family here. We'll have to contact the Census Bureau and Social Security Department on line to get any further. We might as well get started researching your family," Cat suggested.

"All right." Billie grabbed a pencil and piece of paper to take notes. "My parents' names were Daniel P. Waterman and Eleanor M. Downey Waterman. They died in the car accident nearly ten years ago, so my dad would have been... let's see, seventy-six today, and my mom would have been seventy-five. So that means, dad was born in nineteen thirty-eight, and mom in nineteen thirty-nine," Billie explained.

"Wow! Your mom and dad were considerably older than normal first time parents when you were born, weren't they?" Cat commented, realizing had they lived, they would be nearly twenty years older than her own parents, and close to her grandmothers' ages.

"Yeah, they were in their forties," Billie replied.

"Wasn't that kind of rough being raised by older parents?" Cat asked.

Billie shrugged as she searched the shelves for the name Waterman.

"Sometimes," she admitted. "Being an only child, I tended to spend more time with adults rather than with other kids."

She looked at Cat and smiled wistfully. "Sometimes we'd go to the park and I'd see these families with a whole herd of kids and wish I was one of them," she confessed. "I guess I act like such a big kid now because that was missing from my childhood."

Cat placed her arms around Billie's waist and smiled into her azure eyes. "Don't ever change. I love it every time you play with the kids. You are just so damned cute when you do."

Billie smiled at Cat's remark. "Well you're pretty damned cute yourself," she replied. "You know, Cat, without any living relatives, it's going to be tough building a family tree."

Cat released Billie's waist and walked toward the card

catalog of family names and pulled open the drawer marked W. "You may be right."

Billie continued to search the shelves for a book of records containing names starting with 'W' while Cat thumbed through the index of family names in the archives.

"Billie, do you have any personal papers or family bibles that your parents owned?" Cat asked. "That might be and easier place to start than this. There are a few Watermans in this file, but no Daniel born in the nineteen-thirties. Here's a Daniel Waterman born in nineteen fifty-six, but obviously he's not the one we're looking for," Cat explained as she held up the index card containing the fifty-something Waterman's name.

Billie stopped her own search to answer Cat's question. "Actually, no. When my parents died, I had the gruesome task of cleaning out their house, and interestingly enough, they had very few records at all. I thought it was a little peculiar at the time, but my mom was a neat freak and threw everything away before it had a chance to pile up, so I didn't give it another thought," Billie said.

"Did they leave a will, or a marriage certificate, or even birth certificates... theirs or yours?" Cat asked.

Billie frowned. "Cat, like I said, there was nothing in the house. Nothing except photo albums of me as a child and a few random documents," Billie explained again.

"No records at all? *Everyone* has records, Billie," Cat replied incredulously.

Impatient with Cat's line of questioning, Billie replied curtly. "Well, my parents weren't *everyone*, Cat."

Undeterred, Cat continued. "Billie, I find that kind of odd, don't you? I mean, no records at all? Doesn't that make you a little suspicious?" she inquired.

Billie was getting angry. "Just what are you implying, Cat? That my parents had something to hide?"

Cat covered Billie's hand with her own. "Sweetheart, please don't be angry with me. I'm just saying that it's a little odd, and it certainly makes our job harder. We'll just have to start with their death certificates and work backwards, okay?"

Billie slowly shook her head side to side and placed her hands on her hips, erecting a protective shield around her parents' memory. The rational part of her mind knew she shouldn't be angry at Cat's observations but she couldn't help it. For some reason, she felt like she had to defend her parents' actions. In fact, she had been very protective of them all her life. Mostly because they were a lot older than her friends' parents.

Billie's parents told her they had resigned themselves to not having children, however desperately they wanted them. Then she came into their lives. They called her their little miracle. Yes, they were older, but they loved her and protected her in every way possible, lavishing her with all the privileges they could. Their love and attention was the primary reason Billie had stayed married to Brian for so long. She allowed Brian to use her preference for women as blackmail to keep her from leaving him, even though he regularly beat and abused her. She just couldn't let him break her parent's hearts. She was sure knowledge of her lesbian nature would have devastated them.

"Billie. Billie," Cat said, breaking Billie's chain of thought.

"Huh? I'm sorry, Cat. What were you saying?"

"I said we'll have to start with their death certificates and work backwards. Okay?"

"That's a good idea."

Cat looked at her watch. "Damn!" she exclaimed. It's nearly noon. The read-a-thon will be over in a few minutes. Look, why don't I pick the kids up and you can continue the research," Cat suggested.

"No, I think I've had enough for today," Billie said, not really in the mood to continue after the disturbing thoughts about her parents emerged. "Why don't we pick the kids up and treat them to McDonald's for lunch, then go home. I'll dig my parents' photo albums out of the basement and we'll go through them. Maybe we'll find some clues there," Billie said.

* * *

The kids were ecstatic that they were going to McDonald's for lunch. They ate as fast as they could then excused themselves from the table to play in the indoor playground that was attached to the dining room. Cat and Billie ate their lunch at a more leisurely pace.

"Billie, maybe there will be something helpful in that box of albums and old documents that belonged to your parents. Do you think?" Cat asked, pushing a French fry into her mouth.

Billie chased her salad around the plate.

Noticing Billie's lack of enthusiasm and her failure to answer the question, Cat took Billie's hand in hers. "Billie, do you feel all right?" She placed her free hand on Billie's forehead, feeling for fever.

Billie shook off her hand. "Cat, I'm fine. Really. I'm just a little preoccupied right now," she said.

"Wanna talk about it?" questioned Cat.

Billie opened her mouth to speak, then closed it and looked down at her salad. Cat waited patiently for her to say something. She looked at Cat once more, her face contorted with confusion.

"Cat, the whole family tree thing is making me uncomfortable," she said.

"Why?" asked Cat.

"I don't know. I just have this awful feeling in the pit of my stomach, like something bad is going to happen. I can't shake it!" Billie explained.

"Billie, didn't you tell me once that you had absolutely no living relatives?" Cat asked.

"That's right. Both of my parents were the last survivors of their families, and I was an only child. Now that they're gone, there is no one left, except me," Billie answered.

"Did either of your parents have brothers or sisters?"

"Mom had a sister, but she died when she was young, and according to Dad, he was an only child," Billie replied.

Cat frowned as she contemplated their dilemma. Finally,

a thought came to her. "Hey! Didn't you say your Dad was in the army?" she asked.

"Yes. Why do you ask?"

Cat popped another French fry into her mouth. "Well," she said between chews. "Service personnel are required to list next of kin in their records. If we can find his records, we may have our starting point. What do you think?" Cat suggested.

Billie's eyes brightened. "That's not a bad idea, Cat."

"I *do* get them occasionally.... good ideas, that is," Cat stated in her best straight-man voice.

Finally, lunch was over and Cat gathered the children to leave. As they were picking up their mess to throw away, a couple of elderly women stopped by their table and complimented them on how beautiful and well behaved their children were. Cat and Billie accepted the compliments graciously, until one of them added, "Your husbands must be proud of them too!"

The grin on Billie's face was immediately replaced by a scowl, followed by a curled up lip and a low growl emitting from her throat.

Cat laughed nervously as she took the elderly ladies by the arms and led them to the door.

"Here, let me get that for you," she said, and held the door open for them. "Have a nice day ladies!" she called, as they hurriedly left, casting worried looks back at Billie.

Cat turned back to Billie and gave her the sternest look she could muster, given an overwhelming urge to laugh.

"Billie, you are so bad!" she accused. "You nearly gave them heart attacks with that growl."

"Serves them right," she quipped. "Come on, we've got a tree to plant," she said, taking Skylar's hand and led her little entourage out the door.

* * *

As soon as they arrived home, Billie retrieved the box of albums and papers from the basement that she had gotten from her parents' house. She carried the box upstairs, sat on the living room floor and spread the contents out around her.

Cat looked at the assortment of photo albums Billie laid side by side. "Is this the stuff from the first box?"

"The first box?" Billie replied. "There was only one box. This is all I have."

"Seriously? Just one box? Wow! You saw all the stuff we got from Mom and Dad's attic. I guess I'm surprised there was only one box of photos and records."

"Do we really need to discuss that again, Cat?"

"No. I guess not." Cat looked again at the array of albums laid out in front of Billie. "Now I know where you get your anal retentive nature," she commented.

Billie frowned. "What's *that* supposed to mean?"

"Look at these albums, Billie." Cat picked up the first one and read the words penned neatly on the cover. "Billie Jean Waterman, ages one through three," she read. She returned it to the floor and picked up the next one. "Billie Jean Waterman, ages four through six. Billie Jean Waterman, ages seven through ten. Billie Jean Wa—"

"I get the point! I get the point!" Billie interrupted. She grabbed the album from Cat's hand and placed it back on the floor. "So she was anal! So what?"

Cat grinned. "You are so cute when you're ticked off," she teased.

"I'm not ticked off," Billie said in her own defense.

"Yes you are," Cat insisted.

"No, I'm not,"

"Are too!"

"Am not!"

"Are too!" chirped Cat for the third time.

"Okay, you're right. I'm ticked off, but I wasn't until you started nagging me!" Billie retorted.

Cat had the decency to look abashed. "Me? Nag?" she asked.

"Yes, you! Now cut the crap and hand me that album!" Billie insisted, pointing to one that was beyond her reach.

Cat retrieved the album and handed it to Billie, but not

before sticking her tongue out at her.

"Is that a threat or an invitation?"

"I'll show you an invitation!" Cat exclaimed as she reached for the space between Billie's legs.

"Hey neighbors!" came a voice from the kitchen.

"Drats!" Cat muttered under her breath.

"We're in here, Jen," Billie called from the living room.

"Put some coffee on while you're in there, Jen," Cat yelled.

Moments later, Jen popped into the living room. "Put on the coffee. Geesh! You'd think I live here or something!"

"Stop your bitching and get down here." Cat reached up and pulled Jen down onto the floor next to her and Billie.

Jen's attention was immediately drawn to the photo album labeled Billie Jean Waterman, ages one through three. She opened the first book and immediately began cooing.

"Oh, my God! Billie, you were soooooo cute!" she exclaimed. "Ahhhhh—look at this! Your hair was curlier than mine as a baby! It's straight as nails now. What happened? Cat! Cat, look at this–Billie and her little dolly! Billie, you look like such a cute little foo foo," Jen teased.

Billie covered her face with her hands and shook her head side to side in disgust as she good naturedly endured the teasing.

While Jen paged through the first photo album, Cat picked one up labeled, Billie Jean Waterman, ages eleven through fourteen.

"Look at this, Jen!" Cat shrieked, showing Jen a picture of Billie at age twelve, dressed in full riding gear, complete with knee-high boots and riding crop.

Billie looked over Jen's shoulder at the picture. "I just won a blue ribbon in the equestrian riding competition," she explained.

"Beep, beep, beep!" Jen exclaimed.

"Beep, beep, beep?" Billie deadpanned in return.

"Yeah, you know, gaydar! I mean, look at this picture. If I had known you then, I would have guessed it," Jen explained.

"You think so?" Billie asked seriously as she took the

book from Jen and looked closely at the picture.

"Hell, I'm not even gay and I can see it!" Jen replied. "Did you parents know?" she asked.

Billie's eyebrows took up residence high on her forehead as she contemplated the picture again. "I never told them. If they knew, they didn't say anything," she replied.

"Do you think they might have known?" Cat asked seriously.

Billie frowned then sighed deeply. She ran a hand through her hair and looked at Cat. "Well, if they *did* know, I wasted a lot of painful months trapped in an abusive marriage for nothing, just so they wouldn't find out."

Jen looked back and forth between her friends. "So, what's this all about?" she asked, indicating the photo albums and memorabilia scattered around them on the floor.

"We've decided to trace our roots, and...," Billie began.

"Trace your roots?" Jen asked.

"Yeah, you know, we're building our genealogies," Cat explained.

"So, you two have finally gone over the top, huh? Finally bought one way tickets to the loony bin!" Jen joked. "Do you realize how much work you have ahead of you?"

"Well, we know it won't be easy, but I think we're up for the task," Cat replied.

"Why?" Jen queried.

"Jen, I've told you about these feelings of past connections that Cat and I have. We're trying to prove there is something behind it," Billie tried to explain.

Now it was Jen's turn to be impressed. "Really?" she asked in all seriousness. "So you really believe your ancestors knew each other?"

Billie rolled her eyes in exasperation, but before she could say anything abrasive, Cat intervened. "Jen, are you going to keep running your mouth, or give us a hand with this stuff?"

Jen scooted over next to Billie and started going through a photo album. Without looking up, she spoke to Cat,

"Cream, one sugar."

"Make mine black," Billie added.

It took a few moments for Cat to realize they were giving her coffee orders.

"Do I look like your personal maid?" Cat asked in her best Jen imitation.

Jen and Billie looked up from their work, then at one another, then back at Cat. "Yep!" they said together then doubled over with laughter as Cat stomped off into the kitchen.

* * *

Cat, Jen and Billie worked late into the afternoon searching through the contents of the box and cataloging each item. After a tremendous amount of fuss over Billie's childhood pictures— Yes…she *was* tall as a child. Yes…her eyes *were* always that impossibly sexy shade of blue, even as a child. Yes…she *did* look cute in a tutu—the women finally sat back and looked at what they had cataloged.

"Well," Cat commented, "except for these incredibly cute pictures of you, which we will definitely save for later torment, there really isn't anything useful here for research. I mean, no birth certificates for your parents, or you, and no wedding license. The only things we have here are pictures of you growing up, your baptism certificate, and your first communion record. By the way, you looked really cute in the virginal white lace dress and veil in your first communion photograph, sweetheart," Cat commented.

"Probably the only time you could justify wearing white, hey Billie?" Jen teased, earning her a smack in the arm from Billie. "Ow! What was that for?"

Billie just scowled at Jen.

"Damn! Can't take a joke, can you?" Jen asked.

"That's enough, you two," Cat scolded.

"Cat, maybe we can use the baptism and first communion records to research church files for more information. I know my parents were devout Catholics and were intimately involved in the church," Billie suggested.

"That's a good idea, love," Cat said.

"Billie, are these the only photos your parents had in the house?" Jen asked.

"Yes. Outside of the family portrait we had taken when I was about Sky's age, which by the way, is hanging on the wall over there, and Dad's military photograph over there on the mantel, these albums are the only ones they had," Billie replied.

"That's strange," Jen commented as she continued to flip through the photo album on her lap.

"What's strange?" Billie asked, feeling her defenses rise again.

"Look," Jen said, shifting the album so Billie could see while she thumbed through the pages once more. "Chronologically, this is the first photo album. There are no pictures in here prior to your birth, Billie. No wedding pictures, no family pictures, no pictures of your mom and dad together, no pictures of your Mom when she was pregnant. Are you sure there are no other albums around?" Jen asked again.

"I said there were no other pictures, Jen. I went through everything when Mom and Dad died. This is it," she said, lifting the empty box up and shaking it.

Suddenly, they heard a sound inside the box. All three women froze. Billie tipped the box upside down and shook it once more, dislodging a small key that had been stuck under a flap.

Cat picked up the key that had fallen into Billie's lap. She turned it over and looked at it carefully, trying to read any identifying marks.

"What does it say, Cat?" asked Billie.

"It has the number 'twenty-one' etched into it, but nothing else. I wonder what it goes to?" Cat wondered out loud.

"Maybe a locker, or a safe deposit box?" Jen suggested.

"Maybe," Cat said as she turned the key over once more.

"Here, let me have it," Jen said. "Tomorrow is Monday. I'll bring it to the locksmith in the morning and have him check it out. He should at least be able to tell us what type of key it is then we'll go from there. Okay?" Jen asked.

"All right," Cat said. She handed the key to Jen who slipped it into her pocket.

Chapter 6

Billie was deep in thought as she sat at her desk the next morning. Certain things about this genealogy search were bothering her. She hated to admit it, but it *was* odd that there were no important records among her late parents' things. Everyone kept important papers – a family bible, or something identifying their origins. None of those things were in the box.

Billie scanned her childhood memories, trying to recall if anything seemed odd or peculiar to her at the time. As a child, she paid no attention to the details of her parent's private lives, but as an adult looking back on things, she now realized that something was out of sorts.

Billie remembered how different things were at home compared to the households of neighbors. For one, there was generally more than one child, and as a result, chaos was often the rule rather than the exception. The homes of their neighbors were comfortably lived in while things were very neat and orderly in the Waterman household. As an adult visiting the homes of friends, Billie often walked away learning something new about her hosts, often by the way their home looked or through the interaction between family members. Such was not the case while she was growing up. Their house was very clinical and sterile, and her mother was a fanatic about keeping house. There was nothing to learn about the Watermans from a casual visit.

Recalling the decor of her childhood home, Billie realized Jen was right. The only pictures she had ever seen besides her father's military photograph, were taken after she was born. There were no pictures on the walls depicting her parents' wedding, no graduation pictures and no pictures of them as a young married couple. Considering she didn't arrive on the scene until they were in their forties, she now realized the lack of evidence of their life together prior to her arrival did seem a bit odd.

"Good Morning, Charland." A voice spoke from the doorway.

Billie looked up to see Art standing there with his hands tucked deep into his pockets. He was rocking back and forth on his heels like a schoolboy. His innocent nature clashed so much with his football player stature that it always made Billie smile.

"Good morning, big guy," Billie said, flashing her boss a brilliant grin. "What's up?"

"I was just about to ask you the same thing," he said. "You looked awfully lost in thought just now."

"Yeah, just thinking about the quest Cat and I are on," Billie replied.

"The genealogy search?" he asked. "How's it going?"

"We're not having a lot of luck on my side of the family right now, especially considering all of my relatives are dead. I guess I'll have to rely on official city, state and government records for information."

"Search the attic. Everyone keeps historical junk packed away there," he suggested.

"Been there, done that," Billie said. "No luck. When I cleaned my parents' home out after their death, all I found was a few photo albums and some minor records on me but nothing of any significance to tell me about my parents' origins," she explained. "Oh, we did find a key. Jen is taking it to a locksmith today to try to figure out what it goes to."

Art frowned. "That's kind of odd. I mean, everyone keeps some type of historical records around the house."

"I know," Billie said, annoyed with the situation. "You aren't the first one to make that observation."

"Okay, so we start by searching official records. Give me your parents' names, and I will start researching their social security benefits and tax records," Art volunteered.

"Are you sure you want to help, Art? This could end up being a lot of work," Billie warned.

"Of course I'm sure. I offered to help, and I meant it. Anyway, things are a little slow around here right now. Helping you gives me a chance to do something interesting for a change," he joked.

Billie smiled at her friend and reached for a notepaper to jot down the information for him. "Okay, their names are Daniel P. and Eleanor D. Waterman. They would have been born in nineteen thirty-eight and nineteen thirty-nine, respectively," she said as she rose to her feet and handed him the note.

She walked Art to the door and placed one hand on his arm. "Good luck," she said. "While you're doing that, I'm going to run over to St. Mark's Catholic Church and search their parish records. My parents were devout Catholics and attended that church faithfully. Maybe I can learn something about them there."

Billie grabbed her briefcase as she headed toward the door. Before leaving she placed a kiss on Art's cheek. "Thanks, my friend."

Art blushed for a moment before getting himself in gear and heading back to his office.

* * *

Jen leaned across the counter while the locksmith studied the key in his hand. "So what type of key is it?"

"I'd say, it goes to a safe deposit box," the locksmith said.

"Okay, so which one? I mean, can you tell which bank the box is in?" she asked.

"Is this your key?" he asked suspiciously.

"No it isn't. It belongs to a friend of mine. Actually, it belongs to her late parents. She found it in an old box from their attic and I volunteered to research it for her. Why do you ask?"

"Well, there *is* a way to determine which bank the box is in, but seeing as this key doesn't belong to you, I can't divulge that information."

"What?" Jen exclaimed. "Are you saying that I need to drag my friend down here before you'll help us?" she asked.

"Look lady, security is my job. Sorry. The key doesn't belong to you. I can't help you without the owner's permission," he insisted.

"What is this, some type of 'locksmith's' oath or something?" Jen asked sarcastically.

"Something like that."

Jen grabbed the key from his hand. "Gimme that," she said. "I'll be back with my friend. She isn't going to be happy about this," Jen warned.

"Just doing my job, lady," he said.

* * *

"Hello there, Billie," the elderly priest said as Billie entered his office. He stood to shake her hand. "So good to see you again. Sit down, sit down," he said, indicating the chair by his desk. "Why it's been a few years since I've seen you at church. What brings you around for a visit today?" he asked.

Billie settled herself into the chair opposite the priest's desk before speaking. "Well, father," she began. "My wife and I are doing research for a family tree and I was wondering if I could search the church records for information on my parents," she explained.

The priest looked up at her sharply. "What did you say?" he asked abruptly.

Billie took a deep breath. *He's so old, he probably can't hear a word I'm saying*, she thought. She repeated her request. "I said I would like to search the church records for information on my parents."

"No, not that. What did you say before that?"

Billie frowned and thought back to her words of a few minutes ago. Suddenly, she understood what the old priest was asking.

Being careful not to lose her temper, lest she misunderstood the priest's intentions, Billie repeated what she had said earlier. "I said that my wife and I are doing research, and I..."

"I *thought* that's what you said!" he interrupted angrily. "*You* are the devil's spawn! Living in sin and fornication with a woman! I told your parents you would bring them nothing but heartache. I told them it was a bad idea to bring you into their lives. I warned them, but they refused to listen," he ranted.

Billie narrowed her eyes at the old man. "What exactly does that mean?" she demanded.

The old priest sat back in his chair, putting as much distance between them as he could. "I told them it was a mistake... that it couldn't possibly be God's will. It just wasn't right! And now God is punishing them with a she-devil of a daughter," he spat.

Billie placed her hands on the desk and leaned closer. "Explain yourself!" she insisted. "How on earth can bringing a child into your life be a mistake?" she asked angrily.

Traitorous emotions paraded across the old man's face as he struggled to maintain control of his temper. Finally, he thrust his hand forward and pointed toward the door.

"Leave this place, do you hear me! There is no room in God's temple for the likes of you," he shouted.

Billie grew angrier and angrier at each word the old man spoke.

"You are nothing but an evil, bigoted old man," she said in a deep, even voice. "I should have known better than to come here for help. What my parents saw in this church and in this faith is beyond me. You are not the first, nor will you be the last to oppose 'my kind'. You and your beliefs mean nothing to me. Now, I came here for a reason, and I am not leaving until that reason has been satisfied. If you think you can remove me bodily from the premises then have at it, otherwise, I expect you to grant me access to the church records on my parents. If you refuse me access, I will pursue a court order. Is that clear?" she asked, her face a mere inch from the old man's nose, the cords of her neck strained to their limits.

Billie held her stare, daring the old man to call her bluff. Finally, he looked away and swallowed. "As you wish," he said. "Follow me."

Billie followed the priest to a room at the back of the rectory. It was lined with dusty old shelves, filled with file folders and boxes.

Billie looked around skeptically. "Please tell me they're filed alphabetically," she said.

"They are organized by last name. Do your business, then leave," he answered. He stopped at the door and turned around. "You may find what you are looking for, but you may not like what you find."

With that, he was gone.

Billie looked at the closed door, apprehension filling her every pore. *I wonder what he meant by that?* she thought before turning her attention to the dusty shelves before her.

"Okay, let's see how this room is organized."

She pulled a box from the shelf, took it to the table and removed the cover then picked up the document lying on top and read the name Paxton. "Well, I've found the P's," she said. After scanning a few more boxes and folders, she determined that the shelves were organized in a serpentine fashion, with the top shelf arranged left to right, the next one down arranged right to left and so on.

It wasn't long before she found the section containing the W's. "Waitsfield, Walters, Warren, Waterman," she recited out loud until she came across the box containing information on her parents.

She braced herself for what she might find inside the box as she pulled it from the shelf and carried it to the table. Slowly, she removed the lid and placed it on the table beside the box before rummaging through the contents. In it, she found a copy of her baptism record, first communion and confirmation records, as well as certification papers declaring her father a deacon of the church.

"That's funny," she said to herself. "I didn't know Dad was a deacon." She continued to dig deeper into the contents of the box.

The box seemed to be organized by date, with the oldest

material at the bottom, and the most recent on top. About half way through the box, she came across several receipts for church donations, made out to a man named Darren Walton.

"Huh," Billie mused. "They must have misfiled these receipts."

Billie carried the receipts back to the shelves and began looking for a file with the name Walton on it. No such file existed. Billie was perplexed. She returned to her parents' box on the table and continued rummaging through it. A short time later, she realized that all of the paperwork in the bottom half of the box contained the name Darren Walton on them, and a few with the name Emma Walton.

Billie suddenly became sick to her stomach. She sat at the table and rested her forehead on her crossed arms. *What does this mean*? she thought.

She lifted her head and stared at the neat piles she had created, one for Walton and the other for Waterman. A thought suddenly struck her. She quickly combed through each of the documents in both piles and verified her suspicions. All of the documents in the Walton pile were dated prior to March thirtieth, nineteen-eighty, and all of the documents in the Waterman pile were dated on or after that date. Billie went through the stack of papers again and came across a black and white photograph of her parents, obviously taken in their youth. The words *Darren and Emma, nineteen sixty-eight* were written on the back.

Oh, my God, Billie thought. *Were they in trouble? Were they part of the witness protection program? Why did they change their name? And why does the name change coincide with my birth date?*

Billie sat there for several long moments trying to absorb the meaning of the ruse that was her life. In a few seconds, all the security she had known as a child dissolved into a sea of uncertainty. Who was she? Who were *they*? And why did they keep this secret from her?

Billie suddenly felt lost and vulnerable. She looked down at the picture of a smiling Darren and Emma Walton and stared at it until the images blurred through burning eyes.

What does this all mean? she asked herself over and over as she sat dumbfounded for several minutes.

Finally, emotionally drained, she slipped the Walton photograph into her pocket then piled the remaining paperwork back into the box and replaced the lid. She hefted the box into her arms and carried it with her as she exited the room. The old priest was standing just outside the door, waiting for her.

"Did you find what you were looking for?" he asked.

Billie stared the old man down. "Tell me what you know, old man," she insisted. "Specifically, why did they change their names?"

The priest held her stare as he responded in a low, warning voice. "Leave them in peace, Billie. Remember them as they were, God rest their souls. Just know they did what they felt they had to in order to keep you safe. They loved you more than life itself, and they took dangerous chances to give you the life they felt you deserved. They put their necks on the line, and this is how you repay them. Did they know about your heathen lifestyle?"

"If they loved me like you said they did, I would hope it wouldn't have mattered to them," Billie said.

"You have brought shame upon their names. May their souls rest in peace… and may yours burn in eternal hell."

Billie had all she could do to resist strangling him on the spot. Instead, she turned and left the rectory without another word, taking the box with her.

* * *

"Hi Heather," Cat said as she approached the records clerk in the hospital archives.

"Hey Cat!" Heather exclaimed. "How's the family?"

"Everyone is fine. Thanks for asking. Hey, I need a favor. I need to see the maternity records for an Eleanor D. Waterman. She gave birth to a baby girl on March thirtieth, nineteen eighty. They lived in this area at the time of the birth, so I assume she came here. Can you help me out?" Cat asked.

"Cat, I really shouldn't do this," Heather said. "You know it's against hospital policy to allow access to private records. Could I ask why you need to know?"

"Eleanor Waterman was Billie's mother. Billie and I are doing a genealogy on our families, and we are hitting a dead end with her parents. I was hoping that her maternity records would name some relative other than her husband, in the event of an emergency," Cat explained.

"Well," Heather said. "That's a different story. Since she's Billie's mom she's family, so I guess it'll be okay," Heather said as she sorted the hospital archive file by last name and then narrowed the search by using the date range between March first to April thirtieth, nineteen eighty.

"Let's see," she said as she scrolled through the list of names beginning with W. A few moments later, she looked up at Cat. "There's no entry here under that name and date, Cat."

Cat looked perplexed. "Are you sure?"

"Positive. No babies born to anyone whose name begins with W during that date range. See for yourself," Heather turned the computer screen toward Cat.

"Humph, Billie grew up in town, so I assumed she was born here," Cat mused while she stared at the screen. "Can you tap into the state archive files?" she asked hopefully. "Maybe she went to another hospital."

"Sure." Heather called up the state archives web site and once more began her search. Again, she came up empty. "Cat, are you sure she was born in this state?"

"I'm pretty sure she was. Maybe if you search—"

"I'm way ahead of you," Heather interrupted as she accessed the national birth records web site. Cat grinned as she waited for the search results.

"Okay, here we go," she said. "Waterman, Helen, son. Waterman, Julie, daughter. Waterman, Lisa, son. Waterman, Mary, son." She looked up at Cat apologetically. "Sorry, Cat. I'm afraid that's it. No entry under the name Eleanor

Waterman."

"That's odd," Cat commented, a frown marring her forehead. "I wonder what that means?"

"Well, if it's not listed in the national registry, she either didn't register the birth, had the baby out of the country, changed her name, or, she's not the birth mother," Heather said.

Her last comment hit Cat like a ton of bricks. "What did you say?" Cat asked.

"I said, she either didn't register the birth, had the baby out of the country, changed her name, or, she's not the birth mother."

Cat stood there, eyes sightless as she stared at the computer screen, trying to digest what Heather was saying.

"Cat, are you all right?" Heather asked as she snapped her fingers in front of Cat's face.

"W…what? Oh, I'm sorry. I guess I was preoccupied there for a moment." She smiled at Heather. "Thanks for the help, Heather. I really appreciate it."

"Any time, Cat. I'll see you later," Heather said as Cat turned and walked away, deep in thought.

* * *

"Okay, let's see, W...a...t...e...r...m...a...n," Art recited out loud as he typed the name into his computer using just his index fingers. "Damn, I'll never get the hang of typing," he grumbled. He pressed the *enter* button and sat back to wait for the results, tapping his fingers on the desktop while the search engine churned through the list of Social Security numbers. Finally, the screen filled with names and numbers. He scrolled through the list and located two Eleanors and seven Daniels. Using their birth dates, he finally narrowed the list to one of each. "Bingo!" he said out loud.

The next step was to request benefits information on each of them and send it to the printer. He logged off the computer and walked down the hall to the printer room to pick up his reports. He arrived just as the second report was rolling out of the printer. He started reading as he walked back toward his office.

Right in the middle of the hallway, he stopped short and stared at the papers. "What the hell is this?" he said under his breath. He quickly thumbed through the second report until he found the page he was looking for.

"Well, I'll be," he commented as he picked up his pace toward his office. Once there, he logged back onto his computer and tapped into the company's personnel files. Moments later, he had found what he was looking for.

"Charland, Billie. Born March thirtieth, nineteen eighty," he read aloud.

He looked back at the social security reports he printed on the Watermans and at the top of both reports, he read the same information.

Social Security number, date of issue, March thirtieth, nineteen eighty.

Chapter 7

Billie was in a daze. A multitude of questions ran through her mind as she walked across the rectory parking lot toward her car. She imagined various scenarios that might explain her parents' identity change, including the possibility they were fugitives, that they were somehow in trouble with the law, and that they were being protected and had relocated with the assistance of the government. What didn't make sense with those scenarios is that according to the paperwork she found in the box, they didn't relocate after the name change. In fact, it was apparent that they lived in the same community for forty years before the name change, and continued to live in the same community for several years afterward. They obviously weren't trying to hide, at least not physically.

So why did they change their name? What were they hiding? Who were they hiding from? What was it that priest said... they took dangerous chances to give you the life they felt you deserved. What did he mean by that?

Such were the questions that ran through Billie's mind as she climbed into her car. She sat behind the wheel and rested her head against the back of the seat with her eyes closed for a long time. Finally, in no mood to return to work, she headed home, hoping she'd have some time alone to sort things out before Cat arrived home.

She pulled into the driveway, turned off the ignition and gently rested her forehead against the steering wheel in an attempt to clear her mind before going into the house. Intense feelings of disillusionment and betrayal weighed her down as she struggled to drag herself across the driveway and onto the back steps. Before reaching the door however, she noticed Jen running across the lawn while waving to her excitedly.

"Billie, wait up," she yelled.

Billie stopped and waited for her to approach.

"What is it, Jen?" Billie asked.

"Look, I've only got a minute. The school bus will be dropping the kids off soon and I need to be home when they get there, so I'll make this fast," Jen began. "I brought your key to the locksmith today and he seems to think it belongs to a safe deposit box, but he wouldn't give me any clues as to which bank it might be in," Jen explained.

Billie frowned. "You mean, he can tell just by looking at the key?" she asked.

"He seems to think he can," answered Jen. "Anyhow, he wouldn't tell me which bank because I don't own the key. He said the owner, a.k.a., you, will have to make the request in person."

"He said that, did he," Billie said. "Well, I guess I'll just have to pay him a visit tomorrow. Do you have the key on you?"

"Yeah, here," Jen replied as she dug deep into her pocket and handed it to Billie. "Do you want me to go with you?" she asked.

"Sure, if you want to," Billie answered. "I just may need you to stop me from tearing his head off; you know, a little pre-planned damage control, so to speak," she explained.

"Okay, you've got it, Big Guy. Well, gotta go. The bus will be here in a minute. Maybe I'll see you and Cat later tonight. If not, then I'll meet you at the locksmith's at say, noon tomorrow. Okay?"

Billie watched her friend leave then went into the house. She sat down in the overstuffed chair in the living room and closed her eyes.

What did that priest mean when he said he warned my parents about me? Why would they regret having me? I was never a problem child! What bothers me the most is the name change. It implies they're hiding something. If this key really goes to a safe deposit box, maybe I'll find some answers there. I feel like my whole life has been a lie. Who am I?

Who are they? she wondered to herself until she fell asleep.

* * *

As usual, Cat collected the kids from daycare on her way home. She was surprised to see Billie's car there when she pulled into the driveway. It was unusual for Billie to make it home before her. *I wonder if she's ill?* Cat thought and she approached the house, trepidation settling in the pit of her stomach.

"Mama, can I go play with Missy?" Skylar asked before Cat even reached the bottom porch step.

"Sure, honey. Seth, can you walk your sister across the street for me?" she asked her son.

"Sure, Ma. Come on, Squirt," he said to his sister affectionately, taking her hand. Half way down the driveway, he turned back to Cat and asked, "Ma, is it all right if I go to Stevie's after I bring Sky to Missy's?"

"Okay, sure. Just be home by five to get cleaned up for dinner, okay? Oh, and stop to pick Sky up on the way back, if you would," she replied.

"Okay, Ma. We'll see you at five," he said, escorting his sister once more in the direction of Missy's house.

Moments later, Cat made it into the kitchen to find Tara just hanging up the phone. Cat raised a questioning eyebrow to her daughter.

"I just called Karissa, Mama. She's coming over. We're gonna listen to music in my room," Tara announced.

Cat just nodded her head. "All right, just keep the noise down, okay?" she said.

Just then, an out of breath Karissa came barging into the kitchen. She bent over at the waist and rested her hands on her thighs, trying desperately to catch her breath. "I ...ran ...all ...the ...way," she said, breathing hard between each word.

Cat walked over to Karissa and knelt on one knee in front of her. "Karissa, honey, are you all right?"

"Yeah, just a little out of breath," she said as her breathing visibly steadied. "I'm okay now."

Tara took Karissa through the living room and up the

stairs to the bedroom while Cat went in search of Billie. She walked through the living room, with the intention of heading upstairs where she thought Billie might be, until she spotted her sleeping in the chair in the living room.

Cat just stood there and watched her for a few moments. Pleasant thoughts of love raced through her brain as she took in the relaxed pose. Billie's head was back, legs crossed at the ankles, shoes kicked off, skirted business suit creeping to mid-thigh. Her tall frame had burrowed down into the chair, hands clasped and resting on her stomach.

My god, she's beautiful.

Cat moved close and kissed her tenderly on the forehead. Billie moaned slightly but didn't wake up.

No fever. That's good. She looks so peaceful. I hate to disturb her, Cat thought as she went to the kitchen to make herself a cup of tea.

Cat sipped her tea while sorting through the mail she had retrieved from the mailbox at the end of the driveway.

"Junk..., junk..., bill..., junk..., bill," she said as she separated the assorted advertisements from the important mail. "I wonder how many trees the advertising industry kills every year just so they can end up in the trash?" she mused aloud as she dropped the pile of junk mail into the wastebasket.

Cat swallowed the remains of her tea, then placed the cup in the dishwasher. She looked out the window over the kitchen sink, and once again admired the bench that completely surrounded the maple tree in the back yard. Billie had spent long hours perfecting the cut of each board, wanting to get it just right. It was a tedious job and after several failed attempts and many ruined pieces of board, she figured out the correct angle to cut, and suddenly the project took off. She put a lot of work into sanding, staining and varnishing it when the assembly was completed. Best of all, Billie had done this on her day off, to surprise Cat when she returned from work.

Cat smiled when she remembered how Billie looked

when the project was finished… stain covering her hands, blotches on her face and clothes, bandages on several fingers, and scraps of wood scattered all over the ground around her masterpiece. But the most wonderful thing was the look of anticipation on her face when she revealed her gift to Cat. The look rapidly turned to pride as Cat fawned over the treasure Billie had presented to her. It seemed that every day she found more and more reasons to love Billie… more and more reasons to thank her lucky stars that she had chosen this woman to spend her life with.

Time to wake Sleeping Beauty, or she'll never get to sleep tonight.

Cat approached Billie and placed a tender kiss on her lips. Billie's eyes flew open at the touch. "Hi," she said, looking into Cat's green eyes.

"Hi, yourself," Cat replied. "You're home early. Do you feel all right, love?"

"I'm fine. Just a little tired, and a lot frustrated," she said. "I spent some time at the church today, going through records on my parents. I was very confused by what I found, Cat."

Cat frowned. "What do you mean?" she asked.

Billie rose from her chair and walked to the mantle above the fireplace. There, displayed proudly, was a large array of frames, all containing pictures of Seth, Tara and Skylar at various ages, of her and Cat, and of their entire family, smiling happily. Billie removed one of the many family pictures that adorned the shelf and admired it through the mist that suddenly filled her eyes.

"Cat, have you ever noticed that in almost every home there are pictures everywhere of kids and family, at all ages?" Billie asked distractedly.

Cat frowned. "Yes, I have. I guess everyone wants to display reminders of the people they love. It keeps them at the forefront of their thoughts, I guess. But what does that have to do with your parents' records, Billie?"

"Our home didn't have any pictures, except those over there," Billie replied, pointing to the family picture and her dad's military portrait. "Our walls were pretty much bare. I never thought much about it until now," Billie mused.

Cat touched Billie's arm. "Billie, you're scaring me. Sweetheart, tell me what's wrong. What's bothering you?" she asked softly.

Billie's eyes met Cat's. "I am not who we think I am," she replied.

"I don't understand," Cat said. An uneasy feeling was beginning to generate in the pit of her stomach.

Billie captured Cat's face between her hands and looked directly into her eyes. Very softly, Billie whispered, "Cat, do you love me? I mean, truly love me?"

Cat was taken aback by the question. She searched Billie's eyes for some hidden meaning in her gaze. What she saw there was confusion and pain, as well as the need for reassurance. Cat stepped into the circle of Billie's arms and held her close for several long moments.

"Of course I love you, Billie. I always will. Nothing will change that. I don't know what you found at the church, but know that nothing will make me stop loving you. Do you understand?"

"Good, because I am not Billie Waterman Charland," she said.

* * *

"What do you mean, you're not Billie Charland?" Cat asked nervously. "Billie, you're scaring me."

Billie took a few steps away and turned around to look at Cat. "I said I'm not Billie *Waterman* Charland. Cat, I started going through the church files on my parents, and half way through the file, I found that my parents changed their name," she explained.

"They changed their name? Why?"

"I don't know. The file contained numerous documents under the names Waterman and Walton. I thought at first the Walton papers had been misfiled, but then I found a photograph of my parents with the names Darren and Emma written on the back. It was dated several years before my birth. I have it right here." She dug the now crumpled picture out of her pocket and handed it to Cat.

Cat took the picture and looked at it intently. “They were a handsome couple,” she remarked as she strained to see any resemblance Billie might have to either of them. She turned the picture over. “Darren and Emma Walton, nineteen sixty-eight,” she read.

"They would have been in their late thirties in this picture. Obviously, they went by the name Walton at that time. Do you know when they changed their names?" Cat asked as she looked at the names and date on the back of the picture one more time.

"When?" Billie repeated. "March thirtieth, nineteen eighty," she replied.

"March thirtieth, nineteen eighty? Billie, that's your birthday!" Cat exclaimed.

Billie's brow creased as she replied. "Yes it is, Cat. For whatever reason, they changed their names from Darren and Emma Walton, to Daniel and Eleanor Waterman, on, or around the time of my birth."

Cat paced back and forth, her left hand on her hip, her right hand worrying the bangs on her forehead. "Billie, this doesn't make sense. Why would they change their names? If the church had records from before and after the name change, they obviously didn't feel the need to leave town, so they weren't hiding from anyone around here," Cat tried to reason.

Billie sat on the edge of the chair and leaned forward to rest her forearms on her thighs. "My thoughts, exactly. Whatever drove them to change their name must have come from a higher level...maybe the state or national level. I don't know Cat. It's all so confusing. Oh, and that nasty, bigoted old priest at the church said something that struck me as odd," Billie said.

"Nasty bigoted old priest?" Cat asked, confused, yet amused by Billie's description.

"The Honorable Reverend Matthews. Sugar wouldn't have melted in his mouth when I first walked in there, but the minute he realized I was married to a woman, he was all fire and damnation where I was concerned!" Billie explained.

"You actually *told* him you were married to a woman?" Cat asked incredulously.

Billie raised her arms out to the sides. "The marriage equality case we won almost three years ago was smeared across all the headlines for weeks. I would have thought he'd have been aware of my role in it before now. Apparently, he isn't one to stay on top of current events. And besides, it's totally natural for me to refer to you as my spouse. I see nothing wrong with it," Billie said in her own defense.

Cat touched the side of Billie's face. "I agree, but some situations require a little more subtlety, love," Cat explained.

"To hell with him if he can't take a joke!" Billie said, grinning.

"What did he say, Billie?" Cat asked.

Billie's mood immediately damped. "Well, after he assured me I was going to hell for living in sin and fornication, he said that he warned my parents about bringing me into their lives. He said that I would bring them nothing but heartache," Billie said, holding her hands out in front of her in confusion. "Cat, I never gave my parents reason to worry. Hell, I even stayed with an abusive husband to avoid hurting them!" she declared.

Cat saw pain and confusion in Billie's eyes. She walked once more into the circle of Billie's arms and wrapped her own arms around her neck. "You could never intentionally hurt anyone, love. You are too tenderhearted for that." She kissed Billie's gently. "We'll get to the bottom of this. I promise."

Billie wrapped her arms around Cat's waist and squeezed her gently. After placing a delicate kiss on Cat's forehead, she pulled her head back and looked into Cat's face. "Enough about me," she said. "How was your day?"

Cat smiled and brushed Billie's bangs out of her eyes. "Not too bad," she replied. "I had just one surgery to anesthetize. It went well. The rest of the day was filled with meetings," she explained. "Oh, by the way, I visited the records archives today to check on your birth records, and oddly enough, there was nothing listed indicating that your mother gave birth any time between March first and April thirtieth, nineteen eighty. We even checked the state and national registers."

"No records?" Billie asked. "What does that mean?"

"Well, in light of your new information, it means that she didn't register the birth under the name Eleanor D. Waterman. That, or she isn't your birth mother," Cat explained.

Billie broke free of Cat's embrace and took a few steps away before turning to look back at her. "Cat, tomorrow, could you check the birth records under the name, Emma Walton?"

"Of course. I'll get with Heather first thing in the morning," Cat said.

"Thanks. I'm sure my parents had a good reason for changing their name. I just need to know what it is. I'll talk to Art tomorrow about doing some Social Security searches on the name Walton. I won't rest until I get to the bottom of this," she said.

Cat looked at Billie closely and saw the vulnerability in her eyes. "I want you to know that I support you in this, Billie. I'll help you any way I can."

Billie smiled. "Have I told you lately that I love you?"

"Several times this morning," Cat replied. "But, not yet this evening. You're a slacker, Charland! You have some making up to do!" Cat joked.

Billie kissed Cat passionately, her tongue seeking and gaining entrance into Cat's mouth. After their tongues performed an erotic dance of love, Billie worked her way across Cat's jaw and down her throat to her collar bone, nipping at close intervals along the way, leaving a trail of telltale marks in her wake.

Cat's breathing became deep and ragged as bolts of desire shot from the points where Billie nipped her neck, directly to her groin. Billie's hands roamed up and down Cat's backside, pulling Cat's heated center closer to her own.

"Cat, where are the kids?" Billie asked through passion-filled breaths.

Cat suddenly pulled back, a frown creasing her brow. "Damn!" she exclaimed. "Tara and Karissa are upstairs."

As if on queue, a voice came from the stairs. "Mama, can we have a snack?"

Cat turned around in Billie's arms, her face flushed. She struggled to keep a guilty look off her face at being caught. Billie stood behind her; her hands on Cat's shoulders. A head taller, Billie rested her chin on top of Cat's head as she looked at the children and chuckled at Cat's discomfort.

Cat gave Billie a slight elbow in the ribs as she heard the chuckle. Satisfied with the grunt she received, she turned her attention to the children on the stairs.

"Sweetheart, how long have you and Karissa been standing there?' she asked sweetly.

"Just for a minute," the child replied. "Can we have a snack?" she asked again.

Cat smiled. "Sure, come on to the kitchen," she said as she straightened her shirt and headed in that direction.

Billie stood there innocently, with her hands clasped behind her. As the two children passed by, she heard Karissa ask Tara, "Do they always kiss like that?"

Tara nodded vigorously as they followed Cat into the kitchen. Billie chuckled once more then went upstairs to change her clothes and relax for the evening, knowing that at least in this environment, she knew who she was... wife, lover, mother, friend.

Chapter 8

Early the next morning, Billie stood under the shower spray with her hands against the wall; her face tilted upward as the water streamed over her brow and ran in rivulets down her body to the drain at her feet. The slightly hot water felt invigorating after her usual five mile morning run. The massaging action of the sprayer head shot pulsating darts of water across her back and shoulders.

She was lost in thoughts about her parents and the plans she had for a day of records searching. She was so preoccupied in fact, that she was unaware of another presence until she felt small hands snake their way across her abdomen, pulling her backward and drawing her close to the firm naked body behind her. She turned around in Cat's arms.

"You are insatiable, my love. Not that I'm complaining, mind you, but I thought last night would have been enough to last you a day or two," Billie said.

Cat threw her arms around Billie's neck. "I will never get enough of you, love. The more you give me, the more I want!"

Billie placed a gentle kiss on Cat's lips. "As much as I would love to indulge your libido, my love, if we dawdle much longer, we'll both be late for work," she reminded Cat as she handed the bar of soap to her,

Cat looked at the soap and quirked an eyebrow at Billie. "I think you might want to leave. The thoughts that are crossing my mind right now with this bar of soap…"

Billie smiled and reached for the shower door. "I'll get dressed then get the kids up for school. Don't be long, okay?"

* * *

Billie was waiting for Art when he arrived that morning.

"Good Morning, Charland," he said as he accepted the cup of coffee Billie poured for him. He sat down at his desk and took a sip of the rich dark liquid. "Good coffee. A guy could get used to this!"

"Well, don't," Billie warned. "I'm just buttering you up 'cause I need your help," she said.

"So, what's up? You look like you're about to crawl out of your skin."

Art sat back in his chair and stared at her in disbelief as Billie paced back and forth in front of his desk while she told him about her discovery through the church records. Finally, when she was finished, she sat down in his guest chair.

"What do you make of all of this?" she asked.

"Well, it certainly sheds some light on what I discovered yesterday when I researched the Waterman's social security numbers," he said.

Billie's head perked up. "What do you mean?"

"Well, I found out that their social security numbers were assigned on March thirtieth, nineteen eighty, which I happen to know is your date of birth, Billie. That seemed really odd to me at the time, but now that we know they changed their names, we have more to go on. We'll need to do a search on the name Walton," he explained. He rose from his chair. "Let's enlist Jimmy's help on this one. He's a lot more proficient with the Internet than I am, not to mention a much faster typist."

Billie agreed as she followed Art down the hall to Jimmy's office. Jimmy had a knack for finding information on anyone. He was one of the old timers around the firm. Even though he was a full-fledged lawyer, he spent most of his time surfing the net for his employers and fellow workers. Despite his constant grumbling about 'new-fangled technology', his proficiency on the Internet astounded all those who worked with him. Jimmy had been instrumental in helping Billie locate Cat's ex-partner when she and Cat went through legal proceedings to adopt each other's children and needed her to release her claims on Tara.

"Walton... Walton. Let's see. Andrew, Bradley, Carl, Daniel, Darren. Here it is. Darren Walton, born April twenty-ninth, nineteen thirty-eight," Jimmy said as he scrolled through the list of male Waltons born in the country on that date.

"Are you sure it's the right one, Jimmy?" Billie asked as she and Art read over the man's shoulder.

"Place and year of birth fits. Says here he was married in nineteen fifty-six to one seventeen year old Emma Rocque before being shipped off to Viet Nam. He continued to serve in the armed forces as a career officer upon returning from the war. It looks like he was highly decorated too, receiving the Silver Star and Purple Heart. He retired from the service in nineteen eighty with the rank of Colonel," Jimmy read out loud.

"It all seems to fit. I can remember him talking about his days in the service," Billie said. "I just wish there was a way to be absolutely sure."

"Well, you just hold on there one more minute, Missy," Jimmy said. He guided the mouse to a small icon located at the bottom of the screen, and double clicked on it. Within seconds, a full screen, color photograph of Colonel Darren Walton appeared on the screen.

"Daddy," Billie said, almost in a whisper, her legs nearly giving out on her with emotional release.

Art circled his arm around Billie's slim waist. "Don't you dare faint on me, Charland." He directed her to the chair beside Jimmy's desk. "Here, sit down. Are you all right?" he asked.

Billie nodded. "Where do we go from here, Jimmy? I know now that Mom and Dad changed their names, apparently around the time of my birth. The question is, why?"

"Well, you can research their social security numbers and tax records to reconstruct their activities around the time of your birth," Jimmy suggested.

"I've already determined that they were issued social security numbers under their new names when Billie was born. Now that we know their real names, we can do another search under their old numbers. Does that magic file you're looking at there have their original numbers, Jimmy?" Art said.

"Coming right up," Jimmy replied.

Within seconds, Jimmy not only found their original social security numbers, but did a search on their yearly income from nineteen fifty-six to nineteen eighty under the name of Walton, and again from nineteen eighty to their deaths under the name of Waterman. A few keystrokes later and the documents emerged from the printer beside his desk.

Billie scanned the documents carefully for several moments before she handed them to Art. She sat in the chair by Jimmy's desk with one leg crossed over the other, her left elbow propped up on the arm of the chair, her chin resting on her hand, as she waited patiently for Art to comment.

Art looked at Billie after he had finished studying the documents. "Sorry, Billie, but nothing jumps out at me," he said.

Billie nodded. "Yeah, I came to the same conclusion. There's just nothing there that would suggest a reason for the name change, and why it happens to coincide with my birth," she said. "Now what do we do? Do you have any ideas, Jimmy?"

"What did you say your birth-date was, Billie?" he asked.

"March thirtieth, nineteen eighty. Why?"

"Just a moment and hopefully I'll be able to tell you," Jimmy said as he typed her birthday into a search engine. The search result produced six hundred fifty-three sites with her date of birth somewhere in the body of the document. Billie became animated as Jimmy further refined the search by typing her name into the search results.

Billie waited anxiously, she watched the screen go blank, then return a moment later with the words *Billie Jean Waterman not found* in large print across the top. Her hopes were dashed as she looked at the subliminal message on the screen.

Jimmy looked at his friend apologetically. "Sorry! I was hoping it would produce something a little more positive than that!" he quipped.

"That's all right, Jimmy. I appreciate you trying anyway," Billie replied.

"Billie, just what are you trying to do here? What is your goal?" Jimmy asked.

Billie took a deep breath. "Well, I started out just wanting to generate a genealogy for my family, but this mystery surrounding my parents' name change has me perplexed. I feel like I've lost my origins, Jimmy. I need to know why. I need to know who I really am," she explained.

Jimmy looked back at his computer. "Genealogy, huh?" he said. "Let's see."

He punched more information into the search engine. Moments later, he had the results he was looking for. "Says here that your mother had a sister, Clara Rocque, died at age sixteen of tuberculosis. Her parents were French immigrants, Giselle and Jacques Rocque. No information beyond that. Your father had no siblings. His parents, George and Sarah Walton were born in this country in the early nineteen hundreds. Again, no information beyond that point. It's going to be difficult to trace any genealogy beyond the early eighteen hundreds. Accurate records were just not kept back then. Just how far back do you want to go?" he asked.

Billie massaged the infant headache that was growing in her temples. “Jimmy, Cat and I believe our ancestors knew one another in the past, so we plan to go backward until we find the link," she said.

Jimmy raised his eyebrows and whistled. "Wow. Good luck with that one. It’s difficult enough doing one genealogy, never mind two that interlink."

"I'm finding that out," Billie said as she rose to her feet. She hugged Jimmy and kissed him on the cheek to thank him for his help, walking away after seeing the bright red blush rise from the older man's neck to his face.

When Billie returned to her desk, she sat in her chair, crossed her arms on the desk, and rested her head on them. She stayed like that for several moments until the telephone startled her out of her trance.

"Billie Charland," she said into the receiver.

"Hi, love," Cat's voice spoke through the line.

Billie smiled into the phone. No matter what her mood, Cat's voice always lifted her spirits. Billie was suddenly struck by an overwhelming need to be held in Cat's arms as her beautiful wife soothed away her worries and promised to make everything all right.

"Hi, sweetheart," Billie replied. "It's so good to hear you voice. I really needed that right now."

"Billie, are you all right?" Cat asked.

"I'm a little discouraged. We've just hit another dead end with my parents. We found all kinds of information on the Waltons, but nothing that helps me to determine why they changed their name. Also, no luck with genealogical records earlier than the early nineteen hundreds. Did you have any luck with the birth records on Emma Walton?" she asked.

"I'm afraid not. No record of Emma Walton giving birth at all. I'm sorry," Cat said softly.

Billie sighed deeply. "Damn," she said. "Cat, what is happening here? All of the sudden, I don't have a past. My whole life has been a lie," she said.

"Sweetheart, your life is not a lie. *We* are not a lie. Our children are not lies. Please don't feel that way," Cat pleaded, a hint of tears in her voice.

"Cat, I'm sorry. I didn't mean to upset you. I'll be all right. Look, I've got to meet Jen at noon at the locksmith's. Maybe the contents of the safe deposit box will shed some light on this. Can you meet us there?" Billie asked.

"I'll be there. Billie, are you okay? I want so much to just hold you in my arms right now and make everything all right," Cat said.

Billie closed her eyes as her heart pounded in her chest with love for this woman. "There is no place I would rather be right now than in your arms, Cat," Billie replied.

"Do you have to go back to work this afternoon? Can you take some time off? I will arrange to have the afternoon off myself if you can," Cat offered.

"Okay. I like that idea," Billie said. "I'll see you at noon. I love you, Cat."

"I love you too, with all my heart. I'll see you in a while. Bye."

"Bye," Billie said before hanging up the phone.

* * *

"Let me make one thing clear right away," Billie said, leaning over the counter and using her best intimidating voice on the man behind it. "My friend here volunteered to have this key checked out for me. I don't appreciate you giving her a hard time. I trust her with my life. You got me? Now do us all a favor and tell me about this key," Billie said.

Jen stood beside her, arms crossed at her chest, and sporting a smug look on her face.

The man ignored Billie's attempt to intimidate him and took the key from her. "It belongs to a safe deposit box," he said.

"That much I got from my friend, here, but which bank does it belong to?" Billie asked.

The locksmith looked at the key and then back at Billie. "Give me a minute and I'll be able to tell you," he replied.

"You do that!"

The locksmith took the key into the back room as Billie turned around and rested her backside against the counter, crossing her arms and facing Cat and Jen. Billie had a stern look on her face. Seeing her distress, Cat approached her wife and brushed the bangs out of her face. "You really need to let me cut those," she said, "Do you feel okay, love?"

Billie opened her arms to Cat. "I'm fine, just frustrated about this whole mess."

Jen approached them as the locksmith came out of the back room. "I hate to break up this little love-fest, but here comes Mr. Bozo," she said.

Billie turned back toward the counter while Cat busied herself looking at a lock display in a case nearby. The locksmith gave them a knowing look.

"Okay. The safe deposit box is located in the First National Bank right here in town. Just a word of warning, you'll need to prove that you own the box before they'll let you into it," he explained.

Billie nodded her head as she accepted the key from the man. "What do I owe you?" she asked.

"Nothing. This one's on me," he replied.

Billie smiled at him. "Thanks," she said. Turning to go, she stopped before she reached the door. "How did you know which bank the key belonged to?"

"That's easy. There's a small coded number etched into one side of the key. You need a magnifying glass to make it out. All I had to do was cross reference it to a master key list to know which bank the box is in," he explained.

Billie smiled again. "Cool," she said. "Thanks again." With that, she and her entourage were gone.

As they walked back to their cars, Billie turned to Cat. "I'll need to pick up my parents' death certificate and copy of their will to prove I have rights to the safe deposit box before going to the bank."

"All right. I'll follow you home. It doesn't make sense to take two cars to the bank," Cat reasoned.

"Mind if I join you?" Jen asked.

"Not at all, Jen," Billie answered. "We'll meet you at our house in about twenty minutes."

* * *

An hour later, all three women stood in front of safe deposit box twenty-one, which had been removed from the vault and placed in a private room for them to view. Billie paced back and forth, all the while staring at the box.

"Aren't you going to open it?" Jen asked.

Cat stopped Billie in mid-pace. "Billie, honey, you need to open the box. The answers you are looking for may be in there. We're here to support you love. Please," Cat reasoned.

Billie approached the table and lifted the lid on the box.

She stood there for several moments just looking at the contents. Finally, she reached in and removed an official looking document and a letter.

Billie turned the letter over and over in her hands before lifting it to her face. She inhaled deeply and recognized the scent of hand lotion that Eleanor Waterman used to treat dry skin. She closed her eyes and held the letter close to her chest. A few tears escaped her lids as an intense feeling of home-sickness, longing and remembrance filled her heart.

Cat and Jen waited patiently as Billie absorbed her Mother's memory through the letter. Finally, she unfolded the letter and held it in front of her, wiping the tears from her eyes with the back of her hand before beginning to read out loud.

Dear Daughter,

If you are reading this letter, chances are we are gone. We could not leave you alone without giving you the opportunity to know the truth. Please know that we never meant to hurt you. We desperately hope that you will understand why we did what we did. Just know that you were always the light of our lives, a light that will continue to shine in our hearts after we are gone.

Your father and I want you to know that we love you very much. The documents in this box will give you some insight into how you came to us. Please know that you came to us in love, and we loved you dearly every moment of our lives. We do not know all the details of your arrival in this world, only that we were desperate for a child. You were the answer to our prayers. Please do not hate us for loving you.

You should also know that we are not who you think we are. When you arrived in our lives, we felt it necessary to change our names to protect ourselves...and to protect you from the consequences of our actions. Our given names are Darren and Emma Walton. We did this to eliminate the paper trail that brought you to us. Please find it in your heart to understand.

Some day we will meet again. We only hope that you will forgive us and greet us with love on your day of reckoning.

We love you, honey, and we wish you love and happiness in your life. Live your life to the fullest, Billie, and don't settle for anything less than you deserve. Life is too short to waste on unhappiness and regret. We will never regret bringing you into our lives. You brought more happiness to us than you can imagine.

We will love you forever,
Mom and Dad

Billie looked up from the letter with tears in her eyes. Both Cat and Jen mirrored those tears as they fought with their own emotions.

Cat embraced Billie. "It's okay, love. I've got you," she said.

"Cat," Billie said. "Please read the document for me. I can't do it," she pleaded.

Cat nodded and reached for the envelope. She removed the document and quickly scanned the contents, taking a deep breath when she realized what they implied. She looked at Billie with tears in her eyes then read the documents more carefully.

"Cat?" Billie said softly when she looked up from the documents for the second time.

Cat looked back at Billie. Tears rolled down her cheeks as she saw the anguish in her wife's eyes.

"Billie, they adopted you," she said as she heard Billie catch her breath. "Love, this is a handwritten contract between your parents and what looks like a third party agency. I don't know how legal it is."

Billie reached out with a shaky hand and braced herself on the edge of the table. Jen helped her into a chair then sat beside her and took her hand while Cat continued.

Cat continued to read. "It says here that Darren and Emma Walton became the adoptive parents of one baby girl, born March thirtieth, nineteen eighty. The document is dated July eighth, nineteen eighty, roughly three months after you were born."

"If they weren't my real parents, then who were?" Billie asked softly.

Cat scanned the document further. "There is no mention of your birth parents, Billie, but..." Cat hesitated.

Billie looked up sharply. "But what, Cat?" she asked.

Cat continued to hesitate, knowing the information contained within this document would break Billie's heart.

"Cat, please. I need to know," Billie whispered.

"Billie, it says here Darren and Emma Walton paid a fee of ten thousand dollars for you."

Cat cringed at the affect her words were having on Billie. She detested the pain this revelation was causing, but she recognized that Billie needed the truth. Only with the truth would she be able to face the future and heal the pain.

Billie closed her eyes as tears cascaded down her face. "Ten thousand dollars," she said. "A human life, purchased for a fraction of what we paid for our home. Who would do that? Why?" Billie asked.

Cat refolded the legal document then placed it inside the envelope with the letter before putting it on the table beside the box. She quickly closed the distance between herself and Billie and wrapped her arms around her. "I'm so sorry, my love," she whispered, hoping her love and support would be enough to see Billie through the wretched heartbreak that was tearing her apart at that very moment.

Still seated, Billie wrapped her arms around Cat's waist and rested her head between Cat's breasts. Jen joined the tableau and silently offered her support.

After several long moments, Billie relaxed and sat back in her seat.

"Are you all right love?" Cat asked.

Billie nodded as she wiped the tears from her face with the back of her hand. "Cat, is there anything else in the box?" she asked.

Cat reached into the box and picked up a tiny bracelet with a string of small pink beads, each one containing a letter, spelling out the name of the owner. "Suzanne," she said. "Billie, your name was Suzanne."

Billie clenched Jen's hand tightly as the tears rolled down her face. Finally, unable to contain it any longer, she broke down and cried violent tears... tears that shook her to her very soul. Heart wrenching wails tore from her throat as Cat and Jen both wrapped their arms around her and cried with her.

Chapter 9

Billie curled herself into a fetal position on the bed with the blanket pulled tightly around her neck. She stared straight ahead, unblinking. The room was dark, the shades drawn.

"Billie, sweetheart," Cat said from her position by the bedroom door.

No answer.

"Billie, please talk to me," she begged.

Still, no answer and no movement from the bed. Finally, tired of the non-communication, Cat approached the bed and climbed in. She spooned herself in behind her and wrapped her arm around Billie's waist.

"Sweetheart, please talk to me," she whispered into Billie's ear.

Billie responded by covering Cat's hand with her own. Cat took that as a positive sign as she climbed over Billie and lay on the other side so that she was lying face to face with her. She brushed a long strand of hair away from Billie's cheek and tucked it behind her ear.

Billie's eyes focused on Cat. "Cat. I feel so lost, so alone. I don't know who I am or where I came from. I can’t believe my parents kept this secret from me for so many years. Years of deception and trust thrown out the window. I loved them unconditionally. How could they do that to me?” she asked.

"Sweetheart, you are not alone. Do you hear me? As long as I live and breathe, you will never be alone. The kids and I will always be here for you, love. I know your heart is broken, Billie. Believe me, I know, but maybe there's a reason for all of this. I'm sure your parents loved you."

"Then why did they keep this from me for so long? Hell, if we hadn't found that key, I'd probably never know. I would have continued to live a lie for the rest of my life," Billie raged. "Did they think I wouldn't be able to handle the fact that I'm adopted? Were they afraid I'd want to find my real parents?"

"Neither of us can answer those questions, Billie. Unfortunately, the only ones who can are gone. We can only speculate. I'm sure your parents didn't mean to hurt you. I'm sure they were just trying to protect you," Cat reasoned.

"Cat, the adoption part of it I can handle. The lies, I cannot," Billie explained as her voice choked with emotion. She closed her eyes and took several calming breaths in an attempt to compose herself.

Cat patiently waited for her to speak once more.

Finally, Billie opened her eyes. "Cat, what kind of parent sells their child? I could never do that! I could never be so desperate as to abandon my own flesh and blood. Hell, Tara and Sky aren't even biologically mine, and I couldn't do that to them!" Billie said sternly. "No child deserves to be abandoned, Cat… never mind sold like some cheap piece of furniture," she added through an emotionally charged voice.

Cat trailed the back of her hand lightly across Billie's cheek. "Billie, I'm not making excuses for your biological mother, but maybe she had a good reason for doing what she did," Cat suggested.

Billie just looked blankly at Cat. "No, Cat. There can be no good reason for such a heinous act."

"You don't know that, Billie. In all probability, your quality of life would have been much worse if she hadn't. If a woman can be driven to the point of such desperation, she must have been living a lifestyle that was unfit for a child," Cat explained.

Billie turned her face away, not wanting to hear Cat's logic.

Cat took Billie's chin in her hand and forced her to look at her. "No, Billie. I am convinced that she did this to benefit you in the long run. You have to look at this positively, love. You'll drive yourself crazy if you don't."

Billie looked deep into Cat's eyes, desperately seeking

solace. “Cat,” she said softly. “Even if I acknowledge what you say as true, that doesn’t make it right. I still don’t know who I am. My past is still a lie. I was an innocent child, Cat. I didn’t deserve to be sold. I would never do that to my own children,” Billie reiterated.

“I know you wouldn’t, love,” Cat replied. “And speaking of the children, I've told them what happened. They want to see you when you're ready, okay?" Cat asked.

Billie nodded her head slightly then yawned.

Cat kissed Billie on the forehead. "Sleep. Give yourself the time you need to heal and to deal with this. I'll be close by. I need to make supper for the kids and tuck them into bed later on, but I'll be back to check on you throughout the evening. I love you, Billie. I always will. Nothing about your past or your origins will change that. You *do* understand that, don't you?"

Billie nodded her head as she closed her eyes and drifted off to sleep.

Cat kissed her once more before silently slipping from the room.

* * *

Later that evening, Billie awoke to find a slip of paper tucked into her hand. She rolled onto her back, and turned on the bedside lamp. She unfolded the paper and read.

COME, TAKE MY HAND
Come, Take my hand,
And I will transfuse
My ebbing strength
Within your tears,
Transforming two weak
Into one strong voice.
Come, Take my hand,
Burden me with your
Tension and indecision
Which are mine too.
For only by helping

Can I help myself;
Only by seeing others
Do what I have done
Can I gain insight.
Come, Take my hand;
In strength of numbers
We will brave the world.
I love you, Billie,
Come back to me.
Come, Take my hand.

Billie folded the paper and placed it on the nightstand. She stared at the ceiling as tears streamed from her eyes, falling into her ears and onto the bed. Suddenly, she realized just what she had been taking for granted in her life. She had a wonderful wife, who loved her unconditionally, and whom she loved with wild abandon. She couldn't imagine her life without Cat. She loved her with a passion that was beyond description. Cat's words in this poem were proof positive that she felt the same.

She had three healthy children who were the loves of her life and her pride and joy. No one could ask for better kids. She loved them so much, and they loved her. She had wonderful friends... Jen, Fred, Art, Marge. They would be there for her at a moment's notice, and she for them. She had Cat's parents, who loved her as their own. It appeared now that they were much better parents than her own had been... at least they had never lied to Cat. Finally, she had a very stable and satisfying job. She had everything most people only dreamed of.

Here I am, feeling sorry for myself, when out there, beyond that door, are people who love me, people who would die for me if necessary. I have to come to terms with this before I drive Cat away. I have been such a fool!

She threw off the blankets, climbed out of bed and headed for the door.

Billie stepped into the darkened hallway and stopped

short to look around. She listened to the silence that permeated the air. The indigo light on her watch noted the time to be five after twelve-o-five.

It's past midnight, she thought to herself. *I can't believe I slept for so long.*

As she made her way down the hallway, she stopped at each of the children's rooms to tuck them in and kiss them goodnight before descending the stairs to the living room. Her heart nearly burst with love and pride for these children as she thanked the heavens above for giving them to her.

As she approached the bottom of the stairs, she saw a glow coming from the table lamp near Cat's favorite chair. Cat was asleep in the chair, an open book in her lap, her head resting against the wing on the back of the chair. Billie stood there for long moments watching her sleep.

My God, she is beautiful! Billie thought as she noted the silky red-gold hair, perfectly sculptured face, soft china doll features, and creamy white skin. She removed the book from her lap and placed it on the table then turned off the lamp. Slowly, she reached under and behind Cat, and lifted her into her arms, cradling her against her chest.

Cat stirred as Billie lifted her from the chair. "Billie?" she asked sleepily.

"Yes, love. You fell asleep in your chair. Time for bed," she replied as she headed toward the stairs.

Cat snuggled into Billie's neck as she allowed herself to be carried to bed. Billie nudged open the bedroom door and carried Cat across the room then gently lowered her onto the bed. She crawled in beside her and lay face to face with her, neither touching the other.

Cat opened her eyes and looked at Billie sleepily. "How are you feeling?" she asked.

"Better now that you're here with me," Billie replied. She trailed her fingers down the side of Cat's face and smiled. "Thank you for the poem, Cat. It was beautiful. It made me see things in a different light."

"Good," Cat replied. "I love you Billie."

"Why?" Billie questioned.

"Huh?" Cat said.

"Why do you love me, Cat? I have put you through hell over this past year, with my mood swings, hospitalization, brain surgery, and now this mess with my parents. God, Cat, a lesser woman would have jumped ship a long time ago."

"Billie, I could never leave you. I am incomplete without you. Don't you know that by now?" Cat reached for Billie's hand and held it tightly to her heart.

"I have been a fool, wallowing in self pity, Cat. I need to look at what I have in my life *today*, not at the past. The past is gone. I can't change it, but I *can* shape the future. I promise to try as hard as I can to put this behind me."

She pulled Cat into her embrace. "Cat, please forgive me for being blind to all the wonderful things I have. There's so much to be thankful for. I love you Cat. I love you beyond words."

Cat snuggled in close to Billie and wrapped her arm around the Billie's waist. Their legs entwined like braided rope. "I could lie in your arms forever," she whispered before closing her eyes and finally succumbing to sleep.

"Forever," Billie repeated before drifting off to sleep herself.

* * *

Billie was sitting sullenly at her desk the next morning when Art poked his head in.

"Good Morning, Billie," he said. He parked himself on the corner of her desk and watched her go through her e-mail. "How did things go at the bank yesterday?" he asked.

Billie looked up at him with a pained expression on her face.

He placed one large hand on her shoulder and squeezed gently. "Not good, huh?" he guessed.

Billie focused her attention on the screen, knowing that if she looked up at her friend again, she would cry. She had sworn to Cat that she would try to see things in a positive light, but try as she might, it was difficult.

She pulled her bottom lip in between her teeth and drew her brow into a frown. She looked through tear-filled eyes at her hands hovering over the keyboard and realized she owed Art an answer. She shook her head no and bit down on her lip a little harder to prevent herself from crying.

"Want to talk about it?" he asked.

Billie placed her hand over Art's, which was still on her shoulder. Finally, she looked up at her friend. Tears threatened to spill onto her cheeks.

Art opened his arms, an invitation Billie could not refuse, as she flew into them and allowed herself to be enveloped in the safety of her friend's arms.

"Come on, Billie. Let it go," Art crooned in her ear as he rubbed his hand up and down her back.

Billie clung to him like a lifeline, shuddering sobs wracking her tall frame. After several long moments, the crying subsided and her breathing evened, yet she continued to cling to him, her head resting on Art's broad shoulder.

Art turned his head to whisper in Billie's ear. "Are you all right?"

Billie nodded then looked Art in the face. "I've been doing a lot of this lately, huh?"

She inhaled deeply, trying to compose herself before continuing. "Art, I spent the entire evening yesterday feeling sorry for myself. I told Cat that I would try to deal with this, but I'm afraid that I'm not doing a very good job. All I can do is cry. I'm not a pretty sight when I cry, am I?" she commented.

Art wiped away, a tear that had rolled down Billie's cheek. "Charland, I dare say that nothing can mar your beauty. Hell, if I wasn't so much in love with Marge, and you with Cat, your beauty alone would have me worshipping at your feet."

Billie blushed.

Art grasped her by the shoulders. "Now, are you ready to tell me about it?"

Billie sat down in her chair and reached for her briefcase. She retrieved the letter and adoption papers and handed them to Art. Moments later, Art looked up from the documents and whistled.

"Wow, Billie. No wonder this threw you for a loop."

"That's an understatement, my friend," Billie replied. "My entire world came crashing down with that one piece of paper. All the history and security I had as a child is meaningless. It's all a lie. I have no idea who I am. You bet it threw me for a loop!"

Art scanned the document further. "You know this document isn't binding, don't you? What your parents did was basically illegal. No wonder they changed their name."

Billie took a deep breath. "I know." She paused long enough to regain the tenuous grasp she had on her composure. "I just don't know what to do next. I'm not even sure I *want* to do anything."

Art looked up again from reading the adoption papers. "There's no mention of your birth parents' names in this document, Billie. If you do decide to pursue it, we can start by researching the name of the adoption agency, but my guess is that it is bogus," Art pointed out.

Billie looked down into her lap, contemplating her entwined hands for several long moments.

"Just say the word, my friend and I'll start looking," Art offered.

Billie took the document from Art. "No need. I've already researched the adoption agency, and you are right, it was a bogus name. The agency never existed. I've hit another dead end," she concluded.

"And how do you feel about that, Billie?" Art asked.

"Lousy," Billie said, truthfully. "I feel lost. Like my whole existence is nothing but a lie. I hurt inside. How could they deceive me like that? How can two people who professed to love me, deceive me like that?" she asked, as tears formed in her eyes once more.

Art raised Billie's chin with two fingers. "When two people want a child badly enough, they'll do anything to get it, Billie. You said they were older. Maybe they had been denied by adoption agencies because of their age," he suggested. "In any case, you had a good childhood. They *did* love you. You know they did."

Billie nodded her head. "Yes, they did. I just wish they hadn't lied to me," she said. "I don't know if I can forgive them for that."

Chapter 10

"Hello?" Cat said into the receiver.

"Hi honey, it's Mom."

"Hi, Mom. What's up?"

"I just wanted to let you know that your grandmothers will be home for a visit this weekend. They're stopping over for a few days on their way back to South Carolina from Greece," she explained.

"Really? That's great! Billie wants to meet them. How long are they staying?"

"They said a few days, but I'll try to get them to stay longer, of course. How is Billie, dear?" Ida asked.

"I'm worried about her, Mom. She's so depressed about her parents," Cat explained. "She's trying to come to terms with it, but underneath that tough-guy facade of hers is a pretty sensitive heart. She's been hurt pretty deeply."

"Well, I'm sure, given time, she'll be okay. I can understand what a shock it was to her. Be patient with her Cat, she needs you now more than ever," Ida said.

"I know, Mom. I'm doing everything I can, but I look at her and see a stranger in her eyes. She scares me sometimes," Cat remarked.

Ida's voice took on a guarded quality. "Cat, she's not becoming violent or abusive again, is she?"

"No, Mom, she isn't!" Cat said a little harsher than she intended. "Look, I'm sorry, but I don't want to give you the wrong impression. Billie is NOT being abusive. I'm just afraid for her emotional state. It breaks my heart to see her in so much pain," Cat explained as her own emotions threatened to spill over.

"I know, sweetheart. Maybe visiting with your grandmas

will help. You know how distracting they can be, especially Grandma Jo. If anyone can pull her out of the doldrums, it will be Josephine Wycliffe," Ida chuckled. "Okay, dear, I guess I'll let you go. Kiss Billie and the babies for me, all right? Talk to you later. Bye."

"Bye, Mom, I love you."

No sooner had Cat hung up the phone then Billie arrived home from work. Cat smiled at her as she dropped her briefcase and kicked her shoes off by the door.

"Hi, love," she said, going into Billie's open arms.

"Hi, baby," Billie dropped a light kiss on Cat's nose.

The two women clung to each other for several moments, Cat's arms around Billie's waist, and Billie's arms around Cat's shoulders until their heartbeats came into sync as one.

Finally, Cat pulled her head back and looked into the blue abyss of Billie's eyes. "How was your day?"

"Fine. How about yours?"

"Just fine?"

"Yeah, just fine."

Cat noticed the slight frown creasing Billie's forehead. "Billie, I'm worried about you," she said.

Billie abruptly released Cat from her embrace and walked a few steps away. "Cat, I really don't want to hear about this again. I'm fine. Really. So just drop it, okay?"

"No Billie, I don't want to drop it. I hate seeing you like this. You haven't smiled... and I mean, *really* smiled since we started this search. I wish now we had never started it. My heart is breaking for you. Please don't shut me out."

Billie turned to face Cat and saw the pain and tears in her eyes. She immediately took Cat into her arms. "Cat, I'm sorry. I didn't mean to snap at you. I know you are just concerned about me, but it will take time for me to come to terms with this whole adoption mess. Please forgive me?"

Cat nodded and reached up to wipe her tears. Billie pushed her hands away and wiped them for her then pulled her once again into a tight embrace.

“Billie, maybe we should just forget about the family tree, okay? If I had known this genealogy search would bring you so much pain, I would never have suggested it,” Cat admitted.

“No, Cat. Now that we’ve come this far, I have to finish it. There is no way I can let this go now. I can't rest until I know who I am. I am not the only one in limbo here. Seth has a right to know his heritage as well."

Billie walked toward the living room. She stopped at the doorway. "You are right about one thing Cat, we should have never started this quest. Ignorance is bliss I guess. But it’s too late to turn back now,” Billie replied. “Don’t worry about me. Whatever happens...happens. I’ll just have to deal with it.”

"Billie, whatever happens...whatever you discover about your birth parents, please don't allow it change who you are today. You are perfect the way you are. Please don't change," Cat begged.

"I will try my damnedest not to allow this quest to change our lives, Cat. I promise I will try."

Billie headed upstairs to change into more comfortable clothes before dinner.

Cat watched her go with an intense feeling of regret filling her heart. "It already has, Billie. It already has."

* * *

Dinner was an animated affair, with Tara and Seth competing to describe the water fight that had occurred on the school bus that day on the way home. It appeared that students in the upper grades had been planning it for a week. Several of them came prepared that morning to battle it out on the bus. Unfortunately, the entire busload of children was caught in the crossfire.

"George was really mad!" Tara exclaimed.

"That's because Tommy got him in the back of the head with his squirt gun!" Seth said.

"No fair. I wanna ride the bus too!" Skylar exclaimed. Being five years old and only in a half-day, morning kindergarten, Skylar had missed out on the water fight.

Billie worked very hard to contain her grin as Cat turned it into a lesson. "You know, each and every one of you is lucky that George wasn't distracted enough to run off the road. That water fight could have ended in an accident," Cat explained.

"George pulled the bus over and took their guns away," Tara said. "Serves them right."

"You're just mad 'cause *you* didn't have a squirt gun," Seth said to his sister.

"I could out-shoot any of them!" Tara bragged.

Billie interrupted the conversation before it ended in an argument. "I'm sure you could, rugrat, but Mama is right, you're very lucky that George didn't lose control of the bus during the fight," she said.

"Tommy and Chris got suspended from school for starting the fight," Seth explained. "And five other kids have detention after school for a week!"

"I don't want to ever hear of you guys becoming involved in something like that. You'll have one very angry mother on your tail if you do!" Cat exclaimed.

"Make that, two angry mothers," Billie added.

"Don't worry, we won't" Seth said, watching his two sisters nod their heads in agreement.

"All right then. How about ice cream bars for dessert? You can take them into the back yard, okay?" Cat suggested.

Within moments, the children were playing and eating ice cream happily in the yard while Cat and Billie cleared away the supper dishes. Billie rinsed the dishes and handed them to Cat to be loaded into the dishwasher. During this exchange, Cat brought up the phone call with her mother earlier that afternoon.

"Mom called today, Billie. It seems that my grandmothers will be in town this weekend."

Billie's eyes perked up. "Really? That's great! I'm anxious to meet them."

"I know you are. Now you'll get a chance to see just how much you resemble Grandma Alex," Cat said.

Billie smiled at the mention of her resemblance to Alexandra Spirakis. She looked at Cat and grinned from ear to ear. "From what I've heard about Grandma Jo, I'd better say clear of her, huh? I'm liable to get my rear pinched or something, do you think?" she joked.

Cat laughed out loud. "I wouldn't put anything past Grandma Jo!" Cat exclaimed.

Billie took Cat into her arms and kissed her tenderly. "I'm looking forward to the visit, love. I think I need the distraction just about now."

"Well, with those two around, anything is possible. They are going to love you, Billie, but you are right about Grandma Jo, she'll put the moves on you if you let your guard down around her!" Cat chuckled.

"Thanks for the warning, Red. Thanks for the warning!" Billie replied, adding her own chuckle to the fray.

* * *

Saturday found Billie enjoying a cup of coffee and the daily paper in the early morning hours before the rest of the household awoke. She stared at the paper long enough for the printed words to blend into a psychological ink blot test as her mind wandered to the impending visit with Cat's grandmothers.

She looked forward to meeting the colorful Josephine Wycliffe and Southern belle Alexandra Spirakis, and hoped they could help with Cat's side of the genealogy. Ida had already prepped them about their plan to build a family tree, and she was looking forward to hearing about the history that was bound to come from two such richly colorful ladies.

So engrossed was she in the ink blot tests before her, that she was unaware of a presence in the room until Cat wrapped her arms around her shoulders from behind, and planted a kiss on her collar bone, startling her from her reverie.

"Good morning," Cat said, placing her left cheek against the right side of Billie's face. "Sorry I startled you. You seemed pretty focused on that paper. See anything interesting?" Cat asked as she looked at the page over Billie's shoulder.

Billie cupped the right side of Cat's face with her hand. "Actually, I was just staring, caught up in thought about our visit with your grandmothers today," she explained.

Cat slid into the chair to Billie's right and smiled at her wife. "I'm looking forward to seeing them again. It's been about six years. Tara was just a toddler the last time I saw them," Cat explained.

"Your mother hasn't seen them in six years?" Billie asked.

"No, Mom spends a couple of weeks in South Carolina with them every year. Dad drops her off on their way to Florida each winter. This is the first time they've been *here* in six years," Cat said.

Billie nodded her head. "What do you think they'll say about me...about us?" she asked.

Cat grinned broadly. "About you? Well, Grandma Jo will probably make a pass at you, and Grandma Alex will shower you with her southern hospitality and charm. That is, of course, once they get over the shock of your resemblance to her," Cat said.

Billie's brow drew into a frown. "You know, I am really, really curious about the resemblance thing. Everyone is making such a big deal of it. To tell you the truth, it makes me a little uncomfortable," Billie confessed.

Cat rose to her feet and leaned into Billie, resting her upper body on the table. Nose to nose, she looked deeply into Billie's blue eyes. "Sweetheart, you have nothing to worry about. They will absolutely adore you. I guarantee it. Now, where is my morning kiss?" she demanded.

Billie smiled as she drew Cat into her lap. She wrapped her arms around Cat's shoulders and kissed her passionately. "How was that?" she asked, looking into Cat's flushed face.

"Ah...ah...Th...That was good...very good!" Cat stammered. "Got any more where that came from?" she asked.

Billie was about to oblige, when a small voice interrupted their tryst. "I'm hungry!"

"Hold that thought!" Cat said as both women turned to

see Skylar standing in the doorway with her teddy bear in one hand, and her blanket in the other.

* * *

"Caitlain Maureen, come on ova here and give your Grams a big hug!" the elderly southern belle said as she pulled Cat into her embrace.

"Grams, it's so good to see you. I've missed you so much!" Cat exclaimed as she found her face buried in the older woman's generous bosom.

"Let me take a look atcha, child." She took Cat by the shoulders and turned her around. "Oh, my goodness! You have grown into quite a beauty. Hasn't she Josie?" Alex said in her thick South Carolina accent.

"Alexandra Spirakis, you're going to smother the woman where she stands with those breasts of yours. And besides, I'm jealous. You haven't done that to *me* in a long time! Come here, Cat, let me get a look at you," she instructed as she made Cat turn in circles "Yep, I have to agree with you, Al. She's a real beauty. Turn the ladies' heads, do you?" Jo said, winking at Cat and making her blush.

"There's only one head I want to turn, Grams," Cat said, still blushing.

"Oh yeah, we've heard about your lady. So when do we get to meet her?" Jo asked.

"Right now," said a voice from the doorway as Billie chose that moment to enter the room.

Three faces, one young and two old, looked toward the door at the sound of the voice. The sudden silence was so deafening you could hear a pin drop as Billie's appearance caused time to stand still.

"Oh, my!" Alex slid to the floor in a dead faint.

"Holy Shit!" exclaimed Jo, staring at Billie, her mouth wide open.

"Grams!" exclaimed Cat as she ran to the rescue of the unconscious woman.

"Holy Shit!" Jo exclaimed again.

Billie quickly went to assist Cat.

Josephine continued to stare, mouth agape, at Billie. "Holy Shit!" she said for the third time.

"Billie, help me move her to the couch," Cat said.

Billie lifted Alex under her arms while Cat took her feet. Together, they moved her to a more comfortable position on the couch. Once she was settled, Billie came around to stand beside Cat, affording her a closer look at the elderly southerner who lay there unconscious.

The woman was quite literally an older version of Billie.

Billie's face contorted into an intense frown. "Wow, Cat. You're right. The resemblance is uncanny," she said. "I only hope I look that good when I'm her age!"

Cat turned to Josephine. "Grandma Jo," she said. "Please get the smelling salts out of Grams' bag."

With robotic movements, Jo retrieved Alex's bag from the coffee table, found her smelling salts, and handed them to Cat, all without taking her eyes off Billie.

Cat looked down at the object Jo had placed in her hand. "Ah, this is a tube of lipstick. I need her smelling salts."

"Damned purse. She keeps everything in there but the kitchen sink!" Jo cursed as she finally found the salts and handed them to Cat.

Within minutes, Alex was conscious. She looked up into crystal blue eyes that mirrored her own. "Oh, my!" she said, as once again, she fainted away.

Billie looked from Alex to Cat, then back to Alex. "Damn!" she said. "Is that what you call a delicate Southern constitution?" She then looked at Josephine, she asked, "Does she do this a lot?"

"Holy Shit!" was all Jo could say.

Cat rose to her feet and took Jo by the shoulders and looked her in the face...at least she *tried* to look her in the face. Jo was too busy looking around her at Billie. Cat took Jo's chin in her hand and turned her face toward her until they made eye contact. "Grandma Jo, are you all right?" she asked.

Josephine pointed to Billie and stammered, "Sh...sh...she's Alex!"

Cat smiled and said, "No, she's Billie. She just looks like Grandma Alex, at least the way Grandma Alex looked forty years ago."

"Holy Shit!" Jo repeated yet again.

Billie looked at Jo and Cat standing face to face and was suddenly awestruck at what she saw. If she was Alex's double, then Cat was certainly Jo's. Both women were of the same height. Tinges of red-gold remained in Jo's long flowing hair, despite the strands of gray running through it. Although somewhat bent and plumper with age, Billie could imagine Jo firm and muscular in her youth. The most striking resemblance though, were the emerald green eyes, albeit, Jo's were full of mischief and edged with crows feet, but still portrayed a youthful exuberance, even in her late seventies.

Billie's focus was suddenly diverted from the pair by the sound of "Oh, my goodness!" coming once again from the couch beside her.

Cat and Billie immediately went to Alex's side.

"Where are my cigars? I need a smoke!" Jo said as soon as Cat released her.

Cat moved to the middle of the room and looked back and forth between her grandmothers...one reclining on the couch, threatening to faint once more, while the other in a panic looking for the cigars she had given up years ago.

"Okay, time out!" shouted Cat. "Time out! No more fainting. No more holy shitting! No more anything...you got that?"

She looked at a perplexed Jo and Alex, and a grinning Billie. Once she obtained the proper concurrence from the elderly ladies, she reached for Billie, who took her hand and joined her in the middle of the room. "Now, Grams, this is Billie. Billie, this is Grandma Jo and Grandma Alex," Cat said, making the proper introductions.

Jo and Alex looked from Cat, to Billie and then at each other. Struggling into a sitting position, Alexandra was the first to speak.

"Josephine Wycliffe, you didn't tell me she looked like

me!" Alex accused.

"I...I didn't know!" Jo defended herself. "Damn, I need a smoke!" she added.

"Grandma Jo, you know you gave up smoking years ago," Cat reminded her grandmother.

"That's right, I did! Okay, then I need a drink!" Jo replied, causing Billie to laugh out loud.

"Josie, you are going to be the death of me yet!" Alex scolded as she rose to her feet and approached her.

"Al, sweetheart, not unless you're the death of me first!" Jo bantered back.

"Well, where are my manners?" Alex turned toward Billie.

"They fainted to the floor with you a few minutes ago, my love," Jo quipped, making Billie struggle to hide the grin that threatened to spread across her face.

Alex sent a dirty look toward Jo and dismissed her with a wave of her hand.

She turned to address Billie once more. "Don't mind her. I am a little inclined to the vapors. Let me welcome you into the family proper-like," Alex said as she pulled Billie in for a hug. Then, turning to Jo, she said, "Josie, come welcome your granddaughter into the family."

Grumbling, Jo walked over to Billie, one hand shoved deep into her trouser pocket as she reached forward with her other hand to shyly shake Billie's.

"Josie, you are acting like she's a business associate. Now welcome her properly," scolded Alex.

Jo removed her hand from her pocket and reached around with both hands to hug Billie, tweaking her behind in the process.

"Yeow!!" shrieked Billie. She jumped back and rubbed her behind while casting a knowing glance in Jo's direction.

Jo grinned and said to Billie, "Now how 'bout that drink?"

"You're on! Scotch on the rocks, right?" Billie asked.

Jo threw her arm around Billie's waist and led her to the bar. "Girl after my own heart," she said.

Alex was dumb struck at Jo's boldness. "That woman!"

she sputtered.

"Don't worry about Billie, Grams. She'll give Grandma Jo a run for her money!" Cat explained.

"Well, I'd like to see *someone* put that brazen woman in her place for once!" Alex said.

Cat smiled and locked arms with Alex. "Oh, she will, Grams. She will," she said.

Chapter 11

"Josie," Alex said. "Josie, darlin' are you sleepin'?"

"Not any more!" Jo grumbled. She looked over her shoulder at Alex, who was crying softly. She pulled herself into a seated position and felt Alex's forehead. "Al, are you all right? Why are you crying?" she asked.

"Josie, its Billie. There's something about her, something familiar," she tried to explain.

"Well, I should hope there's something familiar, she looks just like you," Jo pointed out.

"No, it's more than that. I can feel a connection to her. I...I...," Alex faltered, not really knowing how to put her feelings into words.

Jo was becoming concerned. "Al, what is it?" she asked. She took Alex's hand in her own. "Sweetheart, talk to me."

"Josie, it is never far from my mind. I think about it all the time. Seeing Billie has caused the memories to come flooding back. Seeing her has renewed my hope that maybe, just maybe, it's true," Alex rambled

Jo grasped Alex's hand and squeezed. "Al, you're not making sense. Now start from the beginning and tell me what's bothering you," she urged.

Alex closed her eyes and allowed the tears to flow, tears that she had held in check for fifty long years. "Josie, please hold me."

Jo reclined next to Alex and took her in her arms, holding the distraught woman and running her hand up and down Alex's arm as she cried. Moments later, Alex had calmed down enough to talk. Jo was lying on her back with Alex's head resting on her shoulder, and her arm draped across Jo's waist.

"Whatever is bothering you, Alex, we'll get through it.

Now talk to me, love," Jo insisted.

"Josie, seeing Billie tonight reminded me of my daughter," Alex explained.

Jo stiffened at Alex's words. "You mean, Ida?" she asked, knowing the answer well before Alex replied.

"No," was all she said.

Jo turned her head and kissed Alex on the temple. "Al," she said softly. "I can understand why seeing Billie would remind you of that tragedy, but sweetheart, don't allow her resemblance to you to send you into a tizzy. Your daughter was stillborn more than fifty years ago. You know that."

Alex sat up and looked at Jo. "Do I, Josie? Was she really stillborn? I never saw her. The midwife told me she was stillborn. I never held her lifeless body in my arms," Alex finished in a choked whisper.

She pulled her knees into her chest and wrapped her arms around them.

"Al, we've been over this a hundred times. You never heard the child cry. The midwife rushed her out of the room as soon as she was born. Maybe there was something wrong with her. Maybe they were trying to protect you," Jo suggested.

Alex just stared straight ahead, shaking her head in denial. "I don't believe that Josie. I know in my heart she is still alive," Alex countered.

"Alex, they all said the baby was dead...the midwife, your Uncle's wife, your Uncle. This is not a case of someone kidnapping your baby," Jo pointed out.

"They are all liars, Josie, every one of them," retorted Alex vehemently.

"Why would they lie to you?" Jo asked.

"To protect my family's name. Josie, I wasn't married. I brought disgrace on my family. I was a young single woman, heavy with child and no husband to give the child a name. My uncle sent me away when my condition became obvious. He sent me to live with his sister in Georgia. Out of sight, out of mind. He could be quite heartless when he felt the situation warranted," Alex explained.

Jo climbed out of bed and paced the floor. "Why would he do such a thing? This was *your* child, Al, not his."

Alex sat with her back against the headboard, hands folded in her lap as she watched Jo pace. "Like so many southern gentlemen of his day, there was nothing more important to him than his reputation. In the South, everything depended on your good standing in society...business deals, acceptance in the community. My child threatened all of that," Alex explained.

"It sounds damned harsh if you ask me," Jo mumbled. "I can't imagine anyone depriving a person of their child. Why would he assume he had the right to make life and death decisions over someone who wasn't even his own flesh and blood?" Jo asked, frustration heavy in her voice.

"Josie, you didn't grow up in the South. You have no idea what it was like. While you were raised a free spirited Yankee, I was protected, sheltered and controlled. The South was very different in those days, Josie. Women had no say at all over their own lives. If you weren't married, your father, brothers, and even your uncles had authority over you. If you *were* married, your husband was your lord and master. With my parents deceased, my Uncle took over the estate until my father's will left everything to me at the age of twenty-five. His position as lord of the manner gave him the authority to make life-altering decision about everyone who lived there. Coming from the North, you just can't understand what I mean unless you've lived it," Alex responded.

"Damned backward southerners! I may be a good-for-nothing Yankee, but in my wildest dreams, I would never treat a person like that," Jo sputtered. "I just wish I could have met your uncle before he died. I would have taken great pleasure in turning him from a bass to a soprano."

Alex looked at Jo with intense love in her eyes, a love born of fifty years together.

"Josie, darlin', you would not have survived in the south. I can't imagine you allowing any man to dampen that Wycliffe spirit of yours. But then, they don't know you as I do. As tough as you'd like to believe you are, you are just a pile of mush inside. I wish I had known you back then, Josie. You would have protected me. You wouldn't have allowed them to take my child," Alex said with conviction.

Josie narrowed her eyes at Alex. "You're damned right I wouldn't! But that's beside the point Al. You don't really know that they took your child from you. She could have been stillborn just like they said she was," Jo pointed out.

"I don't know, Josie. Seeing Billie today caused a terrible rush of memories to return. Land sakes alive! No wonder I fainted. Oh, my goodness, she could be me forty-five years ago! Josie, what if she is somehow related to me? How else would you explain it? Her resemblance is too much of a coincidence," Alex tried to reason.

Josie stopped pacing and looked at Alexandra. "Alex, sweetheart, even I have to admit that Billie's resemblance to you is too strong to deny, but Billie is adopted. She doesn't even know who her mother really is. Considering her age, if she's related to you at all, she'd have to be your granddaughter. How in hell are we supposed to verify anything if she doesn't even know who her mother is?" Jo exclaimed.

Long moments of silence followed. As much as Jo hated to admit it…as much as she wanted to bury the memories and avoid any more heartache for this woman whom she loved more than life itself, she had to agree with Alex. The physical resemblance was indeed too much to deny, and part of her was as convinced as Alex was that somehow Billie was kin.

Finally, Jo climbed back into bed and opened her arms to Alex. "What do you want to do, Al?" she asked.

Alex lay back down and returned to her head to its previous position on Josephine's shoulder. "I need to tell her, Josie. If there's a chance...," Alex replied haltingly, allowing the rest of the sentence to remain unspoken.

Jo was silent for a few more minutes. She could feel the slight shudders emanating from Alex as emotion threatened to overcome her. Alex was right. If there was a chance that she and Billie were from the same bloodline, she had a right to know. They both had the right to know.

Finally, Jo nodded her head up and down. "Okay, Al. We'll tell her." She kissed Alex gently. "Sleep now, sweetheart."

“I love you, Josie, with all my heart. Thank you, my love,” Alex whispered.

“I love you too,” Jo replied.

Jo immediately felt Alex relax in her arms and within moments she drifted off.

It was several more hours before Jo finally succumbed to fatigue and joined Alex in sleep.

* * *

"Well, what did you think of them?" Cat asked.

"I think they're cute," replied Billie.

"Cute?" Cat questioned. "I've never heard them described quite that way before."

Billie was lying face down on the bed with Cat sitting on her low back, her legs straddling Billie's waist.

Billie looked back at Cat. "God, Cat!" she moaned. "You have exactly two hours to stop that."

Cat chuckled at the almost orgasmic look on Billie's face in reaction to the massage. "You, my love, give too much away," Cat warned her.

Billie's eyebrows arched on her forehead. "What do you mean?"

"What do I mean?" Cat repeated the question as she applied a little more depth and pressure to the massage.

Billie dropped her head onto the pillow and moaned loudly.

"*That* is what I mean?" Cat said. "You are way too easy."

"Busted!"

"Busted indeed!" Cat replied before adding, "So, really, what did you think of them?"

Billie shifted her weight and rolled onto her back, then pulled Cat into an embrace. "I liked them, Cat. I liked them a lot. I will say, however, that my resemblance to Alex is kind of scary. I mean, I can see how *you* might look like Jo, but, Cat, why Alex and I?"

"I don't know, Billie. But you're right, it is kind of scary. I thought their reaction to meeting you was funny, though," Cat replied.

Billie laughed at the memory. "Yeah, it *was* kind of funny. Alex acted like a typical southern belle...all delicate and fragile, and Jo ...well, Jo was quite brash. Does she always swear like a sailor?" Billie asked.

"Grandma Jo has been known to turn the air blue on occasion. Much too frequently for Grams' tastes of course. She is quite a character!" Cat explained.

"She's quite a flirt. She either pinched or felt up my butt three times during the evening!" Billie said, a chuckle belying her tone of mock indignity.

"Can't say that I blame her, love."

Billie tilted Cat's chin up to her. "So, is that where your inherited your lusty nature, wife?"

Cat wiggled her eyebrows up and down and nodded her head vigorously.

Billie pulled Cat over on top of her. "Remind me to thank her," she said before claiming her lips once more.

* * *

Cat, Billie and the kids returned bright and early to Doc and Ida's the next morning to take the entire family out to brunch. As usual, Jo was dressed in mannish trousers and a button-down shirt, complete with a bandana tied around her neck and an Australian outback hat propped on her head. Alex, on the other hand, graced her tall slim form with a simple dress belted at the waist, with a wide turndown collar which met at a “V” modestly above her cleavage. Atop her head was a wide-brimmed sun hat, covering her traditionally coifed hair.

All through brunch, Billie took extra caution to keep her distance from Jo to avoid potentially embarrassing encounters that she might have a hard time explaining in public. As it turned out, Billie's precautions were unnecessary, as both Jo and Alex seemed preoccupied.

After brunch, the kids conned Billie into playing a game of football with them in the backyard. Surprisingly, Jo asked to join in. Soon, Alex and Cat were standing on the back deck, watching two grown women playing football against three children.

"No wonder I'm gray!" Alex commented as the children tackled Jo to the ground, two yards short of her goal. "That woman thinks she's still in her twenties!"

Cat looked over at Alex and smiled. She grabbed her grandmother's hand and brought it to her heart. "It's this," Cat indicated by sweeping her hand across the scene in the back yard, "and your active lifestyle that keeps both of you so young, Grams. She's having fun. Don't give her too hard a time when they're finished, okay?" Cat said.

"Okay, I won't," Alex said. "I'll wait until tomorrow mornin' when she can't get out of bed!" she added wickedly.

Finally, the game was over, the children conquering the adults. Cat and Alex stepped off the deck into the yard to meet their respective mates as the children ran into the house looking for something to drink. Jo and Billie walked arm in arm toward their wives, very proud of themselves for even making it through the game.

"I'd give you a victory kiss, but seeing as you lost...," Cat teased.

"I'll take that kiss anyway!" Billie said as she grabbed Cat and dipped her backward placing a wet sloppy kiss on her mouth.

Jo and Alex looked on with knowing smiles, both women reminiscing about times gone by, when they would have done the same thing. Just then, Jo looked up at Alex, "What the hell," she said then proceeded to dip Alex backward for a kiss.

Alex was very flustered when Jo finally released her. "For goodness sake, Josephine Wycliffe! Must you behave so wantonly all the time?" she scolded.

Jo backhanded Alex on the butt as she walked to the

porch swing. "Ah, get over it, Al. You liked it, and you know it. After all, I'm only 'wanton' you," she stated, and evil grin plastered on her face as she sat down.

Alex fussed with a few strands of loose hair as she stammered, "Well...well, yes, I did, but that's beside the point."

"What is the point Al? That even after fifty years together, I still find you sexy and irresistible? That I spend several hours a day fantasizing about making love to you?" Jo said causing Alex to blush to the roots of her hair. She knew she was baiting Alex, but the southerner was so much fun to pick on, and after all, she *did* mean every word of it.

"Oh, my goodness, Josie! How can you talk like that in front of the youngsters?" she said, as she felt a flush rising once again into her face.

"That's a pretty shade a pink, Al," Jo commented. "I'm sure Cat and Billie don't mind that I still find you attractive. In fact, I'll bet they could show us a thing or two," Jo teased.

Now it was Cat and Billie's turn to blush as they looked everywhere but at the grandmothers.

"Josie, you stop that right now. Look, now you've got *them* a'blushing. My word," Alex scolded again as Jo grinned from ear to ear.

Alex needed to put some distance between herself and Jo. All this kissing and talk of fantasies were making her warm and fidgety. She turned to Cat. "Caitlain, honey, would you like to help your old grandma fetch some iced tea for our football heroes here?"

Cat smiled and nodded her head. She winked at Billie and followed Alex into the house.

Billie sat down on the swing next to Jo. She bumped shoulders with her. "You are a wicked woman, Jo. Do you realize the state you have Alex in right about now?" she grinned.

Jo grinned back. "Ohhhhh, yeah!" she said then fell silent, as though she had just remembered something sullen.

Noting the mood change, Billie reached out for Jo's hand.

She enveloped it between her own and placed them in her lap. "Jo, is everything all right?"

* * *

In the kitchen, Alex set about retrieving four iced tea glasses from Ida's cupboard. She looked at Cat. "Sugar, you might wanna go ask your Mom and Dad if they want some. I think they're in the living room with those beautiful children of yours."

Cat went to run her errand as Alex placed her hands on the counter top and tried desperately to compose herself. Jo teasing Billie and Cat brought back memories of how she used to make Ida blush whenever she brought a beau home. Thoughts of Ida, led to thoughts of the child she had lost.

It's time, Alexandra. It's time they knew, she told herself, regaining control as Cat returned to the kitchen.

"They already have some tea, Grams," Cat said as she approached. Noting the forlorn look on Alex's face, Cat reached out and touched her arm. "Grams, are you feeling all right?" she asked.

* * *

Billie narrowed her eyes at Jo. "Okay, spill it," she said. Getting no response, she tried another approach "Look, Jo. You haven't made a pass at me all morning, so either I've grown a third eye in the middle of my forehead, or something is wrong. Now what is it?" she demanded.

Billie's comment was made just as Cat and Alex stepped within hearing range onto the deck.

Jo looked up at Alex and smiled, then nodded her head sideways at Billie. "Well, Alex, she's got your spirit, doesn't she?" she said.

Cat narrowed her eyes at her grandmothers, shifting her gaze between the two women. "Now what was that supposed to mean?" she asked.

"Oh, my!" Alex said, quickly putting the two glasses of iced tea down before she spilled them.

Billie quickly jumped up from the swing.

"Now don't you go do that vapors thing again, Alex," she said as she guided the older woman to the swing beside Jo. She handed Alex an iced tea. "Here, drink this."

She handed the other glass to Jo then took hers from Cat. Billie leaned her backside against the railing and faced the elderly ladies. She reached her free arm out to Cat, who went willingly to her.

"Now," Billie said. "There's been a tension in the air ever since we went to brunch this morning. Jo, you just haven't been yourself, and Alex, it's obvious you're preoccupied. Now something is going on here, and I...no, *we* want to know what it is," she finished, looking at Cat for affirmation.

Alex looked at Jo, looking for support.

"She's right, Al. I guess it's time," Jo said.

Alex sighed deeply while nodding her head. "Caitlain, darlin', please go fetch your mother. She needs to hear this too."

Part II

On Solid Ground

Chapter 12

Billie paced back and forth behind the porch swing for several long moments as Cat and Ida sat there, legs crossed at the ankles, hands folded in their laps. Alex and Jo were sitting opposite them in twin Adirondack lawn chairs. Doc stood near the steps, leaning against the baluster.

Alex looked nervously at the tableau of women before her.

"Nona, what is it?" Ida asked, obviously feeling her mother's distress.

Jo reached out for Alex's hand, and grasped it tightly for moral support.

Billie ceased pacing and stopped directly behind Cat and Ida. She spread her hands out along the length of the swing. Based on the tension, she instinctively knew what they were about to say would turn all of their worlds upside down.

Finally, she lost patience waiting for Alex to speak. "Look, my gut is in knots here. I don't know what's going on, but I have the feeling I'm not going to like it. Please, just get it over with."

Jo rose from her seat and approached Billie. She shook her finger in Billie's face. "You, young lady, had better learn a little patience. Have some respect for this woman here," she said, pointing to Alex. "You'll regret it if you don't," she finished.

Billie stared angrily at Jo. She looked ready to rip Jo's head off, before Alex rose to her feet and stepped in between them.

"Josie, please. Let me handle this," Alex said.

Jo looked at Alex. "Al, I won't let anyone disrespect you, regardless of *who* they are."

"And just who am I?" Billie asked angrily, taking another

step toward Jo.

"Billie, honey, please sit down. There's no reason to be angry," Cat reasoned. This was definitely *not* how she envisioned her grandparents and wife getting along.

"No, Cat. Let her answer." Billie repeated her last question. "Just who am I, Jo?"

"You are my granddaughter, Billie. At least I think you are," Alex replied, followed by gasps from both Ida and Cat.

Billie snapped her head around to look at Alex. "What did you say?" she asked incredulously.

Cat rose from the swing and grasped Billie's arm. "Grams, what are you saying?"

Alex turned her back on the group and walked a few paces away. She turned to face them once again. "Please, sit down. It's a long story. One that is long overdue."

One by one they sat… Billie and Cat on the porch swing, Ida and Jo in the lawn chairs. Doc remained standing where he was, watching the scene with keen interest.

Alex remained standing, positioned at the head of the tableau. She stood there for long moments, unable to find a way to start the discussion. Billie was becoming more impatient with each minute that passed, regardless of Cat's efforts to quell the flames brewing within her.

Seeing Billie's escalating mood, Jo rose from her chair and approached Alex. She cupped Alex's face between her palms and pulled her down for a kiss.

"Do you want me to tell them, Al?" Jo asked.

Alex smiled as a lone tear ran down her cheek. "No. I'll do it. I love you for asking, though," she replied.

"Well, I'm right here if you need me," she said. She took Alex's hand in her own and held it tightly.

"Thank you," she said before looking up at the others gathered before her. "Ah, this is very hard to talk about. The implications are almost unimaginable. It was more than fifty years ago, but the pain is still as fresh as the day it happened," she began.

Jo squeezed her hand slightly for moral support.

Doc, Cat, Billie and Ida looked at her expectantly.

"Fifty-five years ago, I gave birth to a baby girl. She was taken away from me immediately. I was told that she was stillborn. I never heard her cry. I never saw her. The doctor said she was born dead," Alex tried to explain. "They never even let me see her," she repeated, the tears starting to flow.

Ida's eyes grew as large as saucers. She joined Doc at the railing and huddled under the protective shelter of his arm around her shoulder as she steeled herself for the rest of Alex's tale.

Cat's grip on Billie's hand tightened as she felt her wife stiffen with anxiety at the announcement.

Jo wrapped her arm around Alex's waist. "Al, you don't have to do this," Jo said. "Let me."

"No, Josie. I *do* need to do this," Alex said insistently.

Alex looked at her audience and saw how each woman had sought her own sense of solace at the news… Ida with Doc, and Cat with Billie. Tears were clearly visible in Cat and Ida's eyes; however, a cold mask had been pulled down over Billie's features as she sat there on the swing… her right leg crossed over her left, her left elbow resting on the arm of the swing, her chin resting on her fist, and her right hand held firmly in Cat's grasp. She was staring at the floor next to the swing, her brow drawn into a frown.

Ida spoke up. "Nona, how..."

"How did I come to be in the family way?" Alex asked for her daughter. Ida just nodded.

Alex played with the hem of her jacket for a moment before looking into her daughter's face. "I was raped by one of the stable hands after coming home from a ride, Ida."

At the mention of rape, Billie's head snapped up and swung around to look at Cat, who was obviously recalling memories of her own horrific ordeals. Uncrossing her legs, she leaned in toward Cat and pulled the woman close, urging her to rest her head on her shoulder.

Alex paced anxiously. "He was a good looking man. He was always pleasant. I used to stay and watch him groom the horses after a ride. I guess I was lonely, and he seemed so attentive, so friendly," she tried to explain.

Alex took a sip of her iced tea before continuing. "Here I was, twenty-three years old and unmarried, which was unheard of in those days for a woman in her twenties. If a woman of that age was still unmarried, society assumed there was something wrong with her. Anyway, there I was, unmarried, and still under my family's control. Hell, Daddy had given up on marryin' me off years earlier. He couldn't understand why I wasn't interested in all the young men he brought home. I couldn't bring myself to tell him that I preferred women. I don't know how he would have reacted. I wish now I had told him. We lost him about a year before the rape. Maybe if he was still alive, things might have been different," Alex mused sadly.

"Anyway, I came home from a ride one day, and there he was. We were alone. He kept eyeing me funny while he was grooming my horse...askin' me all kind of questions about what I liked and didn't like in a man. He was so bold to ask me if I fancied him. I didn't want to lie, so I told him I liked him well enough, but not as a beau. He kinda became angry with me over that and told me he was gonna prove what a big man he was... prove to me that he could make me feel good."

Cat's knuckles were white as she clenched tightly to Billie's hand while Alex spoke.

"I fought him the best I could," Alex continued, "but he was really a big man and he easily overpowered me. He dragged me into the nearest stall and had his way with me. When it was over, he packed his gear and left. I did the best I could to pull myself together, then snuck into my room through the back stairway...you know, the one that leads from the kitchen to the bedrooms on the second story," she said to those who were familiar with the mansion she and Jo lived in.

"Anyway, I cleaned myself up and kept my mouth shut about what happened. I guess I was too ashamed to say anything. I spent the next week or so hoping and hoping that everything would be all right, but two weeks later, I woke up sick to my stomach and knew in my heart of hearts that I was with child. Of course, in my Uncle's eyes, I was nothing but a wanton whore. I tried to tell him the stable hand raped me, but he blamed it all on me...saying it wouldn't have happened if I hadn't flirted with the man."

Alex stopped short to look at Jo. "Josie, I didn't flirt with him. I promise I didn't. I was just tryin' to be pleasant," she insisted.

Jo squeezed Alex's. "I believe you, Al. I believe you," she replied.

"So two months after it happened, I was shipped off to Aunt Edna's house for the duration of the pregnancy. Seven months later, I gave birth to a baby girl that the doctor said was dead," Alex finished, looking down at the clasped hands in her lap as a deafening hush fell over the crowd.

"So, what does all of this have to do with me being your granddaughter, Alex?" Billie asked, breaking the uneasy silence.

"I don't know that it *does*, Billie," Alex replied, "but the resemblance is too strong to ignore. I can't help but think that you are my daughter's child," she said.

"But Grams, you said your daughter was stillborn," observed Cat.

"That's what I was told, darlin', but keep in mind that I never saw her. Birthin' was a horrible experience for me. I had a very hard time with it. The doctor had me under a heavy dose of laudanum near the end. I was pretty much out of it," Alex explained in a choked voice.

"Nona," Ida said. "Why would they tell you she was stillborn if she wasn't?"

"Sweetheart, ya gotta remember where I come from. South Carolina in the nineteen fifties was ruled by a southern aristocratic patriarchal mentality. My uncle had taken over control of the estate, including me. He was a ruthless man with definite ideas about a woman's place in the home and in society. We were very rich and influential in the community. In those days, a reputation was far more important than family," Alex explained.

Jo became very agitated at this point, pacing back and forth. "Damned southerners," she mumbled under her breath. It was obvious what she thought of Alex's treatment at the hands of the aristocracy.

Alex reached a hand out to stop Jo's trek back and forth across the floor. "Josie, darlin', please stop pacin'. You're makin' me nervous," Alex said.

Jo stopped and looked impatiently at Alex before stomping over to the lawn chair and sitting down again.

“When my uncle found out I was with child, he beat me senseless then accused me of all kinda sinful deeds and bringin’ shame on the family. It wasn’t long after that I was shipped out of state to my aunt’s house to wait out the pregnancy.” Alex stopped to take another sip from her iced tea. It was then that she noticed how hard Jo was working to hold back angry tears.

She walked toward her partner of fifty years and took her hand. She kissed it gently and looked into Jo’s eyes. “Josie, it was a long time ago. All but the pain of losing my daughter has been forgotten. Please don’t dwell on what’s passed us by. Instead, look at the wonderful possibilities that lie ahead. Okay, darlin’?” she asked.

Jo took a deep breath and held back the hateful words she had reserved for Alex’s kin. Instead, she forced a smile onto her face and nodded her head in agreement with Alex’s plea.

Alex mouthed a silent *thank you* to her partner, then continued to pace.

"Anyway, I never saw her when she was born. I never even heard her cry. All I remember is hearin' the doctor say that she was born with the cord around her neck. My family's reputation was very important to them. It would not be inconceivable to eliminate a source of embarrassment by giving the child away," Alex finished.

Billie stood up and approached Alex, stopping directly in front of her. Billie held Alex's gaze for long moments, the audience of three holding their breaths around them.

Finally, Billie reached up and touched the side of Alex's face. "Where did you live at the time, Alex?"

"In Charleston, South Carolina, but...," Alex started to say.

"Thank you," Billie said before turning to Cat. "Cat, I'm going to Charleston as soon as I can book a flight. I'm sure to find a birth record there and a certificate of death for this child, if one exists. I'm going to look for my mother."

Alex took Billie's hand. "Not without me," she said.

Chapter 13

"How long have you suspected that your daughter may still be alive?" Billie asked Alex as they sat side by side on the flight into Charleston, South Carolina.

Alex contemplated the question for a moment before answering. "In my heart, I guess I've always wondered," Alex admitted, "When she was born, I was under strict orders from my uncle not to tell a living soul about the birth, lest shame be brought down on the family name. For two years my uncle set out to brainwash me, convincing himself, and nearly convincing me that the pregnancy never even happened. But I knew. I knew the pain and humiliation of being raped. I knew the pain of believing my child had died. I managed to push it to the back of my mind, but I never forgot it. Then, when I turned twenty-five, my inheritance was awarded and I regained control of my life. I banished my uncle from my home, and refused to acknowledge him until his death several years later.

"Unfortunately, the damage he had done was irreversible. My daughter was gone. Whether she was dead or not, I was not sure. But she was indeed gone, and I had resolved to start my life anew and put the pain of losing her behind me. I have managed to successfully hold that pain at bay for fifty years, Billie. That is until I met you. I don't believe it is possible for you to look so much like me without some biological reason," she explained.

Billie held her gaze for a moment longer before looking away. She leaned her head back against the seat cushion.

"What are you thinking, Billie?" Alex asked as she watched a parade of emotions march across Billie's face.

Billie's eyes held Alex's gaze for several seconds before

looking down at her hands clasped in her lap. "I'm thinking that I'm scared shitless, Alex. I'm thinking that I'm angry as hell that the people who raised me lied to me for more than thirty years. I'm thinking that I don't need another complication in my life," Billie replied before pausing to reflect, and seeing the forlorn look on Alex's face.

Billie took Alex's hand in hers, placing it palm down inside her own. She entwined their fingers and closed her fist, grasping the aged hand firmly.

Alex, whose eyes had been glued to their entwined hands, looked into Billie's face as Billie squeezed her hand.

"Alex," Billie said, "I am also thinking that I am very excited at the prospect of learning just who I am and where I came from, and if that origin starts with you, I am thinking that I couldn't have come from a more perfect place," Billie finished.

Alex smiled and closed her fingers around Billie's. "I truly hope that is the case, Billie," she replied.

Billie nodded before a grin spread across her face.

"What 'cha smilin' about?" Alex asked.

Billie chuckled. "I was just realizing how complicated Cat's and my family trees will become if you and I turn out to be related!" she explained.

"Indeed!" Alex commented. "Caitlain wasn't happy about stayin' home, was she?" Alex asked.

Billie glanced at Alex, and then down at her hands. "No, she wasn't, but she has a busy schedule at the hospital this week, and she couldn't find a replacement for the surgeries she is scheduled to anesthetize. But, she and Jo will be joining us in a few days. I'm glad Jo agreed to stay and fly out with her this weekend."

"You love her very much, don't you?" Alex asked.

"With all my heart, Alex. She is my life," Billie explained.

Alex nodded in understanding. "As Josie is mine. We are lucky ladies indeed."

A moment later, the stewardess' voice announced that they were about to make their final approach into Charleston, followed by the standard safety instructions. Ten minutes later, the wheels of the 737 jet touched down on the runway of the Charleston International Airport.

Thirty minutes after that, Billie and Alex were in a taxi, on their way to Alex's ancestral home on the outskirts of Charleston.

* * *

Billie sat quietly, scanning the countryside on the ride from the airport. Broad fields of tobacco plants could be seen lining the main highway on either side. The taxi suddenly took a turn and drove through an open wrought iron gate, supported by brick pillars. On both sides of the drive, were perfectly aligned cottonwood, magnolia and cypress trees, all standing sentry to the well-traveled road that led to the stately plantation at the end of the drive.

If Billie closed her eyes, she could imagine how this may have looked one hundred fifty years earlier, with well-kept fields of cotton and tobacco plants growing abundantly across the landscape while slaves carefully tended the crops. Thinking back to how Alex had described life on the plantation just fifty years earlier, she wondered to herself how she would have accepted the second class status allotted to women in those days. Having been born two generations after Alex into an era when equal rights for women was in full swing, she found it difficult to fathom how someone as independent as Alex Spirakis could have allowed her life to be dominated by men. She found herself grateful that her arrival on earth came at a time when her worth as a person was not allowed to be disputed.

"Beautiful, isn't it?" Alex remarked as she noticed Billie's fascination with the plantation.

"Yes, it is," Billie agreed. "Is it still a functional plantation?" she asked.

"Parts of it are. My daddy never believed in allowing the land to be fallow, so Josie and I open it to the neighboring communities to cultivate it for their own use. The only stipulation is that twenty-five percent of the yield must be donated to needy folks in the area. Those efforts are organized by the local food shelf in Charleston," she explained.

Billie was in awe of this remarkable woman and the generosity she and Jo so freely allotted to their neighbors. "That is very kind and generous of you, Alex," she remarked.

Alex covered Billie's hand with her own. "It's the least we can do, dear. Two old women have no need to hoard so much when those around us have so little. And besides, our community has been nothing short of remarkable when it comes to my relationship with Josie," she explained.

"They know?" Billie asked.

"I'm not really sure if they do or not. I assume they do. Josie and I have never come right out and declared the nature of our relationship, but then, no one has ever asked. All I know is that we have been quite happy here for fifty years, and if the community knows, no one seems to care. Oh look, there's the house," Alex pointed out as they rounded the last bend in the drive.

Billie gasped as the house came into view. "Holy shit!" she exclaimed.

Alex laughed. "Now you sound like Josie," she said.

Billie turned to Alex, mouth wide open in awe.

"Close your mouth, dear. The bugs will nest in there if you're not careful," Alex said.

"Don't tell me you actually *live* here!" Billie exclaimed.

"Why of course we do," replied Alex.

"Holy shit!" Billie exclaimed again.

The mansion was huge, sporting a three-story center section, roof-high pillars lining the front entrance, and a two-story wing on each side. Spanish moss clung to the brick walls, while yellow jasmine flowers lay in dense, symmetrically arranged beds along the entire facade of the estate. Fierce looking stone gargoyles guarded the gables that protruded from the roofline at periodic intervals across the main part of the house. A circular garden lay directly in front of the house and a cobblestone path led around the periphery, to meet at the carport sheltering the main entrance at the front of the mansion.

As the taxi pulled under the carport, a middle-aged gentleman met them at the car. He greeted Alex graciously.

"It's good to have you back, Miss Alexandra," he said. "You should have called. I would have been happy to meet you at the airport."

A sudden movement from the taxi drew his attention to Billie as she exited the car. He stood and stared in disbelief. He looked back and forth between Billie and Alex, his eyes bulging, mouth agape.

Seeing the man's surprise, Alex smiled and placed a hand on his shoulder. "Chet, this is Billie Charland, my granddaughter," she announced, a little uneasy about how Billie would accept the moniker. "Billie, this is Chet, a trusted employee and very good friend."

Chet smiled broadly. "A man would be a fool not to see the family resemblance, Miss," he said. "Welcome to SpireCliffe Acres, Miss Billie. I'm sure you'll enjoy your stay here," he said as he shook her hand warmly.

Billie thanked the man for her welcome then looked at Alex. "SpireCliffe?" she questioned, eyebrows raised into her hairline.

Alex locked arms with Billie as she led her toward the front entrance. Chet collected their luggage and saw to the taxi. "It was Josie's idea. It's named for Spirakis/Wycliffe. We changed it after I insisted we add her name to the deed. You see dear, I wanted to make sure that Ida inherited the estate when we are gone, and since this backward nation of ours doesn't allow our kind to marry in every state, it was the only way we could legally guarantee Ida's inheritance, especially considering Josie is Ida's biological mother," she explained.

The interior of the house was even more magnificent than the outside, with tall ceilings, winding staircases, marble floors and valuable art decorating the walls. The main foyer alone was nearly as large as the entire first floor of Billie's house. Alex gave Billie the grand tour of the main level.

Billie's favorite room was the library, with leather-paneled walls, a large oak desk, and oak bookshelves lining every wall. There was every title imaginable contained on those shelves, from dusty old history books, to current novels by Danielle Steele and Steven King. This room was obviously designed for a man's tastes; however, touches of Josephine Wycliffe could be seen here and there, including an old worn fedora hanging on a coat rack near the entrance.

As they ascended to the second story, Alex encouraged Billie to choose one of the many bedrooms as her own for the duration of this, and future stays at SpireCliffe Acres.

Alex stood in the doorway of Billie's room as she watched the younger woman flop herself down on the bed. "I'm gonna raid the kitchen and fetch a sandwich or somethin'. Are you hungry?" she asked.

Billie sat up as her stomach took that opportunity to make its presence known. She grinned. "Lead the way!"

* * *

"Do you always eat like this?" Billie asked as she watched the Alex down a thick ham and cheese sandwich. Her appetite reminded her of Cat. Thinking of Cat, she felt a pang of homesickness wash over her.

"I've always had a healthy appetite. It becomes habit after so many years," Alex explained. "At SpireCliffe, if you aren't even the least bit hungry, it is wise not to venture near the kitchen because if you do, Maggie will insist on feeding you a full course meal. If I've learned anything over the past thirty years of eating Maggie's cooking, it's not to cross the woman. You eat what she puts in front of you, or there's hell to pay! It's easier just to eat it, hungry or not!"

Alex chuckled as she spoke affectionately of the long-term employee who ran her kitchen. "Like I said, it's become habit after so many years. I'm just happy that my metabolism can handle it."

Billie abruptly changed the subject. "Alex, do you mind if I call Cat and the kids?"

"Of course not, darlin'. This is your home when you're

here, okay? I want you to be comfortable in it," Alex explained. "Do whatever you would do if you were home."

Billie thanked her as she rose to her feet and planted a kiss on Alex's cheek before heading into the library to call her wife. "Be right back," she said.

* * *

"Hello?"

"Jen?" Billie asked.

"Hi, Billie," Jen quipped. "How was your flight?"

"Fine. Where's Cat?" Billie asked, a little more abruptly than she intended.

"Billie, is everything all right?" Jen asked.

"Everything's fine Jen. What are you doing there so late?"

"I'm having an affair with Cat. What the hell do you think I'm doing here?" Jen replied sharply.

Realizing she had over reacted, Billie apologized. "Jen, I'm sorry. I'm just tired. Really, where is Cat?" she asked.

"Cat is tucking the kids into bed. Billie, let me put your mind at ease, I'm here making arrangements with Cat about the kids staying with Fred and me for the next few days. It seems she managed to find a replacement at work after all."

Billie's spirits soared, but at the same time, she realized she had acted like a fool to their best friend. "Jen, I'm really sorry. I was being a jealous fool. I'm sorry," she said again.

"Billie, you know I love you and Cat very much. I would give my life for you if necessary, but your maniacal life style is too much for the likes of me! No, you two definitely deserve each other. I wouldn't touch what you two have with a ten foot pole. Besides, you'd rip my head off and feed it to me if I tried!" Jen said, chuckling.

"Jen, what would we do without you?"

"I don't know, and I don't plan on giving you the chance to find out. You're stuck with me, Big Guy!"

"I can think of worst things to have stuck to me, my

friend. So, is my wife there or not?" Billie asked.

"Yep, I think I hear her coming down the stairs right now. Oh yeah, here she is," Jen said.

"Don't tell her it's me. I want to have a little fun with her," Billie said.

Jen handed the phone to Cat.

"Who is it?" Cat asked softly, receiving a shrug from Jen in response.

"Hello?" Cat said into the receiver.

Billie started to breathe heavily into the phone, partially covering the receiver with her hand.

"Hello? Who is this?" Cat asked.

"Heh...heh...heh...little girl. Wanna have some fun?" Billie asked in a raspy voice.

"Who is this? Cat asked. She looked at Jen, who was grinning ear to ear.

"Know what I wanna do to you...heh, heh, heh...," Billie continued.

"You are one sick person," Cat started to rant.

"I wanna make you naked...and cover you with whipped cream...heh, heh, heh...," Billie teased.

"I'll contact the police if you call here again," Cat said, slamming down the receiver.

"Cat!" yelled Jen, catching the receiver just before it hung up the phone. She took it out of Cat's hand and held her hand over the mouthpiece. "It's Billie!" she whispered.

Cat's eyes opened wide. "Oh yeah?" she asked, raising one eyebrow at her friend. Cat took the receiver back from Jen and held it to her ear. "Okay. Okay, you want to have some fun? Fine, but *I* run the show, you got that?" Cat asked.

"Anything you say, my sweet," said Billie, still disguising her voice.

"All right. First, we make sure our spouses are out of the way. By the way, are you married?" Cat asked.

Jen was just about busting a gut in the background.

"Billie suddenly realized that Cat was onto her. "Oh, I'm very married, but my wife will never find out."

"Good," Cat answered, now knowing that this game had turned from one of teasing to one of seduction. "Now, take your clothes off, and I'll do the same," Cat continued.

Billie was dumbstruck. "Huh?" she asked.

"I said, take your clothes off. Here Jen, hold my shirt and bra while I slip off my panties," Cat said with the receiver near enough for Billie to hear.

Jen was doubled over with laughter.

"Ahhhh...what are you doing?" Billie asked.

"I'm taking my clothes off. Aren't you?" Cat asked.

"Ahhhh...Cat, Jen is there," Billie said, giving up the ruse.

"I know she is. I kind of thought...you know, the more the merrier," Cat said casually, causing Jen to cringe.

"Cat, I'm only kidding," Billie said desperately.

"Really? I'm not!"

"Damn it, Cat, put Jen on the phone," Billie demanded.

Cat grinned broadly as she handed the phone to Jen.

"Yes?" Jen said.

"Jen, tell me she isn't naked," Billie said.

Jen looked at a fully clothed Cat and said quite flippantly, "Okay, she isn't naked."

"Jen, I'm not fooling any more. Don't bullshit me," Billie warned.

"Billie, you asked me to tell you that she wasn't naked, so I did. What else would you like me to say?"

"Jeeeennnnnnn," Billie threatened with her tone of voice.

"Okay, okay, I give. I value life too much to continue with this. All right, you want the truth?"

"Yes."

"She's naked," Jen said, covering the receiver with her hand and laughing out loud.

"Put Cat back on the phone. Now!"

Jen handed the phone back to Cat. "She is really pissed," Jen said, with her hand over the receiver once more.

"Hello sweetheart," Cat said with a sugary sweet voice.

"Caaaaaaat! I am not very happy right now! Damn it Cat, tell me you're not naked," Billie demanded.

Cat finally decided to end the joke. "Billie, calm down.

Sheesh, you started all this. No, I'm not naked. Look, if you can't take a joke, then don't start one, okay?" she said.

Billie took a deep breath. "I'm sorry," she said into the receiver. "Damn, but I miss you, Cat. The thought of you naked with another woman. Well, damn it, it makes my blood boil!" she exclaimed.

"Billie, we're talking about Jen here," Cat said, getting a *What am I, chopped liver?* look from Jen.

"I said I was sorry, really I am. Look, Jen tells me you found a replacement for your surgeries," Billie said, changing the subject.

"Yes, I did. Grandma Jo and I will be catching an early afternoon flight tomorrow to Charleston. It arrives at the airport at three-thirty p.m., Charleston time. Can you pick us up?" Cat asked.

"You bet. We'll be there," Billie replied.

"Good. How are you settling in?" Cat inquired.

"You didn't warn me about the house. Wow! It's magnificent. Our whole home can just about fit in the entry way!" Billie explained.

"Yeah, I know. We used to love to slide down the banisters when my sisters and I were small. It is kind of overwhelming, but it's pretty comfortable," Cat said.

"It seems to be," Billie agreed. "Look, love, kiss the kids for me, okay? I love you, Cat, and I miss you so much. Alex and I will be at the airport in time for your flight. I can't wait to hold you in my arms again," Billie finished.

"I love you too, sweetheart. Okay, I'll see you tomorrow afternoon," Cat said.

"Kiss Jen for me, okay?" Billie added sincerely.

"I will...on the lips!" Cat said, chuckling loud enough for Billie to hear.

"You will pay for that, woman!" Billie warned.

"Oh, I'm counting on it!" Cat replied. "See you tomorrow. Bye!"

"Good bye my love," Billie said as she hung up the phone and returned to Alex in the kitchen.

Chapter 14

Billie returned to the kitchen to find Alex putting her saucer in the dishwasher. "How are Caitlain and the children?" Alex asked.

"They're fine, and I've got some good news. Cat found someone to cover her surgeries, so she and Jo will be flying out tomorrow. They'll arrive at the airport here in Charleston around three-thirty p.m."

Alex smiled broadly. "That *is* good news," she said. "What do you say we celebrate with a glass of wine while we relax in the parlor for a while?"

"Sure," Billie agreed as she stepped aside to allow Alex to lead the way. As Billie followed behind the older woman she admired the poise and grace with which the elderly grandmother carried herself. As they reached the parlor, Alex walked directly to the wet bar in the corner of the room, while Billie scanned the countless family photographs that adorned the walls.

Silence prevailed as Alex busied herself choosing a wine, allowing Billie time to become acquainted with the ancestors that had been long lost to her. At least Alex hoped they were ancestors. After pouring two glasses of wine, Alex carried them over to where Billie was admiring the photographs. She silently handed one of the glasses to Billie, as she too examined the portrait Billie was looking at.

"That is your great, great Uncle Samuel Spirakis," Alex provided.

"Thank you," Billie responded as she accepted the wine. "Are *all* of these people ancestors?" she asked without taking her eyes from the pictures.

"Every one of them," replied Alex. "Over there is my

mama and daddy–Elizabeth and Jonathan Spirakis. My mama died from cholera when I was quite young and Daddy raised me by myself. He never remarried. He said this land and his baby daughter were the only things he needed in life," she recalled as mist filled her eyes.

Billie watched the older woman as she spoke of her father. "He must have loved you very much," she commented.

Alex wiped the corner of her eye. "Yes he did. That one right there," she indicated by pointing, "is my Uncle Edward. He's the one who sent me away when I was heavy with child. That would never have happened if my daddy hadn't died a year earlier. Life would be so much different for me now if he hadn't died when he did."

Billie looked contemplatively at the older woman. "You may not have met Jo if he hadn't," she pointed out.

Alex's eyes met and held Billie's for several moments as she saw the truth in her statement. A silent nod was her reply.

Not expecting Alex to elaborate, Billie returned her attention to the portraits. "So who are these other people?" Billie asked, captivated by the wall of faces.

"To be honest with you, darlin' I don't really know. This wall has been decorated with portraits by four generations of Spirakis kin. Some of them date back to the 1800's," she replied.

"How many of them have you added?"

"Well, there's mama and daddy, and of course, Uncle Edward, although I'm amazed his portrait is still there. Josie has threatened to tear it down and burn it for years now!" she joked. "Oh, and that one over there, the one of the young girl is me at ten years of age," she pointed out.

Billie walked over to stand in front of the portrait and gasped as she realized it was like looking at a photograph of herself at that age.

"What is it, darlin?" Alex asked.

Billie looked at Alex. "That could be me," she replied. "My fifth grade photograph is almost an exact copy of that portrait."

Alex reached forward to cup the side of Billie's face with her palm. "Well of course it could, sugar. If you are who I think you are, it makes total sense," she explained.

Billie turned her face into Alex's hand and placed a gentle kiss in the palm before turning back to look into exact copies of her own blue eyes.

"Are you all right, Billie?" she asked.

Billie nodded then took a few steps away. "All of this is just a bit overwhelming," she replied. "Throughout my entire life, I have had no sense of roots. My parents went out of their way to avoid discussing relatives. I guess I didn't know what I was missing until now. Seeing this wall of portraits makes me realize that each of us comes from a long line of people who have lived and died... people with a history, many of them nameless – lost in time. Each person on this wall has their own unique genealogy. If I am truly who you think I am, then I am one of them," she continued, pointing to the wall.

"If I am one of them, I have a real family name and a real family history. My son has a real lineage. The whole concept is mind boggling," she admitted.

Alex's heart swelled with pride as she watched Billie wrestle with the complex notion of an ancestry she hadn't know she possessed. Alex took Billie by the elbow and led her to two overstuffed chairs in front of the fireplace. She motioned for her to sit as she returned to the wet bar to retrieve the bottle of wine.

Billie sat down and relaxed in the appointed chair as Alex refilled their glasses. A sigh of relief escaped her lips.

"That's Josie's favorite chair," noted Alex. "I can't tell you how many hours we have spent sitting right here, reading, and discussing historical events," Alex reminisced as she refilled Billie's wine glass.

Billie smiled at the loving look on Alex's face. "The two of you have been together for a long time," she observed. "The love you have for each other is tangible."

"We've been together for more than fifty years," Alex

responded. "I can still remember the first time I laid eyes on her. I arrived at the American Embassy in Saigon, to help with decipherin' some code. I was just a youngster at the time. I was in my mid-twenties, as was Josie. I was so taken by the brash Yankee I could hardly speak." Alex paused and smiled at a memory that had come to her mind.

"So you had the child after you broke the code? Were you with Jo at the time?"

"Yes… and no to your questions. I went back home after we broke the code, while Josie threw herself into the war effort. We didn't meet again for another five years at an historical convention that my family was sponsoring here in Charleston, about a year after I had given birth to the child. The spark was still there, Billie. I took one look at her from across the room and realized my feelings for her were as fresh as they were when we parted way five years earlier. I knew without a doubt that my heart no longer belonged to me," Alex explained.

"Obviously, she felt the same way about you."

"Well, not right away," Alex chuckled. When we met for the first time in Saigon, she saw me as an intrusion the military hired to spy on her and invade her space. You see, she really didn't ask for an interpreter. I was kinda forced on her by the government. So, being quite the rogue, young Josephine Wycliffe decided right there and then that she was going to use her charm not only to control me in the office, but also in bed!" Alex exclaimed as Billie laughed.

Alex lightly slapped the back of Billie's hand for emphasis. "Well, you can imagine her surprise when I was having no part of her plan! In fact, she was quite insulted one day when I picked her up bodily and tossed her aside after she had backed me into a corner and propositioned me!"

"Oh, my god! I wish I had been there to witness that!" Billie laughed.

"I managed to ward off nearly all of her advances. I kind of gave in the day we broke the code, but only for one kiss. Believe you me, darlin', for the few weeks we worked together before that day, it was a challenge working with Josie. Like I told ya, I found myself attracted to her the moment I laid eyes on her, but a proper lady has standards to uphold, so as much as I wanted to, I didn't give in to her advances," Alex explained.

"So you met again, five years later, and bang, it just happened?" Billie asked in anticipation.

"Love at first sight all over again. At least for me, anyway," replied Alex.

"And what about for Jo?" Billie prompted.

Alex took a sip from her wine and pressed the back of her head into the chair cushion as she stared into the recesses of her memories. "Like I said, darlin', in the beginning, Josie's goal was to seduce me into cooperation, but I know in my heart that it was I who seduced her... not with my body, but with my soul. After breaking the code, there was no reason for me to stay in Saigon, so we said our goodbyes. As we parted, I swear I saw tears in her eyes...tears she quickly covered with her signature aviator sunglasses that always seemed to be within arm's reach."

Alex smiled as she recalled her next memory. "I was so hopin' she'd ask me to stay. In a last ditch effort, I leaned in and placed a very light, but tender kiss on her lips while saying good bye."

"What happened next?" Billie asked, captivated by the story.

Alex looked at Billie and cocked one eyebrow. "That stubborn, Yankee pride of hers got in the way. After I kissed her, she took a step back, shoved those blasted sunglasses onto her face and told me to get out of there. I knew she was trying hard not to allow her emotions to get to her, and I guess I should have called her on it, but like I said, a lady has standards. That was the last I saw of her for five years."

Billie sipped her wine then recounted their second meeting. "Okay, let me see if I understand this," Billie said. "You're thrown together in the heat of war, discover there is a mutual attraction that neither of you acted on...," she began.

"Correction, dear, Josie acted on it, quite brazenly I might add! I was the one who resisted. You know, the southern standards thing," Alex interrupted.

"Right. Josie acted, you resisted. So where was I? Oh, yeah, you part company even though it is obvious to both of you that there was something deep between you, then five years later, you meet again at a party."

Alex smiled broadly. "Oh yes. And it didn't take long for Ms. Wycliffe to find her way into my heart all over again, *and* into my bedroom, I might add," she said, blushing a deep crimson red as she refilled both wineglasses. "From then on, we were inseparable. I joined Josie's lecture circuit as an interpreter and traveled everywhere with her. There was no goin' back at that point."

Billie grinned as she noticed the blush that had nicely colored Alex's face. Leaning her elbow on the arm of the chair, she rested her chin on her hand and looked at Alex. "So what happened to the 'a lady's got standards' thing?" she asked, grinning ear to ear.

Alex looked into her wine glass, and coyly glanced at Billie between her eyelashes. "Well, a lot had happened to me in that five years that made me realize there was much more to life than one's reputation. My heart meant more to me than my reputation ever would. Never had that fact become more real to me than when my uncle hid me away during my pregnancy. I felt shamed and degraded, all for the sake of appearances and my family's reputation.

"Don't you see? When Josie came back into my life, my heart looked beyond the fact that she was a woman, and a Yankee woman at that! It looked beyond the fact that my uncle would be horrified that I was one of 'those' women, and beyond the fact that he would have to endure the scrutiny of friends, family and neighbors. I looked beyond all of that into the greenest eyes I had ever seen, and willingly allowed myself to drown in their depths. Standards be damned! I was in love, and that was all that mattered," Alex explained.

"And Ida?" Billie asked, leaving the question hanging.

Alex nodded her head and sipped her wine. "Ida was our gift from God, Billie. As soon as Josie and I committed ourselves to each other, I told her about the child I had borne. She was nail-spittin' angry at the stable hand who attacked me, and at my uncle for beatin' the tar out of me and treatin' me like a common whore. It took a long time for her to get over the hurt she felt for me. It took even longer to get over the anger she felt toward my Uncle for shipping me off to Aunt Edna's and hiding me away like the embarrassment he thought I was," Alex said, a frown crossing her features at the painful memories. Shaking it off, she looked back to Billie, and paused to reminisce. A faraway happy look entered her eyes.

"Anyway," she continued, "about a year after we met for the second time, we committed our lives to each other. I wanted a child desperately, but for obvious reasons, I didn't want to be the one to bear it, so Josie graciously agreed. It was a difficult nine months to say the least!" exclaimed Alex. "You can imagine how impatient Josie was with the whole morning sickness and bulging tummy business! She was very difficult to live with. I think I was more grateful for the end than she was!" Alex explained, chuckling slightly. "That kinda explains why Ida was an only child," she added. "More wine, Billie?"

Billie handed her glass forward for a refill then sat back in her chair. She felt a slight flush rise into her face, and a warm feeling filled the pit of her stomach.

"I'm kind of surprised that living within the southern aristocracy, you managed to secure such a broad education. I mean, you speak several languages and are an expert of Greek history," Billie pointed out.

"As backward as my Uncle Edward was, my daddy was quite progressive and believed women deserved the same rights and opportunities as men, so he saw to it that I received a good education. He was so proud of me when we broke the code."

Billie sipped her wine as a short silence descended over them.

"Alex, could I ask you a question?"

"Of course, dear," Alex replied leaning forward in her seat.

"What is it about Jo that you find attractive? I mean, why Jo? Why not someone else?" Billie asked.

Alex sat back in her chair and smiled as she recalled all of the reasons she loved her life-long partner.

"Goodness! Where do I begin?" she wondered out loud, a faraway look in her eyes. Finally, she focused on Billie once more. "When the Embassy sent me to Saigon to help Josie decipher the code, I was ready to be away from my family for a while. Daddy and I had just had an awful row over some beau he wanted me to marry. 'Course, I was wantin' no part of it, only Daddy didn't know why, and I was too scared to explain it to him," Alex began. She paused to take a sip from her wine.

"Anyway, off I went to 'Nam. Heaven knows I didn't expect it to change my whole life like it did. But then, I haven't met a person who hasn't been changed by the opportunity to meet Josephine Wycliffe. She is truly an extraordinary person, Billie."

Billie smiled at the obvious love emanating from Alex's eyes. She found herself hoping that this would be her forty years from now, recalling her life with Cat with equal fervor.

"So, how did you know you were in love?" Billie asked.

"There was a very strong attraction right from the beginning. I knew how *I* felt. There was no doubt in my mind 'bout that and I had a pretty good idea how Josie felt too, especially when I caught her lookin' at me when she didn't think I could see her," Alex explained.

"Josie was like no woman I had ever met before. In my days, women in the South were expected to be quiet, delicate and dependent. You can imagine how shocked I was to meet a woman who was anything but that. Josie was excitin' to be with. She was strong and bold. And the words that came out of that woman's mouth! Oh, my goodness! It took me weeks before I stopped blushin' during a simple conversation with her. She made me tingle all over with just a look. She still does. Miss Josephine Wycliffe knows how to turn on the charm when she wants to," mused Alex.

"There was many a night that I wanted to strangle her, she was so stubborn. We'd argue for hours while decipherin' that code. She didn't quite trust me to do my job. She had to be intimately involved in every detail. One night in particular, when we were close to breakin' the code, she was all nervous and pacin' back and forth, askin' question after question. She made me so nervous that I just stopped and told her quite plainly that I was fluent in several languages while she herself just barely got by on simple English, so don't tell me how to do my job!" Alex exclaimed, placing her hands on her hips as she demonstrated how she had reprimanded Jo.

Billie chucked at the thought of this southern belle standing up to the tough Yankee. "What did she say to that?" Billie asked.

"Once the initial shock of me confrontin' her wore off, she pushed her hat down into her head and walked right toward me with this stern look on her face. She got close enough that I could feel her breath on my cheek. She pushed me back into my chair and demanded to tell her what I was talkin' about."

"She pushed you into the chair?" Billie said, recalling her own, regrettable excessive force with Cat several months earlier.

"She did. I was so angry, I could spit nails, so I promptly told her to get the chip off her shoulder and to listen to what I was tryin' to tell her."

"I'll bet she didn't take kindly to that," Billie mused.

"Actually, I think I shocked her with my boldness. I know I shocked myself! She simply raised her hands up and apologized. The next day, we broke the code. That night we celebrate our victory and over the next two days, there were so many meetings and publicity shoots that we had little time to spend together. A day later, and I was on my way home, having done my job, and dispensable to the operation from that point on. I could have stayed if Josie had insisted, but as I told ya earlier, she didn't. I was devastated. I went home with a broken heart, wonderin' if I'd ever see her again," Alex finished.

Billie placed her hand on Alex's knee. "That must have been very difficult for you," she said.

Alex nodded before answering. "Yes it was. She wrote to me a couple of times, but Josie was never very good at correspondence. The next few years were very difficult for me. I lost my father. Then the rape and the stillborn birth of my daughter. I had all but given up on life when our paths crossed again. Like I said earlier, when our eyes met from across the room at that convention, everything came flooding back. My traitorous knees once more refused to support me as I fainted away. When I came to, I was in my hotel room, and Josie was there lying next to me, holding me in her arms. She took me to heaven for the first time that night, and I have never looked back."

Billie watched Alex closely as she spoke, smiling as the intense love this woman had for her partner came through loud and clear in her voice and on her face. Finally, unable to hold it back any longer, Alex yawned.

"Goodness gracious, me," she said, completing the yawn. "I guess that flight took more outta me than I expected. Maybe I'll just turn in for now. We have a busy day ahead of us tomorrow."

Alex placed her wineglass on the table beside her chair and rose to her feet. Billie rose as well and accepted a hug from her. "You just relax and make yourself at home, Billie. I'll see y'all in the mornin'," she said. Excusing herself, she left the room.

Billie watched her leave, then approached the fireplace, wine glass still in hand. After watching the flames for a bit, she walked around the room and looked at the fine art that decorated the wall, until she came to a book shelf tucked behind one of the many overstuffed chairs that lined the room. She scanned the contents of the shelf and discovered several photo albums. She pulled the first one off the shelf and opened the front cover. There was a neatly written entry inside. *Alexandra Spirakis and Josephine Wycliffe - Book I.*

Curious, Billie carried the book to the chair she had occupied earlier and sat down, placing her wineglass on the table. On the first page of photos, she came across what could have easily been a picture of her and Cat, except the subjects in the photo were dressed in period garb from the nineteen sixties. Billie gasped as the resemblance became immediately apparent.

For the next several moments, Billie flipped through the pages of the album, enjoying the story told by the pictures, and reading the dates along the way. When she reached the end of the album, she realized that it basically covered the first ten years of Alex and Jo’s lives together.

She closed the book and returned it to its rightful place before reaching for the second book. Not wanting to move too far away from her treasure, she sat cross-legged on the floor in front of the shelf and spent the next two hours watching fifty years of Alex and Jo's lives unfold before her eyes.

By the time she closed the last album and placed it back on the shelf, she was filled with a feeling of awe, peace and respect for the ladies. What she also felt was a connection to Alex that was so strong Billie was now convinced without a doubt that they were family. Seeing these pictures and knowing in her heart that she was part of them renewed her desire and determination to prove it once and for all. She would find Alex's daughter, and her mother, if it killed her. Hopefully she would find a sense of belonging in the process.

Finally, tired and emotionally drained, she rose to her feet and went to bed.

Chapter 15

When Billie returned from her jog the next morning, she found Alex sitting at the kitchen table, sipping tea and reading the morning paper. She let herself in the back door, and dropped a kiss on Alex's cheek.

"Good Morning, Grams," she said, before excusing herself to go shower and dress.

Alex sat there, tea cup suspended in midair. "Did she just call me, Grams?" she said out loud, "I believe she did!" She smiled broadly.

Fifteen minutes later Billie emerged and sat down next to Alex. As soon as she sat, Maggie brought a cup of coffee to her. Billie made eye contact with her and smiled. "Thank you," Billie said.

"Gracious, child! You look so much like the mistress here! You make me feel thirty years younger!" she exclaimed. "Now, how'd you like your eggs, dear?" she asked Billie.

"I don't usually eat a heavy breakfast. Some cottage cheese and fruit would be enough," Billie said.

Maggie looked at Alex, who was cringing at Billie's words. *Uh, oh, Maggie's goin' ta unload on her for sure!* Alex thought as the cook opened her mouth to speak.

"Cottage cheese and fruit?" she remarked. Maggie placed her hands on her hips. "Young people today don't know what good food is. Are y'all sure you don't want somethin' more substantial, Miss Billie?" Maggie asked.

Billie smiled. "No, cottage cheese and fruit will be fine," she said cheerfully.

"Kids today!" exclaimed Maggie as she shuffled away to fill Billie's order.

Alex looked at Billie.

Billie sported a *what did I do?* expression on her face.

"She let you off pretty easy. You may not get way with it at dinner tomorrow night," Alex said. "Josie and Caitlain will be here by then, and I happen to know that Maggie is plannin' a big welcome home dinner."

"So, we start our search this morning," Billie commented, changing the subject. "We'll need to go to city hall, or to the hall of records, wherever Charleston keeps the city's birth and death certificates," Billie explained.

She sipped her coffee and thanked Maggie as she placed the cottage cheese and fruit down in front of her. Maggie clucked under her breath as she walked away.

"All right. I'll have Chet bring the car around in about a half hour," Alex said.

"Grams, I'd rather drive myself, if that's all right with you," Billie replied.

Alex nodded. "Okay. We have several roadsters that belonged to Daddy in the storage garage. They haven't been driven in years, but they all run just fine," she remarked. "Or you can drive the Lexus. It isn't as classy or excitin' as the antique ones, but it is a little more comfortable for longer trips, seein' as it has air conditioning and all."

The roadsters turned out to be a half dozen antique cars, including a nineteen twenty-three Pierce Arrow Touring Car, a nineteen twenty-seven Studebaker, a nineteen twenty-nine Packard Convertible Coupe, a nineteen thirty-one Mercedes Benz SSK Roadster, a nineteen thirty-two Rolls Royce Roadster, and a nineteen thirty-three Willy's Coupe, all in spit-shine condition, fully operational and finely tuned. They had been housed in the storage garage for nearly five decades. Although they had not been routinely driven, they were kept in tip-top running condition by the mechanics staff at SpireCliffe Acres.

Billie felt like a child in a candy store as she walked in between and around the sporty vehicles, running her hand over the still supple leather and shiny exteriors. Finally, unable to resist, she chose the nineteen thirty-two Rolls

Royce Roadster, with its cream colored paint and red leather boot.

Alex asked Chet to pull the car out of the garage and drive it around to the front of the house. Soon, the two ladies were settled in the vehicle and headed to town. Since Billie had chosen a convertible and since it was a pleasant, sunny, eighty-degree day, she couldn't resist putting the top down. Alex pulled a scarf over her hair to protect her perfect coif. Billie, on the other hand, allowed her dark hair to blow in the breeze as the car sped along the highway, reveling in the feel of freedom the wind through her hair gave her.

Alex looked at Billie and smiled at the broad grin and look of joyful exuberance on Billie's face as she pulled into the parking lot at the hall of records. Billie turned the car off, and smiled at Alex. Her grin split her face ear to ear.

"This is one great car!" Billie said.

Alex smiled back. "Its Josie's favorite too. She hasn't driven it for a long time though. I think her eyes are starting to go, but you won't get her to admit that," Alex said, tucking strands of hair into place had been loosened from the windy ride. "Anyway, Chet normally drives us where we want to go. There isn't much need for either of us to drive."

Billie pulled Alex's hand away from her hair. "Grams," she said. "Why don't you wear it down? You have such beautiful hair."

"Oh pshaw, you silly girl. I'm too old for that, and besides, I've always worn it this way," she reasoned.

"Well, I still like it better down," Billie said, looking nervously at the building before them.

"Why do I get the feelin' you're avoiding going into this building, Billie?" Alex asked.

Billie sat back, hands tightly clenched on the steering wheel. Her arms were outstretched with her elbows locked and her back pressed into the seat. She stared straight ahead, her chin tilted slightly down. The muscles in her jaw tensed. Finally, she turned to look at Alex. "Am I that transparent?"

"Well, I really don't think my hair style is that important to you, sugar," Alex observed. She placed her left hand on Billie's shoulder. "If it's any consolation, I'm really nervous about this too," Alex added.

"I'm sorry, Grams, I'm being self-absorbed. I haven't given much thought to how you feel about this."

"I've had a lot of time to think about and deal with this, Billie, far more than you have. Don't be worryin' about me. I have a beautiful granddaughter either way," she said.

"I'll tell you what," Billie said. "Let's get through this together, okay?"

Alex took a deep breath. "Well then, there's no better time than the present to start. Are you ready?"

"Let's go," Billie replied, as she reached for the door handle.

* * *

"June fourteenth, nineteen fifty-nine," Alex answered as the record's clerk asked for the date of birth on the certificate.

"Mother's name?" asked the clerk.

"Alexandra Spirakis."

"Father's name."

"Unidentified," replied Alex, receiving an odd, knowing look from the clerk. Alex squirmed under the scrutiny.

Seeing Alex's discomfort, Billie leaned over the reception desk and said under her breath, "Look, we didn't come here for you to make my grandmother uncomfortable. Now keep your odd looks to yourself and do your job."

The clerk looked at Billie nervously before continuing. "Home birth, or hospital?" he asked.

"Home," replied Alex.

"Okay, I think I have all the information I need for the search. I'll be back in a few moments." The clerk made his way to the archives at the back of the hall.

Alex looked at Billie. "What did you say to that man?" she asked.

"I just reminded him to mind his manners, Grams, that's all." Billie smiled smugly to herself.

Moments later, the clerk returned. "I'm sorry ladies, but I

don't have a birth record on file under that name and date. Are you sure the birth would have been registered here in Charleston?" he asked.

"This is where the birth mother lived at the time. Why wouldn't it be registered here?" Billie questioned, her hands spread wide on the desk.

"Well, that was more than fifty years ago, Ma'am. Record keepin' wasn't at its best back then," the clerk offered.

"Damn!" Billie exclaimed. "Now what?"

The clerk stood by nervously, waiting for further instruction. "Is there anything else I can help you with, Ma'am?" he asked timidly.

Billie looked up. "No. Thank you," she said before looking at Alex. "Any ideas?" she asked.

Alex locked arms with Billie and led her toward the door. "One," she said. "The birthin' was actually in Lancaster, at Aunt Edna's house. Maybe it woulda been registered there," she suggested.

Billie smiled broadly. She kissed Alex on the cheek. "Grams, why didn't I think of that?"

Alex cupped Billie's face in her palm. "Well, you would've after a time," she said. "We'll need to go home and get a bigger car if we're gonna pick Josie and Caitlain up at the airport. We'll talk about the trip to Lancaster at dinner tonight."

* * *

The meeting at the airport was slightly tense. On the way there, Alex had warned Billie that public displays of affection were pretty much frowned on in certain southern societies, Charleston being one of them, and even more frowned on if the interested parties were of the gay persuasion.

"Why do you stay here if that's the way you're treated?" Billie asked.

"This is where I grew up. My roots are here. My money is here. This is where my home is. Josie and I basically keep to ourselves. To our neighbors, we are just two old spinster ladies who share a home. We are seldom affectionate in public. I don't believe many of them give it any thought, and those that do, have so far kept to themselves," Alex explained. “And besides, we travel a great deal, so outta sight, outta mind, so to speak,” she added.

Not being able to take Cat into her arms and kiss her senseless when she got off the plane, was really bothering Billie.

Cat came through the gate, scanning the tops of the crowd for the dark head she expected to see waiting for her. She wasn't disappointed. Catching Billie's eye, she waved her hand over her head and started making her way toward her wife, dragging an irritated Jo behind her.

Cat reached Billie at the same time that Jo reached Alex. Alex greeted Jo by placing a hand on her back and gently rubbing it up and down. Jo smiled into Alex's face, promising much more when they got home.

Cat threw herself into Billie's arms. Billie held her tightly. "Don't kiss me," she whispered into Cat's ear.

Cat pulled back and looked at Billie, confusion clearly written across her face.

Billie smiled into her face. "Look around, love, and you'll see why."

Cat saw several people staring at the two of them disapprovingly. She looked back at Billie, anger brewing on her brow. "Billie, since when have you let this type of reaction bother you?" she asked, her arms still wrapped around Billie's waist.

"Since Alex and Jo have to live here after we've gone," she replied. "Please understand, Cat. I promise to make it up to you when we get to the house," she said, smiling wickedly.

Cat took a deep breath and released Billie's waist. "Okay," she said, smiling crookedly. "But you'd better make good on that promise!"

"Oh, I will. Believe me, I will," she exclaimed. Billie threw her arm around Cat's shoulder and walked her toward the luggage carousel to retrieve their bags.

Billie and Alex had chosen the nineteen twenty-seven Studebaker to drive to the airport. It was the only car large enough to accommodate the four ladies and their luggage, short of having Chet drive them in the limousine. Cat and Billie sat in the front, with Billie driving, while Jo and Alex took the back seat. Cat sat in the center of the seat, tightly against Billie, her hand resting in Billie's lap, roaming up and down the taller woman's leg while her head rested on Billie's shoulder. Billie was having a difficult time concentrating on driving.

In the back seat, Jo and Alex sat side by side, very little room between them. Jo took Alex's hand, raised it to her mouth and kissed the backs of her knuckles. Alex smiled at Jo affectionately. By the time the car pulled into the carport, the atmosphere inside the car was palpable. Making their excuses to each other, the ladies soon disappeared into their respective rooms. Neither pair was seen for the rest of the day.

* * *

Alex and Jo lay entwined in each other's arms. Alex's head resting on Jo's left shoulder, her right arm tucked between them, her left hand trailing a path up and down Jo's bare arm.

"Josie?" Alex asked.

"Hmm," Jo murmured, feeling very relaxed after Alex had 'welcomed her home proper-like', as she liked to put it.

"Josie, darlin', Billie and I hit a dead end at the clerk's office today. Even though I lived here in Charleston at the time, the baby's birth wasn't registered here," Alex said.

Jo looked at the aging beauty beside her. She placed a tender kiss on Alex's forehead. "Wasn't the baby born in Lancaster, Al? Maybe they have a record of the birth," she suggested.

Alex smiled at Jo. "Great minds think alike, my love. That's exactly what I suggested to Billie. But what if we can't find a birth certificate in Lancaster, either?" Alex asked.

Jo absentmindedly played with Alex's hair with her left

hand. "I don't know. Maybe you can ask around for anyone that may still remember you when you were staying there," she suggested.

Alex just nodded her head, starting to doze off. "I didn't socialize much while I was there, Josie. In fact, Uncle left strict orders with Aunt Edna to keep me hidden. After all, I was bringing shame on the family name," Alex replied sarcastically just before yawning loudly. "Goodness me!" she exclaimed.

Jo turned her head and kissed Alex's forehead once more. "Go to sleep, Al. We'll talk about this in the morning," she said.

No response came from the sleeping Alexandra.

"Damned, southerners!" Jo mumbled under her breath.

* * *

Cat lay flat on her back, her left knee bent out to the side. Her left arm was tucked under her head while her right hand stroked back the dark hair framing the head that was lying on her abdomen. Her face was pointed toward the ceiling, eyes closed and a look of serene satisfaction on her face.

Billie was lying on her stomach, partially on top of Cat, her weight shifted to Cat's right side. Her upper body trapped Cat's right hip and leg while her head rested on Cat's stomach, just above her navel. Billie's right arm was thrown over Cat's left hip, pulling her in closer.

"Billie?" Cat asked.

"Hmm?" Billie murmured, feeling very relaxed after welcoming Cat home, 'proper-like', as Grandma Alex liked to put it.

"Billie, love, I'm sorry you hit a dead end today. Grams mentioned you were planning to go to Lancaster to Aunt Edna's. What if you find nothing there either?" Cat asked.

Billie took a deep breath without opening her eyes. "Then we should probably ask around to see if anyone remembers Grams while she was there," Billie suggested.

Cat sighed and nodded her head without opening her eyes. "Good idea," she said, yawning.

Billie kissed Cat's stomach, then said, "Go to sleep, Cat. We'll talk about this in the morning."

No response came from the sleeping Cat.

* * *

Billie woke early, still wrapped tightly around Cat. As tempting as it was to stay in bed all day, the lure of the crisp, fresh morning air that wafted in through the open French doors was irresistible. She untangled her arms and legs from Cat's and climbed out of bed, then walked naked to stand in front of the open doors. She stood there enjoying the smell of cottonwood trees covered in a low blanket of morning mist.

A sense of renewal filled her as she gave into the urge to step out onto the balcony, totally exposing her nakedness to the morning dew. She twirled around several times and finally stopped at the railing. She looked down over the gardens, only to see a fawn lazily grazing in the grass below. She felt a connection to this land and a sense of belonging as she realized her mother may have been conceived on these very grounds.

She decided to take advantage of the comfortable morning temperatures to get her exercise in. Returning to her room, she donned her running gear and headed out for her morning run.

This morning, Alex woke to find Jo's arm thrown over her midsection, pinning her to the bed. She looked at her partner of fifty years and smiled, remembering the woman's frisky nature from the night before. She placed a gentle kiss on Jo's forehead then worked her way out from under the arm across her abdomen.

Dressed in tight-fitting spandex leggings and a button-down shirt with its tails tied in the front, Alex made her way across the yard to the pool house where she and Jo had set up an exercise room, complete with treadmill, exercise bike, rowing machine and several free weights. As she climbed onto the treadmill, which faced an array of French doors that opened onto the pool area, she saw Billie run by, dressed in running shorts and sports bra. Her dark hair was pulled into a pony-tail, which bounced around as she ran. Alex found herself envious of Billie's youth and remembered that she too was once as fit and trim as her granddaughter is right now.

Exercise and morning showers over, Alex and Billie were sipping coffee and making plans for their trip to Lancaster when first one, then the other of their spouses finally roused from bed a full two hours after they had.

Cat was the first to appear. She entered the kitchen, hair all in disarray from sleep, shuffling along in bare feet and Billie's football jersey that hung loosely and came to mid-thigh. "Coffee," she chanted as she plopped herself down in the chair next to Billie and rubbed her eyes.

Jo was the last to join the crew. In a shuffle that matched Cat's, she made her way to the seat next to Alex. Billie looked at the older woman and chuckled at the boxer shorts, oversized T-shirt and ankle socks she wore under a worn terry cloth bathrobe that was left hanging open.

"I need a cigar," commented Jo sleepily. Almost simultaneously, Billie and Alex leaned over and kissed their partners, welcoming them to the morning.

"Al, you tried to kill me last night," Jo said. She reached around to rub the muscles in the small of her back.

"Well, I was just trying to welcome you home, proper-like!" Alex said. "I'll have Maria run you a hot bath to soak in, darlin', then maybe I can be talked into givin' ya a massage later," she said suggestively. Billie and Cat gave each other knowing grins.

Jo looked at Alex through hooded lids. "Did you put something in your coffee this morning, Al?"

Alex swatted Jo lightly on the shoulder. "Goodness, Josie, can't a lady be affectionate now and again?"

"Grrrr," responded Jo as she gratefully accepted the coffee Maggie placed in front of her. She grabbed Maggie's hand before she could walk away. "When are you going to let me make an honest women out of you, Maggie?"

"When pigs fly, Josephine Wycliffe!" Maggie joked as she slapped Jo's hand away. "How do you live with this woman, Miss Alex?"

"It isn't easy, Maggie. It isn't easy," Alex responded with a laugh. She looked at both Cat and Jo. "Well, while you two were sleepin' the day away, Billie and I have been makin' plans to go to Lancaster," she said.

"Driving or flying?" Cat asked around sips of her coffee.

"It's only a two to three hour drive from here," Jo said. "Might make for a nice day out if you don't mind the ride."

"A nice ride sounds good to me," Billie said.

"Ya know, Maggie is plannin' a big dinner tonight. She's likely to poison us all if we're not back on time," Alex said.

"You're damned right I will!" The voice came from the direction of the pantry, causing grins to break out all around the table.

"Well, it's still early. If we leave within the next hour, we'll be back well before dinner," Cat said.

"All right. It's settled then. I'll ask Maggie to pack us a lunch. There's a beautiful park in Lake Marion, right by the water, which will be perfect for a picnic," Alex said.

An hour later, the ladies climbed into the Studebaker, and were on their way to Lancaster.

* * *

The trip to Lancaster was uneventful, except for the frequent pit stops Cat insisted on making.

"I can't help it, Billie!" Cat exclaimed after the third stop and evil look from Billie. "It's not my fault that my bladder is so small!" she said. Finally, two and a half hours later, they reached Lancaster and pulled into the first gas station they came to. Billie went inside and asked for directions to the town hall. Moments later, she pulled the car into the parking lot of Lancaster Municipal Offices and turned off the ignition.

Billie glanced nervously at Cat then looked at Alex in the rear view mirror. Alex had been unusually quiet during the trip, focusing all her attention on the passing scenery and avoiding eye contact with the other occupants in the car. Billie asked Cat to scoot over a bit so she could turn around in her seat. She reached into the back of the car for Alex's hand. Alex put her hand in Billie's, finally making eye contact with her younger copy.

"You don't have to come in, Grams," Billie said. "Cat and I will run in and check it out."

Alex shook visibly.

Jo reached for Alex's other hand. "Maybe that's a good idea, Billie," Jo said.

Alex nodded her approval.

Billie gave Alex's hand a squeeze and then looked at Cat. "Are you coming with me?" she asked.

Cat and Billie climbed out of the car and walked into the town hall and down the main corridor, reading the names of city offices on the frosted-glass windows as they passed each door.

"Constable, treasurer, mayor, superintendent of schools, town clerk. Billie, here it is. Town clerk. Sounds like a good place to start," Cat said as she led the way toward the closed door.

As the two women entered the room, they ran directly into an elderly man who was leaving, causing him to drop the papers he was carrying.

"Oh, I'm sorry," Billie said as all three of them bent down to retrieve the papers from the floor.

After collecting the papers that had scattered randomly at their feet, Billie rose to her full height and handed them to the man, making eye contact with him for the first time. The man's eyes bulged out of his head as the word 'Alexandra' came from his lips, barely loud enough for Billie to hear. Then, like a scared rabbit, he scurried away as fast as he could.

Cat watched him leave. "I wonder what that was all about?"

Billie looked away from the man's retreating form, a

frown on her face. "He called me, Alexandra," she said.

Chapter 16

"Billie, maybe we should go after him," Cat suggested.

Billie noticed an envelope on the floor that was overlooked in their rush to clean up the results of their collision. She put her hand on Cat's arm. "Maybe we won't have to." Billie picked the envelope up from the floor and looked at it carefully. "No, maybe we won't have to," she repeated.

Cat looked at the envelope and then at Billie's face. "This might be an important document, Billie. We can't keep it," Cat said.

"Oh, we're not going to keep it. We'll return it," Billie said, smiling at Cat. "How we return it though, will depend on what we find in the town's records," Billie explained.

Cat smiled and nodded her head. "You are a snake, my love," she said.

"Thank you," Billie replied. She dropped a kiss on Cat's mouth then hissed and snaked out her tongue to tweak Cat's lips.

"Oh, my!" said a voice from across the reception counter, drawing Billie and Cat's eyes to a very disturbed middle-aged woman in attendance there.

Billie turned her face back to Cat's. "Ooops!" she said, causing both of them to break out into huge smiles.

"Damned southerners!" Cat said in her best Josephine Wycliffe imitation.

"Well, let's get this over with," Billie said, as she took Cat's hand and led her toward the desk, right into the disapproving glances they received from the clerk.

"If you're here to request a marriage license, we are not bound by law to provide one," the clerk said.

"Been there, done that. We're already married," Billie said.

"Then how may I help you?" the clerk asked in clipped tones.

"My name is Billie Charland. I am looking for the birth record of a child who was born in this city fifty-five years ago. Now, there is a very good possibility that this child is my birth mother. I am looking for a birth or death certificate to help me resolve this," Billie explained.

"I'm sorry, Miss. I cannot divulge confidential city records to total strangers. I have no way of validating your claim," the woman said, a distasteful sneer crossing her face as she looked at Cat and Billie's clasped hands.

Billie narrowed her eyes at the clerk. "Look, Miss... Slattery," Billie said as she read the woman's name tag. "I just happen to be a lawyer, and I also happen to know that birth and death certificates are a matter of public record. Now, either you tell me where I can access these records, or I will insist on seeing your supervisor and escalating this matter. Furthermore, I will make a point of insisting that your poor treatment of us is due to your intolerant attitude. The choice is yours," Billie finished, continuing to hold the woman's gaze.

Cat held her breath as the woman debated her choices. Finally, she opened a drawer in front of her and retrieved a set of keys. "As you wish, Ms. Charland. Follow me," she said.

Without releasing Cat's hand, Billie followed Miss Slattery to a room at the back of the office. They stood there patiently as the clerk unlocked the door and pushed it open. She motioned for them to enter, and then followed them inside. The room was lined with shelves containing neatly organized file folders filling them to capacity. At the far end of the room were a photocopier, a microfiche machine and three file cabinets containing records on microfilm.

"I think you'll find everything you need right here, Ms. Charland, and...ah Miss..." the clerk said, indirectly asking for Cat's name.

"Caitlain," Billie said. "This is Caitlain Charland, my wife," Billie replied.

Miss Slattery walked quickly to the door, stopping when she reached the threshold. "Please let me know when you are through. Take your time. The office doesn't close until five p.m."

She quickly exited the room leaving them alone.

Cat turned to Billie. "You are a wicked woman, my love. You really know how to make someone squirm, don't you?" she asked.

"Only if they deserve it, Cat...and *she* sorely deserved it," Billie replied. "Now, let's see if this place is any better organized than the records room at the church."

* * *

"Al, are you all right?" Jo asked, turning Alex's face toward her.

"I'm fine, Josie," she said, trying hard not to look Jo in the eyes.

"Then why are you shaking, and why won't you look at me?" Jo asked persistently.

Alex looked down into her lap at her hand that Jo was holding so tenderly. A surge of love filled her heart as she realized her life partner was doing her best to protect her from harm and let her know that she could depend on her for strength. A tear fell from her eye to join the entwined fingers there.

"Al, for the love of God, look at me," Jo said.

Tortured blue eyes met green as tears flowed freely from them.

Jo pulled Alex's head into her shoulder. "It's all right, Al. Cry it out, sweetheart. Damn! If I could take away your pain, I would. You know that, don't you?" Jo asked.

Alex nodded her head from its position on Jo's shoulder.

"Talk to me, Al. You're always telling me to put a voice to my feelings. Now it's your turn," Jo encouraged her.

"It hurts, Josie. After all this time, it still hurts. There are so many bad memories here," Alex cried.

"We should have let the kids come alone, Al. This is too much for you."

Alex breathed deeply and lifted her head from Jo's shoulder. Just then, she saw a man exit the town hall, causing her to gasp.

"Al, what is it?" Jo asked.

"That man! He looks so familiar," Alex said.

Jo reached for the handle and pushed the door open. She had one foot on the ground before Alex stopped her.

"Josephine Wycliffe, get back into this car. You can't just go approaching a total stranger on the street. He looks familiar is all. I may not even know him," Alex scolded.

Jo looked at Alex and got back into the car. "I have no problem with approaching a total stranger, Al. Hell, if I thought it would take away your pain, I'd go door to door at every house in this town asking if they knew you all those years ago," she vowed.

Alex smiled as she lifted Jo's hand to her lips to kiss the palm.

A sensual shiver ran down Jo's spine as her body responded to Alex's touch. "Damn woman! It's been a lot of years since we fooled around in the back seat of a car! Keep that up and the kids are gonna be shocked at what they find when they come back!" she warned.

Alex grinned and placed a tender kiss on Jo's hand. "Josie, my darlin', you are incorrigible!" she exclaimed.

* * *

The small room was neatly organized. It wasn't long before Billie located the section of shelving containing the names starting with S. "Cat, over here," she said.

Together, they combed through the records until they came across a folder labeled, Spirakis, Alexandra. Billie took the folder from the shelf and carried it to the table. She stepped back and drew in a deep breath and stared at the manila colored wrapping.

"Do you want me to open it?" Cat asked as she stood next to Billie and rubbed her hand up and down Billie's back.

Billie shook her head. "No, Cat. I've got to do this. I'm...ah...I'm just a little nervous," she said, as she approached the table once more.

Billie opened the folder that contained a single document. Picking up the paper with shaky hands, she studied it carefully. Cat watched the emotions dance across Billie's features as she read the document. Seeing the emotional struggle Billie was obviously experiencing, Cat circled her wife's waist with a reassuring arm. Moments later, Billie reached out for the table for support as her knees started to weaken. Cat quickly pulled a chair away from the table and guided Billie into it.

"Sweetheart, what is it?" Cat asked softly.

All Billie could do was look at Cat, intense emotional pain speaking volumes from the pulpit of her eyes.

Cat reached forward and took the document from Billie's hands, silently asking permission to read the document.

Billie nodded slightly in affirmation.

Cat read the document carefully. When she was finished, she too pulled out a chair and sat beside Billie and turned her attention to the distraught woman beside her. Billie was staring at her hands before her on the table. Tears were running down her cheeks.

As she ran her hand up and down Billie's arm, Cat spoke softly. "Billie, honey, talk to me."

Billie turned her face toward her wife. "Cat, that document says it all."

Cat just nodded her head and rubbed Billie's back.

* * *

By the time Billie and Cat left the clerk's office, it was nearly two. They decided not to say anything to Alex until they stopped for lunch. When the returned to the car, they found Jo sitting across the back seat, her back propped up against the door, and Alex reclining between her legs. Her head rested on the spot between Jo's breast and her eyes were closed in sleep.

Jo watched the two younger ladies walk toward the car, hand in hand. It was obvious that Billie had been crying. They were carrying a folder, which Jo assumed contained the information they were looking for. Based on Billie's tear-stained face, Jo immediately concluded that what they found was bad news.

Billie opened the door and allowed Cat to climb into the front seat ahead of her. She handed the folder to Cat then climbed in herself. She turned in her seat to look at Jo. "Is she all right?" Billie asked.

Jo nodded. "She's fine. I assume you found what you were looking for?"

Billie nodded her head. "We did. Let's stop at the lake for lunch. According to the map, it's about an hour away. We'll talk about it then, okay?" she asked.

"Okay," Jo said. She kissed Alex on the head as the car lurched forward into traffic.

Alex slept nearly the entire way to the lake, waking up just minutes before they reached their destination. She shifted in Jo's arms and opened her eyes. "Josie," she said.

"Hi, sleepy head." Jo helped Alex into a sitting position.

"Where are we?" Alex asked.

"Nearly to the lake, Grams." Cat turned around in her seat and reached into the back for her grandmother's hand.

"What did you find, Caitlain?" Alex asked.

"We're almost to the lake, Grams. We'll talk about it then," Cat explained.

Alex nodded as Billie pulled the car into the parking lot by the lake.

Jo helped Alex out of the car while Billie and Cat retrieved the picnic basket and blanket. They chose a serene spot under a tree. The area very much reminded Billie and Cat of their favorite tree in the park back home. It was the tree they spent time under while watching Seth rehabilitate from his coma, while waiting out Cat's pregnancy with Skylar; and while Billie mourned the death of her client, Peggy McBride. For these reasons, this particular tree in this particular park seemed like a fitting place to spend time while they dealt with the loose ends of their lives.

The ladies ate their picnic lunch in silence. Afterward, they strolled along the lakeshore, hand in hand, stopping to skip stones into the water. Finally, they stopped and stared out over the lake. The four women stood as one. Billie stood directly next to Alex, book-ended by Cat and Jo on either side.

Strictly by feel, Billie reached for the older woman's hand and squeezed it tight. Staring straight ahead, she took a deep breath. "Grams, she's alive."

Jo was there just in time to catch a crumbling Alex as she sank to the ground.

Chapter 17

On the drive back to Charleston, Alex grasped the copy of her child's birth certificate in shaky hands. She read it over and over. *Certificate of Live Birth*, was printed in bold letters at the top.

Live birth! Alex thought to herself. *I knew she was alive. I could feel it.*

Date: June fourteenth, nineteen fifty-nine, Gender: Female, Height: twenty-two inches, Weight: seven pounds, ten ounces, Mother: Alexandra Spirakis, Father: Unknown. It was all there.

Alex was ecstatic.

Jo was pensive.

Billie sat with her right arm around Cat, her left hand on the steering wheel as she guided the antique car down the highway toward home.

Billie was contemplative.

Cat was apprehensive.

* * *

Chet greeted them warmly at the carport as the four women exited the car. Alex charged into the house, full of pep and energy, directing them all to the parlor for a victory toast. Billie, true to her normally stoic nature, smiled warmly, but internally waged a war that had her teetering on the edge of emotional release. Cat and Jo were unnaturally reserved, both deep in thought about what lay ahead for their loved ones. Neither was looking forward to the emotional upheaval that was sure to come.

Alex enthusiastically filled four wineglasses and handed them out to the other three women.

"A toast!" Alex said, raising her glass high into the air. "To family. May we soon be together again."

Jo, Cat and Billie all looked at each other and reluctantly complied, adding their voices to the toast. However, between them, a silent message passed, a message that clearly communicated doubt.

Jo rubbed Alex's back. "Al, I really hope we find your daughter. I know how much it would mean to you, but you need to be realistic. It's been fifty-five years," she said.

Alex looked into Jo's eyes. "Josie, darlin', I know we'll find her. I just know we will. Billie came to this family for a reason. I have to believe that. Don't you see?" she asked.

Cat's heart was breaking for her grandmother. As much as she wanted a happy ending, she wasn't sure it would happen. "Yes, Grams. We see. We'll do everything we can to find her, but Grandma Jo just wants you to be prepared in case we *don't* find her, or in case we find her and she is no longer with us," Cat said as gently as she could.

Cat looked at Billie as she allowed the warning to permeate the room. She saw shocked realization cross Billie's face as she obviously had not considered the possibility that Alex's child may have been born alive, but over the past fifty-five years, may have passed on.

Alex released herself from Cat's grasp and walked to the fireplace, still holding her wineglass. Long moments passed in silence as she watched the flames dance. The other three occupants of the room held their breath and shifted uneasily until Billie broke the spell. Billie stood in front of Alex and placed two fingers under her chin, forcing their eyes to meet.

"I will find her," Billie said. "I promise."

* * *

Billie and Cat excused themselves well before dinner and retired to their room to spend some time alone, and to think about the events of the day. Once in their room, Billie started to pace like a caged tiger. The atmosphere was very charged.

Billie was strung like a bow.

Cat sat on the edge of the bed watching her wife wear a path in the carpet. Either Billie would stop to talk about it, or Cat would have to force the issue. Cat chose the later.

"You shouldn't have promised you'd find her, Billie."

Billie stopped in her tracks and looked at Cat, piercing blue eyes boring into her very soul. Cat watched a play of emotions ran rampant across Billie's face as she waged an internal struggle to stay in control of her emotions.

"Billie, honey, talk to me, please," she said.

Billie resumed her pacing. The tension was building with each pass across the room.

Cat finally rose from her position on the bed and stood in Billie's path. Billie stopped abruptly in front of Cat. Her breath came in ragged pants, her hands clenching at her sides, her jaw muscles contracting furiously. Cat knew exactly what Billie needed to release this penned up emotion.

She looked into Billie's eyes and said two words, "Take me."

Billie lifted Cat off the floor by her waist and carried her to the bed. The energy building within her chest was nearly impossible to control as she literally tore Cat's clothes from her body. Cat knew what she was in for. When Billie was in this type of emotional rage, she was wild with battle lust. All Cat could do is hold on and ride out the storm, and what a delicious storm it was. Cat reveled in these moments when Billie threw restraint to the winds and unleashed her raw sexual power on her.

Billie ravished Cat from head to toe, biting, licking, nipping, clawing and reducing Cat to boneless flesh in her hands. Cat begged for more, screamed Billie's name over and over as orgasmic waves crashed over her, mindless that her screams of desire carried throughout the house. Billie brought her to climax no fewer than three times before she begged her to stop, afraid that there would be no energy left to return the favor. But, return it, she did. Flipping Billie onto her back, she proceeded to push her to the limits of endurance, only to back off and approach again. After several aborted landings,

Cat circled around once more and dove into Billie, causing her to explode into a thousand tiny pieces, each one throbbing with spent desire. Multiple choruses of Cat's name joined those earlier sung by Cat as all ears in the house tuned into the sound coming from the upstairs bedroom.

Jo and Alex were in the parlor, quietly discussing the day's events, when the sounds of intense lovemaking reached their ears. They looked at each other for long moments, before Jo rose to her feet and took Alex's hand to lead her through the grand hallway, to their room upstairs.

* * *

"So where do we go from here, Billie?" Alex asked, before placing a forkful of mixed vegetables into her mouth.

"Well, I've been on a few cases at work where we've had to find a missing family member for one reason or another. A lot depends on whether the missing person wants to be found," Billie commented. "But my best guess would be to start with the state adoption records. Some states have sealed them from prying eyes, even if those eyes have a right to know. If South Carolina is one such state, then we'll have to take legal action to access the records," she explained.

Cat put down her fork and placed her hands on the table. She looked around the room nervously. Billie noticed her discomfort.

"Cat, honey, what is it?" she asked.

"Billie, Grams, I hate to burst your bubbles, but the only thing the birth certificate proves is that you gave birth to a live baby girl fifty-five years ago. Grams, it doesn't mean that the child is Billie's mother," Cat explained. Then to Billie, she added, "Love, I just don't want to see you hurt if it turns out not to be the case."

Billie held Cat's gaze for several long moments before taking a deep breath. "You're right, Cat. All we have to go on is my resemblance to Alex. I hope that it's enough, but you are right, it might not be." She placed her hand over Cat's and forced a smile onto her face.

"I'm sorry, Billie," Cat said.

"Don't be sorry, Cat. One of us has to stay grounded here, and right now, I'm not the best candidate for that, so you've got the job," she said, this time sporting a genuine smile.

"So, when do we get started?" Alex asked anxiously.

"I've been giving that some thought, Grams. I've already called my co-worker, Art, and asked him to start researching South Carolina's adoption policies. I've also asked our best Internet surfer, Jimmy, to start a missing persons search on any fifty-five year old female adoptee, who may be currently looking for her birth parents. If she is actively looking for you, there is a chance that we may find her relatively fast. For now, however, unless we get lucky, there isn't much we can do until we understand what our limitations are. Also, Cat and I need to get home. All this talk of adoption is really making me miss my kids," Billie said.

"I second that motion," added Cat.

"What can we do from this end?" asked Jo.

"Well, you can try to find anyone who may have known Alex when her daughter was born. That means another trip to Lancaster, of course, but there may be someone around who remembers Alex giving birth, and may even know what happened to the child. News travels fast in small communities," Billie suggested. "Oh, by the way," she added. "While Cat and I were in the clerk's office, we quite literally ran into a man coming out as we were going in. The collision caused him to drop his paperwork all over the floor. He looked me directly in the face and said 'Alexandra'."

“Al! That must have been the gentleman who came out of the Lancaster clerk’s office that you thought looked familiar to you,” Jo piped in.

Billie looked at Cat. A spark of hope passed between them at Jo’s statement.

“Anyway,” Billie continued, “Cat and I helped collect his papers and mail from the floor, but in his haste to get out of there, he missed an envelope. I have it in our room upstairs. Remind me to give it to you before we leave tomorrow. The fact that he called me Alexandra is probably important. You'll have to look for him to return the letter. He may be the missing link," Billie said.

"We can do that," Alex said.

"*I* can do that," Jo corrected. "You said yourself that Lancaster held some bad memories for you," Jo reminded her.

"That was before I knew my daughter was alive, Josie. I will endure any emotional hardship to find her," Alex stated.

Jo shook her head at Alex's stubbornness. "Do you see what I have to put up with?" she asked the two younger women, who both smiled.

* * *

The next day was filled with teary good byes as Cat and Billie boarded the plane for home. Billie sat in the window seat and blew kisses to the two women standing by the fence and waving furiously. Both Billie and Alex clutched copies of the birth certificate in their hands. They were both on a mission to see if those pieces of paper would knit their destinies into one.

As the plane lifted off the runway, Cat took Billie's hand in hers. "It feels good to be going home," she said.

"Yes it does," Billie agreed.

"Billie?" Cat said.

"Yes?"

"You need to remember that whatever happens with this quest, our definition of family has to remain intact. We can't let this change who or what we are. Do you understand?" Cat asked.

Billie touched Cat's face.

"Cat," she said, "we all have families we are born into, but for whatever reason, we sometimes become separated from them and form families of our own, unrelated by blood, but families nonetheless. What you and I have together is a bond stronger than blood could ever be. You and the children are my real family, Cat, regardless of what we find in this quest. Please don't ever forget that," she finished.

“I couldn’t have said it better,” Cat replied. She laid her head on Billie's shoulder for the flight home.

Chapter 18

The plane touched down at four-fifteen in the afternoon. Billie called during a layover and warned Jen that they were coming in, then proceeded to beg a ride home.

Jen picked the kids up from school that afternoon and headed straight for the airport. All five children stood with their faces against the chain-link fence, fascinated by the size of the jumbo jets that taxied across the tarmac. Skylar spent most of the time with her hands over her ears to block out the sound of the jet engines. Soon, Jen pointed out Cat and Billie's flight as it made its final approach.

"Cat, honey, look," Billie said. She pressed herself back into her seat so Cat could lean over her to look out the window. "Look, the kids are over there, by the fence," she said, as they both spotted the children jumping up and down and waving as the plane approached the gate. "Stevie and Karissa are with them too!"

The race was on as the kids ran into the terminal to greet their moms at the arrival gate.

Billie was first to enter the terminal. Skylar threw herself into Billie's arms as soon as she saw her. After a hug and a kiss, Billie passed her on to Cat as she opened her arms to Tara and Seth, who wrapped themselves around their mother. After an appropriate amount of cuddling, they moved on to Cat, as Billie turned her attention to Jen. Jen walked into Billie's arms for a warm embrace. "Thank you, Jen, for taking care of the kids, and for being there for us when we needed you again!" she exclaimed with a smile.

"You're welcome, big guy," Jen said. "How was your visit?" she asked both women as Cat approached them and threw her arm around Jen's waist for a hug as the kids ran off to collect the luggage.

Billie looked at the curly-haired blonde. "She's alive, Jen. Alex's child was not stillborn. We found the birth certificate in Lancaster, where she actually gave birth," she explained.

"So now you know that your mother is out there somewhere," Jen concluded, looking at Billie as they walked toward the exit door of the terminal.

Billie looked at Cat. Remembering the conversation they had had the previous night during dinner, she answered Jen as optimistically as she could.

"Jen, we don't know yet that this child is my mother. The only thing we know is that Alex's child was not stillborn. The only real evidence we have to go on is my resemblance to Alex, which I have to admit, is pretty strong. But to know for sure, we have to find her daughter then probably do DNA testing to establish a link between the two of us… that is, if there *is* a link, *and* if she's willing to do the testing," Billie finished.

Jen nodded as the trio of friends was interrupted by the sounds of the children running toward them. "We found them!" Tara and Karissa chimed together. "Seth and Stevie are coming with the luggage. They found them on that merry-go-round over there," Tara said, pointing in the direction of the luggage carousel, where Skylar was sitting between two large suitcases, happily riding around and around.

"Skylar Jean Charland, what in the world are you doing?" Cat yelled as she rushed forward to retrieve her daughter from the revolving belt before she disappeared behind the rubber strips separating the luggage claim from the unloading area. "Goodness gracious child, I'll have gray hairs soon enough without you rushing them!" she scolded.

Billie thought the whole picture was quite funny, and struggled to keep the grin off her face. She lowered her head to Cat's ear. "You sound like Alex, love...goodness gracious!"

Cat swatted Billie's arm for teasing, as she set Skylar on the floor, where she immediately ran to join the other children.

Soon the eight passenger minivan was filled to capacity

with five children and three adults, heading for home.

* * *

Billie arrived bright and early at work the next morning. As she passed Art's office, she saw that he wasn't in yet, so she continued on to her own. She put her briefcase down in her chair then set the coffee machine up to brew. Back in her office, she laid her briefcase on top of her desk and unlatched the clasps. Inside, there was a single long-stemmed red rose with a piece of paper rolled up and tied to its stem by a pink ribbon.

She smiled broadly, her eyes misting over, as she brought the rose to her face and inhaled its aromatic essence. She gently pulled on one ribbon tendril until the paper fell loose into her hand. She laid the rose down on the table and unrolled the paper. It read:

FROM THE ARMS OF PERFECTION
From the arms of perfection
Does Sunshine spew forth
A thing of beauty none greater
Than that I see
When I rise in the morn
And look into your face
***
From the arms of perfection
Does a Rose blossom deep
Blood red crimson
Compared in beauty
Only to the hue
That colors your cheeks
***
From the arms of perfection
Does a Pearl gently form
In the depths
Of oceans so blue

They are rivaled only
By the color of your eyes
***
From the arms of perfection
Does my love for you grow
Greater than the Sunshine
And the Rose
And the Pearl
And the Oceans so blue
***
From the arms of perfection
Does our love spring eternal
It will endure
And we will be two
Stronger than one
From the arms of perfection
***

PS. Know that I love you Billie, and that I will always be here for you. Think of us and our perfect love when you look at this rose. Its beauty is rivaled only by the love I have for you in my heart. I'll see you tonight. I love you, Fred.

Billie looked at the signature and saw that it was signed "*Ginger*"...an old joke between her and Cat that had its beginnings in their aerobics class days. Billie lowered herself into her chair and broke down into joyful sobs.

Art chose that moment to arrive. He stopped short when he saw her crying then rushed to her side.

"Billie, what is it?" he asked worriedly.

Billie looked up at him and smiled then handed him the poem.

Art scanned the poem quickly, swallowing hard when he reached the end of the PS. He put the note on the desk and looked around awkwardly while he blinked rapidly, his right hand on his hip, holding his suit jacket open. His other hand rubbed the back of his head. He looked everywhere but at Billie. He cleared his throat and swabbed the corner of his eye.

"Ah, damn, I have something in my eye. I'll be right

back," he said before hurriedly leaving the room.

Billie grabbed a tissue from the box on her desk, then leaned back in her chair, smiling broadly while dabbing at her eyes. "Art, you are a bigger baby than I am!" she said under her breath.

She picked up the rose and inhaled its fragrance one more time then closed her eyes. *What a great way to start the day. I love you too, Ginger.*

* * *

Art threw a document on the table in front of Billie. "Okay, here's what we've got," he said.

Billie looked up from the case she was working on. "What it is?" she asked.

"It's South Carolina's adoption laws."

Billie frowned. "That's an awfully thick document, Art," she commented.

"Yes it is, and it looks like pretty dry reading too. Have fun with it!" he grinned and turned to leave.

"Whaaaa... Art, I thought," she stammered.

"You thought I would do the honors for you?" he asked.

"Well, yes," Billie replied.

"Yeah, well, that's just what I planned to do, but the senior partners have seen fit to assign me to prosecute an international drug case. Looks like I've got to fly to Honduras in the morning. Sorry," he said.

Billie sat back in her chair and looked at the imposing document sitting on her desk. "I think I'd rather brave the killer mosquitoes in Honduras than deal with that monstrosity!" she exclaimed.

Art leaned down over her desk and kissed Billie on the forehead. "Why do you think I'm not complaining?" he said wickedly. He backed away just beyond her reach before Billie had a chance to swat him.

"You're getting slow, Charland!" he joked as he turned and left her office, leaving her there to stare at the document in dreaded anticipation.

* * *

"Billie!" a voice rang out across the tops of the cubicles.

Billie turned to see Jimmy's head pop up over the chin-height panel. "Hey, Jimmy. What have you got for me?" she asked. Her mouth was suddenly dry with nervous emotion.

Jimmy motioned her over to join him. "Actually, I need a little more information," he said.

"Did you have any luck with the search I called you about from Charleston?" she asked.

"The search?" Jimmy asked, momentary confusion on his face. Suddenly, he remembered. "Oh, the search. Yes. That's been done for a while now. However, I..." he started.

"It's done? Where is it?" Billie asked incredulously, irritated that Jimmy hadn't notified her when it was finished.

"Right here," Jimmy said, pointing to the report on his desk. He slapped Billie's hand away as she attempted to grab for the document.

"Now you just hold your horses there, young lady. Give a person a chance to explain, will you? Sit!" He pointed to the chair by his desk.

Billie reluctantly sat down, a look of anger and impatience on her face.

"You can wipe that look off your face too. I'm too old and much too impatient to put up with emotional nonsense from the likes of you or anyone else. Do you understand?" he asked.

Billie was shocked into silence, shocked not only by Jimmy's boldness, but by her own rude manner in dealing with the elderly gentleman. It was *she* who went to *him* for help, after all. She had no right to treat him so disrespectfully.

She sat there looking down at the hands in her lap for long moments. Finally, she raised her head. "I'm sorry, Jimmy. I had no right to treat you like that. Please forgive me," she said.

Jimmy was a little uncomfortable with her apology and brushed it off. "Never mind that," he said. "Now, I need more information," he said.

"What kind of information?" she asked.

"Well, I've done a search on all the fifty-five year old women in the country that are looking for birth mothers. I excluded obvious things from the search, like certain nationalities and skin colors, and have been able to narrow down the list to about four hundred women," he said.

"Four hundred!" Billie exclaimed in a raised voice, visibly agitated. "Do you know how long it will take to locate and contact four hundred women?" she said.

"Calm down there, Missy," Jimmy warned again, waiting for her to control herself once more before he continued. "All right, now. If your mother is out there looking for her own birth mother, then it makes sense to me that she might be looking for you as well," reasoned Jimmy.

Billie perked up, amazed at the older man's logic. "That makes sense," she said.

"Yes it does. Now, what I need is your birth date so I can write a macro that will narrow the search field a little more," he explained.

"That's easy," Billie said. "March thirtieth, nineteen eighty."

"March thirtieth, nineteen eighty, it is," Jimmy repeated as he wrote the date down on a scratch pad. "Now, go away and let me work. I'll let you know when I have something."

Billie smiled at the abrupt way she was dismissed. Suddenly a thought came to her that made her chuckle. *If Josephine Wycliffe was straight, she would surely give this man a run for his money!*

She got up from the chair by Jimmy's desk with a big grin on her face – a grin that was missed by the older man, who was already deeply absorbed in his work.

Chapter 19

"Josie, Darlin', are we almost there?" Alex asked nervously.

"For crying out loud Al, you're worse than a child. Even Ida wasn't this bad when she was little," Jo complained.

Alex looked at her hands in her lap, clasped together to keep them from shaking. "I'm sorry," she said. "I'm just so nervous, is all. Josie, what if we don't find anything?" she asked.

"Between us all, we'll find something, Al. If *we* don't, I'm sure Billie will. She has access to all those newfangled computers and the Internet, and besides, we have that letter Billie gave us. All we need to do is find the owner," Jo explained.

"I hope so. I just want this over with, Josie. I want to find my baby and hold her in my arms and tell her I love her," Alex said.

Jo looked at Alex with sincere concern. "Al, sweetheart, it may not be that simple. Your daughter may not even know that she was taken from you against your will. She might think that you gave her away. You have to be prepared to deal with that possibility," Jo explained.

"Josie, I will deal with whatever comes my way in this matter. I have never felt so strongly about anything in my life, except maybe my love for you, and for Ida," Alex said.

Jo reached across the seat and took Alex's hand in hers. She kissed her knuckles while focusing on the road ahead of them.

"Al," she said, "you have my full support. You know that, don't you?" She looked at Alex for affirmation. "Good, we are definitely in this together. But promise me one thing. No matter what happens, sweetheart, we can't lose *us*. We can't lose who *we* are, okay?"

Alex waited for Jo to park the car in the lot of the Lancaster city offices before replying. Jo pulled the car in between the lines designated for visitors and shut off the ignition. Both women turned in their seats to face each other.

Alex touched Jo's cheek. "Josie, darlin', nothing in this world can make me stop lovin' you. After fifty years of me dealing with your ornery ways, you should know that by now. What I feel for you is stronger than anything I know. You are my soul, Josie. I can't live without you. I promise not to lose *us* in the process of finding *we*," Alex said.

Jo smiled and took Alex's hand in her own. "Alex, sweetheart, let's go find our daughter."

* * *

Alex and Jo approached the receptionist's desk in the clerk's office and asked for help. Jo leaned forward to read the woman's nametag. "Ah, Miss Slattery, my name is Doctor Josephine Wycliffe, and this lovely lady here is Alexandra Spirakis."

Alex stood there, very ladylike, not particularly fond of being under a microscope, but willing to bear the scrutiny for the sake of their mission.

"We are here looking for information on an adoption that may have taken place in this town fifty-five years ago," Jo continued. "This woman's daughter was illegally and forcefully taken from her after the birth. She has not seen her since. Can you help us find the records?" Jo finished.

Miss Slattery smiled smugly.

I don't think I like this woman, Jo thought to herself.

"I'm so sorry, Miss Spirakis," the clerk said, addressing Alex for the first time. "I'm afraid I can't help you. Adoption records in this state are sealed," she said.

Alex grasped the counter to prevent herself from fainting into a heap on the floor. Jo placed a hand on her back to steady her and to give assurance that she was there to support her.

"What do you mean, they're sealed?" Jo asked.

"What don't you understand about that Ms. Wycliffe? Sealed means sealed. They are inaccessible to the birth parents, adoptive parents, and even to the adoptee without a court order," the woman answered sarcastically. "It's the law."

"Look, Miss Slattery," Jo said, trying very hard to hold back her intense desire to call the woman a bitch and strangle her half to death. "Our granddaughter came in her just two days ago and found the birth certificate for the child, and you tell us, that even with this information, we cannot see her adoption records?"

"That's exactly what I'm saying, Ms. Wycliffe. The records are sealed. You'll have to take it to the state supreme court to convince them to give you access, if that's what you really want," the clerk finished. "I don't make the laws, I just enforce them. Now, I am a very busy woman. Please excuse me," she said.

Alex was crying by the time they returned to the car. Jo took her hand and led her to a bench nearby and sat with her arm around Alex's shoulders. She pulled Alex's head down onto her shoulder and whispered against her hair, "We're not done yet, Al. We've just begun to fight. Come on. Let's go find a decent room. It looks like we may be here for a day or two."

* * *

It was mid-afternoon by the time Jo and Alex found a suitable hotel room and settled in. The disappointment resulting from their visit to the clerk's office made Alex lethargic. She sat on the edge of the bed wearily, a deep sigh escaping her. "Where do we go from here, Josie?" she asked.

"*You* are going to take a nap. *I* am going to do some research," Jo replied.

"Josephine Wycliffe, if you think for one moment that you are going to rush out and do this without me, you've got another thing coming!" exclaimed Alex.

"Don't get your panties in a bunch, Alex," Jo retorted. "All I'm going to do is find out where one Jonathan J. Simpson lives," she said, reading the name off the envelope Billie had given them before going home. "I promise I won't introduce myself to him without you, okay?" she compromised.

"You promise?" Alex asked.

"I promise. Now lie down and get some sleep. I want you fresh for tonight. I've got *big* plans for you," Jo said wickedly.

"Ms. Wycliffe, you are incorrigible!" exclaimed Alex.

"What?" asked Jo innocently. "Can't I make dinner plans for my best girl?" she asked.

"That depends on what you're planning on eatin' out," replied Alex coyly.

Jo looked at her with a mock expression of shock. "Now who's being incorrigible?"

"Well, anyway, you'd better get outta here now while you still can," Alex teased, raising her eyebrows suggestively.

Jo walked to Alex and stood very close to the seated woman. She took Alex's chin in her hand, and kissed her long and hard, causing Alex to lean back and grasp the bedspread with both hands, crumpling it up into a ball in each fist. Finally, Jo released her and stepped back.

Alex was breathless, eyes closed and her breathing ragged. "Oh, my!" she managed to squeak out as Jo reached the door. She opened her eyes and noticed that she was alone. "So much for taking a nap," she said to herself as she fanned her neck with the magazine on the bedside table.

* * *

Jo drove slowly through the streets of Lancaster, trying to follow the directions given to her by the gentleman behind the counter at the hotel reception desk. She wasn't having much luck finding Forrest Avenue.

"Should've known better than to ask a man for directions," Jo mumbled under her breath as she found herself going in circles again. Finally, thoroughly lost, she pulled into a gas station convenience store and asked the clerk for help. "Ah, excuse me, Miss, but can you direct me to Forrest Avenue?" Jo asked. "The directions I have are just not cutting it," she said.

"Let me see that," the woman said.

Jo gave the handwritten sheet of instructions to the woman, who looked at them carefully. Finally, she handed them back and smiled. "Don't tell me, a man gave you those, right?" she asked, chuckling as Jo nodded her head. "Okay, it's really very simple. Turn right out of the station here, take your second right, and then your first left. That's Forrest Avenue."

Jo thanked her and left the station.

Jo soon found herself on Forrest Avenue. She drove slowly down the street, looking at house numbers as she went, until she located the number fourteen.

"Bingo!" she exclaimed as she committed the house to memory. Jo then drove up and down the street two more times to be absolutely sure she could find it later when Alex was with her. Finally, she turned around and headed back to the hotel.

When she entered the hotel, Jo noticed a small flower shop inside the lobby where she picked up a long-stemmed red rose for Alex. Very proud of herself, she headed to their room, humming smugly. She quietly let herself into the room and tiptoed across the floor to the still-sleeping Alex and gently laid the rose down on the pillow beside her love.

Josephine, she told herself, *you are such a mush ball!*

She placed a gentle kiss on Alex's cheek then went to sit in the chair to patiently wait for her to wake up.

* * *

"Josie, have I thanked you yet for the lovely rose?" Alex asked innocently.

Jo took her eyes off the road for a moment to smile at her

wife. "Sweetheart, saying thank you has never been a problem for you, but I gotta admit, you outdid yourself this time!" she replied, grinning.

"Well, it's not every day that a girl receives flowers from her beau," Alex said. "It's only polite to thank her proper-like."

Jo patted Alex's knee. "Well, love, the next time I tease you about your sense of etiquette, just remind me about the rose, okay?" she joked.

"Here we are," Jo pulled the car to a stop in front of fourteen Forrest Avenue. Jo saw the tension on Alex's face. "Look, Al, let me go in and talk to him. I'll ask him if he knows you, and then we'll decide what to do, depending on what his reaction is, okay?"

Alex just nodded; her mouth suddenly dry from nervousness.

Jo climbed out of the car, approached the house, and rang the bell when she reached the door. She held the envelope in front of her, nervously bouncing up and down on her toes as she waited for the door to be answered. She turned to look toward the car, smiling her assurances to Alex. After a minute or so, she was convinced that no one was home, and turned her back to the door to return to the car. She had taken no more than two steps when the door opened.

"Yes, how may I help you?" a male voice asked.

Jo spun around to face a man in his seventies with medium height and build, and thinning hair. When she realized that she was staring, she cleared her throat and introduced herself. "Ah, I'm sorry. My name is Josephine Wycliffe, and I am looking for a Jonathan J. Simpson," she said.

"I am Jon Simpson," the man said. "I'm sorry, but do I know you?" he asked.

"No. No you don't," Jo said. "I, ah...I have this letter here that belongs to you. Apparently, you had a collision at the clerk's office earlier this week with my granddaughter. You ran off before she could return it to you," Jo explained, handing him the envelope, but not quite letting go of it. "I also have a question for you," Jo said. "Would you happen to remember a woman named..."

"Alexandra!" the man said.

"Alexandra. Yeah, Alexandra," Jo said. She turned to see what the man was staring at and saw Alex making her way up the walk.

"JJ?" asked Alex. "JJ, is that you?"

The man stepped past Jo. "Alexandra," he said, opening his arms to take the Southerner into them, hugging her tight. "Alexandra, it's been so long," he said. "Where have you been? *How* have you been?" he asked.

"I have been fine, JJ, and you?" Alex asked. She pulled back to look at the man's face.

"Oh, I'm fine for the most part. Darned arthritis acts up now and then, but pretty good otherwise," he said.

"Ahem!" came a sound from behind JJ.

Alex looked over JJ's shoulder.

"Ah, JJ, there's someone I'd like you to meet." Alex turned him around to face Jo. "JJ, this is Josephine Wycliffe, Josie, this is JJ." Jo reached out to shake hands with the man as Alex added, "JJ, Josie is my…well, in my heart she's my wife."

JJ suddenly stopped shaking Jo's hand, but did not release it. "Wife?" he asked.

Alex looked uneasily at JJ and then at Jo. "Yes," she answered, expecting a disgusted retort from the older man.

JJ surprised them both by throwing his head back and laughing out loud. Releasing Jo's hand, he threw his arm across her back and extended his other hand to Alex.

"Come inside. I'll put on a pot of coffee. We have a lot of catching up to do!" Soon, they were all sitting around JJ's kitchen table, sipping coffee and talking like old friends.

* * *

Three hours later, Jo had a new understanding of what Alex was like as a young woman. As it turned out, Alex and JJ had been friends throughout their childhood. JJ lived on the farm adjacent to Aunt Edna's house, and had spent a lot of time with Alex when she would come to visit every summer. They'd spent many afternoons walking along the lake, skipping stones and talking about their hopes and dreams. JJ was the only friendly face she saw when she showed up one day nearly fifty-six years earlier, a girl in trouble. He was the one to fetch the doctor when Alex went into labor. He was there when she awoke after a very difficult delivery to hold her hand and comfort her while the doctor told her that her daughter had been stillborn.

Alex reached across the table for JJ's hand as the memories caused her eyes to mist and her heart to break. After composing herself, she took a deep breath and said, "JJ, my daughter did not die that night."

JJ held Alex's eyes for a long time before finally looking down at the table. "I know," he said.

Jo was on her feet in an instant. "Say that again," she said, narrowing her eyes at the elderly gentleman.

JJ looked up at the anger in Jo's eyes. "I said, I know," he replied before standing up and walking around while running his hand nervously through his hair.

Jo was still standing, leaning over the table, her arms supporting her weight while her eyes never left the man as he paced. Alex remained seated, hands clasped in front of her, her eyes locked on Jo.

"You had better have a good reason for ruining Al's life, Jonathan," Jo said in a low angry voice.

"Josephine Wycliffe, he did not ruin my life," Alex interjected in defense of her old friend.

"No, Alexandra. She has a right to be angry," JJ said. "I don't blame her. I look back on that horrible time and cringe in shame at my cowardice," he added.

"JJ, you are *not* to blame," Alex insisted.

JJ walked over to Alex and took her hand in his while Jo looked on; clearly upset, but curious about what the man had to say.

"Alexandra, my dear. I was not the cause of your

trouble, but at the same time, I did nothing to stop it. I will regret that until the day I die," he said.

"JJ—" Alex began again.

"Let me explain," JJ pleaded.

"Yeah, Al, let him explain," Jo added, impatient with Alex for making excuses for this man.

Alex relented as she sat back in her chair and patiently waited for Jonathan to continue.

"It was so many years ago, but I remember it like it was yesterday," Jonathan said. "I was curled up in the corner of the living room by the fireplace when they brought the child out of the birthing room. They didn't know I was there."

Jonathan paused for a moment before continuing. "I saw the doc give the baby to the midwife," he said before Jo interrupted him.

"Where did she take the baby?" Jo asked.

"The doc told her to meet Mrs…Mrs...Damn! What was her name?" he asked himself out loud before it suddenly came to him, drawing a sigh of relief from Alex. "Tanner. That's it! Tanner. He told her to meet Mrs. Tanner at the railroad depot later that evening. He said that she would get her cut when the Society paid him for the child."

"The Society?" Jo asked. "What the hell is that?"

"I wish I could tell you more, but I don't have a clue," Jonathan said. "All I know, is I felt terrible for Alexandra when I realized what they were doing."

By this time, Alex was crying openly as Jo approached her and opened her arms. Still seated, Alex wrapped her arms around Jo's waist and buried her face in the front of her sweater.

Jo looked over at JJ. "Why didn't you do something to stop him?" she asked, her anger coming through loud and clear.

"I couldn't. When the doc realized I had witnessed the transfer, he beat me senseless then threatened me. He threatened to expose my secret to my parents unless I swore to keep silent," he explained.

"Secret?" Jo said. "It had better be a good one to have forced Alex to sacrifice so much!"

"In my mind at the time, it was. Had it happened today, things would be different," he said. Seeing the confusion in Jo's eyes, he added, "You see, I was seeing this…person. Doc caught us in the horse barn one day in a compromising situation. I was so humiliated I wanted to die. Anyway, Doc was pretty discreet about it, turning his back and walking away like he hadn't seen anything. I thought we were safe," Jonathan said, his voice trailing off as he recalled the painful memory.

Jo released Alex and walked over to Jonathan. She stopped in front of him with hands on her hips. "You stayed quiet about Al's child because you didn't want an *affair* exposed?" she asked incredulously.

"Josie, please," Alex pleaded, hoping to diffuse Jo's temper.

Jo kept her eyes trained on Jonathan. "No, Al. We need to get to the bottom of this. So, JJ," she said directly to the man. "Answer the question."

"Doc threatened to expose my relationship if I didn't keep silent. I couldn't let that happen," he explained. "It would have destroyed the lives of several people, including both of our families."

Jo was seething with anger as she started to pace back and forth.

"So let me get this straight," she said angrily. "You sacrificed Al's happiness, and quite possibly that of her child's to cover up an indiscretion?"

She stopped in front of him once more and looked him straight in the face. "How could you do it? How could you live with yourself?" She asked.

Jonathan looked down. "It wasn't just an affair," he said adamantly. "We loved each other very much."

"If you loved each other, why didn't you do something about it? Why didn't you stand up to that doctor and tell him to go to hell instead of making Al pay the price for your silence?" Jo demanded angrily.

"I couldn't stand up to him! I couldn't tell. I couldn't!"

Jonathan replied, his voice shaky with emotion and regret.

"Well, why the hell not!" Jo roared back.

Long moments passed as Jo and Jonathan stood nose to nose, neither able to break the gaze as Alex wept nearby.

Tears rolled down Jonathan's face as he closed his eyes and lowered his chin to his chest. Defeated, he finally replied, "Because my lover was a man."

Total silence permeated the room for several long moments as Jo and Alex absorbed what this elderly gentleman had said. In that one moment, both women knew…both understood exactly why Jonathan acted as he did more than fifty-five years earlier.

Finally, unable to bear the silence any longer, Jonathan raised his head and looked at Alex. "Alexandra, I don't know what to say to you, except I'm sorry. I was a coward. I'm sorry," he said.

Alex rose from her seat and walked over to Jonathan. She forced a smile onto her face, and said, "I understand, JJ. Really, I do."

"If I could find a way to make it up to you, I would. You know that, don't you?" he said.

Jo walked over to the pair and placed her arm around Alex's waist.

"We can't change the past, Jon, but maybe we can shape the future. Come. Sit and tell us everything you know about that night. We need to know everything you saw and heard, and anything you may have learned later. We're trying to find her, JJ. With your help, maybe we can," Jo said.

Chapter 20

Billie was in a hurry to get home that night. Her mind was a jumble of thoughts as she drove through the busy streets. She had been thinking all day long about the beautiful rose and poem that Cat had slipped into her briefcase that morning. Then there was the search that Jimmy promised would be ready by the time she came to work the next morning. He had worked all afternoon writing a program that would narrow the four hundred names he found down to a manageable number. What worried her though, was that in order for her mother to be in the database, she would have to be registered as an adoptee on the Internet, or at least with some agency that could be accessed through the Internet. Such were Billie's thoughts as she pulled into the driveway of her home.

Before getting out of her car, Billie opened her briefcase and withdrew the rose, then grabbed the case and went into the house. As she walked into an empty kitchen, she could hear the sounds of Sponge Bob coming from the family room television in the basement. She opened the closet door in the corner of the kitchen and placed her briefcase inside. When she closed the door and turned around, she saw Cat standing there, a big smile on her face when she saw the rose in Billie's hand.

A wicked gleam entered Billie's eyes as she placed the rose between her teeth and scooped Cat up into her arms. She carried her through the living room and up the stairs to their room, kicking the door shut behind them. Billie gently laid Cat on the bed and lay down completely on top of her. She placed the rose on the pillow beside Cat's head, and kissed her passionately, leaving them both breathless.

"Thank you, Cat. That was the most wonderful thing anyone has ever done for me. The poem and the rose are beautiful, and you're right, the only thing more beautiful is our love for one another."

Billie once again, lowered her mouth for a deep probing kiss–just as the phone rang.

"Damn!" Billie exclaimed as she reached for the phone on the bedside table. "Hello," she said into the receiver, kissing Cat again as she waited for the caller to speak.

"Billie?" the caller said. "Billie, this is Alex."

Billie's head shot up. "Grams?" she said. "Grams, is everything all right?"

Billie rolled off Cat and threw her legs over the side of the bed to sit up. Cat crawled over and sat back on her heels next to Billie, a concerned look on her face.

"Everything is fine, dear," Alex said. "Billie, we're calling to tell you that we had a major discovery today, but it seems that we've hit another dead end," she explained.

Billie motioned to Cat that everything was all right. "So what did you find out"?" Billie asked.

"Hold on a minute dear, Josie has gone to fetch the portable from the front desk at the hotel we're staying in. She'll be back in a minute," Alex said.

"That's a good idea. Cat, sweetheart, run downstairs and get the portable. We'll make this a four-way call," Billie suggested.

Moments later, all four women were on the phone, talking at once.

"All right, all right. Time out here! One at a time!" Jo interrupted, calling order to the chaos.

Once order was established, it didn't take long for Alex and Jo to relay their meeting with JJ to Billie and Cat. Billie's first reaction was anger at JJ for not having the nerve to stand up for Alex all those years ago. Jo was inclined to agree. Between Alex and Cat, however, they made the women see that the world was not as accepting of their kind fifty-five years ago, and that they needed to cut JJ some slack. The only direction any of them could go in from that point on was forward.

By the end of the call, Billie had plenty of information for Jimmy to search on the net in the morning. She had a name, Mrs. Tanner; a year, nineteen fifty-nine; and at least a partial name for an adoption agency, the 'Society'. Billie hoped that it was enough.

After the phone call, Billie flopped down on the bed and looked at the ceiling. Cat climbed in beside her and laid her head on her shoulder.

"Cat, I really want to rip JJ's head off for being so weak. His cowardice cheated Alex out of her daughter," Billie said.

"I'm not angry," Cat said, receiving a nasty look from Billie.

"How can you feel that way?" she asked incredulously.

Cat rolled onto her stomach and propped herself up on her forearms. "Billie, if things had worked out differently...if JJ had stood up for Grams, if she had never lost her daughter, then things would be very different today. There would be no Alex and Jo, no Ida and Doc, and no Billie and Cat. As painful as it was for Grams to lose her child, I couldn't bear to have lived my life without meeting and falling in love with you. I'm sorry if that sounds selfish, but it's the way I feel."

Billie's eyes were wide and overflowing with tears. How could she refute that argument? She took Cat into her arms and whispered in her ear, "Damn it, Cat. Why do you always have to be right?"

Cat raised her head and kissed Billie lightly. "That's what you pay me for."

Suddenly from downstairs, came a loud voice. "Ma! What's for supper?"

Cat's grin hovered over Billie's mouth, before landing one more time. "A mom's work..."

"Is never done," Billie finished for her.

* * *

"Missy, you certainly have one complicated life," Jimmy said as he took down the information Billie dictated to him the next morning. "I have never seen anyone with as much controversy in their past as you have."

Billie saw an opportunity to bait the older lawyer. "Have I actually given Jimmy the Great an assignment he can't handle?" she asked in mock astonishment.

"The day I can't handle a simple Internet search, is the day I'll turn in my resignation, young lady!" he scolded before seeing her grin. "Ahhh. I see what you're doing. Think you can bait me, do you? We'll I'll just show you what Jimmy the Great is capable of. Give me two hours and I'll have an answer for you, or lunch is on me for the rest of the week!" he said.

Billie's eyes opened wide. Jimmy was known around the office for his penny-pinching thriftiness, so that was a serious challenge for him to make.

Billie leaned over Jimmy's desk. "You're on, and lunch is on *me* if you succeed, but let's up the stakes. Double or nothing?" she baited.

"I hope you have a big wallet, Missy. Now scoot. I've got some serious work to do, and I'm on the clock!" he said.

Exactly one hour and fifty-seven minutes later, Jimmy entered Billie's office and threw a report down on her desk. Billie looked at her watch and gulped. She moved her eyes from the report, to the man standing there in front of her desk. "Jimmy?" she asked.

"I'll take a Reuben on rye," he said.

Billie's expression broke into a huge grin. "You found her?" she asked hopefully.

Jimmy picked up the report and started reading, "Sylvia Tanner, owner and director of the Children's Home Society from nineteen forty-seven through nineteen sixty-three. Arrested in nineteen sixty-three for illegally purchasing children for resale on the black market. She sold children for profit, lied about their origins to adoptive parents, altered or created fabricated birth certificates, illegally convinced impoverished birth parents to sign away their rights to their children in order to sell them for profit. She even allowed children to be adopted into homes where they were abused and neglected–some even dying from mistreatment or lack of medical attention." Jimmy paused from his reading to take a breath.

Billie's eyes grew wider with each charge Jimmy read. She hoped in her heart that Alex's child hadn't fallen victim to the last group of children Jimmy described.

"Now here's the important part," Jimmy said. "After Tanner's arrest in nineteen sixty-three, all adoptions records were confiscated and to this day, remain sealed. The only information that has been made public is the distribution of adoptions by area. It turns out that in nineteen fifty-nine, there were three adoptions from Lancaster, South Carolina, and Billie, one of the three is listed as June fourteenth."

Billie began to shake visibly. "Oh, God." She covered her mouth with her hand, her eyes wild with anticipation. "How do I get them to unseal the records, Jimmy?" she asked nervously.

"To be honest, it will take a court order, or off the record, a well-placed financial donation to a hungry politician," he said candidly. "That is, if you can get your hands on that kind of money," he added.

"Alex," Billie said.

* * *

Billie developed a nervous headache soon after Jimmy left her office, grinning from ear to ear at the prospect of free lunches for two weeks. She put her head down on the desk and closed her eyes. It was in this position that Art found her moments later.

"Billie, are you all right?" he asked as he pushed her door open.

Billie lifted her head from the desk and strained to focus on her friend and co-worker. She winced at the pain between her eyes. "Oh, hi, Art. Yeah, I'm fine, except for the pounding in my head," she replied, trying to force a smile onto her face. "I thought you'd be on your way to Honduras by now," she added.

"I'm leaving right now. I just stopped in to say goodbye. You know, you should really go home if you're not feeling well," he said.

"My thoughts exactly, only I'm having a little trouble focusing right now. Care to drop me off on your way to the airport?" she asked.

"My pleasure," he said. "Come on."

Fifteen minutes later, Art pulled into the driveway of Billie's home and let her out of the car. "Do you need any help getting into the house?" he asked.

"No, I'm okay. I'm just going to down a handful of painkillers and hit the sheets," she said. "I should be as good as new by the time Cat and the kids get home."

"All right, then. I'll be on my way. You take care of yourself, Billie," he scolded.

"I will. Thanks for the ride, and have a good trip, Art," she said before turning toward the stairs.

Billie put her briefcase in the closet and slipped off her shoes, padding on stocking feet through the kitchen and living room to her room upstairs. She shrugged out of her sweater, skirt and hose and slipped a T-shirt over her head before crawling between the sheets. She lay there for several moments until she realized that she hadn't taken any painkillers. She staggered to the bathroom and switched on the light. Suddenly, everything in her line of vision seemed distorted and disoriented. She had a very loud ringing in her ears and an odd odor permeated her senses. The throbbing in her temples became almost unbearable as she grasped both sides of her head with her hands. A moment later, she felt her knees buckle as she crumbled to the floor, hitting her head on the door casing on the way down. She lay there for several minutes, her body twitching and convulsing, until finally, she relaxed into what appeared to be a peaceful state of slumber.

It was in this state that Cat found her a couple of hours later when she got home from work. Cat picked the kids up at the sitter, and as usual, they dispersed to their normal after-school hideouts as soon as they got home. Seth and Tara headed directly to Jen's to play with Stevie and Karissa, while Skylar went to Missy's across the street. Cat reveled in the quiet peacefulness of having the house all to herself for a while as she climbed the stairs to her room. The first sight that greeted her when she entered the room was that of Billie, sprawled out on the floor, half in and half out of the bathroom, a large welt protruding from her right temple.

"Oh, my god, Billie!" she exclaimed as she ran to the unconscious woman.

Cat's medical training took over as she quickly went through the list of vital signs. Having verified that Billie was stable, she retrieved a pillow from the bed to put under her head, and a cold compact from the freezer in the kitchen for the bump on her temple. Billie stirred as Cat was administering to the injury.

"Cat? Cat, what happened? Why am I on the floor?" Billie said groggily as she tried to sit up, but laid right back down again as her head pounded with intense pain.

"Billie, don't try to get up, please. I need to ask you some questions so I can figure out what happened here, okay?" Cat asked.

Billie nodded her head.

"All right. First, what are you doing home?" Cat asked.

"I had a really intense headache, so Art dropped me off. My vision was blurry and I didn't dare to drive," Billie explained.

"How did you end up on the floor, Billie?"

"I don't know. I remember climbing into bed then realizing I hadn't taken any painkillers, so I got up again. When I switched on the light in the bathroom, things started to get really weird."

"Weird, how?"

"Well, my vision was all distorted, I smelled this really strange odor and there was a loud ringing in my ears. I remember feeling unsteady on my feet, but then everything just blanked out, until I woke up and found you here with me," she explained.

Cat sat back on her heels and nodded her head. Looking into the worried eyes of her wife, she said, "Billie, It looks like you had a grand mal seizure. I'll check with Daddy to be sure, but all of the symptoms point to it. Boy, it's been a while since you've had one. Fortunately as you know, they are not usually life threatening, except of course, when you pick a fight with the door frame in the middle of one!" Cat added, trying to make light of the situation. "It's a good thing you have such a hard head, wife!" she said through a toothy smile.

Billie smiled back, too weak and tired to argue about it.

"Anyway, we might want to evaluate your meds to make sure you're taking the right dose. It could also be the stress from this genealogy search that is triggering it, but for now, let's see about getting you into bed so you can sleep for a while. I'll call Daddy while you sleep, all right?" Cat finished.

Billie nodded, still too disoriented to hold an intelligent conversation for any length of time.

With a little effort, Cat managed to get Billie to her feet and into bed, kissing her lightly on the forehead as she pulled the covers up to her neck, and promised to check in on her later before leaving the room. Outside in the hall, Cat leaned against the wall and took a deep breath.

I'll never get used to treating family members, she thought before going downstairs to call her father.

Chapter 21

Billie awoke and came downstairs just as Cat was loading the supper dishes into the dishwasher. Cat could feel her presence as she entered the kitchen, but kept her back to her as she rinsed and loaded the dishes. Billie wrapped her arms around Cat's waist and pulled her back into her chest. Cat went willingly, leaning her head back and to the side as she rested it on Billie's left shoulder. Her right hand held Billie's head in place as Billie nuzzled her neck.

"Mmmmmm," they said at the same time.

After a moment or two, Cat turned around in Billie's arms. "How are you feeling?" she asked, looking into eyes of azure blue.

"Headache's gone. Did you call Doc?"

"Yes I did. He also thinks it was a seizure. He'd like to see you tomorrow, to do some tests, adjust your meds, you know, stuff like that. He also said driving is off limits for a while until he can understand and control what's causing the seizures," Cat said, knowing how well received *that* piece of news would be.

"Aw Cat! Do you know how tough it is not to be able to drive?" Billie complained.

"I know, love," Cat replied, "but imagine what could happen if you had a seizure while behind the wheel of a car, or even worse, what if one of the kids was with you?" Cat reasoned.

"I know, I know, but I don't have to like it," she whined.

Cat stood on tiptoes to place a light kiss on Billie's lips. "Are you hungry?" she asked.

Billie grinned. "A little."

"Well then, sit yourself down and I'll fix a dish for you,"

she said.

"Cat, I can get it," Billie began.

"I said, sit! Doctor's orders!" she commanded firmly.

"I really hate it when you pull rank on me!"

* * *

Cat made a pot of coffee while Billie ate, and sipped the rich brew while she kept Billie company at the kitchen table.

"So, other than the seizure, how was your day?" Cat asked.

Billie swallowed the bit of stew she was chewing. "Actually, the morning went great." Billie suddenly remembered the information Jimmy had discovered and became animated. "Oh, oh, oh! Cat! How could I forget! Jimmy found Alex's child!" she said excitedly.

Cat nearly choked on the sip of coffee she had in her mouth. "He did? That's wonderful, Billie! Where is she?" Cat asked, just as excited.

"Well, he hasn't physically found her, but he found the name of the adoption agency that took her from Alex. Cat, the individual records are sealed, but he *did* find out there were three children given up for adoption in nineteen fifty-nine in Lancaster, and one of them was on June fourteenth!" Billie explained.

Cat's eyes were as wide as saucers. "So where is this agency located? It seems like a logical next step would be to visit them to find out as much as we can about the Lancaster adoptions," Cat reasoned.

"I'm afraid that isn't possible, Cat. The agency was closed in nineteen sixty-three when the owner was arrested for selling babies on the black market," Billie said.

"Billie, that's awful!" Cat exclaimed. "How will we find her?" she asked.

"Well, like I said, the records are sealed, and it will take a court order to open them. I'm prepared to take it to that level if I have to, Cat, but I think we should try a direct appeal to the governor of South Carolina first," Billie explained.

"Billie, do you really think he'll listen to us? Heck, we

don't even live in South Carolina," Cat said.

"No, but Alexandra Spirakis does, a very rich and influential Alexandra Spirakis. Now *she's* someone, he'll listen to!" Billie explained.

"You are a wicked woman, Billie. I like the way you think," Cat responded with a smile as she rose from the table to fetch the cordless phone.

* * *

The phone rang three times before it was picked up. "Hello?" The rich southern accent flowed easily from the other end of the line.

"Hi Grams," Cat said.

"Caitlain? Caitlain, honey, how are you?" Alex asked, a smile in her voice.

"I'm fine, Grams. How are you and Grandma Jo?" she asked.

Ignoring Cat's question, Alex launched into a few of her own. "Caitlain, dear, something is wrong. I can hear it in your voice. Is Billie ill? I had the strangest feeling about her around noon. Is she all right?" Alex asked.

Cat looked at Billie with an astonished expression on her face. "Did you say around noon, Grams?" Cat asked.

"Yes. I was sitting in the parlor with Josie, talkin' about her history lecture comin' up in about a month, when all of the sudden, I felt this odd feelin' in the pit of my stomach. I called and called and called, but no one answered your phone. Finally I just gave up... well, actually Josie made me stop. She said if somethin' was really wrong that you'd call me, and now you have. So tell me, child, what's wrong with my granddaughter?" Alex finally finished.

"Cat, what is it?" Billie asked from across the kitchen table as she looked at the confused look on her wife's face.

"Grams, could you hold on a minute?" Cat asked.

"Sure, darlin', but I want an answer when you come back," Alex warned.

Cat covered the receiver with her hand as she looked at Billie. "Billie, she knows that something was wrong with you today. She said she felt it. Should I tell her?" Cat asked.

Billie shrugged. "I can't see where it would hurt, Cat. It is kind of odd though that she actually felt it," Billie said. "Although it does lend credence to the ancestral connection theory."

Cat nodded and removed her hand from the receiver. "Grams, you're right. Billie *was* ill today. Look, we haven't told you this yet, but Billie has a mild form of epilepsy. She had a seizure today around noon," Cat explained.

"I knew it. I just knew it! Josie, I told you I wasn't losin' my mind! Our Billie had a seizure today, and it happened around noon!" Alex said off line to Jo.

Cat could hear Jo grumbling in the background, bringing a smile to her face.

"She didn't believe me, Cat. She thought I was losin' it or somethin'" Alex said. "Sugar, is Billie right there, I'd like to talk to her," Alex said.

"Actually, I called you, Grams, because Billie has some news for you. Here, let me put her on," Cat said. She handed the phone to Billie and took her empty dish away.

Billie caught her arm as she started to walk toward the sink, and pulled her back. She wrapped her arm around Cat's waist and pulled her in for a kiss. "Thank you," she mouthed as she let her go. She held the receiver to her ear. "Hello, Grams."

"Child, you nearly scared the life out of me today," Alex scolded, causing Billie to grin. "Land sakes, Billie, you should have told us you have epilepsy. How are you feeling now?" Alex asked.

"I'm fine Grams, really. It’s not the first time I've had a seizure, and it probably won't be the last. Don't worry about me. Doc will adjust my meds and I'll be fine," she said. "Grams, I have some news for you. We've found the agency that took your daughter from you."

"Oh, my!" Alex said as Billie listened to scuffling sounds on the other end of the line.

"Grams? Grams, are you all right?" Billie said into the

phone.

Jo's voice came onto the line. "Billie? Al's all right, she just nearly fainted again. Are you all right, girl?" she asked.

"Jo, never mind me, is Alex okay?" Billie asked.

"She's fine, in fact, she wants the phone back, but before I hand you over to her, answer the question," Jo demanded.

"Jo, I'm fine. I have epilepsy. I've had it for about a year now. My medication pretty much keeps it under control. Cat thinks the stress of this genealogy search may have brought on the seizure, but I'm fine. Really. Please don't worry," Billie explained.

"All right then, you take care of yourself. Alex, hold your britches on, sheesh," Jo exclaimed before Alex's voice came back on the line.

"Billie, honey, did you say that you found her?" Alex asked in a shaky voice.

"No Grams, we found the agency that took her from you. The adoption records were seized and sealed, but they *do* show a child from Lancaster registered with them on June fourteenth, nineteen fifty-nine. It has to be her, Gram. I just know it is," Billie said. "There is one problem, though," she continued. "Like I said, the records are sealed and it will take either a court order or a decree from the governor to open them."

"The governor?" Alex asked. "You leave this to me, Billie. I'll deal with Governor Jamie Hubbard. He happens to be an acquaintance of Josie and me. You see, we have given generously to his campaigns in the past, and I'm sure he would do anything to keep his constituency happy," Alex said, a wicked tone entering her voice. "Now, give me all the details," she said.

Billie spent the next half-hour telling Alex everything she knew about Sylvia Tanner and the Children's Home Society. She hung up the phone and smiled at Cat. "Your grandmothers can be very ruthless when they have to be, love. Remind me never to cross them," Billie said.

Cat leaned over the kitchen table and took Billie's chin in

her hand, forcing their eyes to make contact. "*Our* grandmothers, love. *Our* grandmothers," she said, causing a grin to spread across Billie's face as she nodded her head.

Billie placed a gentle kiss on Cat's mouth then suddenly frowned. “Cat, where are the kids?"

"They're downstairs watching Dr. Dolittle," Cat answered.

"Dr. Dolittle? With Rex Harrison? That's my favorite!" Billie jumped up from the table and ran toward the basement stairs. She turned back and looked at Cat. "Ah, Cat, can...," she began.

"Yes, love, I'll make you some popcorn! I'll be down in a few minutes." She watched Billie disappear through the basement door. "Kids today!" she exclaimed while pulling the popcorn out of the cupboard.

* * *

Billie called in an unscheduled vacation day the next morning, opting instead to cuddle a while longer in bed with her wife.

"Cat, it's Friday. Why don't you call in a day off as well? We'll have a relaxing three-day weekend," Billie suggested, pulling Cat closer she was nearly laying completely on top of her.

"I can't, sweetheart. It's too short notice to find a replacement," she said. "However, I have only one surgery scheduled for nine a.m., so I don't need to be in until eight, and barring complications, I should be free to leave by noon," she said.

"Will Doc be at the hospital or in his office this morning?" Billie asked. She leaned her head to the side to give Cat better access to her neck.

"Hospital," Cat said.

"Good, I'll go in with you this morning and have the tests done there. Seeing that I can't drive, it'll work out well that way."

"Good plan."

Billie looked at the clock and saw that it was nearly six.

She kissed the top of Cat's head and said, "Love, we need to get up and shower. We still have to get the kids ready for school."

By seven, they were showered and dressed and urging the children to finish dressing so they could eat breakfast at a somewhat leisurely pace. Since Billie couldn't cook worth a damn, she was relegated to lunch duty, making ham sandwiches, and filling lunch bags with pudding cups and apples, while Cat threw together bacon, scrambled eggs and toast. Soon, dressed, fed, and armed with school bags, the kids headed to the end of the driveway to wait for the bus, the adults right behind them.

Just as she was pulled the kitchen door closed behind them, the phone rang. Billie swore under her breath and motioned to Cat that she'd only be a moment, and raced to reach the phone before the caller hung up.

"Hello?" she said into the receiver.

"Good Morning, Billie," Alex's voice said clearly from the other end.

"Grams!" Billie exclaimed, out of breath.

"Billie, you aren't havin' another seizure are you? You sound out of breath," Alex said worriedly.

"Grams, I ran in from outdoors to catch the phone before you hung up. No, I'm not having another seizure," Billie answered.

"That's good dear. Look, I'm calling to let you know that Josie and I have a lunch date with Governor Hubbard today. I intend to make it clear to him that his cooperation is key to future campaign contributions. In fact, I'm even thinkin' of donatin' enough money to build a youth center, named after him," she explained. "What do you think?"

"I think you are an evil woman, Grams," Billie said, mirth filling her voice.

"Thank you, dear. I knew you would approve. I know you're probably on your way out, so I'll give y'all a call later to let you know how things turned out, okay?" Alex said.

"Okay, Grams. Good luck, and Grams, I love you, and Grandma Jo too. You know that don't you?" Billie asked.

"I do know, love. We love you too, very much. I'll call you later this afternoon. Bye."

Chapter 22

Billie spent the morning undergoing a barrage of blood tests while Cat was in surgery. After sufficient fussing over the bruise on her temple, Doc invited her back to his office when the tests were done. Opening the door, he motioned for her to enter before him.

"Have a seat," he said. "How about a cup of coffee?" he asked.

"Doc, you're a man after my own heart," Billie replied. "Please. I'm just about due for a fix anyway."

Doc popped a coffee pod into the machine and brewed a cup for Billie. "So, Billie, tell me, how are things with you and Caitlain?" he asked as he handed the coffee to her.

"Things are wonderful, thanks for asking," Billie said. "We're a little overwhelmed right now with the search for my mother, but we seem to be holding up under the strain," Billie commented.

"Well, young lady," Doc said, leaning across his desk toward her. "Caitlain may be holding up under the strain, but *you* are not."

Billie narrowed her eyes. "What do you mean?" she asked.

"Billie, one of the things that can bring on an epileptic seizure, is extreme stress. Considering that your condition has been well under control with your current level of medication for about a year, the probability that this attack was stress related is pretty high. You need to either end this search of yours, or you need to deal with the stress better. Tell me, have you been to the gym lately?" he asked.

Billie looked guiltily at the cup in her hands. "Well, no, not as much as I should, I guess. This search has been pretty time-consuming," she admitted. "I run most mornings, but then, it's the end of the day when I'm stressed out. Maybe I should change the time of my workout," Billie suggested.

"No, I wouldn't change it," Doc said. "I mean, if you're running every morning now and still having seizures, then changing the time that you're running may not be enough. I would suggest adding a work out at the end of the day, even something as simple as power walking or stationary cycling," he suggested. "If stress is indeed the cause of the seizure, you either need to remove the source of the stress, which by the way is my first recommendation, or, you need to find a way to work off the stress before it affects you physically."

Billie shook her head. "I can't quit the search now, Doc. You know we're very close to finding Alexandra's daughter. We have the name of the agency that took her, and in about one hour," Billie said, looking at her watch, "Alex and Jo will attempt to gain access to the sealed records on the adoption through the governor of South Carolina."

Doc smiled and sat back in his chair. "Well, if anyone can charm the pants off the governor of South Carolina, it's Alex," he said. "I hope she reins Jo in before the meeting, though. When Josephine Wycliffe is on a roll, there's no stopping her. I'd hate to see a tirade on Jo's part ruin Alex's chances with the governor," he said before rising to his feet and brewing a second cup of coffee for himself.

"Do tell," Billie prompted, intuitively knowing there was an entertaining story behind Doc's words.

* * *

Cat found Billie in her father's office after her postoperative debriefing. She pushed the door open and walked in to find Billie holding her stomach, laughing heartily. She stopped in the doorway. "What's up?"

Billie was still chuckling. "Hi, love. Your father was filling me in on the legend of Josephine Wycliffe," she said.

Cat walked to her father's desk and sat on the corner of it. "That grandmother of mine is certainly a character," she said.

"That she is, kitten. That she is. How did surgery go?"

Doc asked.

"Very well. No complications. The patient stayed relatively stable throughout the operation," Cat replied.

"Good. Well, if you ladies will excuse me, I have a lunch date with your Mother, and knowing her, she'll kill me if I'm late. I'll see you and the kids tomorrow then?" he asked, looking at Billie.

"Tomorrow, it is, Doc," Billie said, noting the questioning expression on Cat's face.

Doc kissed both ladies on the cheek before excusing himself. After he left, Cat looked at Billie. "Tomorrow?" she asked.

"Your dad invited us over for a cookout. What could I say? I didn't think we had other plans. Do we?" Billie asked sheepishly.

Cat smiled. "No we don't. It just surprised me, that's all. So, want to get some lunch?" she asked.

"Sure," Billie said, looking nervously at her watch.

"What is it, Billie?" Cat asked, seeing the gesture.

"Nothing, really. It's just that Alex and Jo are meeting with the governor just about now. I hope he cooperates," Billie replied.

Cat grinned. She locked arms with Billie and led her toward the door. "Now who could possibly resist the charm of Alexandra Spirakis and the boldness of Josephine Wycliffe?" she asked between chuckles.

"Who, indeed?" Billie replied as they left for lunch.

* * *

After a leisurely lunch, Cat and Billie returned home, intent on spending a few intimate hours together before the children came home from school. Cat walked into the kitchen, threw her keys on the table and kicked her shoes off into the corner by the closet. Purely by habit, she walked over to the refrigerator and reached for the handle. Billie was there, her hand against the door, holding it closed before Cat could open it.

Cat found herself trapped against the refrigerator door, looking into Billie's eyes. She saw a smoldering fire burning deep within their blue depths.

Billie placed her right hand around Cat's neck and pushed her head against the refrigerator door and lowered her lips to Cat's. Several passionate moments later, both women were breathless from the intensity of the exchange. Billie bent over and placed an arm under Cat's legs, lifting her off the floor and bodily carrying her into the living room. Not wanting to waste the time and energy climbing the stairs, Billie headed for the overstuffed couch, laying Cat down, and then herself on top of her. More passionate kisses followed. Soon, Billie worked her way from Cat's mouth to her throat, and across her collar bones. Cat's head was thrown back into the cushion and her breath came in frantic pants, as Billie reached up to unbutton her shirt.

Just as Billie released the last button on Cat's shirt, the phone rang. Billie raised her head and looked at Cat, wavering between answering and ignoring the rings. Moments passed, their eyes remaining locked as two, then three, then four rings pealed out. Finally, the answering machine picked up the phone. Billie smiled and lowered her mouth once more to Cat's lips.

Suddenly, the sound of Alex's frantic voice came across the speaker on the answering machine, causing an instant pause once more in their lovemaking as both women listened to the message. "Sweethearts, we did it! We did it! The governor graciously allowed us access to my daughter's adoption records. We have a name, Billie! We have a name! Give me a call when you get home, okay? We'll talk to..." Alex's voice rang out.

Billie was on her feet in a flash and grabbed the phone before Alex hung up. "Grams! It's Billie. No, everything's fine. Cat and I were just, ah...a little tied up. No, it's all right," Billie said into the phone as Cat sat back up, smiling at her wife's discomfort while she buttoned her shirt.

"You said you had a name?" Billie asked. She picked up the pen by the phone and wrote down the information dictated to her by Alex.

"Okay. Okay, Howard and Julia McGuire. I think I've got it. All right. Grams, I'm going to call Jimmy as soon as I hang up to see if there's anything he can do for us today, otherwise it will be Monday at the earliest before we know anything. Yes, I know, it will be a long weekend, but Grams, it's been a long fifty-five years. I promise I'll find out as fast as I can. I'll call you as soon as we know something, okay? All right. We love you and Jo too. I'll talk to you later. Bye."

Billie hung up the phone and looked at Cat. Cat was curled up on the couch with her arm thrown over the back, looking at Billie with anticipation on her face.

"Cat, we have the name of her adoptive parents, Howard and Julia McGuire," she choked out before the tears came. Cat rose from the couch and approached Billie and wrapped her arms around her.

"Shhh, it's okay, love. Calm down. That's it, relax," she said as Billie's trembling slowed. "Now, call Jimmy and give him the information, then I want you to relax and take a nap, okay? I'll stay with you until the kids get home," Cat suggested.

Moments after placing the phone call to Jimmy, Cat and Billie were in bed, wrapped in each other's arms, Billie's head on Cat's shoulder, while Cat repeatedly rubbed the arm Billie had thrown over her chest. Billie was soon sleeping, consumed by emotional exhaustion. Cat looked at the ceiling, praying to any god that would listen that this woman was indeed Billie's mother. She dreaded the disappointment that would surely follow if it turned out not to be the case.

* * *

The phone rang as the Charland family sat down to supper.

"I'll get it," Billie said. She had been edgy all afternoon, anxiously awaiting a phone call from Jimmy. "Hello?" she said into the receiver.

"Hi Missy, this is Jimmy. I've got the information you were looking for."

Billie's knees suddenly became weak as she reached her hand out against the wall for support. Cat was on her feet immediately, going to Billie's side to place an arm around her waist. Billie's arm went around Cat's shoulder for balance. Cat looked back over her shoulder to the table, where the three children were watching them with concern etched on their faces.

"Is Mom all right?" Seth asked nervously.

"She's fine honey," Cat said, "Bring a chair over here for Mom, will you, sweetie? Billie, let me take this," she said, taking the receiver out of her wife's hand as Seth pushed the chair in behind Billie's knees.

"Thanks, hon," she said to her son as he stepped back a pace, unsure of how serious the situation was.

"Jimmy, this is Cat. Could you hold on for a minute please? Thanks."

Cat looked at Billie, who was sitting in the chair staring blankly ahead, then looked back at Seth. "Sweetheart, Mom's okay, I promise. She's just a little overwhelmed right now with the search to find her mother. Do you understand? Please don't worry, okay?" Cat finished.

Seth nodded his head and went back to sit at the table, just staring at his supper. Skylar was whimpering lightly while Tara stood by her side, rubbing her back, eyes wide with worry at her mother's strange behavior.

Cat looked at the children and then down at Billie, who was still sitting there staring straight ahead. She raised the receiver to her ear once more and spoke to Jimmy.

"I'm sorry to keep you waiting, Jimmy, but Billie's a bit overwhelmed right now. Why don't you give me the information and I'll see that she gets it, okay?"

Minutes later, she hung up the phone and knelt down on the floor in front of Billie. She placed her hand on the side of Billie's face and softly called out her name. Billie blinked and focused on Cat, clearly confused.

Billie looked at the worried expressions on the children's faces, then looked back again at Cat. "Cat, what happened?"

"You had a petit mal seizure, Billie," Cat said angrily.

"I did?" Billie responded.

"Yes, you did. Damn it Billie! This mission you're on is getting to be way too much for you," Cat said in a raised voice, before remembering their audience of three just a few feet away.

"Damn," Cat said under her breath. "Look, Billie, we can talk about this later, okay? Right now, we need to finish dinner," Cat said, helping Billie to her feet and leading her to the table, still somewhat in a stupor. She then went to comfort the girls who were still tense with worry.

Billie sat down and looked around the table at three long faces. "Hey, what are the sour pusses for?" she said, forcing a smile to lighten the mood.

One by one, the worried expressions started to lift, and soon the supper table turned into its usual sounding board for the day's events, the only notable difference being, the looks of concern and frustration that flew back and forth across the table between the two adults.

* * *

Billie sat up in bed, her back resting against the headboard as she watched an angry Cat pace back and forth across the room.

Cat struggled with herself over whether or not to tell Billie about Jimmy's phone call–a call she obviously did not remember taking place. Finally, she decided to wait until Sunday to tell her. This would give her at least one day to relax and enjoy the cookout her father had planned. Cat stopped pacing and stood at the foot of the bed.

Billie looked down at her hands in her lap while Cat paced. She knew she was in trouble. Doc had warned her to take it easy, and according to Cat, she worked herself into a state when the phone rang, and fell into another seizure.

I really need to learn how to deal with extra stress or I'll be walking on eggshells for the rest of her life. My whole livelihood was at stake here. Being a lawyer was by definition, a stressful job, she thought.

Finally, she made a decision. "Cat, I want to start seeing Dr. O'Brien again," she said.

Cat's brow knit together in confusion. "Why?" she asked.

"Cat, honey, I know you think this search is what's causing the seizures, but in reality, it's the stress brought on by the search. It's the stress doing it, not the search itself. If I can't learn to deal with stress better, this is going to happen every time I get upset about something. I really think I need to see Dr. O'Brien again," Billie explained.

Cat stood there, her arms crossed in front of her. "All right, Billie. Give her a call Monday morning and set it up. I'll go with you, if you'd like."

Billie nodded her acceptance and looked back down at her hands.

Cat stood there, trying very hard to stay angry with her, but failed miserably. The heart-stricken look on Billie's face at the moment was tearing her to shreds. She crawled onto the bed next to her and pulled Billie's head down into her lap. For the next several minutes, she stroked back Billie's hair and hummed an old lullaby Ida used to sing to her as a child. Soon, Billie was sleeping peacefully. Cat slid down onto the bed beside Billie and reached over to turn out the light. Moments later, both women were walking in the dreamscape.

Chapter 23

The cookout was a huge success. Cat kept a close eye on Billie and noted that she was making a conscious effort to relax and enjoy herself, being as playful as ever with the children, and even sneaking up on Doc to spray him with the garden hose. It felt so good to see her at ease. All of this made Cat glad that she had withheld the information about Jimmy's phone call.

Later that evening, Billie called Jen and Fred and made arrangements for the four of them to go out to dinner. They hired a sitter for the five children, then set out to enjoy an evening of dining and dancing. The two couples completely enjoyed themselves, despite the odd looks Cat and Billie received when they hit the dance floor. When they returned home, all five children were sleeping in wild array on sleeping bags all over the floor of Cat and Billie's family room. Instead of waking them, Cat insisted that Stevie and Karissa be allowed to spend the night, giving Jen and Fred a much deserved night alone. Billie shooed their friends out the door to take the sitter home and strict instructions not to collect their children before noon the next day.

All in all, it had been a nice day.

It was a pity the same could not be said of the following day.

* * *

Billie rose early as usual. She donned her running gear and headed out for her five mile run through the park. When she returned nearly an hour later, she stripped off her clothes and jumped into the shower to wash away the sweat from her morning exercise. She briskly toweled herself dry and slipped on a sports bra, button up sleeveless shirt, which she tied in the front with the shirt tails, and a pair of cut-off denim shorts, her mid-section from navel to diaphragm exposed.

She padded through the house in her bare feet to the kitchen where she put on a pot of coffee to brew, then walked around picking up the few odds and ends the kids had left hanging around from the night before… an empty soda can… a paper towel… a piece of paper with some scribbling on it. Billie carried these items to the wastebasket and threw them in. As she watched them fall into the bin, she suddenly noticed the name 'Jimmy' on the paper she had just thrown away. Her heart rose to her throat as the leaned down and retrieved the paper from the bin. She carried the paper to the table where she sat down and started to read.

Jimmy called. He found the address for the adoptive parents:

Laurel McGuire, born June fourteenth, nineteen fifty-nine, Lancaster, South Carolina

Adopted by Howard and Julia McGuire

Current Address: One sixty-three Pine Street, Hazelton, Pennsylvania

Adoption Agency: Children's Home Society

Adoption Agent: Sylvia Tanner

Billie looked up from the note to see Cat standing in the kitchen doorway. Cat's eyes were wide with anticipation, guilt clearly written on her face.

Billie narrowed her eyes and fought back anger. "When did this call come in, Cat?" she asked as calmly as possible.

"Friday night during dinner," Cat replied. She raised her chin defensively.

Billie rose to her feet and turned her back on Cat. She walked over to the kitchen door and looked out the window. "Friday night during dinner," she repeated. She turned around sharply. "And here it is, Sunday morning. When did you plan to tell me about this, Cat?" she demanded angrily.

"Sometime today," Cat replied truthfully.

Billie stood there, totally outraged. She walked toward Cat and stopped just inches from her. She leaned over so that their faces were a mere hair's breadth away. "What gave you the right to withhold this from me? I've lost an entire day of searching because of you," she said in low angry tones.

Cat was pissed. "What gives me the right? What gives me the right?!" she yelled, walking into Billie and forcing the taller woman back a couple of steps. "I'll tell you what gives me the right! Watching you work yourself into a frenzy and scaring the shit out of the kids by falling into a seizure because of it! *That's* what gives me the right, Billie!"

Billie's eyes widened at the revelation. She looked down at the note in her hand. "This prompted the seizure?"

Cat nodded her head.

Billie sank back down into the kitchen chair she had vacated earlier. She propped her right elbow up on the table and leaned her forehead into her palm. "Damn!" she exclaimed.

"Billie, this is becoming too much for you. You either need to give up this quest, or let someone help you with it," Cat said angrily.

Billie's jaw clenched and unclenched repeatedly. "I can't give up, Cat," she said firmly.

"Well, I can't stand by and watch you make yourself sick over it. The kids were terrified Friday night. I'm sorry I withheld the information from you, but you were in no condition to deal with it at the time. Now, you can be angry with me if you want, but given the choice, I'd do it again!"

Billie sat silently for a long moment, contemplating the tabletop while Cat stood by nervously awaiting her reply. Finally, she sighed deeply and said, "I'm sorry I yelled at you, Cat. You were only doing what you thought was best for me."

Cat walked up behind Billie and wrapped her arms around her neck. "I forgive you, love. Now, will you please let me help you?" she asked.

"Help me how, Cat?" Billie asked, still rubbing her temple.

"You've been trying to do this all alone. The last time I looked, we were a team. Let me help. Let *me* make the phone calls. Let *me* ease some of the stress. Please," she said.

Billie nodded her head. "Have I told you lately how much I love you, Cat?" she asked.

"Every time you look at me, love. Every time you look at me," Cat said.

* * *

"Hello?" came the soft female voice from the other end of the line.

"Hello, my name is Cat Charland. I am looking for Howard or Julia McGuire. Am I speaking with Mrs. McGuire?" Cat asked.

"Yes, but before you start, I'm not interested in buying anything..." the fragile sounding woman began.

"No! No, I'm not a saleswoman, Mrs. McGuire. Please don't hang up," Cat pleaded. "I'm calling...well, I'm actually looking for Laurel McGuire. Do you know where I can—"

CLICK, came the sound from the other end, cutting Cat off in midstream.

Cat looked at the receiver like it was an alien creature that suddenly appeared in her hand. "Huh," she said, dialing the number again. For a second time, the frail voice answered the phone.

"Mrs. McGuire, please don't hang up. I have reason to believe that Laurel is the mother of someone very close to me. Please, give me just a few minutes of your time," Cat begged.

"Please hurry," the voice said. "He'll be back soon, and I'll have to hang up again."

It became immediately obvious to Cat that the woman on the other end of the line was afraid for her own safety, not disturbed by the phone call. "Mrs. McGuire. I need to know where Laurel is. Do you know?" Cat asked.

"You say she is someone's mother?" the woman asked.

"Yes, someone very dear to my heart," Cat exclaimed, looking up into smiling blue eyes. "She is ill right now and unable to make this call herself. *So I'm stretching the truth here just a little bit,* Cat thought, as she shrugged her shoulders to Billie. "Will you help me?" Cat asked.

"She hasn't lived here for over thirty years," the woman said. "Threw her out of the house, he did. Told her never to come back, he said. Got herself in trouble! Got into drugs. Bad seed, he said," the older woman rambled into the phone.

"Please, Mrs. McGuire, tell me, where is she?" Cat urged, getting the distinct feeling that she was losing this woman.

"Don't tell him I know. Don't tell him I've been staying in touch with her. Hell to pay if he finds out," the woman said.

"Julia, I won't tell. I promise," Cat replied. "Where is she, Julia?" Cat pushed again. She looked at Billie, who sat there clenching her fists at the obvious abuse that was going on in that household.

"Bay City, fifteen Birch Court, Bay City, Michigan. Got married, she did. Many years ago," the disoriented woman said.

"I need a married name, Julia. Please, give me her married name," Cat said, feeling a sense of urgency.

Suddenly, Cat heard the gruff sound of a man's voice in the background. "Who are you talking to, bitch?" said the voice.

In a moment of lucidity, Julia said into the phone, "I'm sorry Mrs. Stafford, but I'm not interested in buying any magazines. Please don't call here again."

Cat looked over at Billie as she held the dead receiver to her chest.

"Did you get the name, Cat?" she asked, hope filling her eyes.

Cat hung up the phone and reached for the pad of paper and pencil in front of her. She held it so Billie couldn't see what she was writing. *Laurel Stafford, fifteen Birch Court, Bay City, Michigan.* She handed the pad to Billie and smiled. "Which do you prefer, an aisle or a window seat?"

Billie grabbed Cat's face in her hands and kissed her hard

and long, smacking loudly when she released her. "Cat, my love, kick me now for not letting you help earlier. I've been a fool! Thank you, sweetheart."

Cat just smiled. "I'll put it on your bill," she said.

Billie raised her eyebrows. "Bill?" she asked.

"Oh yes, and I'm *very* expensive," Cat said seriously.

Billie reached into her pockets and pulled the linings out, indicating her penniless status. She looked at Cat sheepishly. "Can I take it out in trade?" she asked, a wicked gleam in her eyes.

"Well, it just so happens, Ms. Charland, that I don't accept checks, money orders or credit cards, so that pretty much limits your options, wouldn't you say?" Cat said as she circled around a seated Billie, trailing her fingertips across broad shoulders and finally seating herself in the chair at Billie's left.

Billie turned her face toward Cat. "Trade?" she asked.

"Do you mind if I inspect the merchandise first?" Cat asked.

"No, go ahead," Billie replied as Cat once again stood and circled around her, poking and prodding, squeezing and pinching. Finally Cat looked into her mouth.

"What am I, livestock?" Billie asked with mock indignity.

"Hey, if I'm going to use you for stud service, I want to know what I'm getting," Cat explained.

"Stud service?" Billie questioned sarcastically.

Cat took one more look her subject before saying, "You'll do. Trade it is. Upstairs, two minutes. Be there!" she said, getting up and leaving the kitchen.

Billie sat at the table and looked once more at the name and address on the pad of paper.

"I'll see you soon, Mom," she said before grinning broadly and following her wife upstairs.

* * *

An hour later, Billie was flat on her back, out cold and worn out from paying off her debt to Cat. Cat smiled as she brushed the dark bangs off her wife's forehead then kissed the spot vacated by the hair.

Poor baby, Cat thought. *She's still weak from the seizures.* She placed one final kiss on her forehead then whispered in Billie's ear, "If you push yourself too hard again, you won't have to worry about seizures, because I'll kill you myself. Sleep well, my love."

She rose from the bed and pulled a T-shirt over her head and glanced at the nightstand clock. *Good, time to make a phone call before Jen and Fred bring the kids home from the movies.*

Padding down the stairs to the kitchen, Cat reached for the phone and dialed the number for SpireCliffe Acres, Charleston, South Carolina.

"Yeah?" The greeting from the other end of the line was terse.

"Grandma Jo!" Cat said cheerfully. "You know Grams doesn't like you to answer the phone that way," she scolded.

"Yeah, well, Al needs to loosen up a bit," Jo said. "What's up?"

"Some good news, Grams. Could you ask Grams to pick up the extension so I can tell both of you?" she asked.

"I would, Cat, but Alex is not here. She's gone into town with Maggie to visit the craft fair. Damned craft fairs. Last year, Alex dragged me to four of them. Little does she know, I paid Maggie to go with her this time," Jo said, chuckling under her voice, very proud of herself. "So, you can either call back later, or give me the message and I'll ask her to call you," Jo suggested.

"No, I'll tell you," Cat said. "Grandma Jo, we found Grams' daughter," she said.

"Jumping Jesus! Really?" Jo exclaimed. "Who? Where?" she asked.

"Well, Billie's coworker found the adoptive parents, and the child's name, Laurel McGuire. I called the mother and had a very strange conversation with her during which I obtained Laurel's married name and address," Cat explained.

“What do you mean by strange conversation?” Jo asked.

“I got the strong impression that Laurel’s mother was the victim of domestic abuse. All during the conversation, she was terrified that her husband would catch her talking about Laurel. Apparently, he threw Laurel out of the house more than thirty years ago and has forbidden any contact with her since. I can just imagine the treatment Laurel must have received at the hands of that moron,” Cat said.

“So, what’s next?” Jo asked.

“We now have a married name and address for her, so I guess we either call her or drop in on her unannounced," Cat explained. “In any case, Billie and I want to do this alone before we expose Grams to any major rejection scene.”

Cat was greeted by silence at the other end of the line.

"Grams?" Cat said.

"I'm here. I'm just worried about Al, Cat. What if this reunion thing doesn't go well? What if Laurel is angry about being given up? I swear, if she hurts Al, I'll...," Jo sputtered.

"I know. I've been thinking the same thing about Billie. If Laurel really is her mother, I’m worried about how she’ll feel facing the woman who gave her away," Cat said.

"Well, it doesn't really matter how you and I feel about this. Al and Billie have to do what's right for them, and it's our job to stand by them, even if we don't agree with what they're doing," Jo said.

Cat sighed into the phone. "You know something, Grandma Jo?" Cat said, "Sometimes it's no fun being the sidekick."

Chapter 24

The flight into Flint Michigan was relatively uneventful. After securing a rental car, Billie and Cat drove the one-hour distance between Flint and Bay City in moderate silence. Cat periodically glanced at Billie, concerned about the woman's solitude.

"Sweetheart, are you all right?" Cat asked from her position behind the steering wheel.

Billie nodded without looking at Cat.

"You've been so quiet. Wanna talk about it?"

Billie looked down at the hands clasped in her lap. "What if she isn't my mother, Cat? What, if after everything we've been through over the past several weeks, this woman turns out not to be my mother?" she asked.

Cat reached for Billie's hand.

Billie placed her hand in Cat's and closed her fingers, gently squeezing as she cast a shy smile in Cat's direction.

"If she turns out not to be your mother then we'll keep looking. You are not alone in this Billie. I will be with you every step of the way," Cat said.

* * *

Billie stared out the window, her thoughts focused on the pending meeting with Laurel McGuire. On one hand, she would have preferred to take this trip alone, since she couldn't guarantee what her reaction would be to the woman who could possibly be her mother. On the other hand, having Cat with her was comforting. She really depended on her for strength and support, more than even Cat realized. Billie wondered for the millionth time what she would ever do if this beautiful woman weren't in her life.

Billie squeezed Cat's hand one more time. "Thank you for coming with me, Cat," she said softly.

"There's no way I'd let you go by yourself," Cat replied. "You're stuck with me!" she added.

"I could think of worse things to be stuck to, love," Billie joked.

"Welcome to Bay City," Cat said as she read the sign by the side of the road. We're here love. Do you want to find her first, or check into the hotel?" she asked.

Billie looked at her watch. "It's still early Cat. Let's settle in and then start our search, okay?" she asked, reaching up to rub her temple.

"Headache?" Cat asked.

"Yeah, a small one," Billie replied. "Maybe I can catch an hour or two of sleep before we look for Laurel," she suggested.

Cat nodded as she pulled into the parking lot of the hotel. "That's a very good idea. I could use a nap myself," she said.

While Billie checked them in, Cat went to the information counter and asked for directions to Birch Court. By the time Billie was finished, she had directions in hand, and followed her wife to the elevator.

They had a breathtaking view of Lake Huron. Billie dropped the suitcase on the floor by the door and stood in front of the window. Cat came up beside her, wrapped her arm around her waist, and leaned her head against Billie's upper arm. For long moments, they stood there looking out over the bay, neither speaking, but communicating volumes through their silence.

Finally, the silence became too painful to endure.

"Talk to me Billie. I can feel the tension in your heart. Please let me in," Cat pleaded.

Billie took Cat into her arms. "I'm afraid, Cat. I'm scared out of my mind to meet this woman," she explain

Cat led her to the bed where they sat side by side. She reached up and tucked a stray lock of hair behind Billie's ear, then placed a gentle kiss on the Billie's cheek. "Talk to me sweetheart. Why are you afraid of her?" she asked.

"I'm not afraid *of* her Cat. I'm afraid of what I've been feeling *about* her," Billie tried to explain.

"What do you mean?" Cat questioned, a frown deepening the lines in her forehead.

"Cat, would you say I was a vengeful, hateful person?" Billie asked seriously.

Cat was taken aback by the question. "Billie, why would you ask a question like that? You are one of the most loving people I know. Baby, talk to me," she replied.

"Over the past few days, I have harbored such thoughts. Hurtful, vengeful thoughts," Billie tried to explain.

"Go on," Cat encouraged.

Billie walked to the window once more and looked out over the city, while Cat sat patiently on the bed waiting for her to speak. After a few tense moments, Billie turned around and rested her backside against the windowsill.

"Sometimes I want to hate her, Cat. Sometimes the rage is so great I wish all type of ghastly horrors on her. All my life I believed I was wanted, loved and accepted, and suddenly I find out my mother threw me away. She sold me like a piece of furniture, and the people I thought were my parents lied to me my entire life," she said. Once again, she reached up to rub her temples.

"Billie, you're making yourself ill. Come lay down. Sleep will do you good," Cat urged.

"How can I sleep, Cat? I am so disgusted with the way I feel. Part of me wants to hate them. Part of me is thankful for the happy childhood I *did* have, and probably wouldn't have if my birth mother had kept me. Part of me feels guilty for the anger, and yet another part of me actively fuels the fire of my hatred. I feel like such a monster! I'm so confused. I'm so afraid of which part of me will prevail when I am finally face to face with my mother. I…I…" Billie stuttered as she once again rubbed her temples.

Cat jumped to her feet and immediately went to Billie's side. She cupped her face between her hands and forced

Billie to look at her.

“Billie, stop this right now. You are making yourself sick. Damn it, Billie. Don’t you know by now how wonderful you are? Don’t you realize how much love and happiness you bring to the people around you… to me… to the kids… to our friends and family? Sweetheart, the decisions made on your behalf may or may not have been the right ones for you, but they are in the past. There is nothing you can do about it now but to look forward and make the best of it. Sweetheart, try not to judge your birth mother until you’ve heard her side of the story. I understand your anger, really, I do, but please don’t allow it to control you,” Cat pleaded.

Billie looked into Cat’s face while tears rolled down her cheeks. She closed her eyes and nodded. “I’ll try, Cat. I’ll try.”

“Thank you,” Cat replied as she gently pulled Billie’s face down for a kiss. “Come.” She led Billie by the hand to the side of the bed and pushed her into a sitting position.

Cat knelt in front of Billie and removed Billie's shoes then pushed her shoulders so that she was lying on her back. Cat lifted Billie's feet onto the bed then climbed in beside her, pulling the cover over them from the foot of the bed. "Now come here, love. Let me hold you while we talk."

Billie gratefully rolled into Cat's arms and rested her head on Cat's shoulder. Cat waited patiently for Billie to speak, while she stroked the long dark hair.

"Cat, how can it be possible to hate someone you've never met?" Billie asked.

Cat forced herself to remain calm, even though Billie's question upset her terribly. "Do you really hate her, Billie?"

"Sometimes I hate her, sometimes I don't. I try really hard to understand why she would give me up. How could she do that to me?" Billie asked, crying into Cat's shoulder.

"I don't know, love. She must have had good reason, but we *will* find out, and I will be there with you, holding your hand if you need me to," Cat said softly.

"I *do* need you to, Cat," Billie said before she drifted off to sleep.

* * *

"All right, Billie, where do we turn next?" Cat asked, waiting for Billie to read the directions from her shotgun position in the passenger seat.

"Go through the next set of lights, take your second left, then first right," Billie instructed.

"Second left, first right. Okay, there's the second left," Cat said as she made the left hand turn, followed almost immediately by a right hand turn. "Birch Court. Here we are. We're looking for fifteen Birch Court, right?" Cat asked as she watched Billie's jaw clench and unclench convulsively.

An intense feeling of anxiety had parked itself in the middle of Billie's stomach, threatening a mutiny at any moment. Billie felt a light sheen of sweat build up around her hairline as the taste of bile filled her mouth. A building sense of dreaded anticipation was almost too much for Billie to bear as a light tremor started to form in her limbs.

Moments later, Cat pulled the car to a stop in front of fifteen Birch Court. She turned off the engine and looked at Billie. "Do you want me to do this?" she asked.

Billie looked at her. "No, Cat. I want *us* to do this. Please come with me," she said shakily.

"Billie, are you all right?" Cat asked, noticing the tremors.

Billie nodded. "I'm fine, Cat. Just a little nervous," she admitted.

No knowing whether to believe her, Cat decided to take her word for it as she opened the driver's door and climbed out. She walked to the passenger side of the car and opened Billie's door. She extended her hand to Billie.

"Are you coming?" she asked gently.

Billie climbed out of the car and grasped Cat's hand, and together, they walked to the house. Billie stood behind Cat in front of the screen door and rested her hands on Cat's shoulders while Cat pressed the doorbell. Billie unconsciously dug her fingertip so deeply into Cat's shoulders as they waited, that Cat was convinced there'd be bruising later.

An attractive woman answered the door, her appearance immediately stopping both Cat and Billie in their tracks. Cat guessed the woman to be in her late forties or early fifties. The woman had a slender figure and was nearly Billie's height. Long dark hair, aged by gray, fell in gentle waves around her shoulders. Startling blue eyes stared back at her.

"Yes? How may I help you?" she said.

Cat nearly melted on the spot as Billie's sultry voice came from this woman's mouth. All questions about whether this woman was Billie's mother immediately disintegrated at the sound of her voice.

Billie continued to stand there, silent rage and emotion coursing through her and into the grip she had on Cat's shoulders.

Cat reached up and patted Billie's hand, calling attention to the death grip she had on Cat's shoulder, and immediately felt Billie's hand relax. She turned her attention back to the woman who answered the door. "Ah, are you Mrs. Stafford, Mrs. Laurel Stafford," Cat asked in a shaky voice, already knowing the answer based on the woman's appearance alone.

"Yes," the woman said. "Do I know you?" she asked Cat.

"No you don't, Mrs. Stafford, but I believe you do know this woman," Cat said, motioning to Billie.

The woman pushed the screen door open to get a better look at Billie. Billie made and held eye contact with her immediately.

Laurel's eyes suddenly took on a haunted quality, like she recognized Billie, but couldn't quite place her. Unable to break eye contact, she asked Billie, "Where do I know you from?"

"The womb," was all Billie said.

"Suzanne!" was the only word out of Laurel's mouth before she crumbled to the ground before them.

* * *

"Mom?" a voice said from inside the house.

Everything was happening in slow motion for Billie. Laurel had looked at her and said, 'Suzanne', the name on the tiny bracelet found inside the safe deposit box belonging to Billie's adoptive parents. The next thing she knew, Laurel had fainted away at their feet.

This woman is most definitely my mother, and Alex's daughter, Billie thought. Billie just stood there, looking at the supine body of the woman in front of her.

"Billie! Billie, snap out of it and help me!" Cat yelled at her as she bent over the woman on the ground.

"Mom?" the voice said again, louder and closer. A young man emerged from inside the house. He was tall and lean with a muscular build, broad shoulders, curly blond hair, dimples, and the same blue eyes that resided with Billie, Laurel and Alex.

"Mom!" he said urgently when he saw his mother unconscious at the feet of two strangers.

The young man barged in between Cat and Billie and pushed them away. "What have you done to her?" he asked, bending over to tend to the woman.

"She just fainted," Cat said. "She's not injured."

He lifted Laurel into his arms and he turned to look at Cat. "What are you, a doctor?" he asked sarcastically.

"As a matter of fact, I am," she said. "Bring her into the house and I'll have a look at her," Cat offered.

"No. I don't know who you are, or what business you have here, but I suggest you leave right now, before I call the police," he threatened.

Billie spoke for the first time. "Let Cat look at her. She really is a doctor."

The young man turned to Billie with daggers in his eyes. "And who the hell are you?" he asked.

"Your sister," replied Billie, drawing a startled expression from the boy. "Now bring her into the house so Cat can look at her, or I'll take her from you and do it myself. You got it?" Billie said sharply, nose to nose with her brother.

He looked at his mother and then quickly back at Billie, and suddenly realized she was a younger version of the woman he was holding in his arms.

The young man looked unsure of what to do, until common sense took over and led him to bring Laurel inside. Billie and Cat followed him as he laid her on the couch in the living room, then stood and took a step back. He stood next to Billie, eyeing her suspiciously.

Cat immediately fell into doctor mode. She checked all of Laurel's vital signs, and as expected, found them to be normal. She asked the young man for a cold cloth to place on Laurel's forehead. While he was out of the room, Cat looked at Billie and asked, "Are you all right?"

Billie's jaw muscles were working overtime, clenching and unclenching as she stood there with her arms crossed, a stern look on her face. She looked Cat directly in the eyes, but did not answer.

"Billie?" Cat said again before the young man returned and handed her the cloth. "Thank you," she said as she placed it on Laurel's forehead. She looked back at the boy. "What's your name?"

"Dylan Stafford," he replied, casting another suspicious look at Billie.

Cat extended her hand to the young man. "My name is Cat, and this, as you now know, is your sister, Billie," Cat said.

Dylan shook Cat's hand, but kept his distance from Billie. "I don't have a sister," he said defensively.

"Well you do now," Billie said, staring him down and daring him to refute what she had just said. "And as soon as she wakes up," Billie motioned to Laurel, "she can confirm it for you."

Cat did not like the way Billie was behaving. "Billie, may I speak—"

Cat was about to ask Billie if she could speak to her in private, when Laurel began to stir.

Dylan went immediately to Laurel's side. He grasped her hand and felt her forehead. "Mom, are you all right?" he asked worriedly.

"Dylan?" Laurel asked. She looked around and noticed Cat kneeling on the floor beside her, and Billie standing a few feet away with a cross expression on her face. Finally, her eyes came back to Dylan's face.

"Mom, she claims that she's my sister," Dylan said, motioning to Billie over his shoulder.

Laurel sat up and then with Dylan's help, rose to her feet. She closed the few steps between herself and Billie, and stopped directly in front of her. "Suzanne?" she said again, as she reached up to touch Billie's face.

Billie pushed her hand away. "My name is Billie. Billie Waterman Charland. Does the name sound familiar, *Mother*?" Billie said, lacing that last word with heavy sarcasm.

"Waterman? Yes. They adopted you," recalled Laurel.

"No, they *bought* me, for ten thousand dollars, remember? Where did that money go, Mother, up your nose?" Billie demanded angrily.

"Billie!" Cat said, trying to get her wife to calm down.

Billie ignored her.

"I had no choice. They wanted a child. They loved you on sight," Laurel cried.

"Yes, they loved me and gave me everything a child could ever want, except one thing, the truth. They led me to believe I was theirs. They let me believe I belonged. Do you know what it feels like to find out that your life has been a lie? Do you have any idea how that feels, *Mother*?" Billie raged.

Laurel reached up again to touch Billie's face. Again, Billie knocked her hand away. "I'm sorry, Suzanne. I...I—" she cried.

"My name is not Suzanne!" Billie screamed into the woman's face. "Suzanne died thirty-two years ago when her mother threw her away like a piece of trash!"

"Billie, that's enough," Cat said angrily, coming to stand between Billie and Laurel. Dylan also rose to his feet, ready to defend his mother should this crazy woman become more than just verbally abusive.

Without breaking eye contact with Laurel, Billie put her hands on Cat's shoulders and firmly moved her out of the way. "Cat. This is between my mother and me. Please stay out of it," Billie demanded.

Cat pushed her way back in between the two women. "No, I won't stay out of it. You are my wife, and I will not stand by and let you lose control like this. Do you understand?" Cat said forcefully.

Both women were so distraught that neither of them realized Cat had revealed the true nature of their relationship to Laurel and Dylan.

Billie just reached out with one arm and literally pushed Cat out of the line of fire as firmly as possible without hurting her. "I said, stay out of it, Cat," Billie said firmly. She turned her attention once more to Laurel, who was staring, wide-eyed at her.

Billie was about to unload both barrels at Laurel again, when an intense pain ran through her temple, bringing her to her knees.

Cat was by her side immediately. "Damn you, Billie," she said. "I told you not to work yourself up like this."

"What's wrong with her?" Dylan asked as he watched his sister convulse and twitch on the floor.

Cat and Laurel were immediately on their knees beside her. "Cat?" Laurel said, fear clouding her vision.

"She's having a seizure, Laurel. She's an epileptic," Cat explained.

"Epileptic?" questioned Laurel, her eyes never leaving Billie's face. "Do something!" She urged Cat, fearful that Billie was dying right before her eyes.

"There's nothing I can do, Laurel. It will pass. We just have to wait it out," Cat explained.

Cat was monitoring Billie's vital signs as the seizure wracked her body. She looked at Laurel. "Billie developed epilepsy after she took a bullet to the brain while stopping our daughter's kidnapper, Laurel."

Laurel was confused. "Kidnappers? You have a daughter?" the woman asked.

"You have three beautiful grandchildren, Laurel. A boy

and two girls. Billie and I love them dearly. They are very much a part of what makes us whole. Billie would die for them, as would I, if necessary. Keep that in mind when you think about what happened here today," Cat suggested.

Just then, a particularly violent tremor ripped through Billie's body.

"Will she be all right?" Laurel asked frantically.

"Yes. The seizure will pass in a few minutes. She'll be disoriented for a while, then she'll sleep for several hours. I'll bring her back to our hotel room as soon as the convulsions pass," Cat explained.

"No, please, stay here," Laurel said.

"Mom," Dylan warned. "What about Dad? You know how he feels about...you know," Dylan said, motioning his head in the direction of Cat and Billie.

Cat caught on immediately. "Are you trying to say that your father would object to 'our kind'? Are you saying that he hates gays?" Cat asked angrily.

Dylan just nodded, ashamed of himself for bringing it up.

Cat sat back on her heels and ran a hand through her hair. She sighed deeply, thinking that this whole quest had been nothing but trouble from the start. She looked at Dylan. "Well, you don't have to worry about it. I'm taking her back to our hotel room, right now in fact," Cat said, as she noticed Billie's tremors had stopped and she was coming to.

"Cat?" Billie said weakly, opening her eyes.

"I'm here love. Come on, we're going back to our room. You need to sleep," Cat said. She helped Billie to her feet and walked her out to the car, refusing help from Laurel.

After belting a groggy Billie into the passenger seat, Cat circled around the car where Laurel was waiting. Dylan stood in the doorway of the house.

"Cat. I want to see her again. There is so much I want to say to her, so much she doesn't know. Please, let me see her," Laurel pleaded, tears in her eyes.

"I'm not sure that's a good idea, Laurel. As you saw, intense emotional stress can trigger a seizure. It kills me to watch her go through one of these. Do you know this is the third seizure she's had since she started searching for you just two weeks ago? She hadn't had a seizure for an entire year prior to that," Cat tried to explain.

"Cat, I promise, if she starts to become upset, I will leave. Please let me see her again," Laurel begged once more.

Cat could see the sincerity in this woman's face. Maybe there was more to the adoption than met the eye. Laurel was the only one who could answer that. She took a deep breath. "Laurel, I'll talk to her later tonight, after she's had a chance to recover her strength. If she wants to see you, then I'll call you. Otherwise, we will be on a flight home tomorrow."

"I understand," Laurel said. "Please wait here a moment while I write my phone number down for you," she said before returning to the house.

While Laurel was gone, Dylan approached Cat, who was now leaning against the driver's side of the car, waiting for Laurel to return. Billie was still sitting groggily in the front seat.

"Cat, I want to apologize for that comment I made, and I'm sorry that Billie is ill. I hope she feels better soon. Maybe we'll see you later," he said, walking away as his mother returned to the car carrying a piece of paper.

"Here is the phone number, Cat. Please talk to her. I want desperately to explain things to her. Please encourage her to give me the chance," Laurel said.

Cat just nodded her head and turned to get into the car. Suddenly she stopped and looked at Laurel. "By the way, Laurel, as the fates would have it, we know of someone else who is looking for you. Someone who loves you very much and wants desperately to get to know you."

Laurel narrowed her eyes in a gesture so much like Billie that Cat had to restrain herself from reaching out and touching her face. "Who?" she asked.

"Your own mother," Cat said as she climbed into the car.

Laurel stood there, dumbstruck as Cat drove away.

Chapter 25

Billie slept for several hours. While she was sleeping, Cat spent her time making phone calls.

"Hey Jen," she said when her friend picked up the phone.

"Cat! How are things going? Did you find Billie's mom?" she asked before Cat had a chance to ask about the kids.

"Whoa! First things first," she said. "How are the kids? Are they driving you crazy yet?" Cat asked.

"The kids are fine, Cat. They're all in the pool right now with Fred. So, spill it. Did you find Billie's mom?" she asked again.

"Oh, yeah, we found her all right," Cat replied.

"And…?" Jen prompted.

"It was awful, Jen. It definitely did not go well. Billie was so angry with her," Cat explained.

"Uh, oh! I've seen Billie angry," Jen commented. "I can just imagine how it went."

"No, Jen, you can't. It was worse than bad. Let's just say that Billie worked herself into a grand mal seizure right there in Laurel's living room," Cat said.

"Oh, God, no!" Jen gasped. "Is she okay?"

"She's sleeping it off right now. I knew what was happening, but she nearly scared Laurel and Dylan to death," Cat replied.

"Dylan? Who's that?" Jen asked.

"Billie's brother. Half-brother, that is," Cat said. "He has Billie's eyes and height, but otherwise he must look like his father. Oh, and speaking of his father, the man apparently is an extreme homophobe."

"Wow! Maybe the two of you should just catch the next

flight home and put this behind you," Jen suggested. "It sounds like Billie may be in for a lot of heartache if she continues with this much further."

"I've been thinking the same thing, my friend, but it's really Billie's call. If she wants to pursue this, I will support her, but it is ultimately her call," Cat explained.

"You're right, of course. Wish her luck for me, okay?" Jen asked.

"I will Jen. Look, I still have to call Grams with the news, so I gotta go," Cat replied.

"All right, girlfriend. Kiss the big guy for me and then kick her in the ass for pushing herself too hard. I'll talk to you later. Love you!" Jen said.

"Love you too, Jen. Bye," Cat replied before hanging up the phone.

The call to Alex was difficult. Alex was elated that they had found her daughter, but disturbed by the confrontation between her and Billie.

"Grams, it was awful. Billie was so angry and hurtful. Laurel tried very hard to calm her and to explain what had happened all those years ago, but Billie just wouldn't let her," Cat explained. "The worst part is that Billie worked herself up into such an emotional tizzy, that she fell into another seizure, right there in front of Laurel. Of course, not knowing what was wrong, Laurel was beside herself with worry when it happened. I had to get her out of there," Cat finished.

"Caitlain, where is Billie now? Is she all right?" Alex asked.

"She's fine. She's sleeping right here beside me. The seizures take a lot out of her, Grams. I don't know how long she'll be out this time," Cat said.

"Well, I think Josie and I should get on a plane right now and join you," Alex said.

"Grams, I know you're anxious to see Laurel, but I think we need to resolve the problems between her and Billie first, before we add another contestant. I told Laurel that you were looking for her. She doesn't know any more than that yet. We didn't have time for more, I had to get Billie back to the hotel and put her to bed," Cat finished.

"I understand, Caitlain. Do you think you'll see Laurel again before you leave?" Alex asked hopefully.

"I don't know. She wants to see Billie again. She said there were so many things Billie doesn't know," Cat said.

"What are you going to do next?" Alex asked.

"I'm going to wait for Billie to wake up and then talk to her about Laurel. If she wants to go home, I'll make the reservations immediately. If she wants to see Laurel again, I'll call and set it up. It all depends on Billie right now," Cat finished.

"I really do understand, Caitlain. Please give Billie our love."

* * *

Cat was standing in front of the window looking out over the lake when Billie awoke and called out her name.

Cat turned around. "Hey! How are you feeling?" she asked. She sat on the edge of the bed and affectionately brushed the hair off Billie's forehead.

"Tired, weak, headachy. I had another seizure, didn't I?" Billie asked.

Cat nodded her head.

Billie rolled onto her back and looked at the ceiling. “I’m sorry,” she said.

Cat kissed Billie on the forehead. Sensing the woman needed to speak, she remained quiet.

"Cat," Billie continued, "maybe I should give up this quest and go home. May I should just let Alex deal with it if she wants, but maybe looking for my mother was a mistake," she said.

Cat climbed onto the bed and laid on her stomach, propping herself up on her forearms so that she could look at Billie as she talked. "Do you really want to do that after you've come this far?" she asked.

Billie looked at Cat, confusion etched deeply into her face. "I need your advice. What should I do?" she asked.

"Well," Cat said. "Part of me wants to pack you up and take you home. The seizure you had earlier today was pretty strong and you scared the hell out of Laurel and Dylan. Oh, and by the way, I called Jen while you were sleeping to check on the kids, and she told me to kick you in the ass for working yourself into a tizzy. Remind me to do that later," Cat said, causing Billie to chuckle.

"The other part of me," Cat continued, "would like you to give Laurel the chance to say her piece. You were a little rough on her this afternoon, Billie. She wants desperately for a chance to explain why she made the choices she did. You've come so far in this search, love. I think you owe it to yourself to listen to what she has to say," Cat suggested.

"You think so?" Billie asked.

"Yes, I do. Once you know the truth, you can decide for yourself if you can live with it. If not, we can put this behind us and go on with our lives. If you *can* live with it, you'll have found your mother, and your life will be richer for it. I can't make this decision for you, love, but whatever you decide, I will support you," Cat finished.

Billie ran her forefinger down the side of Cat's face. Nodding, she said, "You're right. If I don't give her the chance to explain, I'll spend the rest of my life wondering. I'll call and ask her to dinner. Is that all right with you?" she asked Cat.

Cat thought for a moment. Dinner was a nice idea. It would give them a chance to talk socially, on neutral ground, and get to know one another a little better before jumping into the private details of their lives. After dinner, they could find a nice quiet place to talk, and hopefully, by the end of the evening, Billie would have her answers, and they would be able to make a decision about how to proceed with their lives, with or without Laurel.

"Do you want to call her now?" Cat asked.

Billie nodded as she sat up and reached for the phone.

Cat dug the phone number out of the pocket of her jeans and handed it to Billie, who accepted it with shaky hands.

"Do you want me to make the call for you, Billie?"

"No, Cat. I have to do this myself," she said as she dialed

the number.

"Hello?" a man's voice said from the other end of the phone.

"Hello, may I speak to Laurel, please?" Billie asked, thinking to herself that this was not Dylan she was talking to.

"May I ask whose calling?" the man said.

"Billie," she supplied.

"Hold on," came the reply.

Moments later, a breathless Laurel answered the phone. "Billie?" she said cautiously.

"Yes, Laurel, this is Billie. First let me apologize for the way I treated you earlier. I didn't give you a chance to explain, and for that I am sorry," Billie said. "Cat and I would like to take you to dinner tonight if you're free. I think we have a lot to talk about. I'd like to start over and do this civilly," she added.

"Yes, I would like that, and Billie, I have so much to say to you, so much to explain. Thank you for giving me the chance to do that," Laurel said.

"Cat and I will pick you up at six, okay? Since you know the area, we'll depend on you to select a restaurant. All right then, we'll see you at six," Billie said before hanging up.

Billie took a deep breath and looked at Cat. "It's a start," she said.

Cat just nodded and smiled.

* * *

The atmosphere at dinner was very tense, filled with polite "safe" conversation, during which they learned of one another’s jobs, hobbies and interests. Billie learned more about her brother, Dylan. Twenty-five years old, he had just completed his degree in veterinary medicine and was now starting to establish a practice. Finally dinner was over and a decision needed to be made about whether to depart company or to continue getting acquainted.

As they walked back toward the car, Billie stopped before reaching for the passenger door handle. "Would you like to come back to our room to talk, or would you like us to bring you home?" she asked Laurel.

Without hesitation, Laurel opted for the first choice. "Please, let's talk. I have so much I need to say to you."

Billie opened the door and slid into the car. Soon, they were on their way back to the hotel.

The first thing Laurel noticed when they entered the hotel room, was the fact that there was only one bed. The thought ran through her mind that she would have to accept and get used to the fact that her daughter was gay if she hoped to be part of her life.

Cat climbed onto the bed and sat cross-legged as Billie stood by the window. Laurel perched herself in the room's only chair. For a long moment, silence permeated the air, making Laurel squirm in her seat. Finally, she took the initiative to start the conversation.

"Billie, I know you must hate me, and you have every right to at this point, but please let me explain what drove me to make the choices I did thirty-two years ago when I gave you up for adoption," she started.

Billie abruptly turned away from the window. "You *sold* me, Mother," she said.

"Billie, please give her a chance to explain," Cat said.

"No, Cat, she's right. I did sell her. That act is the one thing I regret most in my life. I know now that no amount of money in the world is worth losing a child over. It was a hard lesson to learn," she said.

"Then why? Why did you do it? Cat and I have three children and I would die for any one of them. I could never, ever give them up," Billie said passionately.

Laurel wiped a tear from the corner of her eye, rose from her chair and started to pace.

"I'm not sure where to start," she said to herself as she continued her trek back and forth across the room. Finally, she stopped and looked at Billie. "I guess I'll start with my own childhood. A lot of what happened there drove me to make the decisions I did."

Laurel took a deep breath and began her story.

"I knew from an early age that I was adopted. My mother tried very hard to make it sound like I was a heaven sent gift to her and my father. She was a good mother and a loyal wife. She gave me unconditional love. My father, on the other hand, sent a completely different message. He was harsh and strict, ruling our home with an iron hand, liberally administering punishment whenever he felt it was warranted. He was never a very affectionate man, at least not in the way a father is supposed to be with his daughter," she said. "But he was a good provider."

Immediately, a suspicious look passed between Cat and Billie. Their attention was drawn back to Laurel as she continued.

"Unfortunately, he didn't realize that it wasn't his financial support that I needed, it was his love, and *not* the kind of warped love he offered. You see, he started molesting me when I was thirteen."

Billie's fists clenched in anger as Laurel continued. "It started out innocently enough. A few inappropriate touches here and there, an occasional kiss that was just a little too intimate to be coming from my father. By the time I was fifteen, he became bolder, coming into my room at night and touching me while he masturbated."

"Oh, God!" Cat said as she rose from the bed and into Billie's arms. The words coming out of Laurel's mouth were making her ill.

"I'm sorry, Cat. Maybe I shouldn't be telling you this," Laurel said.

"No. No, go on, please. The healing has to start somewhere. I'll be all right," Cat said as she hugged Billie's waist a little tighter.

"All right," Laurel said. "As I was saying, he became bolder and bolder as the years went on. I was seventeen the first time he actually penetrated me."

"Why didn't you tell your mother, Laurel?" Billie asked.

"I did," she said. "Billie, you need to understand

something. My father was a very domineering man. He had total control of his household, and he kept it that way through brute force. Both my mother and I fell victim to his tirades on several occasions. Neither of us dared to cross him, for fear of the punishment that would surely follow. I told my mother about the abuse, but what could she do?" Laurel reasoned.

"She could have taken you and left," Billie supplied angrily.

"Billie, she was uneducated and totally dependent on him. In her mind, she had no choice. I don't fault her for her reasoning. She just didn't know any better." An uncomfortable silence fell over the room for the next few moments.

While Laurel gathered her thoughts, Billie led Cat over to the bed and sat down, her back propped against the headboard. Cat crawled up and sat between her legs, her back resting up against Billie's chest, Billie's chin resting on the top of her head. Finally, Laurel was ready to speak again.

"Okay, where was I...oh yes, I was seventeen the first time he raped me. I felt so dirty and guilty. He convinced me that it was my fault and that if I told anyone, I would be ridiculed and considered a slut and a whore by everyone I told. If I resisted him, he beat me. I was miserable. The rapes continued at a rate of once or twice a week until I left home to go to college about a year and a half later. I was thrilled to be out of the house, but I worried the whole time about what my mother was enduring while I was gone. Her letters indicated things were fine, but by then, she was a master at putting on a good front for the public. She worked very hard hiding my father's sins for several years."

Laurel paused to catch her breath and noticed that Cat had shifted, and was now curled up in a fetal position in Billie's arms. Billie was wrapped around the smaller woman as though protecting her from something. Frowning, Laurel wondered if there was some significance behind the move, but put the thought aside to continue her story.

When I was twenty-one, I came home between the two semesters of my senior year. He couldn't even make it through my first night home before falling into his old habits, only this time I couldn't take it anymore. The next morning, I left and returned to school to stay on campus for the rest of the break. Little did I know at the time, that one night had changed my life forever. By the time the semester break ended nearly a month later, I realized I was pregnant."

Billie gasped, causing Cat to nearly jump out of her skin. She leaned forward, with Cat still in her arms. "Laurel, are you telling me that the man who adopted you is my father?" she asked.

Cat cringed, remembering the abusive tone he had used with Julia when she had called to find Laurel.

Laurel looked directly at Billie. "Yes, that is exactly what I am saying. Your father is Howard McGuire."

Billie sat back again, leaned her head against the headboard and closed her eyes.

My god, she thought. *How would I have handled that? Could I have raised a child that was forced upon me like that? A child that was the product of incest?*

As Billie contemplated these thoughts, another one entered her mind. *Cat had endured being raped, and lovingly accepted the child that resulted from it, our beautiful Skylar, and now, I can't imagine life without her.*

In her mind, Billie reasoned if Cat had the strength and courage to keep her child, then Laurel should have had as well.

Laurel continued with her story. "So, here I was, twenty-one years old, no job, no home. I was too ashamed to return to classes when the spring semester started, so I dropped out of school. I held various odd jobs, including waiting tables and bar tending, but I wasn't able to hold any of them for very long, especially when my employers discovered I was pregnant. I couldn't return home. My father had banned me from the house, probably afraid that I would reveal him as the father of my child. Instead, he convinced the family that I was, in his words, a bad seed, and that I had gotten myself in trouble like the slut he had always warned me I would be. I had nowhere to go, and in my mind, I had no hope and no future, so I fell in with a bad group of people. Soon, I was involved with drugs and alcohol. The night you were born, Billie, I was so high on drugs, that I don't even remember the birth. When you had that seizure at my home earlier today, I was afraid that you had been born with epilepsy as a result of my drug abuse when I carried you. I would have never forgiven myself for that."

Laurel rose from her chair and walked over to the window. Her back was to Billie and Cat, but they could tell that she was crying when she lifted her right hand to wipe her eyes. Cat sat up and looked at Billie, compassion in her eyes for this woman who was obviously in tremendous pain with her memories.

Laurel continued, her back still to the two women on the bed. Her voice was shaky from tears she was trying so desperately to hold back. "When you were born, Billie, I named you Suzanne. It was such a pretty name, and you were such a beautiful baby. I tried to keep you, truly, I did. You were three months old before I finally gave you up. I couldn't support you. My drug habit was more powerful than my maternal instincts, I guess."

Laurel paused to choke back a sob, her shoulders shaking under the strain.

"You were hungry all the time, you cried constantly. Hell, we didn't even have a home. We were living in a flop-house full of other drug addicts. My body was desperate for the drugs I had come to depend on. So I did the only thing I could think of. I sold you. I sold my child for drug money!" she proclaimed, finally breaking down as violent sobs wracked her body.

Billie was there to catch her as she sank to the floor. Strong arms wrapped around the weeping woman, holding her and, rocking her as they both cried out their anguish, shedding tears of lost memories they would never share.

Cat was a total wreck, sitting on the bed, knees drawn up to her chest, arms wrapped around them tightly as she too shed tears of regret. Billie looked up from her position on the floor and saw the naked pain in her wife's eyes. Reaching out a hand, she motioned for Cat to join her. Soon, all three women were sitting on the floor wrapped in each other's arms as they poured their pain into a common font of cleansing.

* * *

The drive back to Laurel's home was relatively quiet, the two women in the car barely speaking at all. Cat came to a stop in front of the house and turned off the ignition. She turned in her seat and looked at Laurel. "Are you all right?" she asked.

Laurel turned her head to look at Cat. "I've been better," she said. "But I'm more concerned about how Billie is."

"Billie is a very strong woman, Laurel. There have been a lot of problems and hardships she has endured in her life, problems that are not my place to talk about. She will have to decide if and when to tell you. But know this, Billie is a survivor. She has such strength and endurance, and such depth to forgive and accept, that I sometimes look at myself and pale terribly in comparison. Her capacity for love is boundless. I have never in my life felt as safe, loved or needed as I have since I met her. She is my life, Laurel. Together we are whole. I can only hope that I have half her strength of character," Cat said passionately. "So, where you are right to be concerned, know that she will rebound, and together, we will go on and be stronger for the experience," Cat finished.

Laurel wiped a tear from her eye. "My heart is so heavy with regret, Cat. I have failed her. I have failed miserably. My only hope is that someday she will find it in her heart to let me in, to forgive me for wronging her so horribly. I hope the Watermans are smiling down on her right now, because they raised one hell of a daughter."

Laurel took a deep breath and slowly let it out.

Cat sat quietly, watching the play of emotions cross Laurel's features. It was so obvious where Billie's physical beauty came from. She found herself wondering if she was looking at Billie in another twenty years. She certainly hoped so; this woman sitting before her was still breathtaking, even at fifty-five years old.

Laurel felt Cat's eyes on her. Turning, she looked directly into emerald green eyes. "What are you thinking?" she asked the redheaded woman.

Cat smiled. "I was thinking about how beautiful you are, and how much Billie looks like you," she confessed.

Laurel blushed and looked back down at the hands in her lap. "She probably considers that a curse, right now," she said.

Cat reached out and touched Laurel's hand, causing the woman to look into her eyes.

"Laurel," she said. "You have given Billie a lot to think about and right now she may be filled with anger and hurtful regret, but give her time," Cat said. Then, smiling, she continued. "Once she's had a chance to think about things, she'll want to talk, and I'll listen. It's one of the things I do best. Well, that and cook. Did you know your daughter can't even boil water?" she added, causing Laurel to chuckle. "There, that's better," Cat said. "Billie has your smile."

Laurel fished a tissue out of her bag and wiped her tears. "I'd better let you go," she said. "I'm sure Billie's watching the clock, wondering where you are," Laurel added.

Cat just nodded.

Laurel shoved the tissue back into her purse and reached for the door handle. Before exiting the car, she kissed Cat tenderly on the cheek, then hugged her fiercely. "Thank you for giving me the chance to set things right with my daughter, Cat. I'll never forget what you have done for me," she said.

Cat smiled through misty eyes as she watched Laurel walk up the path to her house.

When Cat arrived back to the hotel, she found Billie sleeping, curled up in the middle of the bed in a fetal position, the blankets and sheets in wild disarray around her. It was obvious that sleep had been anything but restful. She peeled off her clothes and slipped a T-shirt over her head, then climbed into bed. Billie visibly relaxed as Cat spooned herself comfortably behind her.

Cat whispered into her wife's hair, "Relax my love. You are safe. You are home in my arms. I love you, Billie." She kissed the space between Billie's shoulder blades, then laid her head down and joined Billie in sleep.

Chapter 26

Cat awoke the following morning to find Billie still in bed, asleep. It was a rare occasion when Billie didn't rise first and set out for her morning run well before Cat decided to greet the day. Cat placed her hand on Billie's forehead, checking for signs of illness. There were none.

"Huh," Cat said as she retracted her hand and started to rise.

Cat suddenly found herself on her back, with a blue-eyed monster hovering over her. Apparently, Billie had been playing opossum and grabbed Cat while she tried to get up, pulling her back down in one smooth motion and gaining a positional advantage over her.

"Just where do you think you're going?" the monster asked.

"I've gotta pee!" Cat replied urgently.

"Pee?" the monster asked.

"Pee! Now let me up before I make us both very uncomfortable," Cat warned. She scooted out from under Billie and ran to the bathroom.

Billie chuckled and sat up in bed. She reached for the phone and ordered breakfast for both of them, then settled back down under the covers to feign sleep again.

Cat came out of the bathroom and saw Billie burrowed back under the covers. She revved up her engines and ran full steam ahead at the bed, jumping up and landing right on the prone woman.

"Ooommmph!" exclaimed Billie as Cat landed. Within seconds, Billie had Cat trapped under her again, this time with her sitting on Cat's stomach, a thigh straddling each side, and her hands pinning Cat's shoulders to the bed.

Cat managed to wiggle her hands free and found Billie's

one tickle spot. Billie succumbed to the torture and rolled off Cat, giving Cat the opportunity to gain the upper hand. Moments later, Billie surrendered.

"I give up! I give up! You win. Please stop!" she begged as Cat finally relented and rolled off her.

Billie kissed her soundly. "Thank you, love. I really needed to start my day laughing."

"You're welcome. Now shut up and kiss me again," she demanded.

Billie was more than happy to oblige. Unfortunately for Cat, seconds into the kiss, a knock came at the door.

"Room Service," a voice said from the hall.

Cat looked at Billie questioningly. Billie just shrugged her shoulders and plastered an innocent look on her face. Cat padded over to the door and let the waiter in, pushing a cart in front of him. "Enjoy your breakfast," he said as he left the room.

Cat started taking the covers off the dishes and found a delectable array of pastries and fruits, along with two plates, each containing a fluffy omelet, home fries and toast. The whole meal was complemented by rich hot aromatic coffee. Cat's mouth watered at the sight. She spared a glance at Billie and saw a coy expression on her face.

"You did this, didn't you?" she asked.

Billie just raised her eyebrows and nodded up and down. Cat put the covers back over the food then crawled up the length of the bed to soundly kiss her wife. "Thank you love," she said.

Cat quickly retrieved their omelets and brought them both over to the bed. She sat beside Billie, and together, they feasted while they talked about the previous day's events.

"So, how are you feeling today?" Cat asked.

After taking a sip of coffee, Billie replied, "I'm fine. Still a little tired, probably from the seizure, but I'm okay."

"Laurel and I had a nice talk when I brought her home last night," Cat said.

Billie stopped chewing for a second and looked at Cat.

"Oh, yeah? What about?"

"She feels horrible, Billie. She feels like she failed you miserably," Cat said.

"Yeah, well, she did," Billie replied, becoming a little irritated with the conversation.

"Billie, can you understand what drove her to give you up? She really thought she was doing what was best for you. She couldn't take care of you," Cat explained.

"She could have cleaned up her act, Cat. She should have given up her drugs, not her child," Billie replied angrily.

"Sweetheart, I understand why you're so angry, but think about what drove her to the drugs to begin with. Can you imagine being raped by your own father! Billie, some people just can't get over the trauma that occurs during a rape!" Cat reminded her.

"You did! You did, Cat! You didn't give up. You didn't turn to drugs. You didn't give your child away!" Billie said, tears starting to form in her eyes. "Damn it! I thought I had cried this all out last night," she added, wiping her eyes.

Cat took Billie's hand in hers. She held it close to her heart and looked into Billie's eyes.

"Billie, when Sky was conceived, I had you. You were my rock. Your presence in my life made the trauma so much easier to bear. Laurel had no support network. All she had was a weak mother, and the man who abused her in the first place. Who else did she have to turn to? Billie, think about it. Where would I have been if I hadn't had the support to get through it?" Cat paused, watching Billie carefully as a parade of emotions crossed her face.

"Sweetheart, open that big beautiful heart of yours and try to find a place in it for Laurel. She needs you right now and whether you'll admit it or not, you need her too," Cat finished.

Billie held Cat's gaze with her own, tears threatening to spill from both. Billie's bottom lip trembled with emotion.

"Please, Billie. Please let the pain out. Until you do, there will be no room for anyone or anything else. Please," Cat said.

Billie closed her eyes, allowing the tears to overflow

onto her cheeks as she nodded her head yes. "I'll try, Cat. I'll try," she said.

* * *

"Hello."

"Laurel? This is Billie,"

Silence.

"Laurel? Are you there?" Billie asked.

"Uhm, Billie. I didn't expect to hear from you," Laurel replied, her voice laced with emotion.

"Well, I didn't expect to be calling," Billie answered, receiving a dirty look from Cat, who was standing by, holding her hand for support through this conversation.

"I'm glad you called. I felt so bad leaving you in such a state last night," Laurel said.

"You had no problem leaving me thirty-two years ago, Mother!" Billie said sharply.

"Billie! That was uncalled for!" Cat declared angrily. She abruptly released her hand and walked a few feet away.

"Billie, is that Cat?" Laurel asked. "May I talk to her?"

"Sure," Billie said. She handed the phone to Cat. "She wants to talk to you. Go figure!"

Cat narrowed her eyes at Billie, then took the phone and placed the receiver up to her ear. "Yes?" she said.

"Cat, I just wanted to thank you again for last night, and to say that I deserve everything Billie says about me. Please don't be angry with her. She has the right to feel that way," Laurel said.

"Laurel, she has no right to be disrespectful. What's done is done. It's in the past, and that's where it belongs. You made your apologies last night, and now Billie has to decide whether to accept them or not, but she has no right to be disrespectful," Cat said.

"Let me talk to her," Billie said.

"Hold on, Laurel. Billie wants to talk again." Cat handed the phone to Billie.

Billie took the phone and covered the receiver with her other hand. She kissed Cat tenderly. "I'm sorry, Cat. I'm being an ass, and I know it. I'm sorry," she said again.

Cat looked at her sternly. "It's not me you owe the apology to, Billie." Cat walked away to stand at the window, her back to Billie.

Billie looked at Cat's retreating back and knew in her heart that she was right. She lifted the receiver to her ear. "Laurel, I'm sorry. I've been acting like a fool. I have a lot to think about, and a lot to adjust to, and I'm afraid I'm not handling it very well. Look, Cat and I would like to see you again. We have to make a decision about what to do next, where to go next, and you are part of that decision. Can we meet you somewhere?" Billie asked.

"There's a park on the outskirts of town, bordered by a lake. It's beautiful at this time of year. I can either give you directions, or you can pick me up," Laurel suggested.

"We'll pick you up. Can you be ready in fifteen minutes?" Billie asked.

"I'll be waiting by the curb," Laurel replied.

Billie hung up the phone and approached Cat, who still had her back to her. She pulled Cat back into her embrace and laid her cheek on top of her head. "I'm sorry, Cat. This is so damned hard. Part of me wants to kill her. The other part wants to be held by her. I don't know what to do," said.

"Listen to your heart, not your head, Billie. What she did was wrong. There is no denying that. But what she feels for you is right. She loves you, Billie, and you may never be able to love her back, but you need to forgive her and move on with your own life. This hurt you are feeling right now is like a thorn in your side. It will continue to fester until it consumes you body and soul," Cat said.

Cat turned around in Billie's arms to look her directly in the face.

"Billie, how many times have you told me that I am the other half of your soul?" Cat asked.

"Too many times to count," Billie replied.

"Then keep this in mind... if this hurt and anger consumes your soul, then it will consume me as well."

Billie's eyes opened wide, filling with tears at the realization of what Cat was saying. "God Cat. I can't let that happen. I can't lose you!" she cried.

"Then don't lose yourself. Don't lose yourself to the anger. Let it go. For both of us," Cat pleaded.

Billie forced a smile through the tears. She kissed Cat tenderly, then looked her in the eyes and said, "Let's go get Mom. We've got a lot of talking to do."

* * *

Fifteen minutes later, Cat and Billie pulled up in front of Laurel's house, and true to her word, found her waiting at the curb. Laurel climbed into the back seat and gave Cat instructions to the lake, then focused her attention on Billie, who had turned around in her seat to look at her.

"Billie, I can't tell you how much this means to me. I really appreciate your seeing me again," Laurel said sincerely.

Billie caught a look from Cat out of the corner of her eye before responding to Laurel. "Cat has made me realize that harboring this hurt inside will only damage both of us in the long run. I need to find a way to get through this and come out whole at the end. We all do," she finished.

Laurel smiled at Billie as she nodded in agreement.

The drive to the lake was relatively short. Moments later, the three women were walking along the shore in silence. Billie was holding Cat's hand tightly, using her to anchor her in reality as she strove to find a way to talk to this woman she called mother, without losing her temper. Finally, they spotted a park bench on a grassy knoll overlooking the water and made their way to it.

Billie and Laurel sat on the bench while Cat sat cross-legged on the grass in front of them, randomly pulling the green blades out of the ground. An uneasy silence permeated the atmosphere around them.

Finally, Laurel spoke. "Billie, please talk to me. Tell me what's on your mind."

Billie looked at her mother. "What's on my mind? There's so much on my mind that it would take forever to say it," Billie said.

Laurel touched Billie's hand. Billie flinched, but did not shrug it off. "For you, Billie, I *have* forever. Please tell me," Laurel replied.

Billie lowered her chin to her chest, fighting desperately to keep her emotions under control. Finally, she lifted her head and looked at Laurel. "Did you ever wonder what happened to me? Where I was? How I was doing?" Billie asked, her voice cracking near the end of the sentence.

Laurel took a deep breath. "Never a day went by that I didn't think of you. Never a day went by that I didn't regret the weaknesses and faults that drove me to that most heinous act. I was weak, Billie. I was a coward. A big piece of me died the day I handed you over to the Watermans' lawyer. I felt like my heart was being torn right out of my chest. But I knew that you would be happier in a stable home with two loving parents. I swear, if I had it to do again, I would have done anything to keep you," Laurel explained, whispering that last sentence.

Billie rose to her feet and paced back and forth, clenching her fists repeatedly. Cat watched her cautiously, ready to intervene if Billie got out of control. Finally, she stopped in front of Laurel and looked directly into her eyes.

"I feel like part of me has died, Laurel," she said. "My whole past has been a lie. The only truly real things in my life are my wife and children. I have such anger in here!" Billie raged loudly, her voice deepened and raspy with emotion as she pounded repeatedly at her chest, loud enough to hear thumps.

Laurel held eye contact with Billie through the tirade, regret and pain clearly written in their blue depths.

"I loved you, Billie. I have always loved you. Giving you up was the hardest thing I have ever done in my life. Please forgive me," she pleaded.

Billie broke eye contact and strode away a few paces. Falling to her knees in the grass, she buried her face in her hands and cried out her anguish. Billie's torturous cries tore through Cat's heart as she watched her soul mate rock back and forth, arms wrapped around her middle, and head thrown back, as she cried out her pain. Cat kept her distance to allow the cleansing ritual to work its medicine. Finally, emotionally and physically spent, Billie collapsed to the ground and curled up into a ball, repeatedly catching her breath in hiccupping gasps.

Cat was a total wreck, in nearly as much pain as Billie as she crawled over to her wife and laid her head down on Billie's cheek. Billie was so distraught, that Cat wasn't sure she even realized where she was.

"Billie, sweetheart," Cat said, kissing her cheek. "Sweetheart, talk to me, please."

Billie blinked her eyes, focusing on Cat. "Cat," she said softly.

"I'm here love. I'm right here," Cat said, brushing the bangs off her forehead.

"Laurel?" Billie asked.

Hearing her name, Laurel rose from her position on the bench and approached her distraught daughter, kneeling on the ground in front of her. "I'm here too, Billie," she said.

Billie reached out her hand to Laurel, who took it into her own and held it close to her heart. Tears streamed down Laurel's face as Billie smiled at her.

"Come on, up you go," said Cat as she and Laurel helped Billie to her feet and walked her over to the bench. The three women sat there for a long time, desperately clinging to each other, trying to reaffirm their places in each other's lives, Billie in the middle, bookended by Cat on her right and Laurel on her left. No words passed between them, save the silent communication of their hearts.

Chapter 27

Cat and Billie pulled up to the curb in front of Laurel's home and shut off the engine then turned around in their seats to face Laurel in the back seat.

Laurel looked at the two women and once more marveled at the intensity of love she felt between them. It was the type of love that was rare between a man and a woman… a type of love that was only possible between two people who touched one another's souls on a purely intimate level. It was a type of love so intense, it was tangible.

"Laurel," Billie said. "Would you consider flying to South Carolina with Cat and me tomorrow?"

"South Carolina?" Laurel questioned, glancing back and forth between Cat and Billie for an explanation. "Is that where you live?"

"No. It's where someone very special lives, someone who has been waiting fifty-five years to see you. It's your own mother, Laurel. Like I said yesterday, she and Billie both have been looking for you," Cat explained.

The fear that crossed Laurel's face was a carbon copy of the one on Billie's face a day earlier when they stood on Laurel's front porch for the first time.

"Tomorrow? I… I will have to arrange for time off from work, and then there's Jim and Dylan to think about," Laurel stammered.

Billie immediately read Laurel's hesitation as a reluctance to meet her own birth mother. "Well, maybe some other time then," she said in disgust as she started to turn back around in her seat.

"No!! No, Billie. I *want* to go," Laurel exclaimed as she reached out to touch Billie's arm. "I want to see her. Heaven knows I have spent my entire life wondering where I came from, and who I look like. No, Billie, don't read my hesitation as reluctance. Please. I want desperately to go. Your question just took me by surprise," Laurel exclaimed in her own defense.

"So you'll go, then?" Billie confirmed.

"Yes, of course," Laurel replied. "I just need to make arrangements, and I have a lot of explaining to do to both Jim and Dylan," Laurel explained.

Billie looked again at her mother. "Does Jim know about me?" she asked.

"No he doesn't. I was too ashamed to tell anyone. It has been a very difficult secret to keep all of these years," Laurel said, looking Billie straight in the eyes. "Billie, I am not ashamed that I gave birth to you. Please don't ever think that, but I am horribly ashamed that I threw away the most precious gift I have ever had. It is not something I am proud of. I only hope the love Jim and I share is strong enough to endure this revelation."

Billie frowned, wondering for at least the tenth time if this trip had been a good idea.

"Laurel," she said, "We didn't come here to ruin your life. Please don't do anything that will put your marriage in jeopardy."

"Billie, if there is one thing I am sure of, its Jim's love for me. He has always been supportive of anything that makes me happy. Sure, it will be a shock to him, but you came into my life long before I met him, so this is not a matter of infidelity. He's a good man, Billie, and given time, I'm sure he will welcome you and your family with open arms," Laurel explained.

Billie's eyes narrowed into small slits. "What is it you're *not* telling me, Laurel?" she asked.

Laurel looked at Cat for support.

"Billie," Cat said before Laurel could speak. "Jim has an issue with our lifestyle," Cat explained as gently as she could.

Billie's eyebrows shot into her hairline. "Oh really?" she said before turning to Laurel. "And why's that?" she asked.

"I don't know. He refuses to talk about it. Don't get me wrong. He doesn't actively detest gays. He just prefers not to deal with the issue. I am so glad Dylan never developed the same attitude," Laurel said.

"So what will Jim think about us showing up on your doorstep, and what do you think he'll say about you coming to South Carolina with us?" Cat asked. "He won't try to stop you, will he?" she added cautiously.

"Heavens, no!" Laurel replied. "He would never stand in the way of something I want to do. He's not a tyrant, Cat. His views on gay relationships may need a little work, but otherwise, he's very open-minded."

Going out on a limb, Billie asked, "Do you think he'd considering going to dinner tonight?"

Laurel looked at her daughter. "I don't know, but I will ask him. I'll call you at the hotel in about a half hour, okay?"

"The offer still stands for you and Dylan, even if Jim chooses not to come," Billie commented.

"Fair enough. I'll call you soon," Laurel replied as she climbed out of the car and stood by Billie's window.

Billie quickly rolled the window down and looked up at her mother.

"Do you know your flight number to South Carolina so I can call the airline to see if there are any more seats available?" Laurel asked.

Cat leaned over Billie to answer her mother-in-law's question. "Actually, we haven't made reservations yet. We were waiting to see if you'd go. Why don't you let us make them for all three of us, okay?" Cat reasoned.

Laurel immediately opened her purse to dig out her credit card. Before she could reach inside, Billie's hand shot out and closed the purse.

"Billie…" Laurel began.

"Don't worry about it," Billie replied.

Laurel leaned in and placed a light kiss on Billie's cheek. "Thank you," she said. "I'll call you within a half-hour about dinner."

Billie just nodded as Cat said goodbye. Moments later, they pulled away from the curb as Laurel watched them drive away.

As promised, a half-hour later Laurel called their hotel room and confirmed dinner plans for that evening. As Jim would not be home from work for several hours yet, she was unable to commit for him, but she did confirm that Dylan would be coming along. She also confirmed that not only she, but Dylan as well, would be flying to South Carolina the next day. Laurel surprised them by announcing she had already made reservations for the four of them, leaving at three p.m. the next afternoon.

* * *

Since dinner was several hours away, Billie and Cat relaxed in their hotel room. Cat held Billie in her arms. Billie's head lay on her shoulder, their legs entwined and her arm thrown across Cat's waist. As they waited, they talked about their meeting with Laurel.

"I was very proud of you Billie. How do you feel, love?" Cat asked.

"I'm tired, Cat. My eyes burn, my chest hurts, but my heart feels lighter, cleansed," Billie replied.

Cat smiled and kissed Billie's forehead. "Does that mean you've forgiven Laurel?" she asked.

"It means the anger is gone. Some of the hurt is still here, but I guess in time, it too will fade," Billie answered. "Does that mean I forgive her? I don't know, Cat. What I *do* know, is that I understand her pain and sense of loss. I understand it, because I share it," she said.

Cat nodded her head. "I'm glad she and Dylan are flying to Charleston with us tomorrow. Grams is so anxious to meet Laurel. Imagine, Billie, just imagine after fifty-five years, finding the daughter you thought had died during childbirth," Cat said incredulously.

"Maybe something good will come of this search after all, love," Billie said.

"Something good has already come of it, Billie. You

have your mother, and a brother you didn't know existed. You've always wanted siblings. Now you've got one," Cat pointed out.

Billie grinned when she thought of Dylan standing up to her when they appeared on Laurel's doorstep yesterday. "Yeah, a little brother. I kind of like that idea," she said.

"Do you realize, love, that yesterday morning, you were an orphan, and today, you not only have a mother, but a brother and stepfather! Do you think Jim will come to dinner with us tonight?" Cat asked.

"No, I don't think so. I'm not sure if he'll ever warm up to us, Cat. Only time will tell," Billie observed, yawning.

"Sleep, love. You've had a very emotional afternoon. We all have," Cat said. "I love you, Billie. Thank you for pulling the thorn out of my soul."

Billie lifted her head and placed a gentle kiss on Cat's cheek. "You're welcome, Cat. I love you too," she said.

Soon, both women were fast asleep.

Chapter 28

As suspected, Jim was not with Laurel and Dylan when they met the ladies at the restaurant. Laurel shrugged her shoulders when Billie asked her about it.

"I told him about you, about your conception and birth, and about how painful it was to give you up. He was shocked of course, like I knew he would be. He was quiet for a while then just when I had my fingers chewed down to the first knuckle he wrapped his arms around me and asked me to explain everything to him. By the time I was finished, he was misty-eyed and fully encouraged me to go with you tomorrow," Laurel explained.

"So then, why isn't he here with you tonight?" Billie challenged.

Laurel looked down at her hands, searching for the right words. "For as long as I've known him, he's had a problem with homosexuality," Laurel explained. "For the life of me, I don't know why. He adamantly refuses to discuss it."

"Let me get this straight, he is encouraging you and your son to fly off with a couple of people he has never met? That sounds a bit odd to me, Laurel," Billie commented.

Laurel met Billie's eyes and read the challenge in them. "Billie," she said. "You and Cat are not casual acquaintances. You are my daughter, and Cat is my daughter-in-law. Despite the obvious anger you harbor for me, and heaven knows I sorely deserve it, I have no reason to fear you. Jim trusts my judgment, and besides, Dylan added his voice to the discussion, and verified that neither you, nor Cat was an axe murderer," she said with a twinkle in her eye, trying desperately to end the discussion on a light note.

Despite Billie's best intentions, a small grin formed at

the corner of her mouth at her mother's attempt at humor. She looked at her brother. "Thanks, Dyl," she said. "I appreciate your vote of confidence."

"No problem, Sis. The way I see it, this situation is a result of some unfortunate circumstances that happened thirty-some-odd years ago. We all deserve to know our roots, regardless of how things came to be the way they are today, including Mom. And besides, I'm kind of looking forward to meeting my grandmother."

"Well, hold on to your britches, you're in for a treat!" Cat exclaimed.

Any further attempt to discuss the issue was thwarted by the arrival of the waiter.

* * *

At dinner that evening, the three women, and Dylan talked about Alex and Jo.

"I'm really nervous about tomorrow," Laurel admitted.

"I know exactly how you feel, Laurel," Billie replied. "But there is no need to worry. Alex and Jo are wonderful."

Laurel cocked her head to the side. "Alex and Jo?" she questioned.

Billie quickly looked at Cat. Both women thinking the same thing at the same time.

"Ah… yeah. Alex and Jo. It's short for Alexandra and Josephine, although Grams likes to call Josephine, Josie," Cat explained, watching Laurel's reaction carefully.

Laurel's eyes grew as big as saucers, but silence prevailed as she sat dumbfounded.

Dylan's head snapped up. "Hey! Those are both women's names!" he said, stating the obvious. Then, as the meaning suddenly dawned on him, he asked in a loud and excited voice, "Holy Shit! Are they like… you two?"

Billie and Cat both nodded their heads as their attention bounced between Laurel and Dylan, trying to gauge their reactions.

"Oh, my!" Laurel said, suddenly finding her voice as she reached for her water glass. "I need a drink. Waiter!" she added, waving her hand in the direction of the wait-staff.

Billie spontaneously broke into laughter as Cat, Laurel and Dylan looked at her oddly.

"Don't look at me like that!" Billie said to Cat between chuckles. "Between the 'Oh, my!' and 'I need a drink', she sounds just like *both* Alex and Jo. She is surely Alexandra Spirakis' daughter!"

Still struggling to make sense of the information she had just been given, Laurel shook her head. "So, Alex is my mother?"

"She certainly is," Cat replied, smiling broadly. "Even a blind man could see the resemblance."

"I look like her?" Laurel asked, her interest peaked about these two ladies.

"Exactly. In fact, it was Billie's resemblance to Alex that made us all suspicious about Alex's daughter. You see, she was told that you were stillborn. She never saw you. For the past fifty-five years, she has had the feeling that you were still alive, and seeing Billie was the icing on the cake for her. Billie's resemblance to Alex–through you–is what sparked this search," Cat explained.

"Spirakis… Spirakis. Isn't that Greek?" Laurel asked.

"It sure is. And Jo's last name is Wycliffe," Billie replied.

"So, what are they like?" Laurel wanted to know.

Billie and Cat looked at each other and smiled broadly, causing Laurel to raise her eyebrows and wonder just what kind of family she was born into.

"They are the most unlikely pair I have ever seen," Billie replied.

"You can say that again!" exclaimed Cat. "Like we said, Alex is an older version of you and Billie, at least in appearance. She is tall and slim with piercing blue eyes and thick black hair, graying with age, that flows to the middle of her back when she wears it down, which is almost never. Her mannerisms on the other hand are as far from Billie as you can get in some ways. You see, Alexandra Spirakis is your typical southern belle. She is very feminine and dainty, always dressed as though they were throwing a formal party. She is very matronly, and very proper. Her voice is velvety and heavily laden with Southern charm and etiquette, and never a cuss word passes her lips."

"And Jo...," Billie interjected. "Jo is a streetwise Yankee rebel. If you and I look like Alex, then Cat is Jo's younger twin. She's about Cat's height, has shoulder length graying red-gold hair and an attitude bigger than both of us," Billie said, laughing heartily.

"Oh, and lest we forget, she swears like a sailor, and she's full of the devil. In fact, within minutes of meeting me, she pinched my butt! Of course, that was before she knew she was my grandmother!"

Billie had to pause to control her laughing before continuing. "Oh god, that woman is funny. They are complete opposites. Alex is feminine; Jo is butch. Alex is quiet, Jo is loud and boisterous. Alex is always coifed to perfection, Jo's ordinary attire consists of Khaki trousers, button-down shirt and a tattered fedora. Alex is a perfect lady, Jo is crass and roguish. About the only thing they have in common is their love for each other," Billie finished.

"They sound cool!" Dylan exclaimed. "How long have they been together?" he asked.

"Over fifty years," Cat replied, watching an expression of awe cross the faces of both Laurel and Dylan.

"So they met after I was born," Laurel observed.

"Actually, no. They met for the first time during the Viet Nam war when Jo was on loan from the Citadel to the Navy. Alex was a linguist, and an American liaison for the Greek government. They were assigned to work together to break a secret code that saved the lives of countless troops. Alex became pregnant with you about a year after she came home from that assignment. They met again at a history convention about three years after your birth," Cat explained.

Laurel sat in quiet contemplation for a few moments, absorbing what Billie and Cat had told her about her mother. Finally, she looked once more at her daughter and asked, "Who is my father?"

Billie and Cat looked at each other solemnly before Billie answered. “I think that’s a question you need to ask Alex,” she said. “Just know that there were circumstances surrounding your conception and birth that left Alex devastated. Know also that if things had turned out differently, you would have been raised under a huge umbrella of love. They have such incredible capacity for love. You’ll feel it the moment you are in their presence,” Billie finished, emotion choking her voice.

Laurel reached out and covered Billie’s hand with her own. “Billie,” she said softly. If things had worked out differently, there would be no you, and there would be no Cat, or Seth, or Tara, or Skylar to grace my golden years. You are worth everything I have endured in my life. I just hope you will give me the chance to be the mother I should have been thirty-two years ago. I very much want to be a part of your family. Yours and Cat's… and Alex and Jo’s.”

“I second that,” Dylan said eagerly, adding his hand to the pile; a wide grin splitting his face.

Cat wiped her eyes with the back of her hand then added it to the pile. “Well, we’ve got one more surprise for you, Laurel,” Cat said. “You also have a sister.”

“I have a sister?” Laurel asked incredulously. “How? I mean, I know how, but… but… how?” she asked, thoroughly confused.

“Biologically, she’s Jo’s. Emotionally, she belongs equally to both, and she is my mother,” Cat explained. “How she was conceived is something the grandmothers don’t talk much about. Alex desperately wanted a child, the child she thought she had lost three years earlier, so Jo gave her one. There is nothing Grams wouldn’t do for her.”

Laurel looked down at the table, emotions running rampant across her face. She was a little confused at first that Jo was Cat's maternal grandmother, and that Alex was Billie's. It seems odd, and not at all coincidental that the granddaughters of these two women would meet and fall in love more than fifty years after they had. She found herself wondering if there was some force at work that had brought these four women together.

Billie watched her mother closely as she saw the confusion on Laurel's face. “Are you all right, Laurel?” she asked softly.

Laurel looked at her daughter. “It’s all pretty overwhelming,” she admitted. “I almost expect someone to shout, *Smile–You’re on Candid Camera*,” she joked, looking back and forth between the two women. “It’s a lot to deal with all at once…two mothers, a sister, and three grandchildren! For heaven’s sake, I became a grandmother overnight! And if I’m to be honest, Billie, the lifestyles are a little hard to deal with emotionally. Don’t get me wrong, I am not homophobic. I am thrilled that you have someone as wonderful as Cat to share your life, but learning that not only is my daughter gay, but my mother is too, well, that will take some getting used to,” she confessed.

"I think it's cool," Dylan said.

Billie understood Laurel's discomfort with the gay issue, but couldn’t help but assume some of it was due to her husband's prejudice against homosexuals in general.

"Did you tell Jim about the nature of Cat's and my relationship when you got home last night?" Billie asked Laurel.

Laurel nodded and looked down into her plate with a sad expression on her face.

"I take it, he wasn't very happy about it?" asked Cat.

Laurel looked at her daughter and daughter-in-law. "You guessed right," she said. "Interestingly enough, though, he was more upset about me keeping you a secret from him all these years, than the fact that you are gay," Laurel explained.

"You mean he accepts that we're gay?" Billie asked.

"I wouldn't exactly call it acceptance, sis," Dylan said, making Billie smile at the endearment. "Resignation is a more fitting description. I mean, what choice does he have?"

Laurel turned to her son. "In all fairness, sweetie, we gave your father a lot to deal with last night. I mean, in one evening, he learns that he has a stepdaughter, daughter-in-law, and three grandchildren, not to mention they live a lifestyle that is contrary to what he believes in," she explained.

“Anyway,” she continued, addressing Billie and Cat once more, “he was hurt that had I kept your existence from him for thirty-two years. That was a mistake. I know that now. I should have trusted in his love and shared it with him when we first met. I should have shared it with you, too Dyl,” she said, addressing her son.

Dylan simply nodded his head without speaking.

"Do you think he's capable of accepting us into the family?" asked Cat.

"I don't know, Cat. Maybe when he meets the two of you, he'll come around, but until then, I don't know. I think we need to give him some time to adjust to the whole situation before we arrange a meeting though," she said, watching the three heads of her children nod around the table.

"I'm sorry that our presence is causing trouble in your marriage, Laurel," Billie said.

Laurel touched Billie's face. "You let me worry about that, Billie. Now that I've found you, I will not let anyone come between us again. Not even my husband," she said. "I have to trust in Jim's love for me. If that love is not strong enough to endure this new chapter, then maybe I have reason to question it. Only time will tell."

Chapter 29

Billie, Cat, Dylan and Laurel deplaned in Charleston, South Carolina at six the next afternoon. Alex and Jo's limo driver, Chet was waiting for them at the gate.

"Miss Cat, Miss Billie, it is so good to see you again," he said, taking their hands and bowing slightly in front of them. Then, turning to Laurel, an awestruck look crossed his face.

"You dear lady, must be Miss Laurel. Your resemblance to Miss Alex and Miss Billie is remarkable," he commented. "My name is Chet, official escort to the mistresses when they venture off the plantation. It is nice to make your acquaintance."

Laurel smiled brightly, thoroughly enjoying this man's Southern hospitality.

"And who is this young man?" Chet asked as he reached his hand out to Dylan.

Dylan took his hand and shook it firmly. "Dylan Stafford, sir. Laurel is my mom."

"So that means you are the mistress' grandson. You are in for a treat, young man. You will especially enjoy Miss Josephine. She can be quite incorrigible," he said winking to Dylan as he and the young man collected the luggage. "Right this way, ladies, and young sir," he announced as he led the way to the car.

During the flight, Billie and Cat tried to prepare Laurel and Dylan with what to expect as they approached SpireCliffe Acres, however, all the coaching in the world couldn't prepared them for their first impression.

"Oh, my God! It's beautiful!" exclaimed Laurel as the mansion became visible at the end of the long driveway.

Dylan was speechless. Reaching up, he slid the sun-roof open and stood on the back seat of the limousine, his upper body protruding from the roof of the car. “It’s huge!” he yelled.

Laurel looked at Billie. “I didn’t realize they were so wealthy,” she said. “This plantation is beautiful. I’ll bet it has quite an extensive history.”

“Funny you should put it that way,” Cat commented. “Jo is a professor of History at the Citadel, and the historic significance of this plantation is one of the reasons she agreed to desert her Yankee roots and live in the South. This plantation quite productively produced cotton and tobacco in the days before the Civil War. Alex regretfully admits that this used to be the home to hundreds of slaves that were freed long before her birth. The slave quarters still stand some distance behind the main house.”

“Do you spend much time here?” Laurel asked Cat.

“I used to, when I was a child. We visited for a month every summer. Those summer months were some of the most enjoyable in my life,” Cat replied.

“Maybe you can show Dylan and me around? I just adore historical things,” Laurel exclaimed.

Before Cat could reply, Dylan let out a hoot. “We’re here!” he shouted as the limousine pulled up in front of the large wooden doors. “Holy cow! This place is incredible,” he exclaimed again as he scurried out of the car to help Chet with the luggage.

Climbing out of the car, Laurel became visibly agitated as her nervousness got the best of her.

Seeing the condition her mother was in, Billie reached out and took her hands. “It will be okay,” she whispered. “Cat and I are here for you.”

Laurel smiled and squeezed Billie’s hand as they walked together into the mansion.

* * *

"Alex, will you stop fidgeting and sit down? The house looks fine," Jo scolded as Alex walked around adjusting knick-knacks.

"I can't help it, Josie. I'm so nervous, I can hardly breathe," Alex said, nervously flitting around the parlor, making last minute adjustments to the furniture.

Jo had had enough. Rising to her feet, she grabbed Alex and pushed her up against the wall. She planted a long and hard kiss on Alex's mouth, effectively stilling the woman's fidgeting. Their guests stepped into the parlor just as Jo pulled her mouth away from Alex's. Billie cleared her throat to announce their presence.

There before them, were two elderly women, the smaller one holding the taller one pinned against the wall, their body language making it painfully clear the guests had just interrupted an intimate moment. Both women were looking at them, the taller one's face flushed with embarrassment, the smaller one's bearing a smug expression.

Jo felt Alex's knees begin to buckle. "Don't you dare faint on us, Alexandra Spirakis!" she scolded.

"Oh, my!" Alex said as she sank further down the wall.

Billie and Laurel were immediately at her sides, assisting Jo in her effort to keep Alex from sliding all the way to the floor. Bookending Alex, the two women led her to a chair while Jo went to stand with Cat and Dylan. Turning around, she looked at the three women and was immediately struck by the strong resemblance between them.

"Holy Shit!" Jo said.

Cat threw her arm around Jo's shoulder. "Holy Shit indeed! Kind of overwhelming, isn't it?" she said grinning. "By the way, Grandma Jo, this is Dylan. Laurel's son, and your grandson. Dylan, this is Grandma Jo," Cat said, completing the introductions.

Jo turned to Dylan and put her hand out to shake his. Dylan looked at her hand and raised his eyebrows before wrapping his arms around her in a tight bear hug and lifting her off the ground, swinging her around in a circle. He put her back on the floor and planted a wet sloppy kiss on her cheek before letting her go. "Nice to meet you, Grams," he said, grinning ear to ear.

"Aarrgghh!" Jo said, wiping her cheek while Cat and

Dylan laughed.

While Cat was introducing Dylan to Jo, Billie was making introductions of her own.

Billie knelt down on one knee in front of Alex and took her hand. "Grams, are you all right?"

"Oh, my, yes! No need to fuss over little ole me. Billie, did you bring her? Did you bring my little girl?" Alex asked, not seeing Laurel, who had moved off to the side while Billie was tending to her.

"Yes, Grams, we brought her, and your grandson too," Billie said.

"I... I have a grandson?" she asked, not taking her eyes off Billie's face.

"Oh, yeah, my little brother. He's a cutie too," Billie replied, causing Alex to smile broadly.

"Well, land sakes child, what are you waitin' for? Where are they?" Alex said impatiently swatting Billie's arm with the back of her hand.

Billie rose to her feet and extended a hand to Alex to help her out of the chair. "Grams, this is Laurel, your daughter," she said, motioning Laurel forward.

Alex looked at the vision before her. She released Billie's hand and took a step forward, coming face to face with Laurel. Nearly the same height, build and coloring, they were mirror foils of each other. Both women simultaneously reached their right hand up to touch the cheek of the other. Both had tears streaming down their cheeks. They stood there, staring into each other's eyes until Alex opened her arms and Laurel fell into them.

"My baby," Alex cried. "I thought you were dead. They told me you were dead," was all Alex could say. "I'm so sorry."

Both women cried as they clung together. "Mama!" Laurel whispered as she held Alex.

Billie made her way to Cat and took her into her arms as they, too, cried at the reunion. In fact, there wasn't a dry eye in the room, with Jo and Dylan trying to inconspicuously dry their eyes, not wanting to betray their tough guy images.

"Damn, I got something in my eye," Jo said as she wiped a tear away.

"Me too, damn!" Dylan said, copying his grandmother's movements.

Cat gave Jo a shove forward and motioned for her to join the reunion. Another shove had Dylan heading into the fray as well.

Billie looked at the gathering of people before her and realized that she was now on solid ground. She had found her roots. These people were her home and her family. Motioning to Cat with her head, she herded her wife out of the room and up the stairs while three generations within reveled in the essence of family.

EPILOGUE

The Charland and Swenson clans were gathered in Cat and Billie's back yard for a cookout to celebrate their victorious return. Seth, Tara and Skylar had stayed with Jen and Fred for the entire week that Cat and Billie were gone, and although they enjoyed staying with their friends, they were happy to have their parents home.

Billie and Cat had returned from South Carolina two days earlier after spending a few days with their extended family. The visit went well. Billie and Laurel made their peace, although only time would heal the wounds of lost memories that they would never hold in their hearts. They were exhausted, but feeling emotionally complete.

When Cat and Billie had left South Carolina, Laurel and Dylan were making plans to stay for another week, giving themselves ample time to become acquainted with their new family. The scene at the airport in Charleston when Billie and Cat left was emotional. Laurel still had a sister and three grandchildren to meet and made plans for her and Dylan to visit Billie and Cat in the near future. Whether or not Laurel's husband Jim would be with them, was yet to be seen. Laurel and Jim had a lot of things to discuss and work out concerning her daughter and parents.

"Billie, could you please pass the catsup?" Cat asked as her friends and family sat around the picnic table in the back yard.

Billie passed the catsup to Jen, who passed it to Cat.

"So, this whole quest started because you were convinced you two had a connection from the past. I guess you found it, and it was practically sitting in your own back yard. Who'da thunk?" Jen asked.

“Actually, now that I think about it, it wasn’t that difficult. I mean, with Cat’s unwavering support, a little research with the help of two very good friends, a couple of trips to South Carolina and Michigan… throw in a few seizures, three cases of tissue and a crooked politician, and it was pretty simple,” Billie said.

"Pretty simple, huh?" Jen said. "So you think you're pretty hot stuff now, huh?" Jen said.

"Oh, yeah!" Billie said. "Hot stuff indeed!" she said.

"Ah, would you excuse me for one moment?" Jen said, getting up from the table.

Billie turned her attention back to her meal, talking amicably with Cat, and paying no attention to her friend, who walked away from the table with an evil smile on her face. Moments later, Billie heard Jen's voice from behind her.

"Well, Miss Hot Stuff, time to cool down. Remember the kitchen sprayer? Paybacks are a bitch!" Jen shouted.

Billie turned around quickly and caught a cold spray of water from the garden hose, full in the face.

"Aarrgghh! Swenson, you are *so* dead. Do you hear me?" Billie screamed as she got up from the table and chased her friend around the yard, trying her best to dodge the spray from the hose. After a time, Billie's longer legs gave her the advantage as she managed to wrestle the hose away from Jen, soaking her to the bone.

Cat watched their antics from her nice dry spot at the table. "Ah, it feels good to be home," she said and she enjoyed her hamburger.

Photo Credit: Brad Fowler, Song of Myself Photography

About the Author

Karen D. Badger is the author of On A Wing And A Prayer, Yesterday Once More (a 2009 Golden Crown Literary Award winner for Speculative Fiction), In A Family Way, Unchained Memories, Happy Campers, Collective Identity Sweet Angel and Relative-ly Speaking (Books I, II, III, IV, V and VI of the Commitment Series), The Blue Feather, All My Tomorrows (sequel to the 2009 award winning Yesterday Once More) and her latest novel, 1140 Rue Royale…all released by Badger Bliss Books, which Karen co-owns with her wife Barbara Sawyer (aka, "Bliss').

Born and raised in Vermont, Karen is the second of five children raised by a fiercely independent mother, who remains one of her best friends to this day. Karen earned her B.A. in 1978 in Theater and in Elementary Education, and in 1994, earned a B.S. in mathematics. In addition to her novels, Karen is the author of many technical papers on photomask manufacturing, which she has presented at numerous semiconductor industry conferences, and is the holder if several technical patents. Karen is currently in her 38th year as a Principle Member of the Technical Staff with a prominent Semiconductor manufacturer in Vermont.

Karen and her wife, Barb (a retired Lt. Col., US Air Force) live in the beautiful state of Vermont—home of Ben and Jerry's. They spend their spare time with family as well as doing home improvement projects on both their homes in Vermont and New Mexico. They also enjoy camping, kayaking, motorcycling and singing Karaoke.

Please visit Karen's author website at www.karendbadger.com, or the Badger Bliss Books website at www.badgerblissbooks.com. Also like us on Facebook!

TITLES BY KAREN D. BADGER

www.badgerblissbooks.com

On A Wing and A Prayer
First edition published by Blue Feather Books, Sept, 2005
Second edition published by Badger Bliss Books – Sept, 2014
Third edition published by Badger Bliss Books – August, 2016
ISBN 13: 978-1-945761-01-0, ISBN 10: 1-945761-01-6

Yesterday Once More
First edition published by Blue Feather Books, July, 2008
Second edition published by Badger Bliss Books – Sept, 2014
Third edition published by Badger Bliss Books – August, 2016
ISBN 13: 978-1-945761-02-7, ISBN 10: 1-945761-02-4
2009 Golden Crown Literary Society Award - Speculative Fiction

In A Family Way – Book One of the Commitment Series
First edition published by Blue Feather Books, March, 2010
Second edition published by Badger Bliss Books – Sept, 2014
Third edition published by Badger Bliss Books – August, 2016
ISBN 13: 978-1-945761-05-8, ISBN 10: 1-945761-05-9

Unchained Memories – Book Two of the Commitment Series
First edition published by Blue Feather Books, Oct, 2011
Second edition published by Badger Bliss Books – Sept, 2014
Third edition published by Badger Bliss Books – August, 2016
ISBN 13: 978-1-945761-06-5, ISBN 10: 1-945761-06-7

Happy Campers - Book Three of the Commitment Series
First edition published by Blue Feather Books, Sept, 2013
Second edition published by Badger Bliss Books – Sept, 2014
Third edition published by Badger Bliss Books – August, 2016
ISBN 13: 978-1-945761-07-2, ISBN 10: 1-945761-07-5

The Blue Feather
First edition published by Blue Feather Books, July, 2014
Second edition published by Badger Bliss Books – Sept, 2014
Third edition published by Badger Bliss Books – August, 2016
ISBN 13: 978-1-945761-04-1, ISBN 10: 1-945761-04-0

Collective Identity – Book Four of the Commitment Series
First edition published by Badger Bliss Books – January, 2015
Second edition published by Badger Bliss Books – August, 2016
ISBN 13: 978-1-945761-08-9, ISBN 10: 1-945761-08-3

All My Tomorrows – Sequel to Yesterday Once More
First edition published by Badger Bliss Books – May, 2015
Second edition published by Badger Bliss Books – August, 2016
ISBN 13: 978-1-945761-03-4, ISBN 10: 1-945761-03-2

Sweet Angel – Book Five of the Commitment Series
First edition published by Badger Bliss Books – June, 2015
Second edition published by Badger Bliss Books – August, 2016
ISBN 13: 978-1-945761-09-6, ISBN 10: 1-945-761-09-1

Relative-ly Speaking – Book Six of the Commitment Series
First edition published by Badger Bliss Books – March, 2016
Second edition published by Badger Bliss Books – August, 2016
ISBN 13: 978-1-945761-10-2, ISBN 10: 1-945-761-10-5

1140 Rue Royale
First edition published by Badger Bliss Books – Sept, 2016
ISBN 13: 978-1-945761-00-3, ISBN 10: 1-945761-00-8

www.ingramcontent.com/pod-product-compliance
Lightning Source LLC
Chambersburg PA
CBHW070837250626
47159CB00003B/817

* 9 7 8 1 9 4 5 7 6 1 0 8 9 *